SMOKE AND TRANQUILLITY

ROBERT SWANN

ISBN-13: 978-1542765466
ISBN-10: 1542765463

ACKNOWLEDGMENTS

My thanks go to the vast number of people I have had the pleasure of meeting in the fifty or so countries in which I have worked and lived. It is they who are the inspiration of the characters portrayed in this and my five preceding books. The characters are, in general, a mosaic of personalities, few if any of which are recognisable even to the who know them. Their make-up is founded on the concept that each personality can be sculpted to filter out inconsistencies which would otherwise detract from the purity of the character being portrayed. Nobody is perfect.

AUTHOR'S NOTE

Writing each character in the first person helps to illustrate that people misinterpret each other's intentions. All too often the conclusions reached after a discussion will be interpreted by the participating individuals in their own way – to support their personal point of view. Sometimes the misinterpretations are caused by blind bias and sometimes because the language of discussion is found wanting.

THE BEGINNING OF A DANGEROUS QUEST…

Eyes gleaming with the demented fire of fundamentalist passion, the leader of 'New Light' rants about his mission to his enthralled followers.

"We will go forward and slaughter the white heathens as we will the Arabs, the Indians, and all Asian races and we will drive out from our country the colonial invaders, by exterminating them. They are all heathens and our sworn enemies. We will be strong and our 'New Light' religion, the only true religion. We will dominate the globe."

As he makes this declaration he holds aloft the severed head of an 'infidel'. The onlookers howl their approval; whipped up by fundamentalist followers of New Light, using physical and mental persuasion fuelled by strong alcohol and fanaticism.

Simon Hunter:

I am horrified by the news agency video clip; it is gruesome and will quickly be taken off social media. My catching it is fortuitous for those threatened by it. After the clip ends I can still hear in the echoes of my mind the animal howling of the onlookers as the leader of the cult, Benningo Dagobah, brandishes the severed head and whips his audience into a frenzy. Like the invasion of my mind the awful pictures presented are burned into my retinas, leaving a picture of inhuman horror which will never be fully dispelled.

I realise as I watch the clip, that addressing this situation is to be my next project. Inner demons drive me to help people who fall through the cracks of our self-absorbed international society and have no defence against the actions of self-appointed despots such as Dagobah.

Tefawa Belawa:

My mission in Paris is interrupted by a call from Sir Michael Westinghouse, the head of MI6 and, my boss. He instructs me to put a hold on my current project and go to Golas, my original West African home country, to collect information on Benningo Dagobah who is based in Benejado City. It is a long time since I have visited my old home but I keep up to date with what's going on there and I am only too familiar with Dagobah and his band of fundamentalist thugs.

City is an inappropriate appellation for Benejado; it is far from deserving that accolade. It resembles a remote collection of slum-like buildings in the centre of which is a mud brick structure occupied by the leader of the 'people's' council. He is also the mayor and commander in chief of the Benejado state military and police establishments.

Getting to Benejado City has its challenges; there are two ways of accomplishing this task. To fly to Algeria, rent a 4WD vehicle and drive across virgin desert scrub on non-existent roads, or I can fly into the capital, Golas City, in the south, and take a long drive north to Benejado. Neither option is better than the other and with the flip of a coin I elect to fly into Golas and take the long drive north. Foreign currency is in short supply in Golas and renting a car will be easy enough, but the road vehicles on offer are desperately old and unreliable, like the roads.

Simon Hunter:

I meet up with Tefawa in Paris where he is currently on MI6 undercover work. We meet in the buttery of a small private hotel on the left bank of the River Sein on Rue Jacob. I spent some of my youth living in this hotel in St Germaine du Prez while I was attending the Sorbonne and it is a place which occupies a special place in my heart.

It is some time since I last met with Tefawa and his handsome face splits into a huge grin when he sees me. We shake hands and embrace like the old friends we have become, thrown together in adversity.

"It is good to see you, my old friend." Tefawa's voice is deep and fruity.

"Likewise, my friend. It has been too long." I sigh deeply. "We lead demanding lives and all of our good intentions about meeting up are frequently difficult to keep."

"Exactly so." He takes a chair opposite mine. "Sir Michael sends his best wishes to you."

"Thank you for passing them on, I had also intended to keep contact with him but…"

Tefawa interrupts. "But there is not time to do so."

"Exactly so," I echo his words.

He becomes business-like. "As instructed by Sir Michael I have compiled a dossier on Benningo Dagobah and comments on the country in general. It does not make comfortable reading and my advice to you is to leave dealing with him and his organisation to somebody else – he is unpredictably dangerous."

"And who might that somebody else be?" I look at him with my head on one side.

"That's exactly what Sir Michael said you would say." He gives a knowing smile.

"We all know each other so well, do we not?"

"We've been through a lot together, so yes we do." He nods his head sagely.

Rather than going over the dossier with him I put it to one side to read later and we spend an hour catching up with news since our last meeting.

"Time for me to get moving, Simon, I've got a lot on." He stands and prepares to leave. "I've put as much in the dossier as I can but my time there was limited and I am sure there is more to be found." He pauses as we shake hands and gives me a concerned look. "Simon, I grew up in Golas and I found the visit I have just made to be very disturbing. It has changed beyond all measure since our previous visits. It was a scary place then but it has since become terrifying. I urge you to leave this problem to somebody else; you are unlikely to survive opposing the Dagobah regime."

I will be using the West African protectorate of Nematasulu as a bolt hole should my work in Golas turn sour; Nematasulu is under the protection of my Colony homeland of Recovery Island. Most world governments consider the Colony to be a threat because we refuse to share our powerful technology with them, because of its potentially world-changing properties. We learned the hard way that possession of the technology by others would be exploited to give the user an all-powerful political edge. No government or organisation could be trusted to use it for the good alone it can do for humanity.

I travel to Nematasulu the long way around by flying to Algeria where I buy a state-of-the-art, all-terrain, safari-equipped, 4WD vehicle for the long drive to Benejado City. I am using this long journey to acquire a natural deep tan which will enable me to blend in with the Arab population of the province. I speak good Arabic as well as French so unless I meet an academic linguist I will be able to get away with my intended deception of being an Arab. I also speak the national language on Nematasulu because of a previous project in the country. An initial drawback is that I have bright blue eyes which will, in my guise as an Arab, draw unwanted attention. To overcome this, I use brown contact lenses which are tailor made for me by Dr Carlina Tanterelli's workshop back in my Colony home. I can wear these specially made, soft, breathable lenses, even in the dusty environment of the North African sands for long periods of time without discomfort.

On my drive to the border between Algeria and Golas I avoid most of the towns and villages, only stopping to replenish my food and water supplies and to purchase a simple wardrobe of Arab clothes. The ten days which the journey takes gives me the opportunity to brush up on my Arab vocabulary. By the time I reach Benejado my naturally already dark skin has turned deep mahogany which is an important part of my disguise but has the effect of making my teeth gleam in contrast, which is yet another problem. The local Arab food and drinks discolour their teeth with black and brown overtones. I produce the same effect for myself by chewing berries purchased from village markets. By the time I reach Benejado City not only do I look like a native of the desert, but I also smell like one.

Benejado City, in Benejado Province, is a collection of crumbling buildings of uncertain origin and no architectural merit. It is a legacy of African tribal, British, and French colonisation in a unique undesirable blend. The outlying areas are sparsely populated and scattered with a handful of widely spaced, mostly derelict buildings. The centre is fortified as a citadel with long and high, baked mud, block walls between the many roads giving gated access to the city centre. The wooden gates have long since been devoured by termites and the arched porticos which support them have in the most part crumbled into disrepair.

The occupants of the city are, for the most part, of African descent, but its chequered history also produces a curious mixture of ethnic appearances, some of which are exotic and others which are an unkind amalgam of less desirable elements. These undesirable people, I learn from Tefawa's dossier, are the outcasts – the untouchables – in a population searching desperately for a national identity which remains elusive.

I leave my 4WD vehicle in a rickety lock-up in a remote village outside Benejado City and hitch a camel caravan ride into the city, enabling me to blend in. I begin by observing the Arab population at close quarters. They are tolerated by the Benejaden authorities because they provide the commercial acumen so necessary for city life, an ability which is not abundant in the indigenous peoples. I frequent the Arab-owned tea rooms and coffee shops where local Arabs smoke the hookah as a social catalyst. I forsake the hookah but enjoy the local lemon tea and thick, aromatic, caffeine-laden Arab coffee which is so much part of their distant cultural roots.

There are many subtle dialects of Arabic spoken in the city, some of which I find it difficult to fully comprehend. By trial and error, I find the cafés occupied by those who speak the dialects I do understand and begin my own fact finding about local happenings. Before long I recognise regular patrons and I hear them talking about local events and scandals. The customers are exclusively male and their topics of discussion include politics, women, and foreign cars. One telling subject is absent from the conversations and that is religion. This omission tells me that my original thoughts, confirmed by the observations of Tefawa Belawa, are accurate.

Sir Michael Westinghouse:

Tefawa Belawa, otherwise agent N11, gives a verbal report which is both thorough and disturbing. He is a very level-headed agent of whom I take a great deal of notice. His saying that I should warn Hunter off becoming involved with either New Light or Benningo Dagobah, is a matter of great concern to me.

I feel the need to give some 'backup' to Hunter but as I am doing this off the books I can't go to the PM for his affirmation, but at the same time I can't ignore what is going on in Benejado Province. It has ramifications for us as a country, in the longer term. Benningo Dagobah is a threat to African stability which can easily spill over into neighbouring countries of some influence like Kenya and Nigeria as well as Algeria, Tunisia, and Chad. These are all countries with which we do significant trade and they are important to our economy.

I can't share this with the PM because we are not supposed to have an active presence in that part of the world because of a treaty we have in place with China stating that we will leave the governance of the region to itself and not interfere with them in any way. Our relationship with China is tenuous at best and in his last year in office as PM he wants to ensure harmony so that he can retire on a successful high.

The only thing I can do is to keep a long-distance eye on Hunter and hope that he doesn't get himself into any trouble by inflaming the situation. I realise as I cultivate this theme that any hopes of controlling Hunter are just pipe dreams, he's his own man.

Simon Hunter:

Two weeks immersing myself in Benejado City is enough for me to comprehend the hold that New Light has over the whole population. I have witnessed things that make my blood run cold. Foreigners, except for pure-blood Arab traders, are treated appallingly by followers of New Light and Benningo Dagobah's excessive zeal. Selected foreigners and some Benejadens who have mixed parentage are treated as a subspecies and in some cases slaughtered openly in the streets without the perpetrators being brought to book in any way. Benejado City is an inhuman and brutishly lawless place. The hold the New Light followers have over the general population increases as my one-month tenure draws to a close.

The New Light activists have recently taken to wearing head and face coverings as a badge of office – it makes them recognisable as a united force but indistinguishable as individuals. They swagger about the city in groups and intimidate members of the population at random for no discernible reason except that they are not pure-bred Benejaden. The group leaders are armed with scimitars and the troops under them are armed with machetes. When I first see these, I realise that they are the weapon shown sickeningly on the video which is still vivid in my imagination.

I become a recognisable regular at what is my favourite and most productive café, the translated name of which is *House of Smoke and Tranquillity*. The Arabs I meet there realise very quickly that I am not a local Arab. The café proprietor is a fount of local knowledge which is invaluable to me.

At first the proprietor is cautious; he doesn't know me and recognises that I am not an Arab from his branch of the culture. After a short while and a lot of assurance from me he begins to open up and we become well enough acquainted for him to impart interesting titbits of information. Some of what he says is disturbing and some horrific. Followers of New Light are full-time terrorists and they earn a living by extorting payment from local businesses in return for protection against the excesses of members of New Light. This pressure has recently been applied to Arab businesses as well as unprotected local businesses and has resulted in the closure of some of them, which increases the financial burden of the fewer businesses which still operate.

Arab traders had, in the past, been ambivalent about the extortion aimed at Benejaden businesses, but now that it also directly affects them there is a growing ground swell among the Arabs to counter the extortion. This resistance takes the form of subtle sabotage which will dilute the power of New Light and its followers. Being from trading stock back in their own home countries, they use all their historic wiles to decrease New Light's income from local businesses by a war of attrition. Instead of buying the materials of their trade from local sources they secure them from across the border in Algeria where businesses are not subjected to Benejaden extortion. The combination of all Arab businesses covering not just the cafés but also restaurants, construction, garages and petrol purveyors, maintenance companies and all their offshoots, has an immediate effect on commercial stability across the city.

This action throws cold water on the lawless bands of New Light militia and their hangers on who are acting without co-ordination and lack the knowhow to retaliate against the unified approach of the Arab traders, without whom the city would cease to function. This more than any other single thing leads me to a cold conclusion, as my alter ego *binary one* character, that I am going to have to fly in the face of my *binary zero* nature and stop Benningo Dagobah in his tracks by force and render New Light unviable. Unless he has a peaceful change of heart I must take physical action against him and afterwards live with myself.

Abu Haider:

At first I was wary about the newcomer; he looks like an Arab and his vocabulary is very good but his accent is as indeterminate as his true origin. He comes to the House of Smoke and Tranquillity each day, morning and evening; he takes Arab coffee in the morning and lemon tea in the early evening. He listens a lot and speaks little; as a regular he soon becomes accepted even though he chooses not to partake of the hookah like all other customers. My customers are exclusively male, their womenfolk, like mine, remain at home with the household and children as is their sole responsibility.

This morning he enters, nods to me and takes his customary seat in the corner furthest from the door and facing it. I prepare his coffee and have one of the serving boys deliver it to him. He lifts the small cup and salutes me to signify his thanks for my attention to his needs. As is his custom he unfolds a week-old French newspaper which he has purchased on his way here and begins reading while he samples the coffee with relish.

After finishing his coffee and newspaper he comes to the counter to pay me, exchange pleasantries and to catch up on the local news. We speak to each other in Arabic mixed with North African French, it is an exotic mixture which lends itself well for political discussion and we express our views freely. He has not, in all the time we have been talking, told me his name, so I refer to him by the name which I and some of my other customers who speak to him; Monsieur L'Etranger.

"Monsieur, you are looking pensive. Are you well?" I ask him with concern.

"I am well but the time has come for me to move on and I will be leaving here in a few days; I shall miss our discussions."

"Will you be returning at some time?"

"You can count on it; I am intrigued by the strange mixture of customs here."

"I will give you any information I can before you leave and if it is the will of God, after you return."

Simon Hunter:

Leaving the café, I head back to my rented rooms to prepare for my journey to the civilised, independent, and friendly country of Nematasulu to lay the foundation of a bolt hole. Before the great global financial collapse Nematasulu had been the southern part of a now defunct region which was hived off to enable recovery from the catastrophic financial failure. The move failed. On the short journey to my rooms I come across a small group of New Lighters in their customary long robes. They are in the process of beating a young man who is alone and defenceless against their brutality.

Having knocked him senseless they swagger off, leaving him lying on the ground in a pool of blood. Each New Lighter kicks the supine figure, laughing as they leave to find fresh victims. Other townsfolk, studiously ignore the departing thugs and walk around the figure on the ground without offering to assist him in any way. They all have haunted looks. I kneel beside the unconscious figure and feel for his neck pulse, and despite the significant blood loss his heart rhythm is slow and steady. Satisfied that he is not in imminent mortal danger I go to a nearby shop and use their telephone to call for medical assistance.

The first question I am asked by the emergency operator shocks me. "What is the nationality of the injured person?"

"I don't know his nationality, he is unconscious – why is his nationality important?"

"You are obviously not a Benejaden citizen or you would not ask such a question." The call was disconnected abruptly without resolution and without any offer of assistance.

The injured man stirs and tries unsuccessfully to stand, finally collapsing back to the ground. I do my best to determine the extent of his injuries but I am no doctor. He appears not to have any life-threatening injuries that I can detect. As he begins to recover I sit him up and then assist him to stand. He weaves drunkenly and clings to me until his head clears enough for him to stand unsteadily but unaided.

"Don't try too much too soon." I speak to him in French as he appears to be a local.

"I need to sit somewhere." He shakes his head groggily.

"Here." I place his arm around my shoulders. "I'll take you to the House of Smoke and Tranquillity from where we can get you medical help."

"That is an Arab House." His voice is full of concern; he looks me up and down. "And you are an Arab; if they catch me with you or in the Arab café they will beat me again. I cannot risk that."

"If we go quickly and are careful nobody who can harm you will see us."

With some reluctance, he allows me to guide him to the café; I make sure we stay in the shadows as much as possible. There are no other people about at what is normally a busy time of day. It seems that the locals stay away from the town when the New Lighters are on the rampage.

Abu Haider shuffles towards us as we enter his premises. "Monsieur L'Etranger, who have you here?

He has need of assistance?"

"This man was beaten by a group of thugs and he needs medical attention."

"Through here, quickly, before anybody sees us." He ushers us through bead curtains which lead to his living accommodation. "If New Light sees him in here he will be in big trouble."

"That's the impression he gave me, but I don't understand why." I look at him enquiringly.

"New Light believes in what they call racial purity which they take to the extreme by denying the right of people of different nationality to band together. This man is Benejaden but I suspect he has other blood in his makeup which is probably why he has been treated so badly."

"So where does that leave me?"

"You are an Arab, so you are welcome in here but would not be so welcome in establishments owned or run by other nationalities. New Lighters tolerate us because we look after their commercial interests but even we are limited in our freedoms."

"Why have I not been aware of this before now?"

"Because the New Light leaders have been down country, infecting other populations with their brand of separatist religion. The hard core of New Light and its leader Benningo Dagobah have just returned from a recruiting drive. Tomorrow there is to be a rally outside the Almighty Golden Shrine which must be attended by all Benejadens, who are required to show their solidarity and support for the movement. Only pure-blood Benejadens are permitted to attend; any interlopers will be flogged and that includes us Arabs."

"What can we do about this man's injuries?"

"Officially nothing, but unofficially, well, that's a different matter."

Benningo Dagobah:

I find the need to raise funds by raiding towns and countries outside Benejado province and city a tiresome distraction. Having to take steps to raise money to fund our activities is caused by our squeezing the Arab traders too far, which has had the unforeseen effect of slowing down of city businesses. It has reached the point where we are unable to extract sufficient revenue for the needs of New Light from non-Arab businesses. My visit to outlying areas has been useful but raising funds by these means is a short-term solution. I need to find something longer term if I am to expand the influence of my sacred movement.

On my return to the city after a relatively short absence I can see the continued deterioration of local trading, which makes my funding situation even worse. The only businesses which have not suffered are those run by the Arab contingent; if anything, they are more prosperous. My instinct is to whip them into line by imposing heavy local taxes but I am conscious that without their input the city would fall into ruin structurally and commercially. I take a tour of the city to re-establish the hold over the citizens, which seems to have slipped during my brief absence.

I tour the city in my official limousine which is old but the best available. Automobiles are rare in our city; the roads are not constructed to take them and the people cannot afford them. The outriders forming my bodyguard have bicycles; I would rather they had motorcycles to give them more presence but money is tight and imported motorcycles are expensive. In the Arab Quarter, I stop at the biggest establishment on the street, the House of Smoke and Tranquillity. Their lemon tea is the best in the city.

I am greeted by the proprietor, Abu Haider, and invited into the area which he reserves for people of importance, and he provides me with lemon tea and a plate of sliced melon and mango with a scattering of cinnamon, just the way I like it. We speak in the usual patois of French.

"Welcome to the House of Smoke and Tranquillity, Your Excellency." He treats me with the respect which I both expect and deserve.

"I choose your establishment because it suits my purposes and I know I can always rely on your courtesy." We go through this ritual whenever I visit.

"Your Excellency is too kind and I offer sustenance to you without expecting anything in return except, of course, for your continued patronage."

I partake of the refreshments and look around the establishment. The hubbub which was so evident when I first arrived has ceased completely and the other patrons finish their refreshments, smoking, and games, and leave quietly. Within five minutes the only people in the establishment are in the VIP area. They comprise of me and my entourage, Abu Haider, and a guest Arab with whom he had been in conversation on my arrival. I take Abu Haider aside and ask him who the other guest is and whether he can be trusted.

He looks at me and then at the other guest. "This is a compatriot of mine who travels through here on his way south."

"What is the name of this stranger and how long will he stay?" I ask in a voice loud enough for the stranger to hear.

He rises from his seat and approaches me, stopping before his proximity causes my body guards to react to him. "Excellency, I am Simon L'Etranger and as Abu Haider has told you, I am passing through on my way south and have paused so that I may enjoy his generous hospitality." He lets down the hood of his long tunic to reveal a strong dark mahogany face framed by long, straight, dark hair which is contrasted by a trimmed beard which gives him a slightly demonic look. His chocolate brown eyes look directly at me; normally people look away from me, fearing a confrontation.

"This is not a good time for visitors. I advise you to be on your way, this is not a place for those who don't belong." I keep my face wooden to emphasise that I am not making a suggestion but giving him an order.

Simon Hunter:

Dagobah is the man I had journeyed to see and quite by chance we meet face to face and I have an opportunity to observe him. After receiving his barely veiled threat concerning my departure, I calm our conversation and give myself a chance to further my cause.

"I thank you for your concern, Excellency. I will not be here for much longer and I will make sure that

I do not place myself in any dangerous situations." I purposely misconstrue his threat as an offer of advice for my safety. "I have some trading to do which will take only a short time and it is to the advantage of your great city because it will bring great prosperity to it and your people."

His interest in my words is immediate. "All business of any significance in this city is conducted through me and through nobody else, but I am not aware of the potential to which you refer."

"That is because I arrived at a time of your absence. Abu Haider did inform me of the importance of your position here and I have been waiting for an opportunity to contact you so it is my good fortune that you have come to this establishment today." I am trying to keep cool and relaxed but I am inventing this conversation on the hoof and the stress level of doing so is high.

"What is the nature of this business you wish to conduct?"

I must think quickly; I have no such plan and the stress inches up perceptibly. I need to propose something which will benefit him but which I don't have to follow through on immediately – or at all. "I am considering building an international business centre here which will start with the construction of a hotel with conference and leisure facilities, here in Benejado city, which I can later expand into a manufacturing and production facility. All of this will bring great wealth to the city and its administrators." As my stress level lowers I can see his greed level rising.

Abu Haider:

I now know Simon L'Etranger well enough to see that he is thinking on his feet. The building of a hotel and conference centre is news to me and I'm sure that if this is his intention he would have told me. I remain impassive and make no comment about the conversation. He who runs the House of Smoke and Tranquillity must always exercise discretion.

After Dagobah and his entourage leave I take Simon to one side; I need to warn him of the danger he is putting himself in by associating with this unprincipled man.

"My friend, take care! This man to whom you talked is most dangerous. My advice to you is to leave this place, forget any dealings with Dagobah, and never to return."

"Abu, there are some things we can walk away from and others that it is impossible to overlook. Dagobah is the latter; I understand you cautioning me but I have no option but to continue on the path I have chosen."

"The choice is yours, my friend, but be aware that this man has no morals and he will stop at nothing to get what he wants."

"I know that and I intend to exploit it." He offers no further explanation and I do not seek more of him.

Benningo Dagobah:

This man Simon L'Etranger is of interest to me and I will exploit him. The facility he intends to build must of course be financed fully by him and the permits he needs to realise this intention are within my gift alone. He must be of low intelligence to want to build such a facility in this place which is populated by ignorant people, and I cannot imagine international business people wanting to travel here to what is, even by my country's standards, a primitive city with none of the trappings of infidel civilisation.

On the day following our meeting, L'Etranger arrives punctually as one in my position would expect. I tell my serving man to explain to him that I am having telephone discussions with international business people who wish to invest in the city and the discussions are running over, so he must wait until I am ready to see him. I continue with my breakfast and indulge in a third cup of thick, sweet Arab coffee while I plan what I will do with the money that is to be generated by my building permits.

After an hour or so I tell my man servant to show the visitor in. As he enters I speak into my telephone. "You are not offering enough; this discussion is at an end; I have other interested parties to speak to." The person to whom I speak is of course imaginary. I finish the 'call' and wave my visitor into a chair. "Speed in this is all-important," I tell him. "There are others who have designs like your own and they are all the time trying to bribe me to let them in. But I will not succumb to their cheap efforts to have me use my influence in their favour." I let him make of what I say as he will.

"Excellency, I am grateful for being given the opportunity to talk to you, I know you are a very busy man so if you will forgive me I will not go through any meaningless overtures, I will get straight to the point."

His attitude piques my interest; he is dispensing with the usual Arab preambles and customs.

"Feel free to be direct in your discussions. I am ready to listen to any reasonable proposition."

Simon Hunter:

Subtlety is not in Dagobah's make-up, although he undoubtedly thinks it is. He kept me waiting for an hour to show that he is boss and when I enter his room he pretends to be talking pertinent business. What he does not realise is that I can hear the dial tone as he speaks to nobody.

"Excellency, you are a busy man so I will not employ the usual small talk but rather get straight to the point."

He accepts my direct approach, seeing it as a complement.

"Excellency, I can generate the necessary payment to meet your documentation costs but it will of course take time. International rules for the transfer of cash between countries are tight."

His brows knit in disappointment and frustration. "Time is something I don't have, if you are unable to satisfy my demands I will have to go elsewhere to do business."

"Excellency, doing this in cash is difficult but there is another way."

His brow smooths again as he grasps the lifebelt I have thrown him. "What is it you propose?"

"I have many international business interests and I'm sure that through one of them I can arrange for the import of strategic goods which will be of interest to you."

"What do I need of your western goods? Life here is simple, we have no need of your overindulgenccs." His voice rises with a passion borne of an inner fundamentalist demon which he nurtures.

"I have interests in construction, food manufacture, oil harvesting, and refining…" I can see that he is losing interest but I continue purposefully. "Engineering, power generation, automobile manufacture, armaments, mining…"

He interrupts me, suddenly animated. "You may have something that will interest me, not food or engineering or automobiles or the other things, but there is one thing that may be of passing interest, if what you propose is thought-provoking enough."

"And what might that be, Excellency?" I ask, feigning innocence.

"I might be interested, a little, in acquiring some armaments, just small things. This is to protect our citizens from harm, you understand; I have their interests at heart." He does his best to look pious but is unconvincing.

"Of course, Excellency. Your motives are impeccable and because of this I'm sure I can satisfy your requirements in good conscience. Please let me know what they are and I'm sure we will be able to do business of mutual interest."

The bait is swallowed whole and the meeting comes to what is for me a very satisfactory conclusion. I've found a chink in Dagobah's armour. The only funds to which he has access are in Golacian Dinar, for which there is no international market; this is something I can turn to my advantage. I have an opportunity to become his monetary exchange source which will allow him, he believes, to buy arms from me to further his quest for power. I have other ideas.

Having recently sold my London consultancy business, I am awash with cash. I'm talking billions, which is available to fund my obsession. I have a chance to put it to good use and stop this maniac before he gets to be big enough to become a continent-wide and then a world-wide threat. I intend to clip his wings before he reaches that status and then put him out of business for good.

Benningo Dagobah:

I am told that the Arab community is where the business brains lie but my meeting with Monsieur L'Etranger proves that premise to be wrong. With very little effort I have secured a supply of arms and ammunition at no cost to me. This strengthens my hold over the people in Benejado City and Province and beyond into neighbouring areas. Using new firearms instead of the mismatched crude weapons currently at my disposal against machetes, knives, and spears guarantees an easy ride to victory.

It will be simple enough for me to give L'Etranger what he wants because my control over local affairs is absolute and permissions required for building anything can be sped up or slowed down by me alone to suit my purposes. This makes me feel better because the lack of general subservience in the general Arab business community has hurt me in a way which I will soon be able to control. When my position is stronger, as it will be when I acquire the arms, I will make the Arab business community pay for their disrespect.

The Arab is very keen to develop the business centre because he returns to me later in the day to tell me that he has arranged for a shipment of arms to be made within the next three weeks, and he has acquired all the items on my list. I have only asked for side arms and combat rifles with a modest amount of ammunition for 'defence' purposes. My next order will step up the requirements to include more substantial things like RPGs and anti-personnel mines, again, of course, for 'defence' purposes.

Simon Hunter:

Dagobah is typical of many other would-be tyrants who are so focussed on their illicit objectives that they don't feel the need to work at subterfuge. They believe that their force of personality is enough to obscure their actual intentions. He fits the pattern exactly.

Before engaging any enemy, I must find any weaknesses that I can exploit but at the same time, I must ensure that the enemy does not adopt a similar strategy. My big advantage over Benningo Dagobah is that I know he is my enemy but he doesn't know that I am his. Having learned that he is in town to spread his vile xenophobic message, I decide to delay my departure to Nematasulu to observe my adversary.

His nominal advantage over me is that he is on

home territory and he has hundreds, maybe thousands of followers supporting him. My task, therefore, is to take away the advantages which he has and either turn them to serve me or to negate their advantages to him. To do this I must find a way to gather intelligence about him and his movement. Mustering an army of helpers would attract retribution and accepting that I can never outnumber his forces, I must work alone or with a minimal, carefully chosen force. Rather than trying to recruit a local force myself I intend to talk to my contacts in Nematasulu who are more likely to be able to help me. To establish the type of people required I must first get closer to Dagobah and New Light.

So long as he thinks his subterfuge is working it is easier for me to manipulate Dagobah in the way he believes he is manipulating me. When I tell him that the arms will be shipped to him very shortly he pretends to be offhand but I can tell that he is excited by the prospect. The arms that I have ordered for him, modified to my detailed performance specification, will be supplied from Nuovostan, the small state located on the Russian border with Manchuria, with whom I have had a long working relationship. Their off-the-wall President, Irena Pelochev, has agreed to help me. I have asked her to have all the manufacturing identification marks removed from all items, including the cartridge cases and all documentation. The source of the equipment will be untraceable. In the intervening period between now and the time of supply I will travel to Nematasulu. One of the senior members of the Nematasulu legislature is Noah, son of Chester Gilliland who is the principle founder of my Colony home.

The time I have available to make preparation for the task ahead is extremely limited and getting into Nematasulu is not straight-forward because of the link-up the country has with the Colony, which is in international terms considered to be a pariah. I opt for driving to the capital, Golas City, and arrange for a Nematasulan helicopter to come and collect me. Fortunately for me the security operation in Golas is patchy so it is easy enough to evade the regulations and falsify the source country and destination of the flight.

The helicopter that is used to ferry me is, to others, unusual. It bears the Nuovostani insignia of the country of manufacture but is designed and owned by the Colony and secretly based in the protectorate of Nematasulu. The unusual element in the design of the helicopter, apart from its unconventional shape, is its means of propulsion. The noise-free engine is a compressed sodium power unit and the pair of over-under countermotion rotor blades is skilfully configured to operate as silently as the engine.

Although I have flown in this type of craft before, I am still struck by its noise-free effortless power. The odd shape of the fuselage reflects that it is covered in a series of ram parachute compartments and contains the sodium-fuelled engine. It can fly at the speed of a fighter jet because the rotors can be retracted and swept wings can be deployed which allows the special engine to act like a jet.

The journey to Nematasulu is completed inside half an hour, in smooth silence. Jubil radios ahead and arranges for the defence shield which covers the entire country to have the landing passage from the north east opened. This entails making an opening in the energised defence shield big enough for the helicopter to fly through in safety. The shield which breaks up anything attempting to pass through it. Our helicopter is guided through the invisible opening using GPS. Even though I am aware of the safety protocols in operation to prevent harm to those flights passing into the Nematasulu air space, I am still nervous. Jubil has unshakable confidence in the 3D radar display in the air traffic control centre.

Noah Gilliland:

I was surprised to hear from Simon. I understand from my father that Simon is no longer a seeker for the Colony and he no longer carries out overseas missions to acquire specialist personnel to supplement the Colony's workforce. I also know that his position in his English base was compromised after a particularly difficult assignment during which members of his family were kidnapped and their lives threatened. He undertook by personal intervention to have them released from captivity but in doing so lost the anonymity so necessary for his work as a seeker. He was further compromised by being pressganged into doing intelligence work for the USA and UK which in the end made his situation untenable.

I have met him on several occasions when visiting my parents at our Colony home and know him to be a close friend to them and the other founding members of the Colony. His communication with me to arrange a visit to Nematasulu was terse. Up to now, although we have never been that close, he has been warm and open and I cannot help but wonder about the nature of his visit. Yesterday I received an express parcel from my old friend Ed Pickering, who is the Colony's brilliant chief engineer, which is addressed to Simon and marked most urgent. Ed radioed me to make sure that I deliver the parcel to him.

When Simon is shown into my apartment I am shocked by his appearance. He wears malodourous Arab clothes which are of a dirty brown coarse material which has seen better days. His usually neat hair is unkempt and his former tanned appearance is now burned black by exposure to the sun. His eyes are wrong; they are a dark fathomless brown – not the startling blue which is one of his trademarks.

"Noah, thank you for seeing me so quickly and for not asking awkward questions."

"Simon, I hardly recognise you. It's good to see you but what are you doing here?"

"I need some strong manpower and I'm hoping you can help me. Please don't ask me too many questions, the fewer people who know what I am doing, the safer my operation will be."

"I do trust you but I need to know a little more of what you want before I can help you."

Simon leans forward and bows his head, when his head is lifted again he holds out his hand in which nestles two contact lenses. "I'm glad to be able to take these out for a moment," revealing his familiar piercing blue eyes. "What do you know about Benningo Dagobah?"

"Other than that he is a depraved unprincipled oppressor – not a lot. Why is he of interest to you?"

"The man is a bigoted terrorist…"

"Is there any other kind?" I can't help myself interrupting him.

"Some are driven by a fundamental belief which is wrong but at least fathomable; Dagobah has no principles other than the promotion of his own self-interest. He murders out of some sort of blood lust and appears to enjoy doing it.

"My original question still stands. Why is he of interest to you?"

"What I can divulge is that my circumstances have changed radically since we last met. I am no longer a seeker for the Colony and I no longer run the London-based consultancy. I am a freelancer and the task I have given myself is to prevent Dagobah from murdering any more of his own people and to stop him from spreading his evil to other parts; not just of Africa but of the world. Goodness knows there are enough miscreants in the world that will follow his twisted philosophy to what he considers to be its glorious conclusion."

"Surely that's what the international security agencies are for?"

He gives me a resigned look. "By the time they become involved, if they ever do, it will be way too late for anything but damage limitation; history is littered with such people and their influences. I'm not prepared to wait for that to happen. It is my intention to stop him dead in his tracks with a minimum of delay. I've already set the ball rolling and I need to follow up on what I've done already. I will appreciate help from you to do this but if you feel unwilling to help I will understand."

"What is it that you want me to do?"

I am gratified to see the tension leech from him.

Simon Hunter:

As I begin my discussion with Noah it is as if the intervening time has evaporated in an instant; he possesses the same stoicism as his father, Chester, and he has the same sharp mind as his mother, Penny.

"When did you last see my father?" he enquires.

"A few months ago on my last visit to the Colony."

"Did you find him well?"

"I did, he is in remarkably good health." My response tails off.

"You were about to add 'for his age', I presume."

"No, age is something I have come to terms with. I was going to say – considering the difficulty he goes through in running the Colony. His advanced age – like my own is held at bay by the Colony's unique health regimes."

"I don't want to mislead you, Noah. I am doing this without the full knowledge of your father; he has enough on his plate without having to be concerned with my problems."

"My father has always trusted you implicitly and I trust his instincts so as I said. What do you want me to do?"

"I'm dealing with people who have no morals or conscience and I am going to be stirring up a hornets' nest. I may well need outside support from time to time."

"Consider it offered without reservation."

"Thank you. It may be dangerous for the people I need to assist me and I will understand completely if you feel unable to provide me with the manpower I need."

"Tell me what you need and the nature of the danger."

Benningo Dagobah:

The arms have arrived as promised; the consignment is marked 'agricultural implements' and I make sure that the crates are not opened until they are safe from scrutiny in the underground storage facility in my compound. There are three crates; one with assault rifles, one with two types of side arms, and a third with ammunition for all three types of weapon.

I feel the satisfying power of my possessions when I distribute them to my three trusted commanders and I am gratified by the look on their faces when they see the gleaming weapons. For each commander, there is a machine pistol and for each of their six-man groups there is a smaller side arm. One of the assault rifles, a small side arm, and a sniper's rifle are mine and I have them on display for all to see and understand my seniority.

Future executions will not be by the sword, although it is an effective way of instilling fear. With this assault rifle I can despatch unbelievers in groups rather than one at a time and frighten many more people at the same time. The commanders will no doubt be going to the beer halls and celebrating their new-found power. I expect to hear shots being fired as soon as they are drunk which does not take much time. The raw alcohol brewed here in the city, under my control, takes effect very quickly.

To make sure I can handle the weapon with ease I decide to fire a few practice shots in the secrecy of my underground facility. Fitting the ammunition clip into the weapon is easy enough and I caress the oily smooth weapon which gives me a feeling of great power. The rifle can be used with the extended skeleton butt nestled into the shoulder or by modifying it so that it nestles into the crook of my arm. It is this second mode which I favour and after making a simple adjustment I feel at ease with the weapon. Pointing it at one of the earth walls, I squeeze the trigger; there is no give in the trigger and nothing happens. I try again with the same result; in disgust, I throw the weapon at the earth wall and watch it bounce off and come to rest at my feet.

There is a manual in the packing crate and on flicking through I find that it is written in several languages, one of which is French, which I read tolerably well. After sifting through the instructions, I find that there is a catch which must be manipulated to make it work. I unlock it. I am very pleased; my superior intellect has enabled me to operate this highly technical piece of equipment. I hold it one-handed and squeeze the trigger; there is an angry buzzing sound and the gun flies from my grasp after hitting my upper arm with painful force. The weapon falls to the ground; there is a stitch pattern of bullet holes running diagonally across the wall. My arm is numb and the magazine, now empty, has been automatically ejected from the gun along with the spent shells.

Further examination of the instructions tells me that there is a slide control which enables me to select single, double, five-shot bursts, or whole-magazine discharge. This is a powerful weapon indeed and I must treat it with the respect that I expect others to treat me now that I am all-powerful. I decide to forgive L'Etranger his transgressions because that's what powerful people can do.

Simon Hunter:

Together with six hand-picked members of the Nematasulu defence forces I take a Jetstream helicopter ride back to Golas; the operation proper has at last started. During my short stay in Nematasulu I considered something I should have done earlier. My wish to stop this mindless organisation from being a serious threat to the rest of the world undermined my normally logical planning process. I came to Golas without having first determined a clearly defined strategy; the time has come to put that right.

Once we are airborne I open the package from Ed Pickering. Inside the box is a tear-shaped medallion which has a fine black enamel neck chain. In the centre of one face of the teardrop is a button and in the box, is a note from Ed. It simply instructs me *'to prevent disaster press the kill button'*. The dry humour is typical of Ed. I place it around my neck and inside my robe. There is a selection of other items in the package which I delight in inspecting.

It is important that the strategy I pursue makes sure that I am not falling into the age-old trap of simply pursuing a wish list. My strategy is to prevent the propagation of the doctrine of 'New Light' which is a simple aim but what I must do to fulfil my objectives is to do so in such a way that the organisation is not just abandoned, but that it is fatally and permanently crippled. In this respect the importance is that the tactics must satisfy the strategy.

I must disable the New Light hierarchy and discredit them so that there is no chance of them re-emerging as a credible organisation. Financing the operation is not a problem, my own reserves are more than adequate. Arming those I intend to defeat flies in the face of logic, but there is method in my madness. My intention is to appear to throw my lot in with Benningo Dagobah and to have him see me as an ally. Financing him will help me achieve that aim providing he believes I am doing this corruptly – in accordance with his lamentable moral code.

I am not prepared to sit back and wait for the events to unfold outcome, I will ignite Dagobah's passions to accelerate him towards his own self-destruction. He is a man of great ambition and limited intelligence so I must rush him into pursuing his goals more quickly than his limited intelligence can handle so that he will make mistakes. Timing is of the essence and the speed of action must be accelerated to keep him off balance.

Back in Benejado City I give my six Nematasulan troops the arms I had had delivered to Nematasulu. They are better than those which I have provided to

Dagobah and ensure that they are openly displayed in as intimidating a manner as can be achieved. I let Dagobah know that we are here to help him. He is caught off balance by our unexpected arrival and the displeasure shows on his churlish face.

"What you are doing?" he remonstrates in his customary bad tempered way.

"Excellency; I come to you with good news." I speak with a deference which the strength of our presence belies.

"What is this good news?" His speech falters as he sees the armaments being sported by my six companions. "Those guns," he points to them, "they are not like them ones you have presented to me. Why is this so?"

"These guns are the very latest to be produced and I am testing them for the manufacturer. Out of respect I have saved one for you." I hand him a chamois leather pouch containing a side arm like the ones worn by my companions. "These are so much in short supply that I have no spares and so I present my personal one to you, as a sign of my respect."

He looks at me haughtily. "I expect nothing less; as the head of New Light it is my right." He replaces his original weapon with the new one and turns to look at my companions. "And who are these people? I don't recognise them, they are not Golacian and they are armed which is against the law. I cannot allow their presence either armed or unarmed. They must be questioned and dealt with."

"Excellency; these are a hand-picked bodyguard for you. They are the best and most loyal professional soldiers in the whole of Africa; they will ensure your safety in the coming days when your aims will be accelerated. You will defeat your enemies before they are even aware of your presence."

"We will talk in confidence. Tell these men to stand guard outside my residence and ensure our safety."

Benningo Dagobah:

When L'Etranger appears unbidden, I am alarmed to see him with armed men. He quickly apologises and I decided to grant him an audience so that I might interrogate him. I feel more comfortable when he tells me that his armed men are here to act as my personal bodyguard and I feel even happier when he tells me that they will carry out their duties without recompense. I will move forward with the permissions he requires to build his hotel complex. In view of his generosity I will make sure he pays in full for all the favours I will grant.

The new side arm he gives me is so much better than the earlier model and will impress my subordinates, but it would be better if my bodyguards had weapons inferior to my own just to underline my superiority. I can show them off to my advantage and let my people know that they are trained assassins who will do my bidding without question. A little fear among the ranks of my supporters will keep them on their toes.

Tefawa Belawa:

I've been unexpectedly called back to the MI6

offices in London for a meeting with Sir Michael; this is unusual, I hope that I am not in trouble. When I learn that the meeting is to be held in one of the small sound- and bug-proof meeting rooms my concern levels ratchet up. When he enters the room, he looks care worn and is not at all his usual urbane self; I worry a little more and wait to learn of the reason for our unusual meeting.

"I am sorry to have dragged you away from your overseas duties." It is very unlike him to start off a discussion with an apology. "Something disturbing is going on in Golas. There is a shift of power which is not to my liking. Somehow 'New Light' has been able to acquire sophisticated armaments which could easily change the delicate political balance there." He passes his hand over his face in a dry washing motion. "I am concerned about Simon's safety."

I am relieved that he wants to talk to me about this situation and not about something I have done in contravention of one of the many regulations which blight the service. "How is it possible for them to get weapons? They have no foreign currency and their own money is worthless on the international market."

"My contacts don't know how Dagobah was able to purchase arms and pay in dollars but he did. My concern is that Hunter is in the home of New Light, Benejado City; it was unsafe for him when they were not armed but now that they are his position could be critical. I want you to make sure either from your homeland contacts or by you personally that Hunter will come to no harm."

Simon Hunter:

It is fortunate that Dagobah is essentially unintelligent but that state also can be dangerous for me in that he can be unpredictable and illogical. Simplistically I could simply take him out of the equation by physical means which is something I would not relish or actually condone. To adopt that course could lead to him being made a martyr which would run counter to my intentions. I need to employ methods which will bring him and his organisation down permanently and nip in the bud any consequential offshoots; all of this without revealing that I have been instrumental in his downfall. To do so would make me recognisable and jeopardise any future projects. To achieve these aims it is necessary for me to think in the same illogical way as my adversary. Dagobah is anathema; he aims to be a leader of men but is unable to communicate on anything but the most basic of levels. Any actions I take must be contrary to anything he could possibly perceive as being threatening to him.

On the day following the meeting with him and the new bodyguard, I get a demand from Dagobah; he requires my presence in his compound immediately. On arrival, I am ushered into an interior room with no windows or natural light. I get an unnerving feeling that nasty things happen in this room. I make sure that I am facing Dagobah and have sight of the single door, I have no wish to be ambushed. Dagobah's weapon is in plain sight; I too am armed but my flowing Arab robes make it impossible for me to access the weapon quickly.

Dagobah is relaxed in his own lair and does not

give off vibrations of ill intent, but I am still wary. I make sure by my countenance that he is not aware of my unease. After a long pause, he waves me into a seat with a dismissive gesture. "I accept your small gift of upgraded arms; this equipment is adequate but I am a man of sophistication and I am disappointed that the gift you have offered me is not of the quality which a man of my standing deserves. The guards you have provided to me are equally equipped as I and this is not proper. You will disarm your men of the weapons they have and replace them with the same quality as those of my foot soldiers."

This is not a request and I have to respond carefully if I am to begin my mind games with him. "Excellency, the side arms they have are their own property and they are soldiers of fortune with great experience. What you wish cannot easily be done."

His response is harsh; his eyes glint with a glimpse of his underlying madness as he shouts at me. "This is not a request, it is an order." He draws his weapon and points it at me.

Benningo Dagobah:

This infidel must be out of his mind to resist my orders. To my surprise, I do not see a look of concern on his face as I point my side arm at him and flick off the safety catch. My voice is intimidating. "We could have worked together and had the greatest of success, me with New Light and you with your hotel and conference centre. This is not to be so." I squeeze the trigger and take up the first pressure, as the manual advises.

"Before you do that; just consider what I can do for you." He points at my gun. "The side arm I give you just yesterday has already been superseded. What I have for you is a weapon which is the envy of even the topmost fighting professionals – including your new bodyguards. It is a twenty-five shot, nine-millimetre NLG Surekill which was delivered to me by special courier overnight. I have it for trial purposes; it is the first one produced and as a mark of my respect I would like to present it to you… if you will permit me to get it out. I had intended to present it to you later but you quite rightly want to be armed with very latest weapon as befits your station."

To my annoyance, even though I am pointing a gun at him he does not look afraid, which is disrespectful and annoying but I unexpectedly find what he says piques my interest. "Be very careful when you take the weapon out and when you do hold it between finger and thumb by the end of the barrel, with your left hand." Infuriatingly he smiles as he does what I ask and he produces an ugly, menacingly black pistol between thumb and finger, which he offers to me. I indicate to him with a wave of my side arm to place the weapon on the nearby table and to retreat to a safe distance.

As soon as he is far enough from the table that he would be unable to reach the weapon before me, I step forward and pick it up. Still covering him with my original gun, I lift the ugly piece with my left hand; the pistol grip which I assume carries the twenty-five-shot magazine is much heavier than I expect it to be.

He watches me, still with the infuriating half smile.

"Excellency, I have only your best interests at heart. I bring this new weapon with me as a gift to you and to give you even more superiority than you have been given by nature."

This man clearly understands that I am the chosen one. I smile at him and lower my gun. "I realised you were trying in your puny way to test me, and I was equal to the task. I saw through your deception and defeated you by pure understanding, which I don't expect you to be able to comprehend."

This man is useful to me because of his contacts and access to foreign money, but he is no match for my superior intellect.

Simon Hunter:

I can't remember the last time I was forced to think so fast and without a prepared plan. When Dagobah draws his gun on me my head is empty of ideas, but adrenalin gives a wondrous jump-start to initiative. The NLG Surekill I carry was never meant for him but it certainly got me out of a hole when the idea of a making it a gift struck me. A useful thing is revealed by my fast thinking; his reaction to the situation. This man is even less astute than I thought; he is under the illusion that he is the chosen one and that he is my intellectual superior. I file this away for future use, such knowledge may be critical.

He hefts the NLG Surekill from hand to hand, revelling in the feel and weight which I know from handling the piece myself is a striking part of its ownership. He places his original firearm in the drawer of the small table and slides it shut. The new weapon is placed in the belt clip.

I wrestle a custom-made holster from under my robes and hand it to him. "This is the correct holster for your new piece; please accept this also with my compliments."

He accepts the gift gracelessly and within a few moments the old holster joins the old weapon in the table drawer and the new one sits more comfortably and elegantly in the larger holster. Glancing at a full-length fly-specked mirror, he squares his shoulders and admires his image. "You will supply me with more of these fine weapons and I will ensure that the permissions you require will be forthcoming." His statement invites no response.

"It would be better, Excellency, if you were the only one in your country to have such a fine weapon. Providing them for all your people would put them on the same level as you." I watch and listen carefully for his reaction to my words.

"Let it be so for the moment. I will review your suggestions at my leisure." He dismisses me with an impatient gesture of his hand.

Benningo Dagobah:

I must be wary of Simon L'Etranger he does not think in the way of other men and he is not easily intimidated. My initial thought is to shoot him or to have him shot by others. For the moment, I will hold back. He is not only a source of weapons which are otherwise denied to me but he is a source of foreign currency for which there are no other avenues – for the moment.

Until I can find alternatives it is my choice to allow him to live and be of use to me. It occurs to me that he might have other uses. He is not Golacian and my detractors from outside Golas have labelled me racist because I strive for national purity. It would suit me to dispel that impression even though it is true. I need to garner more international standing and using L'Etranger as a prominent part of New Light will help me in this regard.

I will grant him the permissions he requires and as a part of that process I will insist on him becoming a visible part of New Light and of his appearing at my promotional gatherings. I need to appear, to my international audiences, to take a softer approach to assuage the fears of those outside my sphere of direct influence. The rally for the faithful in Golas City will be my platform for launching L'Etranger on the international stage to disprove claims of xenophobia. This will show the world that I am not the butcher shown on the world news, holding the severed head of one of my detractors. Allowing a new image of racial tolerance to be released into the soft western world is a way of mitigating my past actions. I will select a person that I can blame for this misrepresentation and have him executed publicly for falsely accusing me of intolerance.

Tefawa Belawa:

I report back to Sir Michael Westinghouse as he instructed me – not electronically because the issue is too sensitive to leave a traceable footprint – on the situation regarding Hunter and what he is doing in Golas. He is not happy when I tell him that Hunter is supplying arms to New Light and that additionally he has now become part of the organisation and is appearing at a rally in Golas City to promote the organisation.

"What is he up to?" Sir Michael looks exasperated. "He went there to stop New Light and so far, he has armed them and he is speaking up on their behalf. His methods have always been unconventional but this goes beyond anything I can tolerate. He's making a bad situation far, far worse."

"I find that difficult to accept, sir. The Simon Hunter I know and have worked with under some very challenging circumstances would never betray his principles in this way; he must have a strategy in mind that we don't see."

"I like the man and have sympathy with him for the way he has been treated by us and the Americans in the past, but my fear is the pressure has got to him and that he has turned." He looks as dejected. "What you must do is keep tabs on him and if he is acting in a way which is harmful to us he must be dealt with. Do you understand my meaning?"

"I understand fully, sir, and I will analyse what he is doing and keep you informed."

I don't like the way this is going. Sir Michael's unspoken instruction is that I arrange for Simon's elimination if he is seen to be going over to the other side.

Seeing the look on my face, he narrows his eyes and addresses me by my MI6 code name. "N11, you will be professional about this matter and you will not allow the fact that you know Hunter, to influence your work. If he must be eliminated I expect you to carry out your part of the assignment, is that clear?"

Simon Hunter:

The last week has disappeared in a blur of activity. Moving at a speed that I didn't think possible in this comparatively sleepy backwater, the rally to promote New Light has been set in motion. The venue for the rally is Golas International football stadium, decorated to further the image of New Light. I have been told that I will make a speech extolling the virtues of New Light and to underline that it is an organisation which will promote the interests of Golas to the wider international community.

Dagobah's speech writer will guide me through the process by writing what I must say word for word, and my sticking to the script is an unwavering demand. When I finally see it, I am not surprised that its contents and the message it sends are a confusion of lies, half-truths and wishful thinking. Basically, I am to reach out to the international community as one who is not borne of Golas and extoll the virtues of devout living which is a requirement the New Light experience. I am to explain that the despicable images of cruel execution were faked by an individual who was in the pay of foreign interests and that that person had been taken care of.

Developing the next stage of my plans, I contact Ed Pickering in the Colony by satellite phone. He is a truly inspirational engineer – although the simple word 'engineer' does not begin to cover his talents. He is an inventor of extraordinary talent and I asked him to devise for me and send items to a PO Box in Golas City; I chose this location because the package I request from him will be delivered during my week-long stay in Golas City. To have chosen to have it sent to Benejado City risked it not reaching me or a PO Box. The package is a vital part of my immediate and future plan of action.

On the day of the rally I stand on what is used as a boxing ring. Around me the 18,000 tiered seats are full to capacity with brightly clothed locals who are looking forward to a junket; they have been provided with free beer and local fast food. There is a steady buzz from the crowd punctuated from time to time with outbreaks of loud African music which grows wilder in line with a rise in beer consumption.

In opening, Dagobah is greeted by rapturous whoops and joyous shouting which is the local way of showing approval for the show so far. In reality it is prompted by 'encouragement' from soldiers of the order of New Light. He accepts the accolades, impassively soaking up the mounting adoration. Around the perimeter of the arena are various radio and television station microphone clusters and cameras; mostly they are local outfits but I can see a sprinkling of European and American stations.

Dagobah stills the crowd by hitting the microphone and flapping both hands up and down. Finally, the crowd hushes and Dagobah being the showman he is, pauses in the sudden absence of crowd sound and turns slowly to embrace the whole of the watching stadium with his mesmeric stare. He takes a deep breath and begins his oration.

"Fellow members of our great country and fellow

members of New Light, I greet you and thank you for coming together today to listen to words of great wisdom."

The crowd are prompted to indicate eagerness and he continues his presentation which builds up in both momentum and volume, whipping the watching crowd up into a beer-fuelled fever of adulation. He tells them what they want to hear. He tells them of a bright future for them and for their children and their grandchildren. He denigrates the political elite of the country and tells the listening crowds that their interests are not being addressed by the establishment, their only aim being to feather their own nests and to continue to bleed them dry with ever increasing taxation.

The more he castigates the government, the noisier the roars from the crowd. He holds them in his hands; he is a powerful orator and the noise in the stadium and the effect of what he says are magnified by his few hundred followers who are planted about the stadium. I am impressed and at the same time appalled by the power he commands.

Finally, he finishes his diatribe and introduces me to the crowd as an impartial non-national who has seen the 'New Light' and supports the efforts to take the people of Golas out of the dark ages and to have them emerge into the New Light of prosperity and international influence.

I wait for the wild whooping and singing to die down. I can't help thinking that I am to be the act after the lord mayor's show. He has whipped them up and now surely I am going to bring them back down to earth with a jolt. What Dagobah has done so skilfully is to magnify the mood of the crowd for the sake of local media and now I am to pique the interest of international media by being an impartial outsider who has converted to the true meaning of New Light. There is a greater depth to Dagobah than I had previously thought.

I deliver my speech, word for word as written, to a largely disinterested crowd who have turned the rally into a carnival of dance and music. Their disinterest is not important to Dagobah, what is important is that I am delivering carefully crafted words of encouragement formulated to give the message of his choice to a listening international press corps hungry for reassurances that New Light is not going to be yet another in the long line of terrorist organisations which will harm exo-African society. Reluctantly, I acknowledge that Dagobah is achieving that aim. He is buying himself time to bolster his strength in depth and he is doing so at my expense. I can only hope that I can control the implementation of my tactics and make sure that the victory is mine.

Benningo Dagobah:

Back home in Benejado after the rally, I muse that further success is now assured; I have access to foreign money and arms – and now I have the ear of the international media organisations which are no longer baying for my blood. They seem to have accepted my ruse that the execution which took place so publicly was staged by one of my rivals and that New Light is not a threat. I also demonstrated that I am not a racial purist by having an Arab speak out in defence of New Light. These people can be manipulated so easily.

Monsieur L'Etranger tells me that he must depart from Benejado City to collect some belongings he has left in an outlying village which he visited before coming here. An offer to take him there is not made to help him but so that my people can make sure he is up to no mischief. I am not able to accept the motives of an Arab to be anything but a ruse. He accepts the offer; I have once more shown that my cunning is more than a match for his puny attempts at deception.

Simon Hunter:

The journey to the village where I left my vehicle for safekeeping is made uncomfortable by the appalling condition of the road. Like all the vehicles in Benejado City the one I am in has been cobbled together from several models which had become defunct by age or accident or both. The front half of the hybrid is a crash-damaged Peugeot and the rear a Toyota, both of indeterminate age. Because of this unholy marriage of disparate parts there is a violent disagreement between the functions of the gear box and the differential which causes it to whine incessantly and give a very unsettled ride. Despite the challenges we complete the journey in one piece and without incident.

We arrive at a lockup which I had hired – together with a local guard – to make sure that the vehicle would be safe. As an extra precaution, I had disabled the engine so that it will not start and the steering and all doors are locked. It is as I had left it and the covering of dust shows that it has not been tampered with in my absence. Under the watchful eye of my driver I go through the motions of unlocking the doors and attempting to start it. The starter motor turns over the engine but it fails to catch; I look at the dead engine, feigning disappointment. My driver who obviously admires a vehicle of such beauty feels genuine concern that it won't start.

"Do you know anything about making engines work?" I ask him.

He shakes his head and looks sorrowful.

I open the back of the 4WD and take out a tool box and while the driver's attention is distracted I slip into it the package I had received from Ed Pickering containing the kill switch and other items. Lugging the heavy box around to the engine bay, I open it up and take out a torch which I shine into the dark recesses of the engine. This is all for show and after a little play acting tinkering I try to start the engine again. As I have not actually done anything the engine again refuses to fire up. The driver looks disappointed.

I spend the next two hours using the contents of Ed Pickering's package which enables me to lock out the vehicle's ignition system and replace it with one which can only be activated by me. Using the on-board processor of the engine and navigation system I program the starter button so that the ignition will only operate if it is pressed using my right index finger, using fingerprint recognition. As an added safety precaution, I also program the button to operate by recognising the chemical composition of my DNA. The same technology of skin chemistry is applied to sensors on the steering wheel.

To test the operation of the new system I ask the driver to sit in the driver's seat and start the engine. His joyous expression at being able to sit in this magnificent vehicle and start it is comical. He presses the starter and the engine turns over but does not fire. His look of joy is replaced by one of disappointment. I bang around in the engine bay once more and ask the driver to watch the engine for any excessive sparking while I try to start it. It fires first time and my satisfaction is matched by that of the driver but for very different reasons. The next phase of my mission will be both thrilling and frightening; it launches me into the dangerous heart of the project.

Benningo Dagobah:

The man I had instructed to drive L'Etranger to collect his equipment tells me the whole story on his return. I already know a little about the excellent vehicle because L'Etranger arrived back in Benejado long before the driver of the old car the driver. The impressive 4WD is parked in my compound. It is truly magnificent, fit for a leader of men and I will use it to underline my exalted position by being driven around Benejado in full view of my adoring public. L'Etranger becomes my chauffeur and changes into a new white robe for the occasion. The tour is a great success and the citizens of Benejado, my citizens, are wildly enthusiastic to see their leader expressing his superiority.

When we return to my compound L'Etranger tells me that he is going back to the House of Smoke and Tranquillity where he has rented a room.

"How do you intend to secure your vehicle against harm?" I ask him casually.

"It has a good security system and it will be parked on the land behind the café."

"This is not secure enough in these unlawful times. You will leave it here in my compound where vagabonds will not dare trespass."

He looks at me speculatively, his eyes narrowed and his head slightly on one side. "Whatever you think is best." He acquiesces, which is just as it should be.

"You should leave the keys so that the vehicle can be moved should it be in the way."

"This is a generation of cars which does not require keys; it is customised to the driver alone."

I do not believe him; I have never heard of such a thing but I want him to be gone so that I can get my mechanics to look over it and understand its workings.

Simon Hunter:

Dagobah is easy to read but I must not be fooled into forgetting his animal cunning and still try to be one step ahead of him to anticipate his next moves and remain ahead of his game; as much as his inconsistencies will permit. He did as I expected when he instructed me to leave the car with him; it makes him the envy of his peers as well as his underlings and fuels his self-importance.

I am awoken early next morning by one of Dagobah's emissaries pounding on the door of my room shortly after sunrise. "His Excellency requires you to be with him immediately."

I dress with haste which is something I can now do more easily, no longer feeling the need to shave by the adoption of my new Arab persona. I glance in a smeared mirror as I leave my room and am satisfied that even my own family would not recognise me even with close inspection. My beard is bushy and unkempt which hides my jawline but does not disguise the loss of weight in my facial area; my skin colour is as dark as it has ever been which, together with eyes which are now slightly sunken, makes me look ever more convincingly Arab-like.

Dagobah waits impatiently, pacing up and down in his private quarters. When he sees me his eyes flash angrily. "It is not convenient that you should live so far away from me. I am too busy to have the time to wait for you. While we do another tour of the city I have instructed my men to remove your personal things from the café and put them into a room I have put aside for you here. I do not expect you to pay me any more than you pay Abu Haider."

I see when we get to the 4WD that somebody has attempted to gain access to the vehicle; there are fingerprints and smears around the customised door locks which bear witness to the unsuccessful attempts. As I approach the rear door of the car to give access to Dagobah I feel his piercing gaze as he inspects my method of opening the door. I see puzzlement on his face when I open it without any apparent unlocking effort. He is bursting to ask how I do this without any sign of a key but I don't offer an explanation and neither will his pride allow him to ask the question that burns within him.

He directs the route we take with imperious

barked instructions from the isolation of the back seat. He buzzes down the rear side window and tells me to slow down when we draw near people on the beaten earth sidewalk. When he is satisfied that he has communicated his intent to his doting public – whom I note in my rear-view mirror are gesturing in a less than supportive way now that he cannot see them – he instructs me to return to the compound.

Tefawa Belawa:

What I discover sends chills down my spine. Acting on Sir Michael's orders I make my way to Benejado City, and dressed as a local, I set about tracking Simon down. The task is much easier than I had anticipated. My local contacts confirm to me, as Sir Michael supposed, that Simon is in deep with Dagobah and that not only has he given support at the rally, he is now acting like a second-in-command by driving Dagobah around the city in his personal car.

I am shocked when I catch up with them during their drive-about. Simon looks as if he is enjoying Dagobah's company and they appear to be talking easily. I am further shocked when my Nuovostani informant tells me that Simon has imported the latest model of the NLG Surekill which are now presumably in the hands of New Light.

Sir Michael looks even worse than he did during my last lightning visit to London and he looks desperately unhappy when I fill him in on what I have learned from my visit to Golas and from my Nuovostani informant.

"You need to drop everything else and concentrate solely on Hunter." He looks at me soulfully. "If he has turned you will need to be resolute."

"Do you need to get clearance from the PM?" I ask this because I am playing for time; this is an assignment I don't want.

"If I consider it necessary to involve the PM I will do so at the appropriate time. In the meantime, you will do the job you're paid for. Understood?"

"Understood!"

Sir Michael Westinghouse:

For the moment, I have decided not to tell the PM about my fears concerning Hunter's defection to New Light. It is better to keep it between Belawa and me until the actual situation develops and becomes more clearly defined. The more I find out about the situation the more disturbed I become. Hunter, the new Hunter who has lost his usual compassion, has done some things which appear to be harmful to the interests of the UK. My fervent hope is that I have failed to understand his motives and that there is a valid point to what he is doing.

Belawa is another source of concern. He formed a strong bond with Hunter when they worked together in the field and I am not entirely convinced that the bond will not cloud his judgement. I consider but dismiss the notion that it would be better to take Belawa off the mission and replace him with somebody who does not have an axe to grind. Increasing those who know about my hidden agenda is not prudent.

Simon Hunter:

Progress is not as rapid as I want, although it is advancing at the pace I expected. I upgrade my approach to Dagobah by appealing to his vanity and his voracious need to have his ego fed. Having moved out of the café and into the compound, I am with Dagobah for long periods of the day. This proximity gives me the opportunity to further sycophancy.

"Abu Golas," I address Dagobah in a way which will feed his ego once he is aware of its meaning. "There are matters I would like to discussed with you."

"How did you address me?" He looks at me with confusion. "What is the meaning of this name?"

"Forgive me, Excellency, I am forgetting myself. I called you by the name that my Arab brothers call you, the name you have been given by them is Abu Golas which means father of Golas. It is how we see you."

The look of confusion is replaced with one of satisfaction. "Of course, I am the father of Golas. Your Arab friends are quite right to recognise me in such a way." His look is soon replaced by one of arrogance. "It is my destiny to lead Golas out of the darkness of its oppressed history and into the New Light. This I am destined do."

"His Excellency is truly great." As I say this I realise that I am elevating him in his own eyes to a yet higher plain of arrogance.

"You will meet and work with Oginga, my second-in-command. You and he will follow the programme I have set and further the greatness of New Light."

"Abu Golas, Excellency, I have many plans to

make and much work to do in planning my hotel and business complex. If I am to be successful I must plan carefully and quickly before somebody else steals my initiative. Doing what you say will be very difficult for me."

"That is of no importance to me and nobody can steal your ideas because they will need to get my permission to do so, and while you are working for me I will not give them my permission." He picks up a bell from his table and rings it furiously.

The door opens and a small African bushman enters. He ignores me completely. "You wish to speak with me, boss?"

"I do, and do not call me 'boss'. You may call me Abu Golas because I am the father of my country. You will be working with Monsieur L'Etranger here in supporting my efforts."

"Abu Golas, sir, this is an Arab, not a friend. Is it not his sort we intend to expel from our country? How can I work with him?"

"You will do so because I tell you to. Monsieur L'Etranger accounted for himself very well at the Golas City rally and he represents the changing face that New Light wishes to show the world. Take care about criticising my choice of a supporter who is foreign – you too are foreign and I tolerate you – so enough of your dissent. You will do as I say or the consequences will be unfortunate for you."

Oginga:

This strange-looking Arab has turned up at exactly

the wrong time for me and I must make sure that he does not get in the way of my carefully laid plans. Dagobah is being his usual irrational self, which I am used to, but this time what he proposes will seriously delay my personal plans for expansion. My private enterprise, part of which goes to funding Dagobah's ridiculous plans, relies on me being able to use Dagobah's facilities without any interference from him if I keep providing him with an income.

Communications between the Arab and I are difficult. He speaks North African French with which I struggle, whereas I speak six of the southern dialects; Zulu, Shangaan, Sutu, Xhosa and Matabele, with Afrikaans and a little English. He is less concerned about me than I am about him which in its way gives me a slight edge over him.

He starts to speak to me in French and quickly realises that I am having difficulty in understanding him. A patois of French is the second language here and he speaks to me very slowly so that I can understand the gist of his question. He is asking me where I come from.

I respond to him awkwardly in my poor French.

"*Afrique de Sud.*"

"*Praat ye Afrikaans?*"

"*Ya Mineer, ek Afrikaans praat baie lekker.*"

He begins to talk to me in passable Afrikaans which is a surprise to me because even in my homeland of South Africa this language has been dying out rapidly since that long-ago era of Nelson Mandela which brought about the beginning of the dilution of Afrikaans culture.

"We will be working together for His Excellency, Abu Golas and I have other things to take care of, as I am sure you have. It is in both our interests that we are seen to be working together in harmony; doing so will make both our lives easier."

"I agree," I say to him reluctantly. "His Excellency will make it difficult for us if he believes we are not doing his bidding without question."

"We will talk again after Abu Golas makes clear his requirements of us."

He is dismissing me! It appears that he has appointed himself to the role of leader in our relationship. I cannot allow this trend to develop and I will nip it in the bud before it becomes an accepted relationship.

"I have a conference with Dagobah later today, I will determine what it is you are required to do and instruct you accordingly." I have laid down the gauntlet.

Far from looking uncomfortable about my asserting my seniority over him, he seems to be amused by my words.

Simon Hunter:

In my former life as an international strategy consultant I became accustomed to people in Oginga's position reacting in the way he has by trying to protect what they perceive to be their 'position'. I can now compartmentalise him as being insecure about his place in the hierarchy which means that he will shield his position by opposing me at every opportunity. Even though I have the measure of him it will still be necessary to ensure that he doesn't get in my way by being the filter through whom I must pass to manipulate Dagobah.

Dagobah contacts me a little later to tell me that he requires Oginga to drive him about the city to demonstrate to the locals and his widening membership that he still believes in the notion of African superiority. He tells me that I am useful on the international stage to demonstrate that he is not xenophobic but I am confusing his people by being so high profile.

His instructions make no allowances for the car being mine or that I might not want Oginga or any other person to drive it. Not wishing to rock the boat at this early juncture, I acquiesce to demonstrate my apparent subservience to him.

When the time comes and Oginga fails to start the car, Dagobah becomes agitated. "Why are you unable to do a simple thing like start the motor?" he admonishes Oginga.

"It will not work, Excellency… Abu Golas." Oginga is crestfallen.

Dagobah turns to me. "Why does your vehicle not work? What nonsense is this?"

"I don't understand, Excellency; it was working earlier. Let me try." I slide into the driver's seat and start the engine at the first attempt.

"Now that it is started, I will drive." Oginga opens the driver's door and pulls at my arm.

"Oginga will drive, move out and let him in." Dagobah helps Oginga eject me from the driving seat.

Oginga slides into the driver's seat once more and places his hands on the steering wheel. The engine cuts out immediately. I hide my smile as best I can; the effort I made fitting sensors, not just to the starter button but also the steering wheel, have done their work. He looks crestfallen once more.

"This car is no good, Excellency; we should use our usual car to tour the city." He says this as he attempts in vain to start the vehicle and shows his displeasure by hitting the steering wheel.

"The other car is not suitable for Abu Golas." He seems to like his new name and speaks of himself in the third person. He turns to me. "Until this can be sorted out you will drive me." Turning to Oginga, he frowns impatiently. "I will talk with you later."

Oginga:

I am humiliated in front of Dagobah by this Arab and I will do something to redress this situation. Until now my position as the confidante of Dagobah has enabled me to further my own business ambitions without distraction. My arrangements for tonight's soirée are complete and I will not allow the Arab to interfere with them. I need him to be out of the way tonight because unlike Dagobah he might just be able to understand what I am doing and cause problems for me.

In Dagobah's absence, I have control of his troops and they will follow any orders I give them. Instead of distracting the Arab I decide that it would be best to remove him permanently. I meet with three of the most pliable senior officers in Dagobah's security detail and instruct them. I tell them that I have uncovered a plot against their leader which will, unless action is taken, cost him his life. The officers concerned have no fondness for Dagobah but he pays them, which they prefer to the alternative abject poverty they would otherwise suffer.

The plan is simple as all good plans should be and I explain it to them in simple terms. The three officers are to lay in wait for the Arab at the point where he parks his 4WD overnight. Once parked he will take a rifle from the back of the vehicle and with it he will assassinate our leader. They will all three shoot him dead in such a way that it will not be possible to identify the actual killer except that it will be one of the three. They will all be rewarded for their vigilance.

While all of this is taking place, I will be hosting my event at the other side of the compound so that no involvement will be attributed to me. At a later meeting, I instruct the three regular overnight guards to be vigilant against four gunmen who will enter the compound to do evil and that they must shoot to kill if they see interlopers, and each are to select a different one of the four targets, the fourth being L'Etranger. The three officers and the Arab who they will see is armed, will be killed and the guards will say, because I have planted it in their minds, that they believed the four to be interlopers and they did their duty to protect His Excellency against harm. Simple and effective.

I am happy that I have made the necessary arrangements to eliminate the Arab who was, I will advise Dagobah, in cahoots with the three officers as an assassination team. That will dispose of him and will move me even closer to Dagobah so that I can meet my aims; it also means that I will have the opportunity to appoint three new military leaders who are more to my liking than the three I am about to have eliminated. All that remains to be done now is to set up the Arab to act in the way I have predicted.

Simon Hunter:

Keeping the 4WD out of Dagobah's clutches so that I continue to have exclusive use of it has the disadvantage of my having to be at his beck and call after he fulfils the urge to fuel his ego by parading in front of his people. I need to keep exclusive access to the vehicle because if my longer-term plan works I will need to be able to leave Benejado City at a moment's notice to avoid what could be a baying crowd, by having the fastest vehicle in the city.

We head back to the compound after yet another parade around the city which is unusually crowded.

"Let me out at my villa and then take the car to the usual parking place, then you can take the rest of the day off, but do not leave your quarters in case I have further need of your services."

"Why are all these people here?" I ask, puzzled by the crowds.

"Tonight there is a fundraiser arranged by Oginga to help defray the many costs of administering New Light." He steps out of the vehicle and walks the short distance to the entrance of his villa without a backward glance.

I trace Oginga to the entrance to one of the warehouse structures at the edge of the compound against the stout mud block walls which guard this exposed flank which is bounded by open scrub land between the compound and the city wall. He is meeting and greeting a diverse group of visitors, some in tribal costumes and others in western-style garb both formal and informal, but all are looking excited.

"What do you want here?" Oginga is clearly unhappy to see me.

"I am interested to see your fundraiser in action so I thought I would come and see for myself."

"This is no place for you and your presence here would discourage the donors from being generous. They don't like foreigners. His Excellency Abu Golas would not be happy if you were to cause a drop in donations." He turns his back on me and enters the darkened interior of the warehouse.

I stand looking for a moment at the door which he has closed in my face. The action of closing the door expels some of the air from the interior; I detect the familiar smell of ganja and an overlying aroma which I cannot immediately place. I recognise unwashed bodies and the cloying aroma of the cheap perfume used to disguise it. My curiosity is piqued by what is going on in the warehouse but it remains unsatisfied with my being denied access.

Finished for the day, I leave the 4WD in its now customary parking place close by the entrance to Dagobah's villa and as I turn to leave one of Dagobah's rag-tag army approaches me with a long-barrelled assault rifle dangling from its carrying strap, and stops breathlessly before me giving me a comical wavy salute.

"Sir, I am instructed to give you this rifle which is to be kept in the trunk of your very fine vehicle, and is to be given to His Excellency Dagobah when he leaves his villa at 11 of the pm this night. It is for his protection when he goes to collect the money from the event." He looks pleased with himself for remembering the lines he has so obviously been taught.

I take the rifle from him as he turns away from me with disjointed gracelessness, to return to his barracks. I check the breech of the weapon and see that it is ready for action and the safety catch is on. Satisfied that it is safe, I place the weapon in the back of the 4WD, it is now safe from tampering or purloining hands, me being the only person who can unlock the vehicle. I find the request strange but I dismiss it as being just one more illogical action that I am beginning to accept as the norm.

Benningo Dagobah:

Soon I must go to the warehouse and collect the takings for the night's activity overseen by Oginga. He is becoming more skilful, as is evidenced by each month's cash takings increasing as time passes. I don't like Oginga, he thinks he is one of us but he is a foreign infidel even if he is African. He thinks he fools me but I know he does not truly follow the religious teachings of New Light and that he lives by the rules of some other false god or maybe no god at all.

Soon I will get somebody else to collect this cash for me; it will all be in local currency which has no value outside Golas – I now have access to foreign currency. Local currency can be used for local purchases of all kinds but with dollars I can buy things from beyond our borders, the sort of things that I can use to press my will upon Golacians and the self-styled 'legitimate government' of the country.

When I leave my villa on my way to collect the proceeds from Oginga I can see from the illumination of the compound lights that there are three of my military men approaching the 4WD and that L'Etranger is standing by it. As they approach L'Etranger opens the back of the vehicle and removes what looks like a rifle from it. He approaches me with the rifle which I find alarming. I am defenceless, my side arm is back in the villa. At the same time four overnight compound guards begin running towards me, weapons drawn.

One of the three approaching military men shouts something indistinguishable and begins to run towards L'Etranger, gesticulating wildly drawing his side arm as he does so. The next things that take place are in slow motion. The whole scene is lit up by simultaneous muzzle flashes and L'Etranger clutches at his chest and falls like a dead weight to the ground followed, after a momentary pause, by the three military men who have assassinated him. They are shot dead by my brave compound guards. There is blood, a great deal of blood. The stunning silence which follows is broken by the sound of the running feet of the compound guard.

I am in shock. I see the four lying on the ground, I see blood and smell it and the cordite on the night air and I hear the approaching guards who are jabbering excitedly. They run to me and surround me facing outwards.

"Excellency, are you hurt? Do you need assistance?" One of the men, breathless from running, gasps at his chest heaving.

"His Excellency Abu Golas is unharmed and has the protection of God to thank, you were obviously sent by him to deliver me." I try to keep the wonder from my voice because I now have confirmation that I am the chosen one.

It seems that L'Etranger has not had the same protection as me; he lies dead on the floor. I am saddened that the opportunities that he could have given me will now not happen but God in His infinite wisdom will guide me and grant me the strength to carry on with my holy fight.

I despatch the guards to get a clean-up team to remove the bodies and tell one of them to get Oginga to report back to me. Already the blood is beginning to soak into the porous compound floor and the flies were homing in on the unexpected opportunity. I find it difficult to take in what has just happened. Was L'Etranger an innocent bystander in a futile coup? If so, why did he have a rifle? I will never know, there is nobody alive left to tell me.

Simon Hunter:

Thanks to my inbuilt sixth sense I detected that something was seriously wrong. When Dagobah saw me as he left the villa I retrieved the rifle to give it to him as I had been instructed. It was his immediate reaction that made me suspect that all was not as it should have been. His response was one of fear, not what I would expect of a man who knew that I was charged with giving him a rifle for his peace of mind. He clearly feared that I was going to use it against him; in the microseconds that follow my mind went into overdrive, calculating the situation. I could see the three officers who approached were preparing to shoot either me or Dagobah or both of us. I can also see that the four guards heading my way are either going to be doing the same thing or they are going to shoot the three military men and me.

Desperate action needs desperate measures. To take care of this my timing must be just right. In defence reflex I fell to the floor clutching at my chest. As I arc down I saw the muzzle flashes from the three men. I hit the ground and the hand that had been clutching in my chest area is loosened, and at the same time I see almost simultaneous muzzle flashes from the compound guards followed instantaneously by the toppling of the military men.

I lie on the beaten earth, my breath knocked out of me, momentarily in a state of semi-consciousness. As I recover I give heartfelt thanks to the genius that is Ed Pickering; the teardrop-shaped pendant around my neck, hidden from view, rests over my heart. I pressed the kill button set into the teardrop which activated the disabling mechanism of the side arms being used against me. This ingenious piece of design activates hardened steel spikes which spiral along the inside of the barrel and protrude into it so that when the specially manufactured soft compound bullets pass along them they are shredded into a mist of tiny parts which are discharged without doing any harm. The timing of activating the teardrop was such that I had stopped the weapons of the military aggressors being effective against me but in falling I had let go of the teardrop button and the other three men, not protected by the safety mechanism, perished. I stay supine, judging that if I move the guards will certainly shoot me again and I don't want to rely on the same risky ploy twice. As soon as they have left the area I sneak a look around. It's just Dagobah, me, and three dead soldiers under the black velvet of an African sky.

When I judge it is safe to do so I stir and my movement causes Dagobah to start.

"I mean you no harm, Excellency Abu Golas; I am just pleased that you are safe."

"W…what is this?" he stammers in alarm. "What magic causes you to rise from the dead?"

Never one to miss an opportunity, I stand up and dust myself off and speak to him as though nothing had happened. "I am able to avoid bullets and when I saw they were shooting at you I took the necessary action to prevent you from being harmed."

"What sorcery is this?" His voice becomes aggressive. "No man can avoid a bullet; if it is not the will of God."

"Perhaps then it is the will of God that I am spared so that I may serve you."

"Yes!" he exclaims in sudden revelation. "It is the will of God that you serve me. God is great." His eyes shine with the light of his relentlessly fermenting madness.

Benningo Dagobah:

It is a sign from above, this man has been saved from harm so that he might further my cause and I will not go against divine intervention. Any thoughts I might have harboured against L'Etranger are no longer a consideration; he was clearly not part of the plot to harm me and it was divine intervention that saved us both.

"Your life is at risk," I tell him, "and it is my intention to protect you as I have been guided to do by the almighty power. You will move from your present quarters into the villa where we can work together in harmony and safety to do the will of the almighty and bring order and salvation to the world. The guard you have provided for me will protect us."

I despatch runners to collect the belongings of L'Etranger and bring them to the guest suite adjacent to my living quarters, and I tell the same runners to tell Oginga to come immediately to me and tell me why the men he leads are so untrue to my cause.

Oginga comes scurrying to me with a look of great concern on his face.

"Explain yourself, Oginga." I give him a long hard look so that he knows I am displeased.

"Forgive me, but what do I have to explain, Excellency?"

"Are you such a bad leader of men that you do not know what your own people are doing? An attempt has been made on my life and that of Monsieur L'Etranger and but for divine intervention we would both be dead. The perpetrators of this treasonable act are senior officers in your militia who are now dead thanks to the actions of the loyal compound guards. You have failed me and I must now consider what punishment is appropriate for you. I am displeased, very displeased, with your incompetence. Go to your quarters and do not leave them until I give you permission to do so."

"Excellency, I…" His words are cut short by my sharp slap to his face.

"I do not wish for discussion, Oginga; do as I say and return to your quarters."

I turn to L'Etranger who has witnessed this whole episode in silence. "You, my friend, will go to the warehouse, collect all the money waiting there, disperse the guests and their entertainment and bring the money here to me. Now both of you go and do my bidding."

I turn away from them both. Mission accomplished.

Oginga:

Dagobah's insults are made worse by the Arab witnessing them. After all I have done for New Light it is unfair that I should be blamed for what has happened. The fact that I did arrange this whole thing and that it backfired is neither here nor there; how can everything I had arranged so carefully go so wrong? The Arab has survived the assassination which destroyed the plans I had for laying the blame at his door. How he did this, at point-blank range, is a mystery. I am sure it is not what Dagobah attributes it to – divine intervention – but I have no idea what it is.

The Arab is impassive as we traverse the

compound, me on my way to my quarters and him to the warehouse to collect the spoils of tonight's debauchery. I have a problem with him going to collect the money for Dagobah. The sum involved will be three times what he expects because I was called into the presence before I could cream off my usual cut. This could lead me into a very dangerous place. I am only too aware that to incur the wrath of Dagobah by stealing from him would only lead to one fatal conclusion.

Simon Hunter:

The communication difficulties existing between Oginga and I are both linguistic and cultural. Linguistically it makes meaningful conversation during the journey across the compound stunted. We go our separate ways, he to his accommodation and me to the party warehouse. There are faint strains of music seeping out from the warehouse through the ill-fitting doors. They yield to light pressure and once more the cloying smell from within envelopes me; it is not pleasant. My eyes adjust to the dim red-tinged lighting and the unpleasant odour is stronger within the oppressive interior. Nobody in the room takes any notice of me and they all continue with what they are doing. Some are shuffling what is meant to be a dance, some are comatose on the floor or on items of miscellaneous furniture, some are drinking and smoking themselves into oblivion, and yet others pursue carnal activities without noticeable embarrassment. All the men I can see are Golacian and all the women are of far-eastern origin.

Ganja and unclean body odour are partially

masked by the cheap perfume worn by the women but not to the extent which makes it palatable. Deeper into the interior of the warehouse I see what looks like a cocktail bar constructed from odd scraps of material thrown randomly together. Behind the bar are two hard-looking women whose looks and age appear to preclude them from involvement in the activities on this side of the bar.

They both observe my approach with suspicion; I am not and do not look Golacian so it is hardly surprising that they are wary.

"Mesdames." I address them in French and receive blank stares in return. "M'Frau." I try a Dutch, Afrikaans, and Germanic approach and as expect I receive the same blank stare. "Ladies." The universal language elicits a response.

The older of the two acts as spokeswoman. "What are you doing here? You are not a member and if you're not a member you have to get permission from Oginga to be here."

"I am not here to enjoy the festivities, I am here to claim what rightly belongs to His Excellency, Dagobah. Oginga is not able to do this right now, he is doing something else for His Excellency."

"You expect me to just hand over the money to you? I don't know who you are; you could be a crook who will run off with the takings." She looks at me through narrowed eyes.

"Either you give me the money or I go back to His Excellency and he will come here himself as he normally does." I smile and adopt my non-confrontational face. "If I do that I would not like to be you when His Excellency has to leave his villa after he has already instructed me to get it for him. He is not in the best of moods."

She looks at me wooden-faced and I can see that she is assessing her options. She looks over my shoulder and beckons one of the guests. He comes to her and they walk along the bar to the far end where they have a conversation. The guest leaves and the woman returns.

"He is a soldier of New Light and he recognises you as the driver for His Excellency and says that you are close to him so I will do your bidding. Usually it is Oginga who hands over the night's takings. Which of the two bags do you wish to take, the large or the small?"

"Which one does Oginga usually give to His Excellency?"

"I think it is the small one, the other one goes into the safe." She points over her shoulder to a large old-fashioned safe, the top of which is covered with bottles of liquor.

"Okay, I'll take the small one and you will place the bigger one in the safe."

"I don't have the key or combination so I can't do that."

"Give both bags to me and I'll take care of them."

She hesitates for a moment and then relents and hands both bags over to me but she looks uncomfortable about it. "If this is not what Oginga wants he will seek you out and kill you."

"Oh, this is so much what Oginga wants." I give

her a broad friendly smile. "As a reward for your cooperation you can keep any other money which you collect tonight, I won't tell Oginga."

Both women look delighted at this windfall and they begin looking around to see if they can drum up some extra trade and capitalise on their opportunity. The change in their demeanour is telling.

Tefawa Belawa:

Sir Michael looks at me, askance. "He's done what?" He can hardly comprehend what I have said.

"It looks like he is Dagobah's number two. He appears to have seen off Oginga, who did hold that position, and he's moved up from being chauffeur to being second in charge of New Light." I repeat what I had already said to him, it's difficult for me to believe too.

"Are you sure of that? Because if he has joined New Light, which is a banned terrorist organisation, he must be eliminated." He looks completely devastated by his own pronouncement.

"I am simply reporting what I have seen but I have no background to support the impressions I have gained."

"Is this information second hand or have you actually witnessed what you have reported?" He looks at me intently.

"I have given you a first-hand report; I have actually witnessed him appearing to get closer to Dagobah. As a native Golacian I mingled with the crowds watching Dagobah's campaigning and observed Simon's part in it. Word on the street is that Simon saved Dagobah's life during an attempted coup and he is now looked upon with favour, more so than any of the other New Light disciples."

"My god!" He buries his head in his hands. "We've created a monster. I warned the PM that this could happen during the last project we forced him into, and it looks as though it has." The last words are him talking to himself rather than to me. He must be distraught – he wouldn't normally expose his feelings so openly.

"Before we get carried away, sir," I interrupt him, "I think we should verify what is going on. I know Simon as well as anybody and I still don't believe he would do any of this without a good motive."

"What's to verify? He went to Golas to stop this despot from doing his evil and he has fallen under his spell and become at one with the organisation." He shakes his head. "We, the British government, are responsible for this. Hunter was pushed much too hard, much too soon, by us, to be able to survive intact. He's not a trained agent like you, he has not been taught to compartmentalise the unpalatable things to protect his normal life. I fear his morals have become blurred. He is a lost asset, a lost cause."

Simon Hunter:

This whole thing is happening much faster than I would have thought possible even when I am engaging the side of my personality which has little by way of conscience and does not allow my natural humanity to get in the way. I have gone from being an unknown Arab wanderer to being ostensibly second-in-command of what could become one of the most hated quasi-religious terroristic orders – and all in a matter of weeks.

The fly in the ointment is Oginga; I have made a deadly enemy of him by deposing him. I need to neutralise him to keep myself on the fast track. My opportunity revolves around two bags of money and what I intend to do with them. Obviously Oginga was doing more than skimming the cream off the top carrying out the exercise in the warehouse. He has been keeping twice as much money as he was passing on to Dagobah and that is my route to controlling Oginga.

Although it is now the early hours of the morning, I strike while the iron is hot. The entrance into his quarters is a hole in the wall covered with what looks like sacking. Security is obviously not high on his list of priorities.

"Oginga," I shout before entering his room.

He looks up in alarm from where he is sitting as I enter. When he sees me, his look deepens into pent-up fury and he half rises; arms curved away from the sides of his body, fingers arched like the talons of a bird of prey, eyes narrowed, teeth bared. He looks and acts like a wild animal.

"Be calm," I say to him in Afrikaans. "I come to you with news of your salvation."

He stops in his tracks at my words and puts his head on one side, wondering why I would offer him salvation. He waits for me to continue.

"I was, as you know, asked to collect your takings

from the warehouse and pass them on to His Excellency. I did as you would have done."

He rotates his head until it is upright and the puzzlement turns once more to aggression. He looks as if he is about to attack me.

"I gave him the smaller of the two bags," I say quickly to stop him from escalating his aggression into a physical act.

I see a slow dawning of understanding on his face. The aggression and anger turn into a smile of pure evil as he realises that Dagobah has not learned of being bilked and that he is off the hook. His new look is now calculating. "So now you want to be my partner and you want a cut of the proceeds." He says this with satisfaction. He has obviously, he thinks, found my weakness.

I hand the bag of money to him. "I don't want your money; it has no value to me. You can keep it."

He accepts the bag with a look of incomprehension. "Why would you do this for me?"

"I don't do it for you, I do this for us. It is far better that we work together to make the best of our situation. Just a word of advice; it is better for you to accept working together with me…"

"Why would I want to do that?" He interrupts me, his bravado has returned.

"Because if you don't, your life will come to a sudden and painful end." I turn and leave him without a backward glance but I can feel his eyes boring into my back.

Part of me would never act the way I am now

doing; my sensitive side is switched off.

Oginga:

For the moment, I am safe from the wrath of Dagobah. For some reason the Arab has decided to protect me. He thinks he is being so smart by having one over me but he doesn't realise that I am a master of deception. I will play along with him just long enough to set him up for a big fall. First off, I must silence the two bar girls in much the same way I just did with the three military leaders who were stupid enough to underestimate me. With them out of the way there is nobody who knows that I have been keeping back money from the party nights except the Arab. Sadly, my first attempt at assassinating him failed, but the next attempt will succeed and I will assume my natural place alongside Dagobah. In the meantime, I will appear to go along with what the Arab thinks is a deception but just until I can set him up for a fall.

Disposal of the two bar girls will be easy. I can either ship them back to Golas City where I plucked them from the back streets, or I can simply have them killed. The first is easier because it will not need involvement from anybody else and therefore be more secure from leakage. The second has the advantage of their removal being permanent but involves input from others so that I can have an alibi; but those others would then pose a security risk. I need to sleep on it before deciding.

Tefawa Belawa:

Dressed in regional clothes, I mingle with the crowd who are waiting silently for the Dagobah entourage to pass by. It has been well heralded and the waiting crowds who will cheer him on as he passes, have all been 'persuaded' to be here and be vociferous in their support for His Excellency. I listen to the conversations that take place quietly, away from the ears of the New Light fanatics. They talk of an attempted coup which was foiled by the strange Arab who had recently appeared on the scene and of how he, despite replacing the feared Oginga, still chose to be the driver for the leader of the sect.

When the cortege finally appears a dozen or so ill-assorted men armed with the modern weapons my under-cover man in Nuovostan informed me about. There is a similar rag-bag group at the rear which are obviously what Dagobah would dub his security forces. Simon is driving the 4WD with Dagobah in the passenger seat and four armed men in the back. The men in the back seat look like professional troops; they are smart and look alert – their watchful eyes darting right and left. The guards are wearing shoulder insignias which I don't recognise; I memorise the design and keep it in mind until I can get to a search engine to determine their origin.

What I can see of Simon's face looks relaxed but without knowing it is him I would not have recognised him; gone are the piercing blue eyes, they have been made to look a muddy brown. The hood of his robe is down and his usually smart hair has grown into long flowing black locks which barely move in the gusting breeze. I can't tell whether it is natural or a wig. His skin is burnt a deep mahogany brown either by exposure to the sun or by skin dye. With his slightly aquiline features he passes convincingly as an Arab.

The most damning thing about how he appears is that although relaxed he has a cruel look on his face which was not evident when we last worked together. It is also the look of a man who is possessed of a personal demon. Much as I don't want to, I must send a report back to Sir Michael which will not make his decisions any easier. It seems that Simon is in uncharted territory.

Oginga:

When the two bar girls see me enter the party barn they look startled and fearful. It is two days since the last party and they are still clearing up the mess left by the partygoers; the next party is next week so they do not feel the need to rush.

"Sir, it is good to see you, sir." The older of the two speaks timorously and her hands flutter uncertainly about her face.

The other girl tries to hide behind her companion, looking fearfully over her shoulder, trying and failing to judge my mood.

"You spoke to the Arab when he came to collect the money for His Excellency?"

"Sir, yes, we did, sir." The older one replies with raw fear in her voice.

"What did he say to you?" My voice becomes intentionally sharper.

"He asked us about the money for His Excellency and we gave him a choice of the two bags." Her voice is now quivering with pent up fear.

"And what did he do with the bags?"

"He took them away, sir, but we don't know what he did with them." Both girls cling together for mutual comfort. "He said he would take the smaller one and put the bigger one in the safe but we don't have the safe key so he took both bags with him."

Maybe I don't need to have them assassinated, if I keep on interrogating them they will very likely die of fright. That is but a passing fancy; I have made my decision about how they will be taken out of the picture. Their fate is sealed.

Sir Michael Westinghouse:

I'm just hoping I haven't left it too late to wriggle my way out of this problem; I now have no option but to tell the PM about the Golas situation. My hope that I was mistaken about Hunter's intent has backfired and it looks as though we have a renegade on our hands. I find it difficult to accept that we have turned a reasonable rational human being into a rabid terrorist but there is no escaping the facts presented. I must let the PM know about Hunter and I must have a credible plan to deter Hunter from following the path he has chosen, without having him eliminated. The more I think of it the less likely the softer option appears to be.

The telephone conversation I have with the PM is scratchy and is not helped by his being under fire on several fronts from both allies and enemies on other matters of state. There is also a looming election which is finely balanced in favour of the opposition. One advantage for me is that he is so distracted by what is going on in his political life that he tells me to get on with it and to use my own discretion to deal with Hunter. This is good because it gives me the freedom to do what I will and not so good if I make the wrong choice; I will be left holding the baby and without access to a life raft.

I need to establish a timeframe for any action I deem it necessary to take and to do. I need further conversations with Tefawa Belawa, to see how far down the line of terrorism Hunter is and whether it is still possible to turn him back to the path of righteousness.

Benningo Dagobah:

I have the blessing of the almighty and I have real money and arms and I have a partner who can dodge flying bullets; the time is ready for the next move. I consult my divinity to help me formulate a plan to convert the world's heathens to our great cause; New Light. The money will enable me to buy professional soldiers who will efficiently promote my cause. I will also be able to purchase new and even better weapons than those provided by L'Etranger which will in turn persuade more of the better-quality soldiers to join the cause. A bigger and better army will give me the power to spread my influence maybe to start up an air force which I will have known as the Golacian Air Force, GAF. We will dominate the air and the land; domination of the sea is for the future.

The finances I need will come from internal fundraising using the party warehouse model which will be duplicated across the country and then surrounding countries. Finance from L'Etranger will enable me to purchase outside services. His entry onto the scene has proved to be providential; he has arrived at just the right time and using my formidable skills, I will manipulate him in the same way I am able to persuade the people of Golas to follow my lead. As my second-in-command he will represent the international component needed for New Light to have broader acceptance, and when he has done this and the need for his money has been dispensed with – so will he be, and my quest for racial purity will be realised.

I summon L'Etranger to my chambers to tell him of his part in my tactics, not of course including my intention to dispense with him and his services at a time of my choosing. When he appears, he is dressed as usual in his drab Arab robe which is becoming an aromatic problem.

"You should change and wash," I tell him. "You stink."

"I am not aware of such a problem, Excellency." He looks crestfallen.

"Then there is a problem with your nose. Before we discuss further you must go to the bathroom and shower and change into one of my old robes." I wave the back of my hand, fingers and thumb together in dismissal. He makes no comment but walks to the adjoining bathroom.

Simon Hunter:

I have recently neglected to take care of my personal hygiene and have been living and sleeping in my robes. The other me would have been offended by this but the present incarnation is not bothered. As with the first time I used this bathroom, I am struck by its opulence which is beyond that enjoyed by the rest of the property. There is a family-size shower, a deep Jacuzzi, a low-level WC and a bidet. All are blood-red and have gold fittings. Part of the room is set aside for undressing and has wall pegs and hangers which are also gold.

I strip off my robe and my Arab drawers and hang them on the pegs. Looking at myself in a full-length wall mirror, I am hardly recognisable. My hair is long and unkempt, my face and hands are burnt deep mahogany; by contrast the rest of my body is a pale European which, if seen by anybody else would instantly reveal that I am not truly Arab. The fake tan that I had initially applied to my body has worn off.

Once I have had a hot shower I realise how in need of cleansing I am, I become aware of the offensive odour of my robes. I cast around in the wardrobes, as suggested by Dagobah. They are filled with local garments which are a riot of clashing colour. I try several until I find one that fits; it is obviously one which he has had for several years and has grown out of. I top the whole lot off with a soft brimless hat which matches the material of the garment. Once more I look at myself in the mirror; I look like a rogue but beggars can't be choosers so with a last look I leave the bathroom and return to Dagobah's chambers.

Benningo Dagobah:

L'Etranger reappears; he is wearing traditional Golacian clothes. They are old, I can tell by the design, but in appearance he looks far more suitable now and will also do so to the Golacian people who will see that he has forsaken the Arab style of dressing.

"Forgive me, Excellency, I took the liberty of borrowing some of your clothes as you suggested. You were quite right, my own robes are offensive. I will have these laundered and returned to you as soon as we have had our discussion."

"What you are wearing is most appropriate. You may keep this garment and I will have others of the same size delivered to your rooms by a wench. I no longer have use of clothing of this size; they used to fit me when I was a callow weakling and now I am a properly developed man." I slap my manly stomach and hips to illustrate my point.

"Your Excellency is too kind." He simpers in gratitude at my generosity.

"I intended us to speak here in the privacy of my apartments but I think it more appropriate for us to continue our conversation in a more public place where my people can see that you are embracing our culture. You will drive me around the city and we will have the people see us as allies, me as Golacian and you as an adopted brother of Golas and important member of New Light."

We set out on the usual zig-zag circuit of the city so that we can be seen and admired by the citizens from all sections of the population. I decide this time to ride in the back which is the fitting place for the leader to be. The professional guard take up positions ahead and behind us using an old American Jeep in front and a hybrid Citroen Renault taking up the rear-guard position. This specially selected formation is more impressive than the ruffians I usually employ for such a task. The professional soldiers are smart and they carry modern assault rifles which will impress all of those who watch. This demonstrates the new me.

As we drive, slowly so that the crowds can see their leader and his newly acquired ally and troops, I talk to L'Etranger. The windows are closed and the excellent air conditioning hums softly as it does its work.

"Simon," I use his given name with the French pronunciation. "I have important matters to discuss with you. Now that you have become a fully-fledged member of New Light and have also opted to dress like us, we must embark on the next stage to promote the movement." I outline to him my immediate plans to enlarge our community and make it more powerful. My discussion is so long that we make three circuits of the city before the plan is outlined to him.

Simon Hunter:

Dagobah's plans are little more than an elaborate wish list, most of which is unachievable, but one thing is clear from his stated intentions. The relatively mild-mannered man who talks to me now will be transformed into a ravening despot as his sociopathic tendencies blossom. He must not be allowed to inflict them on his countrymen and later the wider world. Behind the attempts to make his philosophy acceptable to the international community, is a steely and unwavering intent to destabilise as much of the world as he can colonise. He does not have the intellect to carry through his random ideas but my fear is that he will pick somebody powerful along the way who will be able to capitalise on what he has started and throw Africa and beyond into turmoil.

It seems that I have less time than I had initially anticipated to stop this madness and it occurs to me that in my haste to infiltrate his organisation I have unleashed a madman. I will need more support for my endeavours than the six-man army at my disposal and I need to assemble them quickly. I have a secure satellite phone which I use to contact Noah Gilliland in Nematasulu to discuss options. It is not my intention to travel to Nematasulu; the time that would take will be better used securing things on the ground here in Benejado City.

Dagobah has an assortment of clothing delivered to me by what he calls a serving wench. I decline her offer to bathe me and assist me with trying on the robes. My refusal is taken as an insult to her attractions and she turns her mouth turns down at the corners while giving me a sullen look. Not wishing to insult the girl, who is probably no more than fourteen or fifteen years old, I give her an assortment of local currency which probably represents a month's wages for her and maybe more. She leaves somewhat mollified by my overgenerous reward, but does not understand why her offer of companionship has been rejected.

Dagobah wants me to appear on local television and then on national and ultimately international news channels. He has also demanded more and better weapons, throwing into the mix RPGs and launchers together with land mines and other more powerful ordinance. It is possible for me to supply these via Nuovostan and to have safeguards attached to them such as making the explosive content of the weapons time-limited degradable. My main concern though, is where this is leading. If this plan should get away from me and he were to go to another external supplier, no such safe-guards would be feasible so I must continue to meet his demands.

I will arrange for what he wants but I will build in delays so that I can deal with him before the weapons are due to be delivered. His disposal must be such that he leaves behind no successor and that his organisation is valueless to other self-seekers. I need to do this before other terrorist organisations see New Light as a vehicle for the furtherance of what might be better planned, more heartless objectives.

I become aware that the humane side of my personality is trying to impinge on the unfeeling one which is in the ascendency. It fails and I relish the capability. I have to destroy this heathen concept and the people who promote it without the slightest prick of conscience and without remorse.

Sir Michael Westinghouse:

The news from Golas is far worse than I had imagined was possible. Hunter has gone native and now is fully immersed in the terrorist organisation. The report tells me that he has adopted local customs and dress and has been seen parading in triumph with

Benningo Dagobah and has provided a professional armed guard for the security of both the terrorist leader and himself. It seems that he is beyond redemption and I must find a way to stop him and New Light from becoming too powerful to contain – whatever it takes.

With reluctance, I must devise a way to rid ourselves of one whom I had until now considered to be a friend. I will discharge my duty no matter what my personal feelings are and I will try to accomplish that aim without doing him any physical harm. As I formulate that scenario I must also have a fall-back plan should my peaceful plans not succeed. I need to include N11 in this phase of the planning and I know he will do all in his power to protect Hunter's life but will, if the situation demands, carry out his elimination.

Oginga:

The bar girls have been taken care of, I took the safest option and disposed of them. The most pressing thing for me now is to dispose of the Arab in such a way that he is discredited and I am given credit for his removal. How I do this is to be decided and I will not be rushed into it, the Arab has proven himself to be too wary to be taken care of by anything other than a perfect plan.

I will watch and wait and when the opportunity arises I will strike. To start with I will poison the mind of Dagobah against the Arab. A little word here and a little word there will lodge in his dull mind and ferment until it germinates the fertile seeds of doubt.

Using the excuse of arranging the next warehouse party, I visit Dagobah in his private quarters. His reception of me is cool and I know of old that I cannot expect forgiveness for what he sees as my being unable to control my troops. I will need to bury his disapproving thoughts by replacing them with a more positive impression.

"Excellency, I have an excellent idea for improving the finances provided by the warehouse parties and I would value your wise thoughts."

"I am always ready to listen to improving our finances."

"When I returned to my quarters with the Arab foreigner who was going on to collect the money from the warehouse, we talked a little of the parties. He gave the impression that they are ill-advised and that we should stop such things." I give no emphasis to my words but they form the first drip of information to discredit the Arab. I do not back them up at this stage with further information.

"This has nothing to do with him so you can ignore his words." He begins to look impatient. "What is it you propose to do to improve our finances?"

"I have gathered together those who visit the parties from Golas City and the villages immediately around us. I have calculated that if we move beyond the small villages and into the larger ones, we will be able to double and maybe even treble our rewards."

"Why do you bother with such talk? If you think it will work you should do it without bothering me with trifles."

"Thank you for your advice, Excellency. I will do

as you suggest."

I allow myself a moment of satisfaction as I leave his chambers. I have sowed the first seed of criticism which he has not overtly noticed but when I saw more it will lead to the conclusion I seek.

Simon Hunter:

The recording of my appearance on television is a fiasco. The sound and lighting are of poor quality and the interviewer has no perceivable plan of action. There is an unoccupied chair which I would have thought would have been removed but wasn't. His questions are random and pointless and I can see from a dusty monitor that focussing is a problem. I respond to the questions without enthusiasm and ultimately the interview doesn't conclude as much as it falters to a stop.

Dagobah is delighted and he gives me a congratulatory smile. "You have done well, my friend. When this goes out on the news it will have been edited to take out some of the less polished moments."

By my reckoning, for that to be accomplished they will need to edit out at least 95% of the content. Dagobah is satisfied and I join him in his residence where we watch the finished news item; when the item is broadcast I hardly recognise it. The editor has taken such liberties that the meaning of what I said has been entirely lost. The inept questions I had been asked were carefully crafted in a way which had not occurred to me. Dagobah, who hadn't been in the interview with me, dominates the programme; they had separately recorded an interview with him and the meaning of the empty chair becomes obvious.

The interview which appears on the screen gives the clear impression that by superimposition of our images, Dagobah and I share the interview. The questions to which I had answered yes or no or had constructed more complex answers, appear to be in response to some outrageous statements by Dagobah. The tenor of the interview is very different in its presentation to that which I had intended. It portrays me as a bigot who believes that there should be only one religion; New Light.

It is with the greatest of difficulty that I do not physically attack Dagobah. My words have been twisted beyond all recognition and portray me as a monster as well as a bigot who is being controlled entirely by Dagobah, which in this instance is true. I will need to be wary of taking his proposals at face value in the future. The only saving grace about this episode is that the programme is for national rather than international consumption and what the Golacians think of me is of no consequence. I can only hope that this piece to camera is never aired internationally.

Tefawa Belawa:

I am appalled by the television news item; to use Sir Michael's expression, Simon has gone over to the dark side. During the interview he appears to be bored even when he is agreeing to the most outlandish statements from Dagobah. When Dagobah suggests that there is justification for the assassination of unbelievers without the necessity for trial, Simon nods sagely.

I make a copy of the news broadcast and send it to Sir Michael. It gives me no pleasure to do this but it is my job and judgement concerning Simon's motives is not for me to make. My greatest concern is that I may be given the order to arrange for the assassination of one I consider be a friend. Given the order, I will do so as part of my job as an MI6 operative; decisively.

Within an hour of sending the recording to Sir Michael I get a response from him, it comprises of the single word – '*Terminate*.'

Oginga:

I must step up my offensive against the Arab. His television appearance surprised me and even more, his statements and responses to Dagobah are far more radical than I would have thought possible. What was an irritation has now become a direct threat to my resuming my former position in the New Light hierarchy. To speed up the process I must implant more harmful information in the mind of Dagobah.

Getting to see Dagobah is now more difficult than it was before the interference of the Arab. I can no longer march in uninvited, I must justify a reason for an audience. I have the advantage of being more intelligent than Dagobah so it is not that difficult to get his attention to gain an audience. I simply let it be known that I have been listening to the rumours in the streets and cafés, something that he cannot do himself. When he learns of this he summons me to his presence.

"I believe you are keeping information from me,"

is his opening gambit.

"I hesitate to pass information to His Excellency because it is not favourable to one of his most trusted lieutenants and I have no wish to incur the wrath of His Excellency."

"You will incur the wrath of His Excellency if you do not pass on this valuable information." Dagobah is becoming more and more remote by talking of himself in the third person.

"If His Excellency insists I will pass on what I have heard, but let me say I have no reason to suppose that what I hear is true. It is said by many people in the marketplace that His Excellency is favouring an Arab over one of his own people for the second most important position in New Light. They are unhappy that a foreigner is in a position of so much influence. They would prefer that position to be taken by one of their own."

"Such as you?" Dagobah's voice is full of cynicism.

"No, sir," I say with as much humility as I can fake. "I am not of this country although I have taken it as my country of choice. You have now and always have had my loyal support." I watch the cynicism drain from his face to be replaced by one of dawning understanding of what my words mean.

He wrestles with his thoughts before responding. "Apart from your recent indiscretions it is true that you have served me well and I suppose you can redeem yourself by continuing to serve me but in a different capacity. You must mingle with my people and learn more of their concerns about my wellbeing. You must find out if I have enemies, which is the lot of one who is great."

"I will do that willingly, Excellency, but before I do there is one more thing I have heard which causes me to fear for your safety, but I hesitate to reveal it."

"Do not hesitate; tell me of your fears."

There is a rumour that the foreign guards that the Arab has provided you with are loyal only to him and not to you, and it is thought that they do not have your best interests at heart."

"Are you saying that Monsieur L'Etranger is a threat to me?" His demeanour is suddenly frosty and he looks at me with suspicion.

"No, Excellency, that is not what I am saying. It could be that the Arab is not aware of their evil intentions. I pass this information on to you knowing that His Excellency is able by his own wit to discover if there is anything underhand going on."

Having sown more seeds of doubt, I leave Dagobah to ponder his options.

Benningo Dagobah:

What Oginga says to me is disquieting and I do not believe that L'Etranger bears me any malice, but I cannot be so certain about the guard he has provided. One way to eliminate any threat from them is to have them replaced immediately by a hand-picked selection of one hundred percent Benejaden warriors who will carry out my orders without question in return for a generous stipend in our worthless currency.

I will consider to who can make that selection for me. It cannot be L'Etranger and it would not be prudent to have Oginga to do this. I still harbour suspicions that he is not all he pretends to be. Try as I might nobody reliable springs to mind and after much soul searching I conclude that the only person I can trust to do this is me. I let it be known among criminal elements of the general population that I am seeking an elite guard to oversee my security and that I am prepared to pay handsomely for the right people.

Within hours of releasing this requirement into the underworld I am approached by three of the city's gang leaders. As ever, I have been astute; the criminal element applying will do anything that I ask of them, including termination, to control the citizenry. I am also approached by one named Kofi who is not a member of any known gang. This initially bothers me but he impresses me with a cold and emotionless personality and obvious cunning.

I arrange to meet a selection of ten candidates to get five plus a chief. The interviews are individual and I ask questions which will give me a guide to their corruptibility. If they have any morals, they are immediately eliminated. I make a selection quickly and easily; they are all corrupt and have no signs of morality. One man stands out above the rest; it is the lone wolf Kofi. In the anteroom, where they wait after the interview, he stands aloof from the others who talk amongst themselves. They all exchange the pleasantries of comrades in crime. He does not laugh or show any emotion except displeasure at their chattering.

I make my selection and dismiss the rejects. Of the remaining five, four congratulate themselves on their success and the fifth, Kofi, looks at them coldly with disdain.

"This man," I point to Kofi, "is going to be your leader. You will obey his orders as if they are mine."

The four not chosen as leaders look at Kofi with hatred but then hang their heads and assume sullen expressions in my presence. I have spoken, they are also intimidated by this stranger in our midst. My choice is good.

"Stand to attention!" Kofi snaps in his intimidating rasping whisper. "You are part of the elite guard and will act accordingly – or you will be punished."

Confusion reigns; the four look as though they are going to attack Kofi; they are not used to being told what to do.

"Those of you who do not wish to work under my command, as ordered by His Excellency, will leave now and be replaced by more suitable candidates. Now," his rasping voice raises, "as I said, stand to attention. If I have to repeat myself you will be dismissed immediately." He pauses a beat and stares coldly at the four.

In an uncoordinated movement, they shuffle to what passes for attention. My choice of leader is immediately justified, the reasons they comply are threefold; one is that they are being offered a large sum of money for an easy job, another is that they are intimidated by Kofi who is clearly not averse to physical violence, and thirdly and I think most importantly, they fear reprisals from me. I think I have chosen their leader very well; once more fate has intervened to send me the right stranger at the right time.

Simon Hunter:

The guard I provided for Dagobah has been replaced by five thugs. For the safety of my Nematasulan guards I send them back home and I accompany them. Dagobah is not happy with my decision as much because I have made it independently than because I am doing it at all.

He looks at me through narrowed eyes. "I require you to remain here to attend to my needs. You do not have my permission to travel to Nematasulu." In his view, simply uttering this makes it so.

"Excellency, I go to their homeland with them because it is from there that I can arrange for the finance you require to further your glorious cause. It is something that I cannot do by any means other than being face to face with those who can help me to help you." My response gives him a difficult dilemma with which he struggles. Which is the more important to him – having me comply with his wishes or having me arrange foreign currency for his use?

His response indicates 'no contest'. "I will allow you go to this foreign place and arrange for my finances but I require you to be back here in four days. My personal bodyguards are ready to be presented to my public and as we speak their uniforms are being made for a grand unveiling parade in five days. The commandant of the guard has designed the uniforms and is training the elite squad in matters of hard military discipline." As is usual for him he dismisses me with an imperious wave of his hand; our discussion is at an end.

I arrange with Noah Gilliland, using my secure satellite phone, to have the helicopter sent directly to Benejado City to take me and the unwanted guards back to Nematasulu. The arrival of the helicopter causes quite a stir; Benejado has no airport. With Dagobah's permission, the craft lands in open ground behind the House of Smoke and Tranquillity. He gives his permission on the understanding that he attends both the arrival and departure of the flight and will give a speech about support being received from the government of Nematasulu in recognition of the importance of New Light.

His speech to a pressganged crowd which goggles at the never-before-seen magnificent flying craft, is full on bluster which whips the crowd into a fervour of support for the cause. They do so after a little prompting from the extremist followers of New Light who find it necessary to knock to the ground a few less than enthusiastic onlookers. The noisy cheering from the avid supporters is ultimately echoed by the less enthusiastic who see that they are likely to be physically persuaded if they do not join in.

The helicopter rises gently into the air and I watch the ground appear to tilt dizzyingly as we turn onto the course set for Nematasulu. There is no discernible noise from the sodium-powered engines or the super-fast, shallow-pitch, double counter-rotating ultra-high speed fan blades. This is yet another innovation from the master engineer Ed Pickering. The flight over the barren plains of Golas underlines to me why the country is so poor, there is no government or private funding available to develop the land for agricultural use, and no political will to change that situation anytime soon. People like Dagobah and the country's President use whatever finance they can lay their hands on to promote their own personal causes rather than to develop their country.

As we cross from Golas into Nematasulu the landscape is painted using a different colour range which changes abruptly from a lifeless withered brown, apart from a narrow olive-coloured coastal fringe, to a stunning verdant green. Nematasulu has an active irrigation system constructed using the multi-capable advanced technology provided by the Colony.

Noah does his best to mask the shock he feels at my increasingly dishevelled appearance, but he fails to accomplish that feat. I glance at my reflection in the glass wall of his office and see a ragged dirt-encrusted hobo with straggling hair and a drawn, almost skeletal face. Before my departure I changed my Golacian costume for my original Arab guise and I am once more aware of the rank odour which emanates from them.

Noah Gilliland:

I try to hide the shock I feel at Simon's appearance but am unable to do so. He does not respond in any way to my reaction except to wrinkle his nose and frown at some inner thought. I thought him to be intense during our last meeting and now I see before me a man who is haunted and driven by inner turmoil. He gathers his robes around him and settles into a guest chair looking at me intently; he raises his hands to his face and removes his contact lenses.

"I can't tell you how good it is to have respite from

the hell-hole in which I have been living. It is taking all my reserves of strength to keep everything together."

"What can I do to help?" I can hear the concern in my voice which I intended to mask so as not to cause him any more anguish.

"Just helping me with your soldiers and giving me a haven is more than I have a right to expect." His eyes cloud over slightly. "I am setting in motion things which even my evil other self finds it difficult to reconcile." He sits up straighter and takes a deep breath. "But I don't want to bother or involve you in my problems any more than I must."

What is beginning to emerge as we speak is that his natural civilised side is still there but he is keeping it under tight control. I feel for him; I find it impossible to comprehend how difficult it is to walk this tightrope.

"How can I help you?" I ask again.

"One of the difficulties I have to come to terms with is that there is nobody with whom I can discuss my options without endangering their lives. This existence is solitary and unforgiving." He pauses and considers what he is about to say before unburdening himself. "Before I started this particular project I read up on the history of a selection of despots through recent times and I realised that there are common denominators which are present in the fate of tyrannical oppressors. Two examples in the twentieth century and two in the twenty-first century demonstrate that dictators who cruelly subjugate their peoples are finally brought to book by the very people they are oppressing. The four that spring to mind as an example are Benito Mussolini, Adolph Hitler in the twentieth century and Saddam Hussein and Muammer Gadhafi in the twenty-first. One way or another they were killed by the people they oppressed. Mussolini, Saddam, and Gadhafi were physically murdered by the masses and Hitler was driven to suicide by the masses which deserted him when all was finally lost."

He dry washes his face and I am aware of ingrained dirt under his fingernails. "Benningo Dagobah fits neatly into this pattern and will ultimately suffer the same fate if he is allowed to continue. My quandary is that he will do irreparable damage if he is permitted to run the course that I have outlined. My chosen task is to make sure that the outcome I seek is achieved; to do so I must ferment popular unrest to the point where the crowd will take care of him and he will be discredited as will his legacy."

I am appalled by his proposition; he is advocating the murder of another human being by third parties but I do not voice my distaste. Instead, I ask, "Why do you torture yourself by taking on this inhuman task? It is destroying you. Leave it up to the international community and have them take care of it."

He gives me a tired, patronising smile. "Ask the Italian, German, Iraqi, and Libyan people how they handled the same situation historically and they will tell you that they all left it too late to stop the problem in its infancy, and in each case the thinking of the dictators grew out of control and led to unrestrained catastrophic bloodshed. Dagobah must be stopped in his tracks and by his own kind; foreign intervention will only lead to greater division and distrust and the escalation of terrorism.

He is here for two days and he obviously needs some TLC. I suggest to him that he should go to the medical centre for a check-up and although I don't say it to him, a clean-up. He seems happy enough to do as I suggest and in an unusual show of compliance he allows me to make the arrangements on his behalf. I take his compliance as good news; I have never seen anybody from the Colony age as quickly as Simon is in the process of doing.

Simon Hunter:

I attend the medical centre in something of a daze; it's as if I am watching somebody else going through the procedures. I'm stripped down to my skivvies and a nurse takes my temperature and checks my heart. I look down at my body as she takes blood samples and am conscious that my ribs are more prominent than they should be and my upper arms and legs have lost muscle definition. Just before I started this mission I was the epitome of a healthy late thirty to early forty-year-old that most people thought me to be; my real age is so much more. My formerly youthful appearance is down entirely to being brought up in the Colony with its clean air and living and a medical regime and diet and lifestyle which considerably extends life expectancy. My time away from the Colony has exposed me to toxicity, stress, and corrosive foods which have advanced the ageing process significantly. I don't look my real age but neither do I continue to look my previously apparent age. I now look the same age as the Colony founders; they look to be in their mid-fifties but are significantly more than that.

The nurse hands me over to a doctor who gives me a thorough going over. When he compares my current state to that which was transmitted over from the Colony he tut-tuts and shakes his head. The nurse's findings are delivered to him and he looks them over carefully, comparing them with the results of my last examination.

"What have you been doing to yourself? If I have the right information, you have aged twenty years in the last two." He looks at me in puzzlement.

"No, doctor, I haven't aged twenty years in the last two years, it has all happened in the last few months."

"In the last few months." He echoes my words in amazement. "If you carry on as you are you will show your true outside world age within months. We must stop this rapid decline; you must resume your proper diet and stop eating toxic chemicals. You must sleep in your natural rhythm and you must stay out of the burning sun, your skin is a seared mess. You condition has not yet reached the point of no return but you are accelerating towards the danger zone at a perilous pace."

The news the doctor has given me comes as no surprise. The choice I made when leaving the Colony years ago left me open to what is now happening. I am becoming as mortal as those who have not enjoyed the beneficial health promoted within the Colony. They, the outsiders, have an expected life span which averages eighty-three years or so compared with the hundred and thirty or more enjoyed by the first generation of colonists; that is one hundred and thirty and counting, as conditions and understanding advance – so life expectancy increases.

My quarters in the VIP visitor hotel are so far from that which I have experienced in Benejado City that any comparison is meaningless. I have the penthouse suite which has a balcony the size of a tennis court. A large circular table capable of seating twelve people has a sun umbrella which covers it and the seats around it. In one corner of the balcony is a small well shaded self-service kitchen complete with refrigerated store cupboards and a juice bar. There is also voice communication with the hotel kitchen from which any item on the menu can be ordered at any time. I do not overindulge because it will make settling back into Benejado all the more difficult.

The other more reasonable me, which is subjugated for the moment, would wonder why I would be so crazy as to choose the deprivation in Benejado City over that which I now occupy in Nematasulu. Instead of thinking inwardly I begin the projection of what next? The time has come to recharge my batteries by employing the meditation techniques beloved of my mentor Carlina Tanterelli. To set the scene for this I need to find a location which gives me solace and the opportunity to reflect on the way my life is developing. The solution to this comes to me in a flash of inspiration based on a recollection of a fleeting glimpse during my road journey from the airport of a scene which gave me instant serenity. We followed the river road into the western quarter of the city and came across a riverside shack which looked abandoned but which had about it an air of appeal which lodged itself in my subconscious. It occurred to me that this is a good place for me to recharge my batteries.

Using Noah's officials, I learn that the property is on an experimental farm owned by the Nematasulu government and that it was currently unused which accounts for its air of gentle neglect. It was a simple matter to get Noah's agreement to have the small thatched building cleaned out and prepared for brief habitation. One advantage that Nematasulu has over Golas is that there is no red tape or bribery required for me to arrange for the use of this place of refuge.

Later in the day I am ensconced and I sit on the rickety balcony overlooking the wide, slow river. I feel for the first time since arriving in Golas a sense of wellbeing.

During the brief time of my tenure I can feel the tensions slipping away.

Abu Haider:

Simon strides purposefully into my café looking like an entirely different person. He pushes back the hood of his coarse robe and reveals a smiling face; his teeth now that he has briefly stopped eating the local berries are startlingly white in his mahogany face which is less lined than I remembered from only a few days ago.

"Abu Haider, my friend." He places his hands on my shoulders and gives me the traditional Arab three-cheek kiss. "I would talk to you about important things."

"I will always have time to talk to you my friend, *Seemon.*" I use the Franco Arab pronunciation of his name. For some reason, I understand that this strange man, who appears to be but is not Arab, means me no harm even if he does work for the hated Dagobah who is a xenophobe except when it suits him to be tolerant of foreigners, such as *Seemon.*

We adjourn to the parlour in my living quarters where a hookah awaits me and offers tranquillity. I offer him a smoke tube which he declines with a grace which takes the sting out of his refusal of my friendly gesture.

"What is it you wish to discuss with me, friend." I close my eyes and take a deep draft of the perfumed smoke from the hookah.

"I speak openly with you and trust that you will keep the confidences I share."

"Take care, my friend, with whom you share such a confidence, if it means that you put your life in a place of danger. I can only think that what you want to say concerns the despicable Dagobah and should he learn of it he will have you executed." As I speak the smoke drifts from my lungs to be replaced by another deep and relaxing draft.

"We have spoken circuitously of the situation here and how the people are being drawn into an ever more dangerous situation without their realising it."

"This is so but I would not speak of it openly, it is too dangerous." My warning is in languid tones as the smoke works its magic.

"The situation will only get worse as new Light has an ever-stronger grip on the way society is conducted. It will suck down into the depths of depravity all of those who are not wary of the words of bigotry." He stares at me intently as though trying to read my thoughts.

"Speak softly, my friend. Should your words be heard by others without discretion they could lead to your demise." I warn him once more.

He is unmoved by my warning and outlines to me a plan of action which is breath taking in its conception and extremely dangerous to him and perhaps to me should it fail during any one of its complex steps he asks me to take.

Benningo Dagobah:

When L'Etranger returns after his business meeting in Nematasulu he is a changed man. I don't know what lies beyond the borders of Nematasulu but I intend to find out either by invitation or alternatively if needs be by means of invasion. He is more relaxed and his face is not so drawn and haunted looking. I am disappointed that he did not come straight to me on his return. My emissaries tell me that he chose rather to seek out the company of Abu Haider at the House of Smoke and Tranquillity.

I have called together all five of my newly appointed personal guards to show L'Etranger the quality of the men and their new uniforms which make them look as chilling as their newly appointed leader; Kofi, the strongest and most fearsome of them all. The uniforms they wear are black as befits the image I wish them to portray. They are a mixture of African and Arab fighting uniforms with wide flowing pantaloons wrapped tightly at the ankles and a loose top. Most menacing of all is the head-dress which covers their heads and faces except for the eyes. Kofi's eyes cannot be seen because he alone wears sunglasses. His distinguishing feature is a large gold coin bearing the imprint of a soaring eagle which is attached to his forehead by a gold chain which disappears into his head covering. His appearance is truly sinister, just as I knew it would be when I appointed him, and the whole image is topped off by his very visibly wearing a holstered NLG Surekill.

There is an atmosphere of extreme tension when L'Etranger and Kofi's men come face to face. I am even more impressed by Kofi when he speaks in his intimidating gravelly whisper – using the local dialect which L'Etranger does not speak. The two men who are lately in positions of great power in New Light circle each other warily like boxers at the beginning of a title fight.

I have no wish for there to be a conflict between these two. I will promote a clash when L'Etranger is no longer of use and the time comes for him to be removed from office and life. In the meantime, it suits my purposes for there to be cooperation between the two but not harmony; harmony among my minions is counter-productive.

Simon Hunter:

There is something about the leader of the guard which is disturbing. His general appearance is intimidating and his strange hoarse whispering has a chilling inhuman quality. It seems clear to me that he sees me as a threat of some kind and I don't know why, I have done nothing to antagonise or threaten him. That he has been chosen by Dagobah for his appointed task tells me that this warrior has no scruples. He is like others with whom I have had to work in the past – so I will treat him with caution.

The four subordinate guards are typical of their type. Standing to attention with shoulders back does not come naturally to them. When their leader shepherds them out of the room the last in line tries without success to keep in step with his three colleagues, but no matter how he hops and skips he is unable to fall into synchronisation.

Dagobah watches them leave the room through narrowed eyes. "Kofi is a good commander and he will lick his troops into shape given a few weeks."

"Will they be as good as the guard I provided for you?"

"They will be better when they are fully trained, and they are local men who feel loyalty to me; the guard you supplied are foreign and I am not sure I can trust them." He is right but for the wrong reason.

Dagobah changes tack and takes me aside conspiratorially. "We are ready now to move forward with greater pace. I have my trusted guards and yourself in place; with their protection and your contacts we can begin to move towards our destiny. You have the necessary finance in place after your visit to that foreign place?"

"Everything is in place," I assure him while at the

same time I begin my own plan of action. "The armaments you need will be supplied as soon as you can demonstrate that your army is skilled enough to use them."

"The skill of my army is a matter for me to consider, it has nothing to do with the armament manufacturers." His voice and face are pinched with disapproval.

"I know this to be so but we must convince the arms suppliers that these advanced weapons will not be allowed to fall into the clutches of other military groups who would have the weapons copied." This is complete hogwash but I say it with all the sincerity I can muster.

He pauses and looks annoyed. "This is not at all satisfactory. I purchased these weapons without haggling about the price, how dare they apply restrictions."

I smile inwardly at his words; he has deluded himself into thinking that he has purchased the weapons. "Excellency, they have only your interests at heart. Should these weapons fall into the wrong hands they could be used against you by seasoned troops who will do you great damage. I have negotiated with the suppliers to send their top trainer to make sure that your soldiers can be better than any other."

What I say to him feeds his ego and he puffs out his chest in false pride. "You have done well to negotiate such a deal. It is true that my army, once trained by specialists, will be a match for any army in the whole of Africa and even the rest of the world. Make the training happen without delay." He is already tired of the conversation and he turns away and ignores me.

My delaying tactics have begun, now I must put the rest of the plan into operation. What comes next is very difficult compared with the simple moves which have been made so far.

Kofi:

Basic training for the four special guards is a slow and frustrating process; they have been chosen not for what they have got but what they don't have – morals. The equipment available for training them is limited in both scope and quantity. The side arms and assault rifles provided are the best currently obtainable and as far as I know these models are not being released until further proving trials are carried out by the manufacturer. The weapons are of top quality but the men at my disposal are not; they are sullen and they resent me, an out-of-town interloper, being put in overall control of the training of our small 'elite' group.

Before I get a chance to train the men I need more ammunition. Whoever it is who scoped the ratio of projectiles to firearm got the numbers wrong; there is not enough ammunition to prepare any kind of training programme. I presume it is the Arab, as Oginga calls him, who arranged for the supply, and I must wonder at the reason for the lack of planning which has caused the shortfall.

Word comes to me from Dagobah that we are to have training specialists and the reasons he gives me for this do not make sense. I tell Dagobah that given the right amount of ammunition I can train the private guards and the rest of what he calls regular troops without any outside intervention. He doesn't even consider my suggestion; he seems to be impressed that his army is to be trained by foreign specialists who will turn them into the best troops in all of Africa. I don't know where he gets that idea from, it is a complete nonsense; no amount of training will turn them into anything other than the thugs they are.

Abu Haider:

I am fulfilling the part that Simon has asked me to play. I have collected together a selection of my trustworthy fellow Arabs and explained to them the danger that we as foreigners are in should Dagobah become as powerful as is his intention. Discussion within the confines of the House of Smoke and Tranquillity are secure and the freedom of expression that exists here holds no dangers for us from those of lowly intelligence like Dagobah; but his power grows.

There are potential dangers which lurk in the shadows of local society and the thuggish leader of the guards, Kofi, is thought by Simon to be a source of such danger. To guard against his incursion I have posted guards of my own, looking like customers, to make sure that we know if he or any of his men or any strangers should be anywhere near. From within this cocoon we speak freely about protecting ourselves from Dagobah because we are not pure-born Golacian, no matter how many generations some of us have been here. It is understood that for the moment we are not in danger but should

Dagobah become more powerful and amass a larger military force our position will be far from secure, and his interpretation of the laws which protect other nationalities are, as far as he is concerned, far from being fixed.

Our band is small and any moves we attempt to diminish the power which Dagobah craves must be subtle and effective. Our brief discussion is drawn to a close with each person present accepting that they have a contribution to make to safeguard their own security and that of their families and valued friends. Acting on Simon's advice I have kept our numbers down to those of established integrity and influence in the community.

Simon Hunter:

The specialist trainers arrive from their home in Nuovostan. Before departing from their homeland, they were briefed by Irena Pelochev, President of Nuovostan, on the degree of training they must provide and that their country of origin must remain obscure. The leader of the team of three is Karin, a striking young woman with a fierce passion for her country, and her mother who is President of Nuovostan. The team are multi-lingual including French in its modern form, unlike that of the local dialect which is the original language, unchanged for centuries and which is peppered with Swahili phrases. To my amusement my disguise is now so convincing that Karin, who I have met on several occasions in Nuovostan, does not recognise me.

I set the team to work immediately and introduce

them to both the special guard and the regular troops and I can see from the look on the team's faces that they are not at all impressed by the calibre of their pupils, but they don't show disapproval in a way that their pupils will comprehend.

At the end of the first training session the team reports back to me on the progress they have made. They are hesitant to be truthful because they see me as being on the side of the trainees but after a little persuasion they open up a little and tell me that training them to an acceptable standard will be an uphill battle. I give them solace by telling them that they have as much time as is required to get the best out of them and that no time pressure will be place on them as trainers. I tell them that I will report back to His Excellency and advise him that the trainers are doing a good job and that training the troops to a high standard may take a little time but that reasonable success is assured.

With luck, I have bought myself some more time.

Benningo Dagobah:

Everything is in place for me to take the next big stride forward. I have weapons, access to finance, an Arab who will keep the other Arabs quiet, a first-class bodyguard and troops that are being trained to be the best in the world. I intend to strike while the iron is hot. I am now in a position to challenge the government of Golas and make a move on them. They are corrupt and will be easy to manipulate when they see me as a means of further securing their hold over the country under my patronage.

Arranging a visit to Golas City is made easier by my being a recognised political force. I have support from the entire population of Benejado City and have placed sympathisers in every important position in the capital's administration. Some of the old guard were persuaded by monetary reward to retire from office, others who were more reluctant to comply had second thoughts when persuasion was applied, and those who refused to submit to my will have joined the growing number of the disappeared. The President is too old and incompetent to be aware of what I have done.

To give me the international credibility which has, until just recently, been denied me, I take L'Etranger with me. This will not only help internationally; it will help to persuade those corrupt members of the Golacian government who are not Golas nationals to believe that I am prepared to work with foreigners. With their significant influence not being used to oppose me, I can taste the success of my mission. Once I have control of the entire administration I will dispense with the foreign element.

Simon Hunter:

Dagobah is very insistent that I accompany him to Golas City for negotiations with the Golacian government and this does not suit my plans. Abu Haider has briefed his small team and has commenced with his part in shaping the future of a post-Dagobah country.

"You will accompany me on my visit to Golas City and will support all of my propositions." Dagobah assumes that I will comply with his wishes.

He shows his annoyance when I choose to disagree with him on the next steps we should take.

"Excellency, much as I would like to accompany you on such an important mission I think I can be more useful to the cause by remaining here and working with the troops and training."

"Nonsense, you will accompany me and give me the support I deserve."

"Forgive me, Excellency, but the negotiations you intend will be conducted in the Golacian language which I have not mastered and so it will be difficult for me to be convincing in my support for your proposals."

In truth, I have been in Benejado City for long enough to have a working grasp of the country's simple language and limited vocabulary which I choose to keep to myself. He spends a little time pondering my words before an idea dawns on him. "Your assertion is right but it need not be of consequence to you; I will provide you with an interpreter who will translate for you and translate your responses." He looks at me and sees doubt in my expression. "I will not discuss this further. You will accompany me and that is an end to this discussion."

As is his usual way, he turns abruptly on his heel and walks away, already thinking of other things.

I have been given little notice of the order to travel with Dagobah and I use a little of that precious time to get an update from Abu Haider. I find him in his customary position behind the counter in his café.

"Salaam alikum," I greet him.

"Alikum salaam." He makes the traditional Arabic response and greets me with a treble cheek kiss. "It is good to see you, my friend. We should go to my parlour to speak in private." He leads the way and I follow.

"What do you have to say to me?" I invite him to speak when we are safely in his parlour.

My people," he drops his voice to a whisper, "are spreading the word as you suggested but the response from the locals is not as good as from the Arab population."

"This is no surprise to me but please keep up with the approach we agreed, it is a slow process but also very necessary. Are you yet making any progress at all with the locals?"

"We are but at this pace it will take far too long to expect any positive results. We have identified a group of city residents who do not approve of the way New Light are hijacking their religion which is a moderate branch of Islam such as we the Arabs follow. They are against Dagobah but will not make their opposition known; they are too few to be able to resist openly." He looks depressed at the lack of impetus.

"This is as we discussed it might be. You are already into the second stage of the strategy and I congratulate you for this, it is actually happening more quickly than I had anticipated." I give him a smile of encouragement.

"Fast for you but slow for me." He returns the

smile to me but his is self-deprecating. "My people, now that we have found a nucleus of discontent are carefully spreading the word among the less fanatical members of the population to try and swell the ranks of the discontented and have them grow into a reckonable force. I must give a word of caution; as Arabs there is only so much we can do. Among a significant part of the population there are those who resent that we are successful traders and are unlikely to support our cause."

"Stay strong, my friend. If my plans work, and I am sure they will, your position after all of this is over will be stronger than ever."

"I hear your words but I fear that Dagobah is like a rogue camel. He may rear up and unseat us before we have all our plans in place." He shakes his head slowly and unhappily.

Benningo Dagobah:

I quickly overcome L'Etranger's objection when I insist that he drives me and the bodyguard to Golas City. I need to impress those I am meeting by having a 4WD fit for a king, a personal bodyguard with modern weapons, and an Arab chauffeur; I will eclipse the President. I intend to show them that they are not dealing with a nobody from a northern province but with a VIP having considerable power representing a growing city with significant foreign investment.

The journey is long and tiring. I can see in the rear-view mirror that my bodyguard is sleeping, they roll from side to side as we drive over the uneven road surface. On closer inspection, I see that four of the five are sleeping but the fifth, Kofi, is wakeful; I am unable to see his eyes because of his dark glasses but the attitude of his head shows that he is alert; the gold coin at his forehead glistens when it catches the sunlight as he sways to the motion of the road. Once more I congratulate myself on attracting such a professional into my service.

After the long bone-shaking journey with three comfort stops along the way, we arrive at the government house complex of Golas City. The soldiers at the gate house are sloppy compared with my guard whom I have shouted into wakefulness on our approach. I must address the guards because of L'Etranger's inability to speak Golacian. I must do something about that, it is not fitting that a man in my eminent position should be required to address lowly soldiers. I wave the gate guard around to my side of the 4WD so that I may address him.

"I am Abu Golas from the great city of Benejado and I am here to see the honourable president of our beloved country. I am here at his invitation so I expect you to open the barrier without any delay." I intend to show them who is boss.

"I will look on the list to see if you are expected." He is an insolent man and I intend to have him punished for his tardiness.

He returns to my side of the 4WD at a slovenly pace after an insufferably long time. "You are on the list but I will need to see some form of identification papers before I can let you in."

I am not accustomed to being treated in such a way and decide to stop this peasant from causing any further delay. I turn to indicate to Kofi that he should take control of the situation. Kofi and his four-man team leave the vehicle by the back door, first picking up their combat rifles. Their sinister black uniforms with their combat boots and face masks make an instant impression on the ragged ill-disciplined gate guards whose side arms are like peashooters by comparison. I see the look of uncertainty on their faces as they realise they are out-gunned. They hesitate and physically jump when Kofi shouts at them; the gold coin resting on his forehead has a strange mesmeric effect on them. I am unable to hear what he says but their response is immediate. The barrier is lifted.

Word spreads quickly and our passage through the rest of the road checks and barriers is problem free. We reach the main door into government house and park in the prime position which is normally, I imagine, reserved for the car of President Jacob Wellbeing. All seven of us alight from the 4WD and mount the steps to an imposing main entrance, the double doors of which stand open to reveal a grand marble-floored interior. The opulence of the interior is marred by a lack of housekeeping which has allowed the expensive floor to be littered with the debris of everyday living and the paintwork on the grand staircase which leads up to a working gallery is chipped and peeling. Once it was great but it no longer is.

Members of the presidential guard walk untidily down the staircase and look as though they have just woken up. Their side arms are the same as those worn by the gate guard and are vastly inferior to those carried by my guard. I allow myself a smile of assured ultimate victory; compared with my men these are amateurs. I am confident that my plans to take command of the government will be much easier than I had imagined.

Simon Hunter:

Government House is shambolic; the lack of coordination is staggering and their security virtually non-existent. I must take care and be flexible; their inefficiency could derail my plans catastrophically because they are likely to be unpredictable. The ease with which we got through the government house guard bears testament to the vulnerability that would make an attack on the government a simple matter. The plan I have devised requires a government which is more switched on than Dagobah but right from the start that ideal is scuppered.

My original plan was to ferment unrest in Benejado City to destabilise the home of New Light and then to involve the government in dethroning Dagobah by using them to scuttle his organisation. That idea lies in tatters and although the destabilisation is in progress government intervention is unlikely, from what I can tell, to follow. Right now, I don't have a plan B which is a disaster of my own making. Getting my tactics back on the rails is something I must do without delay otherwise my building up Dagobah to topple him as a figurehead will have exactly the reverse effect – I will have made him stronger than he could ever be under his own steam.

I am wheeled into an audience with President

Wellbeing – like a prize boar's head at a medieval feast. I sit not reacting to the discussions, pretending not to speak or understand Golacian dialect. There is an overabundance of point scoring from both sides of the table to which I cannot react, except when what are considered relevant issues are translated for me. The president and Dagobah begin the dance of power, each trying to assume a position of ascendancy, each trying to outdo the other with innuendo and hints of hidden power which are not convincingly tangible.

After an hour of sparring Dagobah tables his proposals full on and he seems to have the measure of Jacob Wellbeing, who appears comparatively slow witted and hesitant. My interpreter is not present to translate for me what is being said between the two at the culmination of the discussion, it is private and not intended for my ears.

Dagobah commences his opening gambit. "Mr President, the time has come for us to talk seriously about our country and what drives us forward. We need to have unified religious and political belief and we need the lead from the government to be strong."

The response from the president is slow. "What little money we have is used up in looking after our people. Until our currency has some international standing there is little we can do to promote either our religion or our politics on the international stage."

"It is not money that is required for such promotion, it is the will to impress on our people that it is their duty to be united behind its leaders both religiously and politically without questioning our motives." Dagobah turns to look at me, still talking in his own language. "This is one who can help you in the matter of currency; he has powerful contacts in the outside world which will enable us to be an international trading nation. He has been financing me and with a little coercion he will be persuaded to help our government. It is within my power to do this." He leans back in his chair and assumes a pose depicting great wisdom.

It is difficult for me not to react to his fanciful words; he describes a situation which even he must understand does not and cannot prevail. I manage with difficulty to look impassive and not to give away that I understand what they are discussing. At a signal from Dagobah the interpreter who has been lurking on the periphery re-joins our small group.

Jacob Wellbeing:

Dagobah is an upstart. He is a peasant who believes he has risen to the exulted position of leadership but it is in an unimportant organisation in an inferior city. I agreed to see him because there are reports from my information gatherers indicating that he is in absolute control in his provincial city and his recent antics in the media have brought him a certain notoriety which is not to my liking. They also inform me that he has access to advanced weaponry which is, disquietingly, superior to that available to the Golacian army; hence my allowing him an audience.

As is my custom I play the part of a bumbling uneducated tribal dictator. None of my countrymen know that I am university educated in America and have a doctorate, I changed my name and my history to hide that fact. It suits me to present myself in the way I do because a slow response gives me time to weigh up the situation before offering any opinions.

The Arab is a different kettle of fish; I can't make my mind up whether he is disinterested or just pretending to be. On the other hand, Dagobah is so easy to read. I have no fear of Dagobah but I am wary of the Arab. At the commencement of our discussions an interpreter is called forward to translate for him. Our conversation is conducted in Golacian which he does not speak but rather than interpreting into French, the second language of our country, he translates into English, the hated language. Dagobah informs me of what he can do for Golas by promoting international dialogue and using his influence to make us a great and progressive nation.

Simon Hunter:

The interpreter mangles the English language and his whispering makes understanding him almost impossible. I tune out from what he is saying and listen in to the conversation between Dagobah and Wellbeing. Very quickly I realise that the translation I am getting from the interpreter bears little resemblance to the promises being made to Wellbeing of what I can do for them. He promises that I can be manipulated into doing anything without recompense because I am so focussed in building facilities in Benejado City that I will do anything they require. This is interpreted to me as Dagobah saying that by helping New Light I will be given unlimited access to facilities not only in Benejado but also in Golas City and any other area of the country.

I am enthralled by the range of the conversation in which they discuss freely what can be done using the finances and facilities that my bottomless purse might fund. Jacob Wellbeing catches the enthusiasm that emanates from Dagobah and begins to weave a graphic picture of what they can achieve together. Their discussion grows ever more fanciful; they talk of having an air force and a navy and of creating a free port which will attract customers from all over the world and bring in more international currencies. Ultimately they will not need the finances provided by me, their income will be self-generated and they will rival the great shopping cities of the world.

In their imagination, they will be rich beyond avarice and will be able to promote their country and, most importantly to Dagobah, their one unrivalled religion. Dagobah's eyes light up with a burning fanaticism that consumes his inadequate intellect. Jacob Wellbeing joins in but without the fanaticism. I must take care not to underestimate the danger of Jacob Wellbeing.

Benningo Dagobah:

I have made my point and the fool Jacob Wellbeing has fallen for my ploy completely. My ability to appear to promote his interests will earn me a place on his team from where I will be able to promote my own agenda and assume not only the religious throne but also the political throne of my country. All of this because of a chance meeting with a lowly Arab; my deity smiles down on me with the beneficence I truly deserve.

We make the journey back to Benejado City immediately after the meeting with Wellbeing. When we arrive back I decide not to parade around the city, to let my people see me in my splendid 4WD, this provinciality suddenly does not appeal to me. I am to become a man of national substance with perhaps an apartment in government house and proper servants dressed in uniforms.

I do not intend to waste time. Moving to Golas City will happen as soon as I have secured things here in Benejado. I have decided to give Oginga another chance because I can't think of anybody else to whom I can give the task I have in mind for him. To start with I will have L'Etranger work with him because I need to have somebody I can trust to make sure that Oginga looks after my interest rather than his own. He is a devious man but not in my class, as he will learn. Once things here have moved to Golas City I will have L'Etranger join me at some lodgings close by so that he can front the foreign propaganda effort.

When, at my bidding he comes to my apartment, Oginga is clearly still angry about his position being taken away from him. I can divine this even though he tries to hide it from me. He believes he has been summoned to be further chastised and he looks distressed. I put his mind at rest, not through any weakness on my part but because I want him, out of gratitude for my forgiveness, to comply with my instructions.

"Oginga, I have a task for you and it is very important and will need all of your skills. I am to go to Golas City for some considerable time and I need to have somebody take care of my affairs here. I am putting you in charge of all council matters in my absence. You will be assisted for a short time by Monsieur L'Etranger who will later join me in Golas City when the situation here is under control."

The look of contrition he had when he first came in reverses to one of elation at being given another chance. I am not famous for doing this and so it means more to him than forgiveness from somebody else, this is clearly written on his face.

"Excellency, Abu Golas, I will do as you command and serve you well. I have no need of assistance from the Arab; I am capable of doing what you wish without interference from him." He has been emboldened by his return to favour.

"This is not a matter for discussion; his presence is not intended to interfere with what you are charged to do; it is to provide the necessary finance for you to take over the council duties and do the other tasks required of you."

"Tasks, Excellency?"

"Yes, the council can take care of the day-to-day running of the affairs of the city, under your supervision of course. Your task is to make sure that every citizen understands that he must work endlessly and tirelessly for the good of New Light. Any citizen showing a lack of respect will be cast into prison and if he does not repent his ways immediately he will be dealt with by the harshest means you can devise." I observe that he can envisage building up great personal wealth and will be given the opportunity to indulge in the barbarism that I know he likes to practice.

"Excellency, I am honoured that you bestow on

me such trust."

Oginga:

The news from Dagobah is better than I could ever have imagined. The Arab spending some time here when Dagobah has gone to the big city is an irritation but it will not stop me from carrying out my orders in my own way. I am ignoring Dagobah's bodyguard and appointing one of my own now that I have the freedom to do so. I don't trust Kofi and his four men to do my bidding without them going to Dagobah for clearance. I will not appoint a head man in my new guard, that is a position I will assume myself and the people I choose will not be locals. Locals will have allegiances and the only allegiance my guards should have is to me.

Dagobah is in a real hurry to be in Golas City and he leaves the day after he appoints me to look after his interests in his absence. The Arab drives him there and then returns straight away. I don't expect any real difficulty from the Arab now that he does not have the protection of Dagobah. I take on board my new guard of ten men who are paid for out of city funds and I arm them with the older guns; I give them a limited amount of ammunition so that the treacherous rogues amongst them will have limited fire power.

I brief them and tell them to round up any citizens who do not pledge full allegiance to New Light and have them thrown into jail, and to do it noisily to encourage others to be more compliant. Their second task is to collect special taxes from those who do not oppose New Light but neither do they wholeheartedly support it. After they have undertaken these tasks I will instruct them to extract taxes from the Arab population; my reason for doing this is because they are Arab.

Simon Hunter:

I imagine that Dagobah does not want me to remain with him in Golas City because he intends to do mischief that I might discover. On my return to Benejado, Oginga has already started to magnify his presence. He has a phalanx of guards who would look more at home in the state prison than out on the streets. Kofi and his guards have remained in the city and will accompany me when I return to Golas City; I presume that they will watch over me to make sure I follow the orders of His Excellency.

Kofi's guards and those of Oginga do not mix. If I thought the original guard was disturbing I now know what disturbing really means when I see the new group. They are uniformed but instead of wearing black they wear the dark green of another religion and their faces are visible under the traditional turban worn by Golacians. I presume that this is because they all bear tribal face scars, some of which are hideous, adding to the visual heartlessness of the group.

Oginga ignores my presence which suits me fine, I have other things to do which do not include having Oginga as a confidante. After resting to recover from the rigours of my journey to Golas City I visit Abu Haider in the House of Smoke and Tranquillity. He greets me like a family member and beckons me into his private parlour.

"It is good to see you back here so quickly, my brother. Things are moving along very quickly and we are doing our best to contain the situation. Oginga has instructed his thugs to make examples of those of the population who do not show absolute obedience to New Light. Already they have thrown scores of people into jail without any sort of trial, at the whim of the guards. My people have told the locals to pretend acceptance of the new regime and to do exactly as is required of them so that they do not suffer the deprivations of jail. Most accept our advice but some of the hot-heads do not and several have been severely beaten and thrown into jail, and I am afraid some of them did not survive the beatings." He concludes his words with a sigh.

"Do not be too hard on yourself, Abu; but for your advice there would have been many more injuries and deaths. Keep with the plan we discussed and we will beat this injustice."

Oginga:

Instant success! I have jailed and beaten the dissenters. It happened with a speed that illustrates that the population is weak willed and will not offer resistance. Next is the task of extracting taxes form those who have not yet been jailed, including the Arab traders who have not, so far, been affected by the change in administration.

Although I have not appointed a leader of my guard group one of their number has made his way to the top as a spokesman for them all. This man has truly frightening tribal scars which extend from his hairline to his neck and chest, and I assume on to his body which is covered by his uniform. I hear from other sources that he bears his disfigured torso when confronting his adversaries and is given to uttering bloodcurdling screams as part of his reign of terror. He is a man after my own heart.

Scar Face, as I think of him, reports back to me his successes. He has anticipated my intentions and started to apply pressure to the Arab traders, and it is as I thought – they crumble before this frightening man. He passes on to me large sums of money which the Arabs have donated without resistance. It no longer matters to me that the Arab L'Etranger is here, his people, like the Golacians, are weak-willed and from the lack of reaction from the Arab – so is he.

I donate one third of the monies collected to the government exchequer with two thirds going into my personal account. This is the same proportion that I paid of the income from the warehouse parties. I arrange to hold more warehouse parties and to make sure that failure to attend such parties is to become a serious contravention of the new rules and regulations which I am in process of drawing up. I will become very rich in a short time, especially as it is my intention to hold the warehouse parties seven days a week.

Simon Hunter:

I am summoned by Dagobah to join him in Golas City. Together with the guard group, I take the 4WD on the dusty journey. I indicate to Kofi that as senior guard he can travel in the front passenger seat; he declines my invitation and travels in the back with his companions. His refusal to accept my offer of a more comfortable ride for him is hissed out through his face coverings in a frightening explosion of whispered words. The gold coin on his forehead has a mesmerising effect as it dances to the rhythm of his frowns.

The journey is mind numbingly boring and I notice again that four of the guards sleep through it but Kofi remains alert, even though I can't see his eyes because of his ever-present sinister black sunglasses. His head shakes as the 4WD negotiates the uneven road but does not loll as it would if he was sleeping. After what seems like an interminable drive we at last arrive at Government House. When the guards on the gate see Kofi sitting in the back they raise the security barriers with frenetic haste.

Since arriving, Dagobah has insinuated himself into the heart of Jacob Wellbeing's government. He has done this by applying his strong will on those members of the government who are weak and by financial reward offered to those who are more resilient but easily corruptible. Inside the government structure he is a rabid nationalist; outside among the general public in Golas he is a fervent religious zealot. To the rest of the world he is now represented as being a re-enlightened moderate who is no longer threat to wider society. Largely this impression is because of the way I am inaccurately represented to the international community. For now I must go along with this representation but I look forward to the day I no longer have to do so.

Benningo Dagobah:

It is like taking candy from a baby. The government members accept the story I put forward without challenging any of the issues arising from what I propose. I indicate to the weaker members of the government that I can make them more powerful by giving them more weight within the structure of my proposed governing machine. The others who are willing to take my bribes can be controlled by financial considerations. Jacob Wellbeing is a different matter; he is clearly stupid and has no vision but influencing him to follow my lead is not an option, he will be surplus to requirements.

When L'Etranger re-joins me in the city, along with my personal guards, I take him straight to an audience with the president. Our conversation with him is very one-sided; I talk and the president listens without giving any indication the he agrees or disagrees or even understands me. To move the discussion along I switch from Benejaden to patois French which the president, of course, understands, so that L'Etranger can make a contribution.

"What M. L'Etranger brings to the meeting is his contacts with the outside world, which is something you have tried to do for so many years, Mr President, but which has so far eluded you. With international acceptance, we can extend our sphere of influence. From my perspective, I can promote the interests of New Light and from yours you can invite inward investment which will allow you to expand your influence and become a leading African politician, perhaps even *the* leading politician."

It is difficult for me to judge how Jacob Wellbeing

feels about my proposal because his demeanour betrays none of his thoughts, but I am sure that when he realises how much his upgraded influence will improve his standing in his community he will go along with using L'Etranger's influence.

Jacob Wellbeing:

Dagobah makes the mistake of thinking that my thoughts are driven by the same objectives as his; that is far from the truth. I will listen to what the Arab says and in the unlikely event that he has anything useful to propose I will consider making use of it. I have no great wish to have to rely on foreign money for my country to operate successfully; foreign money means foreign interference.

There is nothing lacking in my life. I have total control of my country and its citizens which will surprise Dagobah because he is under the impression that he is in control of what goes on in Benejado City. I am happy enough for him to think that, I am safe in the knowledge that his hold over city is just skin deep. At any time, I can send in troops to overwhelm him with vastly superior numbers.

"What magical things can you do to make my life better?" I ask the Arab after Dagobah has left us, at my insistence.

"There is nothing magical about what I do, Mr President. I have access to the outside world at a high level and I have access to foreign money. I can use my influence in any way you wish, as I am doing for His Excellency Abu Golas."

It amuses me to hear the use of his newly adopted

name. The use of it confirms that Dagobah has an ego which is far beyond reality, and I am wondering who put him up to using such an inappropriate soubriquet. The Arab intrigues me; he is a newcomer to our country and in a short time he has wormed his way into the trust of Dagobah, and I wonder why he has done so and what his true intentions are. I understand that Dagobah is holding the potential of permission to build a conference centre in Benejado City over the head of the Arab; my problem with that is it is difficult for me to understand why a businessman with so much wealth would want to build such a centre in what is a backwater. It would be difficult for me to justify building one in Golas City which is much bigger and more suitable. The Arab is obviously rich and I assume therefore more intelligent than this lame duck enterprise suggests.

I dismiss the Arab after a short discussion to consider what lies behind the support he is giving Dagobah; it makes no sense. Dagobah wants to extend his power and is using the Arab to do so, a strange thing for him considering his hatred of all people who are not Golacian. The Arab must know that Dagobah is not sufficiently intelligent to manage any kind of international operation but he insists on going forward with his support, I need to know why. I give the task of finding out about the Arab to my most trusted intelligence operative. Only I know of the operative's existence and he is resourceful enough to be able to dig up background on the Arab and of course Dagobah. I wind him up and set him on his course.

Simon Hunter:

My brief conversation with President Wellbeing leaves me feeling puzzled. The lazy way he asks questions of me belies the astute nature of their content. Dagobah has underestimated the cunning of this apparent country bumpkin. I will need to be wary of him and take care that I do not fall into the same trap as Dagobah.

President Wellbeing has put forward that he has no wish to extend his powers; he is the unelected unopposed president of a country which barely makes its way financially and this is a situation which clearly suits him. He has all the power he can handle and all the money he needs without being beholden to any foreign power. His country is a threat to nobody and there is nothing in his undeveloped country which is coveted by any other.

Dagobah is on the wrong tack when he tries to tempt the president with offers of more of everything. What the president wants is the status quo and he sees Dagobah as a threat; I can use that little nugget to my own advantage.

Oginga:

In the few days that the Arab has been away I have made great strides. The warehouse parties are up and running daily and my specially selected helpers are encouraging any of the reluctant rich to join in with the fun. Doing so brings happiness – not doing will bring retribution.

My helpers tell me that the Arab population is putting up little resistance to the pressure being applied to them to swell the coffers, at my usual commission rate. The few that do resist, along with those of the general Golacian population, find that there is a sudden upsurge in unexplained damage to their businesses and their homes which ceases as soon as they make the requested contributions. It concentrates their minds wonderfully.

Abu Haider:

In line with what Simon suggested my small group of factfinders who endeavour to ferment unrest to test the reaction of Oginga and his cronies pass on their information to me. I in turn pass the information on to Simon for his assessment. He underlines that he does not want to put my people in harm's way and that once they have established the boundaries of Oginga's coercion they should refrain from going beyond the limit, for the moment.

Slowly and meticulously I build up a profile of what Oginga is doing and a list of people who are supporting him, a list of those who are resisting him, and of those who are neutral. What he intends to do with this information is not clear to me but I trust his motives in the same way that I trust him when he says that the armaments he has supplied to Dagobah are not all they appear to be.

Jacob Wellbeing:

My intelligence man has come up with some interesting and disturbing pieces of information about the Arab. Research shows that he is super rich without the source of his wealth being revealed. What is disturbing is that there is no record available about his general background and no record of any kind of history more than six months old. I am presuming that he is travelling under an assumed name, which does not unduly bother me. After all, I too am living under an assumed name. What is disturbing, is that he is lavishing so much money on a nonentity like Dagobah.

In an endeavour to shed some light on the mystery I decide to talk with Dagobah about the Arab. At my instruction Dagobah visits me at breakneck speed, happy that I have summoned him into my chambers.

"Mr President," he addresses me breathlessly. "I came with all haste as soon as I was told you wanted to see me."

"There was no need to run, Benningo; I would have waited for you." When he hears me use his given name he simpers like a subservient woman and looks very pleased with himself.

"For you, Mr President, time is a precious commodity which I have no wish for you to waste."

I find his obsequiousness sickly sweet but make no comment.

"I am wondering about your man L'Etranger. He seems to have come from nowhere and has rapidly climbed in your estimation so that you trust him in a way which I find surprising in one as astute as you."

He preens himself at what he sees as a compliment from his president. "Sir, I can understand your hesitancy in accepting him and I would have shared your concerns but for the fact that he is willing to do so much to help me in my cause and now to help you also."

"Why would he offer that help? What is he looking for?" I leave the question hanging in the air and give him time to consider his answer.

After a long pause, he answers. "He offers to help me and as I have already mentioned to you, because he wants permission to build a business and conference centre in Benejado City. Only I can grant him the necessary permissions to do this and it is contingent upon his ability also to be of assistance to you and our great country."

If he believes what he says he is a greater fool than I thought. My decision to keep him close to me, which is where I want my potential enemies to be, is proving to be a wise choice. There is no way that one as astute as L'Etranger would support a nonentity like Dagobah based on the reasons he has put forward. There is obviously another agenda which may or may not be a danger to me but one which I need to get to the bottom of.

"You know little of this man in whom you place so much trust. Are you sure he is not a danger to you – and perhaps me?"

"The moment he shows anything other than full and unconditional support I will eliminate him using the very weapons he has supplied to me. I like to think of this as poetic justice, having a man killed by using the illicit weapons he has supplied me with to kill others." He finishes his explanation with a wide smile.

When he is gone from my office I think on what Dagobah has said. In my estimation, he continues to be a bumbling fool. The cover story used by L'Etranger is weak; his motive is not yet clear but it does not appear to be of immediate danger to me. He was introduced to me by Dagobah for his own purposes; he did not seek me out, so I feel no threat from the Arab but I will have my people keep a watchful eye on him just in case. All that remains now is for me to find out what it is that Dagobah wants from me. If recent events are anything to go by it will not be anything complicated, he is a simplistic man to the point of being a moron. Nevertheless, care is needed because morons can be dangerous.

Benningo Dagobah:

Inexorably, my plans move forward. The president is old and out of touch – ousting him will be a simple matter. By appearing to be subservient at the start of our meeting I get him to drop his guard to such an extent that he asks me for information about L'Etranger; when I become president, I will never succumb to such weakness. He doesn't comprehend that L'Etranger is completely under my control and that I can get him to do anything.

The president now looks upon me as a staunch ally because I have agreed, in his eyes, to share my good fortune concerning finance and world influence. Once I have insinuated myself into the upper ranks of the government I will bleed L'Etranger dry, in financial and promotion matters, and then dispose of him and by doing this show the president that I am a man of strong will and resolve. As soon as my elevated position is consolidated I will in like manner dispose of the president.

This has been an excellent and satisfying day's

work. Tonight, I will celebrate in the fleshpots of the capital city, the city which will soon be mine to command.

Simon Hunter:

I need to monitor and progress the situation in Benejado City and find a way of getting Dagobah to send me there without my having to ask. He had spent the previous evening enjoying the extreme social life of the capital city and he has surfaced late this morning looking considerably under the weather. His eyes are bloodshot and the aroma of stale alcohol is oozing from his pores. I decide that his hangover will be distressing enough for him to be distracted and to agree to my suggestions just to get me off his back.

"Excellency, I have received information that there are problems in Benejado which Oginga is unable to control, and I believe it is necessary for His Excellency to return to his people to take control." I ignore the look of distaste he gives me. "Sir, it needs your strong hand to stop the problems there from developing into something more serious. I strongly advise you to intercede."

"More serious, you say? Why must I always have to do everything myself when I have others who are not as busy as I?"

"It is the lot of all great leaders."

"It is also the lot of great leaders such as me to delegate responsibility down to those whom I sponsor."

"Sir, it is your right to delegate but to whom can

you entrust such a task?"

"That is such a naïve question! The answer is it must be you – as the only other person here who is trustworthy, I charge you with restoring the situation and you must leave here immediately to take care of the situation." He collapses back into his seat suffering the grip of a monumental hangover.

"Of course, Excellency. I will do as you wish but I am just one person and there are many enemies in Benejado, I will need some form of protection."

"Take my personal guard, I will order them to ensure your safety."

My immediate mission is now complete. I have my orders and it amuses me to think that Dagobah thinks that the decisions are his.

Abu Haider:

I receive a brief telephone request from Simon which I'm sure he will explain when he arrives. I do as he requests and set the scene for his arrival. What he asks me to do involves my small group of supporters. They will need to be nimble-footed to do as he requests and not fall foul of Oginga's thugs; their task is to spread unrest among the population both Arab and Benejaden. Both groups are by now alarmed by the totalitarian regime that Oginga is imposing and the activists within are tipped over into action by the prompts given by my loyal agents. The situation is volatile and it is stressed to those who feel unrest that they must act collectively in a way which allows them to outthink the police and Oginga's guard. It is arranged that a demonstration will take place on the following day to coincide with the arrival of Simon into the city.

Simon Hunter:

Communications are not good; there are few reliable landlines and communications are not secure against government snooping. I have my own satellite phone, which allows me to evade government snoopers, and I have no intention of broadcasting its ownership. I need to arrange for my return to Benejado and risk a call to Abu Haider so I keep the call brief.

At 11.30am we arrive at the town centre in time to see a crowd of locals carrying placards demanding the return of confiscated goods and the freeing of political prisoners held without trial. The mood is sombre with supressed rage and the crowd significantly outnumbers the scant security forces who look uncertain about what to do when confronted like this. It is obvious that Oginga's thugs are not prepared for resistance and they don't know how to react to being significantly outnumbered by armed citizens. Abu Haider has done what I asked of him, he has selected a group of sixty or so and has armed them with firearms from the cachet I had secreted in my living quarters, a mixture of new weapons from Nuovostan and the old ones which had been exchanged. Most of the original weapons are inoperable, but not all, so Oginga's guard cannot tell the good from the bad. Oginga's men back off and one of their number – the ugly one with the tribally scarred face – runs off either for reinforcements or new orders. This part of my loose plan has worked like a dream; I pray that the next part will go as smoothly. Within minutes, Scar Face returns with an angry-looking Oginga in tow.

"You are all under arrest!" Oginga screams at the crowd, brandishing one of the new Nuovostani NLG Surekill side arms. He points his weapon in the general direction of the crowd and squeezes the trigger; the weapon discharges but he appears to miss the dense crowd; he fires again with the same result. He empties his weapon but to no effect. The reason for his lack of success is because I am pressing the kill button on the pendant on a chain around my neck.

Oginga instructs his men to follow his lead and begin shooting. They comply but with the same result. The crowd which they had been trying to quell break out into gales of derisory laughter and begin mocking their aggressors. Some of the crowd show anger brought on by the fear they had felt when they thought they were going to be shot. I leave the 4WD and face the approaching crowd. I hold up both arms and face my palms towards them and tell them to stop in a firm voice.

"Show peace to your enemies as your religion demands. Do not do them harm."

The crowd stops advancing and begins to mutter less threateningly.

"You, Arab," Oginga screams at me. "You are a traitor to our cause. You have provided us with weapons which are inferior. Dagobah will be informed of this and you will be punished by him." He runs at me, brandishing his weapon which is empty.

I tell one of his men to hand over his weapon so

that I may demonstrate that it is they, not the weapons, which are at fault. Oginga looks at me with deep suspicion but instructs one of his men to do so. I take the weapon and check the magazine – it still has six shells in it. I rack one of the shells into the chamber and point it at a pottery mug on the table outside one of the drinking houses. I squeeze the trigger and now that I am no longer pressing the kill button the pot shatters into a thousand fragments. There is a stunned silence.

"As I said, it is not the weapons which are at fault, it is you and your poorly trained men."

The crowd are enjoying the discomfort of the hated Oginga and his thuggish guards and once more they laugh derisively. Oginga is beside himself with rage and he turns to one of his men, seizes his NLG Surekill and discharges it at me. The kill button is still depressed. When he appeared to miss me, the crowd howls with renewed mirthful vigour. Oginga is horrified by the howls of the crowd and mystified by how he had been made to look like a bumbling fool.

Oginga:

I will kill this Arab scum. He has deliberately made a fool of me and what makes it worse is, I don't know how. I am sure of one thing, I will kill him one way or another. Nobody makes a fool of Oginga and gets away with it. After the fiasco with the guns and my inability to hit him at point-blank range, I hear murmurings from the crowd saying that the Arab is protected and that he is immortal. As long as they think like this he is a danger to me. He must be terminated before he leaves here again.

I decide that the best thing to do is to lure him to a place where I can be in control and then to simply assassinate him. Shooting him is the best thing I can do but not with the gun I used earlier, that is obviously faulty, so I take one from Dagobah's private collection which I am sure he would not have tampered with, and to make sure I test it and I know that it works every time.

Satisfied with my preparations, I contact the Arab and tell him to come and see me in Dagobah's apartment which in his absence I have taken over. He agrees to meet me and to come alone for a confidential meeting. Unlike the Golacians I am not superstitious and I don't believe he possesses any special powers.

Simon Hunter:

I get a call from Oginga. He insists on seeing me right away to discuss some important business and for me to meet him in Dagobah's apartment. My suspicions are immediately aroused. I contact Abu Haider and tell him about the meeting and ask him to gather together a small group of trusted men to make sure that I am safe during the discussion with Oginga.

Oginga greets me in sullen silence when I join him in Dagobah's apartment. He has made significant changes to the layout of the room; it is as if he is expecting his tenure to be on a more permanent basis. There is no offer of tea or strong coffee, no niceties, no glimmer of friendship, no sign of any kind of welcome; he looks at me with slightly bloodshot dead eyes.

"You have tried to make a fool of me but I can see through your methods. You intend to alienate me from my people but they have more wisdom than you allow for. They are loyal to me." His voice is as dead as his eyes.

"On the contrary, you made a fool of yourself by missing at point-blank range and your people, far from being loyal, were mocking you. Do not blame me for your shortcomings; you have brought about your own downfall." I realise as I say this that I have adopted their archaic form of speech.

His dead eyes suddenly blaze in anger and his cold voice is now filled with harsh passion. "You are a fool to provoke me and it will give me great pleasure to kill you and let it be known that you tried to attack me and failed, and I had no choice but to defend myself." He can see from my light Golacian robes that I am not carrying any firearms.

His smile of satisfaction turns into a grimace of hatred and he raises his NLG Surekill to shoulder height and points it right between my eyes. When my reaction was not one of fear he begins to look puzzled. "What madness is this? Do you really expect me to believe that you are immune from bullets? I have tested this gun thoroughly and I know it is fully operational."

Still not reacting to the danger, I reach inside my tunic for the pendant and realise to my horror that the pendant is not around my neck, I had taken it off to shower and it is still hanging on a hook in my bathroom. I am without defence and at his mercy. Abu Haider and his men are outside in the anteroom and there is no way I can summon them in time to save me. My face obviously gives away my predicament and Oginga advances towards me. I back away but there is nowhere to go.

Oginga:

This Arab is crazy; he has taunted me and is aware that I am armed. I can tell that he is not armed and still he taunts me. He reaches in to the front collar of his tunic and for a moment he appears to be reaching for an unseen weapon; he stops and the look on his face changes dramatically, something is not the way he expected to be and the look on his face changes from indifference to horror.

I advance towards him and he backs away, keeping his eyes firmly fixed on the gun. His breathing has become quick and shallow; his superiority has evaporated. He stumbles back into a small table and almost falls; I savour the moment and decide to taunt him in a more conclusive way than he did me. For a while I can play with his emotions and fears and make his last few minutes on earth like a living hell.

He thinks I don't know that he has some Arab cohorts outside waiting for his summons but if he chooses to call on them they will not be able to gain access through the door that separates us in time because I have locked it from the inside.

Simon Hunter:

I am trying desperately to fathom a way out of this dilemma. Impotently I reverse back from him and ultimately back into a small occasional table. I have an adrenalin-fuelled flashback which gives me a glimmer of hope. The table I have backed into is the same table into which Dagobah had deposited his old side arm when I gave him his new NGL Surekill shortly after I arrived.

Reaching behind me, I find the drawer handle and slide it open. I need to buy a little time so I try to distract him. "If any harm comes to me Dagobah will be informed and you will be punished." It is a weak repost but it is enough to make him pause.

"Dagobah will only find out about it if any of your supporters, like the ones outside, survive my purge after you are eliminated." His demonic smile grows. "They are next on my list."

During this fleeting interlude, I have managed to reach into the drawer and get hold of Dagobah's old pistol. I push myself away from the table and square my shoulders. Oginga is immediately aware that something has changed. He takes two paces back to move out of physical contact range and sneers at me.

I grip the gun in my right hand and thumb the safety catch off. Oginga seems to be mesmerised by the subtle change in our relationship and looks indecisive. I turn sideways on to him and whip my stiff right arm up to shoulder height and squeeze the trigger in a fluid movement, I see the look on Oginga's face change to emulate the horror that I had felt when the tables were turned. The eerie silence of the room is shattered by the sharp click of the firing pin of my revolver hitting an empty chamber. There is a second click a fraction of a second later. The gun is empty.

Oginga wakes up from his momentary dream state

and raises his gun at point-blank range. The last thing I see is a muzzle flash and the last thing I hear is a thunderous detonation which echoes in the room.

Abu Haider:

Because the room is so hollow I can hear the conversation between Simon and Oginga and it is obvious that it is not going well for Simon. From what I can hear it seems that Oginga is holding Simon at gunpoint and that Simon is unarmed. I try to open the door but it is locked and it would take a tank to batter it down.

Having been in Dagobah's living quarters several times before I know that there is a less secure side entrance which is used by Dagobah when he wants to slip away without being detected by unwanted visitors. I leave my men in the anteroom and run the few metres to the hidden door in a corridor wall and burst through it into a room which leads off the parlour.

I hear a strange double click which I cannot identify and then a sound that is all too familiar, it is the sharp crack of a pistol, which bounces around the room like a deafening roll of thunder and I see a body on the floor with a man with his back to me standing over it there is a fast-growing pool of blood. This much blood can only mean death. My horror at what has happened freezes me momentarily.

Simon Hunter:

My ears are ringing with the sound of the percussion and I am dazed. When I come to, my vision is blurred by muzzle flash. I cannot understand why I am still alive, I was fired at from point-blank range and I had stupidly not had my kill button with me. I should be dead. When my vision clears, I look down expecting to see my blood but there is none, I am unscathed. Lying at my feet is the grotesque form of Oginga; from the quantity of blood he has lost it is clear he is dead, or he soon will be.

It all happened so quickly that I am stunned. Looking around, I see Abu Haider scurrying towards me with a look of confusion on his face.

"Thank you, my friend. Thank you for saving my life." My voice is ragged.

He looks as confused as I feel. "I am unarmed, it was not I who saved you."

After what has just happened there are things to do that I did not expect and there are changes to be made to the loosely constructed aims which I had discussed with Abu Haider. The first priority is to dispose of the remains of Oginga; then I will advise Dagobah that his former number two has been killed. My intention when I returned to Benejado City was to assemble resistance to Oginga's reign of terror and to water down his impact on the city's citizens in readiness for dealing with Dagobah.

With Oginga gone there will be another crony appointed by Dagobah to continue with his subversion of the population; I will need to ascertain who that person is and hope that I will be able to contain him. With difficulty, I manage to make a landline call to Dagobah and I explain the Oginga had been assassinated by a person or persons unknown and that a vacuum had been left which needs to be filled.

Dagobah does not express any surprise that Oginga has been murdered, he rather complains that the event is a further burden on his precious time and it will slow down his programme which I suspect is wheedling his way deeper into government circles. He instructs me to take temporary command of what had been Oginga's job and to send the head guard of Oginga's protection squad to Golas City where he would be debriefed.

This course of action changes my plans for deposing Dagobah and I have once again to reconsider my tactics. It had been my intention to stir up unrest against Dagobah's regime with a view to toppling him through popular dissent, fuelled by my equipping the dissenters with a means of self-defence against his thugs. Overseeing the administration of the city means that I cannot proceed with my plans and remain anonymous.

I despatch Scar Face to Golas City to meet with Dagobah. It takes several attempts for me to get him to understand that his journey is not a request but a summons which if he refuses, will land him in jail. Ultimately he agrees to make the journey but to make sure he completes it I have him driven to the city under armed escort for which I use Dagobah's personal bodyguard. The head of the guard accepts my orders, which I tell him come from Dagobah direct. Apart from his accepting the order with his chilling, sinister, whispered response, he shows no emotion, good or bad. It is impossible for me to assess any visual reaction because his eyes remain hidden behind his large opaque sunglasses. He is anxious to leave my presence and gives me a feeling that he does not enjoy my presence. Life is too short for me to take offence at his reluctance. With that task out of the way I discuss my changed intentions with Abu Haider.

"We must change our plan of attack," I tell him. "I have been given the task of administering Benejado in Dagobah's absence so we must come up with an alternative approach.

"I can make unilateral decisions about what we can do but when I have achieved my aims I will be leaving here. You and your fellow Arabs will be staying; it will be in your own interest to come up with something which will meet the objectives of both yourselves and of the Benejaden people post-Dagobah. Think on, my friend, and I will talk to you again tomorrow."

"I will." He looks at me strangely. "But I do not understand you; just hours ago you were close to death and now you act as if nothing happened. Are you not interest in finding out about who made this attempt on your life?"

"What Oginga tried to do would only have been of consequence to me if he had succeeded. The fact is, he is dead and I am not. He is of no longer of consequence."

"Simon, my friend, you have a cold heart and I must remember never to cause you to use it in my direction." There is no humour in what he says, neither is there any hint of fear.

Benningo Dagobah:

I know something of the man referred to by L'Etranger as Scar Face, I have been briefed by a family member who remains in Benejado looking after my interests. He is a man of little intelligence but high cunning and I intend to find out from him what happened to cause the death of Oginga. The situation with Oginga is most unsatisfactory, not because he is dead, and I cannot be sure that L'Etranger is telling me the whole story.

Kofi ushers Scar Face into my presence. He looks shifty and is obviously not comfortable in the presence of one who is as venerated as I. He waits in obvious trepidation for me to speak and it is clear to me that had L'Etranger not insisted on his being delivered to me by my personal guard he would be, by now, in some faraway place.

"Tell me what you know of the death of Oginga." I purposely make my voice cold and authoritarian.

"It wasn't me." His voice is full of fear.

"If I thought it was you, you would now be dead. You are not, so I don't think it's you. I will ask you again; tell me what you know of the death of Oginga."

"He was in a meeting with the Arab, just the two of them, and there was an argument and a shot and Oginga is dead."

"Are you saying that the Arab killed Oginga?"

"They were in your chamber alone and Oginga is dead so it must have been the Arab." He shrugs his shoulders.

"How do you know they were alone if you weren't

in there with them?"

He shrugs his shoulders again and continues to look miserable. "I was along the hallway watching the anteroom from the shadows. Abu Haider was outside the chamber door and he was listening to the conversation through it. He suddenly ran past where I was hiding in the shadows and disappeared through a side door. There was the sound of a gun and the next time I saw him was when he walked through the chamber door into the anteroom followed by the Arab." He exhausts himself with what was probably as long a speech as he had ever made.

"So the Arab could have shot Oginga?"

He screws up his face in concentration, trying to come to terms with the complexity of what I have asked of him. After a long tortured pause, he responds reluctantly. "It is a possibility, I suppose."

It was clearly a mistake to bring Scar Face all the way to Golas City but at least I have found out some interesting possibilities. It could be Abu Haider who had shot Oginga but I can imagine no reason why he would do so. Monsieur L'Etranger, on the other hand, has issues with Oginga and if anybody is wily enough to outfox Oginga, it is him. I need to think on the implications of this; it may be prudent for me to arrange for the demise of L'Etranger and blame it on his Arab compatriot's jealousy of his position of importance in Benejaden society after such a short period of residency.

Abu Haider:

I have tried to do what Simon asked and come up

with a plan of action but nothing I think of will bear scrutiny of any depth. While I ponder this issue from my perch behind the bar of the café I am approached by a Benejaden whose face I recognise but I am unable to put a name to him. He introduces himself to me using the name 'Jabido' which is unfamiliar to me.

"I would like to sample some of your excellent lemon tea and learn things of interest from you." He speaks French tolerably well and he is dressed in high-ranking ceremonial robes.

"You are welcome in my house and I will prepare lemon tea for you. About things of interest, I know very little." I turn and begin the preparation by cutting the small dried lemons which are to be infused in large-leaf tea.

"Your hospitality and your preparation are tradition at its best." His words say this but his eyes portray a different meaning. "There is word among the local people that you were witness to the killing of Oginga in the house of Dagobah."

"That is so." I admit this without making any comment and wait for further questions.

"There were just three people there in the room – Oginga, yourself, and L'Etranger, so which of you killed Oginga?"

"It was not I."

"Then it must have been L'Etranger."

"It was not Simon L'Etranger, nor was it I."

"Are you saying that Oginga shot himself?"

"Neither was it Oginga; he did not shoot himself."

"You are saying it was some supernatural being?"

"I believe there must have been another person present who escaped unseen through the dressing room."

"So there was a fourth person in the room!"

"Not that I saw. The shot could have come from the wardrobe room after which he disappeared."

"That is very convenient for you, it absolves you of blame over the death of Oginga and there is nobody to contradict what you say, except perhaps L'Etranger – but then you and he could be in league in this matter."

"You are welcome to the tea and to the few words I have given you in this matter. I have no more to say." I get off my stool and walk away from him. "You may find other premises in the town to be more to your liking."

Benningo Dagobah:

The telephone message I get from my cousin Dangajabido was "Abu Haider tells me that there was another person in the room, or rather the next room, who was the assassin. It is my belief that Abu and L'Etranger were jointly responsible for the death of Oginga. These two men are Arabs and they are working together, my cousin, against your interests. I believe both men are a danger to you. If you so wish it, I can arrange for them to be eliminated."

I can hear the slight slurring in his voice which means he is either under the influence of drugs or alcohol or both, and even if I thought him competent to carry out such a task I would not entrust it to him in his present condition.

"Thank you, cousin, for what you have done. I would ask you to take no further action in these matters until I ask for your further assistance." My words seem to satisfy him.

My words might have satisfied Dangajabido but they did little to help me. I now have alternative scenarios to work with, each of which will need a different course of action – or one course of action if I should decide to have them both killed.

Simon Hunter:

Abu Haider is agitated; he tells me that he has not been able to come up with a solution to the problems we discussed.

I broach the subject with caution. "Let us consider what we want to do and why, to see if we can agree on what to do about Dagobah and New Light, presuming of course you agree that they are the priorities we need to consider."

"There are other things but these two are of prime importance." He looks relieved that we will be working together on a solution.

"We can discuss the other issues later but for now let us consider what we can do to totally discredit Dagobah and at the same time draw the teeth of New Light." I can see that he is relaxing more, so I continue. "There are many ways of disgracing Dagobah but we must select the approach which will finish him completely. Do you agree on this?"

He pauses before replying, weighing up options about what I have proposed. "I agree he should be discredited but if it is your intention to cause him physical harm I cannot go along, I am a man of peace."

"Relax, my friend; it is not my intention to use brute force to accomplish our aims unless there is no credible alternative. There are many more subtle approaches which we can employ and in any case, it is far more likely that he will come to harm at the hands of his own people. The choice of how he can be made to pay for his brutal excesses is in the hands of the Benejaden people and perhaps ultimately the Golacian government."

My words seem to satisfy him and he once more relaxes and contributes his thoughts. "Dagobah has many enemies among my Arab brothers but we are a peaceful people and they will not consider doing anything that contravenes the covenants of our religion. If any form of overt coercion is required, you must look to others for satisfaction." In a simple sentence, he has set out his stall very clearly. He will help but only under very specific peaceful conditions.

"I respect your words and if I ever ask you to do something which offends you ethically you must tell me and I will make alternative arrangements."

"My people will protest peacefully, if you wish, but they will not resort to physical violence except to defend themselves against harm."

"Let me outline to you an approach which I intend to take providing you agree with my proposed actions, because it will involve you and your people."

He accepts the conditions and sits back in his chair

to listen intently to what I intend to do to free his people and the Golacians from this brutal despot. His eyes open wide and his brows are raised when I outline my proposition to him.

Benningo Dagobah:

There are not enough hours in the day to do all that I must do. Scar Face and Dangajabido are looking after things in Benejado and keeping tabs on L'Etranger; they do not know that they are both charged with the same task which gives me the opportunity to get two different perspectives on what he is doing.

This allows me to make progress with discrediting the old fool Jacob Wellbeing. I have identified the members of his cabinet who can be persuaded by judicious payments of money from Benejado city funds and have elicited their unconditional support for my foray into government control. This is the first of my many objectives, the second is to deal with those members who are reluctant to help or are avid supporters of the old fool. To do this I must use the wiles of those members who have agreed to support me for substantial rewards; they are planting information in many places to implicate them in misdemeanours, and in some cases felonies.

The undermining of the president is a matter for my personal attention and I have already started that task now that I have my two collaborators taking care of monitoring L'Etranger. Those who are with me against him, not just for the money but for the positions they will hold in government when I become president, are already starting rumours in the corridors of power. They are doing well. I am already hearing from un-associated sources that the president is up to no good and is bleeding the country dry. There are already rumblings of discontent which I and my followers are magnifying by innuendo.

Simon Hunter:

I can now return to Golas City and resume my assault on Dagobah. The journey is tedious, dusty, and the oppressive heat is only assuaged by the excellent air conditioning. Once more the back compartment of the 4WD is full of Dagobah's guard and as ever Kofi remains alert and impassive during the whole of the journey; the other three sleep. After the dramatic episode with Oginga I ask Kofi if one of his men shot Oginga; he makes no comment and just shrugs, and as ever, I can judge nothing visual from him hidden as he was by the ever-present full face covering. Clearly he has no intention of discussing this or any other matter with me.

We arrive back at Government House a little after dusk and although the temperature has dropped it is still oppressive and cloying when we step out into the open. The usual night scent descends; it is an earthy mixture of stagnant water and rotting vegetation which I find impossible to grow accustomed to. The guards are by now familiar with the 4WD and we are waved through without any checking. I drop off the guards near their accommodation block but I decide to contact Dagobah in the morning. By then I will be rested and be sharp enough to deal with his deviousness.

What is, to me, late this morning, to Dagobah is early. I meet with him to be debriefed about my visit to Benejado. He is not fully compos mentis and the early discussion goes badly. He seems to have got out of the wrong side of bed.

"You were gone long and your visit was a disaster." He both looks and sounds crotchety. "How did this thing happen? Why is Oginga dead?"

"I have no understanding of what happened. For no apparent reason Oginga decided to pull a gun on me and threaten to shoot me. I was unarmed so I thought I was about to die and then I remembered that you had put your old side arm in the desk drawer in your chambers. I retrieved the gun and tried to defend myself but for some reason it didn't work. I thought I was done for when I heard a gun go off but I was unharmed and when I recovered I saw Oginga lying on the floor in a pool of blood."

"You were indeed fortunate that somebody came to your rescue. The reason my gun didn't work, by the way, is that it was not loaded, it was only for show." He peers at me through narrowed eyes. "So it was Abu Haider who came to your aid in your time of need?"

"Yes, it was very brave of him. He tried to come to my assistance even though he wasn't armed. He is a true friend."

"If you were not armed and neither was Abu Haider, who is it that shot Oginga?"

"I do not know who but I am grateful to whoever it was. Without his intervention, I would not have survived."

"Your gratitude is well placed," he says thoughtfully.

I notice a big change in his demeanour; it is as if something important has just occurred to him.

Benningo Dagobah:

Sometimes small statements can be more persuasive than long speeches. What L'Etranger has said in a few words has set me on a different course. If neither he nor Abu Haider were armed they did not go to meet Oginga for the purpose of killing him. If that is the case and providing what they say is true – I have no reason to doubt their word – there is another reason that Oginga chose to eliminate L'Etranger.

Neither of the accounts given to me by Scar Face and Dangajabido appear to be accurate; this should not surprise me. After all, they are Golacian and they have been brought up to be conniving. I am more inclined to believe L'Etranger even if he is a foreign devil. Foreigners are not capable of inventing such stories. To test this theory, I must give L'Etranger a task which will tell me if he speaks the truth.

"Whoever it is that did this thing has done me a favour," I say to L'Etranger in an offhand way. "It is clear to me that Oginga did not have my best interests at heart. He was obviously up to something underhand and he was caught out by a superior intelligence." I give him a penetrating look. "If that somebody was you or Abu Haider then I should reward you for doing me a great service."

"It was neither of us. Abu Haider believes that there must have been another person present, it is he who deserves your thanks."

"There is no need for you to be modest. If it was you there are many ways I can reward you."

Simon Hunter:

As devious politicians go, Dagobah is a pushover. If only he knew that I have experience of real political cunning as displayed circuitously by the President of the USA and the British Prime Minister, or the subtler innuendo-based approach of Sir Michael Westinghouse. Had Dagobah known this he would have taken a different approach. He wants me to take credit for ridding him of Oginga; that is something I will resist because not only is it not true but his weak attempts to manipulate me confirms that he has another agenda and that will not be in my interests.

Obviously, something has been said to make him change his mind about me or Abu Haider or both. I don't know what that something is but it shows up in his facial expression towards the end of our initial conversation. Having assumed this, I must not think that my assessment is invincible, maybe he is playing me a different way. Only time will tell.

Abu Haider:

I talk to some of my more knowledgeable contacts in the Arab business community to try and find out about my unexpected and slightly unpleasant visit from the man calling himself Jabido. I know his face but still can't place his name. On the third attempt, I hit the jackpot. I am told that Jabido is the short name for

Dangajabido and a person of that name is the cousin of Dagobah. Casting my mind back, I try to recall our conversation, the one which had made me feel uneasy. He had been angling to find out who had shot Oginga which in itself is not alarming but allied to his being the cousin of Dagobah sets me to thinking.

Simon is once more in Golas City and I decide to pass this bit of information, which may or may not be of value, on to him. I am frustrated by the indifferent quality of the Golacian telephone system and it is not until later in that evening that I contact him and pass on the information. Simon is quiet for a moment and after reflection he asks me to find out as much as possible about Jabido or whatever it is he calls himself. From the tone of his voice I gather that this information is of interest to him and he thanks me profusely.

Simon Hunter:

Abu Haider's information registers almost immediately in the recesses of my mind and lights up a small but bright synapse. What he says explains some of the questions that Dagobah asked me during our last conversation. Something that Jabido had said to Dagobah had a bearing on my response to his questions, and his to my answers. I can't help wondering if I will ever find out or whether what it is has any significant bearing. Introspection is not good for me at this stage, I am behind programme in dealing with Dagobah and New Light and I need to bring the programme back online.

I know enough about Dagobah now to be able to

divine that his immediate aim is to push aside Jacob Wellbeing and assume the presidency. Once in a position of supreme power he will manipulate parliament in his usual arrogant way. Dagobah has failed to detect the cunning of the president and I believe that error on his part is the weakness I have been looking for. There is one thing Dagobah has read correctly, and that is Jacob Wellbeing has structured the parliament to be completely subservient to him; it is both a strength and a weakness. His strength is that he holds absolute sway over cabinet decisions and his weakness is that the cabinet is feeble and their support can be bought by anybody willing to demonstrate that what is on offer is better than what they've got. Dagobah is an arch manipulator and will take advantage of the chink in Jacob Wellbeing's armour. Wellbeing is cunning, possibly more so than Dagobah is as a manipulator.

I am under constant scrutiny so a meeting with Jacob Wellbeing is difficult to arrange and there is no guarantee that I can get a meeting with him without being accompanied by Dagobah. The time has come for some duplicity; I need to tempt the president to meet me without our being accompanied. I don't know him well enough to cook up something subtle so I must come up with something succinct and irresistible. Money is not a motivator for him, what money he lacks he can simply have printed for his personal use. His advanced years make it unlikely that he can be tempted by pleasures of the carnal variety and even if he can be tempted his exulted position in Golacian society offers him all the opportunities he could handle. I need to give careful thought to how I can tempt him.

Sir Michael Westinghouse:

Reports from Golas are becoming more and more disturbing. They tell me that Dagobah has moved into residence in the grounds of Government House and has been appointed to the cabinet of Jacob Wellbeing. He is obviously setting out his stall to promote New Light as the religion of Golas with himself remaining at the helm. I can only guess at the damage that he can do once he assumes a position of high responsibility. For the moment, he has stopped the religious slaughter but he will no doubt resume his extreme prejudice against all foreigners in his country once his position is secured.

My immediate problem is that I need to find out what part Simon Hunter is playing in this odd game. On the surface, it appears that he is bankrolling Dagobah which continues to bother me. I can't see how arming and financing New Light is going to enable him to bring down Dagobah. It is logical to think that the support he is being given will stabilise and encourage New Light rather than discourage it. I have allowed this to happen without informing the PM, whom I believe needs to be able to deny all knowledge of these troubling events; he needs to be protected by deniability.

Experience demonstrates that intervention by foreign military powers is counter-productive in that it foments rebellion rather than quelling it. The PM has made it clear to me and anybody else who will listen, that intervention of that kind is absolutely forbidden which is why I countenanced Hunter going it alone. I had not reckoned on him going rogue, it is something that I find hard to reconcile. I need to consider the position very carefully but the more I think about it the more I conclude that Hunter must be taken out of the equation before he does any further harm. New Light is dangerous on its own but doubly dangerous with Hunter's support.

Jacob Wellbeing:

Monsieur L'Etranger has made direct contact with me and wishes to talk to me in confidence about matters of great importance. I am not inclined to meet with him because I don't believe he can bring anything of value to our discussion, especially if he wants to keep Dagobah out of whatever he wants to talk about. I fob him off, saying that I am too busy to attend any but the most important meetings.

"Mr President!" He speaks these two words with an authority which causes me to sit up and take notice. "I can understand your reluctance to meet me, after all you hardly know me, but what I have to say to you can make your life more pleasurable and I can offer this to you alone and, in confidence, not to His Excellency Dagobah."

This riddle intrigues me. He wants to offer me something that he chooses not to offer Dagobah and it is something to my advantage. After a moment of thought I agree to see him.

I see the Arab in the room set aside for casual discussion. He is dressed in Golacian costume including the headdress, which looks out of place on one whose dark features are noticeably un-African. He treats me with deference and bows as he approaches me and waits to be invited to be seated. But for the fact he is Arab I would like this man and his style. I wait for him to speak. He goes through all the sycophantic meanderings before he gets to the point of the meeting.

"Mr President, since I have been working with His Excellency Dagobah I have witnessed the difficulties that are experienced by yourself and the people of Golas because of a lack of access to foreign currency."

"If you are about to offer me money do not do so, you are wasting your time and more importantly mine." I interrupt him in mid-flow.

He in turn interrupts me before I can continue. "Mr President, I would not insult you by offering mere money." He looks pained. "A man in your exulted position should be free to travel the world in style but you are unable to do so not because you don't deserve it but because the currency of your country is not accepted by other nations. I can offer you a way around this hurdle." He pauses and waits for me to respond.

"Continue with your thoughts." I am intrigued by his proposition.

"I am able to provide you with serviced air transport which will enable you to travel freely and which carries with it the wherewithal to pay landing and take-off fees which are valid anywhere in the world. No payment will be needed from you and you will also be provided with an experienced senior pilot and crew who will take orders directly from you."

"Your proposition is tempting." I do my best to remain casual. "My question must be, why would you do this for me? What do you want in return?"

"I do this in the interest of my project to build a conference centre in Benejado and of course a second one in Golas City when the time is right."

"What you request is a simple matter for me but I am intrigued to know why you cannot offer the same opportunity to Dagobah?"

"It is a matter of protocol, sir. You are the president and you deserve this. His Excellency is but a servant in your government and it would not be fitting for him to display the privileges that are your right. You could, of course, if you wish, offer to have him accompany you on your journeys or you could allow him to use it on his own with your permission."

"This will cost me nothing and all you want in return are some building permissions?" My scepticism shows in my tone of voice.

"It will cost you nothing but there is one more thing." He leaves the sentence hanging in the air.

"And what might that be?" I knew there would be something else, there always is.

"There is one simple thing." He gives me a relaxed smile and I wait for the sting in the tail.

"I would like our arrangement to be between us, it is better that His Excellency believes that this is something you have been able to arrange privately under your own steam."

I can hardly believe my good fortune; I have no wish to travel the world, there is nothing out there for me, but the ability to travel within my own country by air will serve my purposes very well. Such ability will stamp my position with more authority and it will earn me more loyalty from my government members. It will also underline my seniority to Dagobah who misguidedly thinks I am not aware of his ambitions.

Noah Gilliland:

I think that nothing Simon Hunter asked of me will surprise me but I am wrong. He has become a very off-the-wall kind of character, but his request for a Hovering Jetstream complete with a crew of two on unlimited loan certainly takes my breath away. He gives no indication of what he wants it for but as he is a valued member of the Colony's privileged inner circle I have no qualms about granting his wish.

Later, in the day of the request, I make my regular contact with my father thousands of miles away on the Colony's main island. It still feels creepy that my dad is head honcho of the Colony and he holds the welfare of thousands of people both there and here in Nematasulu in his hands, but it doesn't faze him in the least. It is something he has grown into over the decades since the Colony was formed. In its early days, the Colony was known as Recovery Island; the name was changed because of the erroneous global perception that the island's advanced technology was a threat to the international status quo. It isn't – but grasping politicians who wanted the technology for less than honest use decided to ostracise the Colony and its technology. If they couldn't control it, they didn't want anybody else to be able to profit from it.

As is the way on the Colony I call my father by his given name, Chester, but I still think of him in my head as Dad. He greets me with his usual enthusiasm when we talk and I fill him in with what my wife Naomi are doing here in Nematasulu and our children Jasper and Kristin who are both at the local college. He is, as ever, hungry for news of his two grandchildren and his interrogation of me about them and their achievements is intense. He in turn fills me in with what he and my mother Penny are doing. Both of my parents are amazing; they and the other two founders still run the Colony on a day-to-day basis as well as having a very active social and sporting life, not at all bad for people in their late nineties. In that respect, they are no different to many of their island colleagues and friends, all of whom benefit greatly from the Tanterelli health regimes which prevail in their everyday life.

After we have dealt with our family happenings I approach him about what Simon Hunter is doing, and I do it in such a relaxed way as not to invite too many probing questions. In that mission, I fail miserably and he immediately goes into chief executive mode and begins to interrogate me. I tell him about Simon's request for a Hovering Jetstream complete with pilot and landing rights. Chester knows nothing of this and is silent for a long heartbeat; he tells me he'll get back to me and he sounds uneasy which is very unlike him. I feel a problem brewing.

Benningo Dagobah:

Scar Face has taken it upon himself to look after my interests without being asked to and he passes some interesting information on to me. He followed L'Etranger to a private presidential office in

Government House and saw him being admitted by one of the presidential guard. He waited until L'Etranger left after a short while and minutes later the president also left by the same door. It did not necessarily mean that there had been a meeting between the two but it was not a possibility to be totally excluded.

There is no room in my life for distractions at this time and if L'Etranger looks like becoming a distraction he will have to be removed. I am too close to success to leave anything to chance. Before I take this situation to its final stages I will need to find out if the meeting took place, and if it did, to find out what it was they discussed. I cannot rely on any of my own people to be discreet about investigating the subject matter in their meeting; it is something I will need to take care of myself. It is necessary for me to outfox the president and I am confident that I can do so.

I have made very rapid progress with the members of the cabinet that I have gathered in to my fold. As for the few who remain outside my influence and are not swayed by the rewards I offer, which are either financial or power based, I am slowly building allies. I have already started my programme of elimination. Each of these individuals has a weakness, in my experience all men have a secret which they cannot afford to broadcast because of the damage it will do to their standing. I have given the job of finding the weaknesses to Scar Face. He is cunning enough to find out the things they are trying to hide but not smart enough to use the information for his own purposes. Now I prepare to put L'Etranger to the acid test; if he fails he is as good as dead. I despatch

Scar Face back to Benejado to work with Cousin Dangajabido and I send back my personal guard to watch over them and report back to me.

Jacob Wellbeing:

True to his word the Arab arranges for an aircraft to be put at my disposal. It is delivered straight into the compound of Government House. This is made possible because it is a helicopter but like none I have seen before in the flesh or on the world news. The pilot wears a lapel badge telling me that his name is Jubilee and that he is a leading pilot. Like the machine he looks smart, his mid-blue uniform is tailored and his hair is cut military style. I am happy that he will do his job well.

I decide to give myself a trial run and I instruct him to fly me to the city of Bando which is nearly five hundred kilometres from Golas City and is the second largest city in the country. The flight is comfortable and I am pleasantly surprised by my first trip in a helicopter; I had expected the journey to be noisy and slow but it is neither of these things. In the movies I have seen helicopters are very basic and not at all comfortable, this one is smooth and silent and the cabin is cooled to a comfortable level, and the girl serving drinks and a light meal is both pretty and efficient. She smiles a lot, showing even white teeth which glisten in the sunlight we are sliding quietly through.

It is comforting for me to be alone, except for the serving girl. Moments of solitude in my working life are few and far between and I savour them like fine wine and delicate western food. The journey to Bando takes less than an hour; by road it would have taken me fifteen hours in an uncomfortable car and I would not have had the attention of the very pleasing serving girl. On arrival, I am greeted by the Mayor of Bando. The mayor is aghast at my means of transport; he had assumed that I would be travelling by road and is mightily impressed by my luxurious mode of transport. Perhaps the Arab has a greater understanding of my people than I had at first thought.

The mayor is even more impressed when I invite him on board and show him into the small but beautiful executive room and his day is made even more memorable by his being served with refreshments of the kind not available anywhere in Bando or indeed Golas. We discuss civic matters and I learn that Dagobah's acolytes have been to the city and his position as mayor had been challenged and threats had been made of retribution against those who did not subscribe to New Light. I put his mind at rest and tell him that I will provide him with protection from the army which I will send within a week.

Bando, being the second largest city is of great importance because of the tax revenue it contributes to the country's coffers – which are indistinguishable from mine. I will need to contact all cities to see how far New Light has gone in plundering my territory and my purse. Our currency may not be acceptable throughout the world but it is still the mainstay which props up my government and my lifestyle. I value this independence even if it does mean that we are unable to import goods from overseas except by bartering, and as we have very few natural resources bartering is a rarity that is limited essentially to me and is on a very limited scale.

Dagobah wants to change all of that and turn us into a second-rate world power, I know this because some of my close allies in government have been approached by him to support what he calls the rebirth of our nation. Those same allies questioned my allowing Dagobah into a position of power; what they fail to understand is that they are close to me as friends but it is in my interest to have my enemy even closer to enable me to counter any moves he might make. It suits me to have Dagobah think of me as a weak and old leader because it enables me to keep my powder dry for the head-on collision which is inevitable; it is for me to decide when and what form the collision will take.

Noah Gilliland:

My father gets back to me having done what he said he would by considering the developing situation with Simon. He is troubled by what his research has uncovered; on the surface, it appears that Simon has suffered some sort of breakdown and has gone rogue. He has provided Dagobah with arms and finance which will give added strength to the organisation which is clearly in the business of expansion. Simon's lending him international credibility which he does not deserve is in my father's estimation responsible for the changes in Dagobah's philosophy and are a short-lived convenience; his ultimate goals of racial cleansing and religious unity are still in place but now they are below the surface. Unusually I disagree with my father's reading of the situation; I believe that

Simon has an agenda which is far subtler than it appears to be on the surface.

When I express my view my father's thoughts take a different direction, he brings into the equation his deeper knowledge of the character of Simon Hunter; he agrees that there is likely to be a hidden meaning behind Simon's methods even though this is not the view of Sir Michael Westinghouse, who I do not know. He had a long conversation with Sir Michael who expressed some alarm at the direction that Simon is taking. Unlike my father he believes that Simon has come off the rails and has gone to the dark side.

Father tells me to keep watch on the situation but to acquiesce to Simon's demands providing they are within the law and the bounds of reason. When I tell him what I have done in that respect he gives me one of his rare belly laughs. His reaction makes me feel good and the father-son bond which has always been strong strengthens even more.

Simon Hunter:

Providing air transport for the president is more successful than I dared hope. On the first day of its possession he makes a promotional tour as if he were the President of the USA having access to his version of Air Force One. He goes up in the estimation of his people and from the look on his face in his own estimation as well.

"There are advantages to having this transport which I had not considered." The president gives me a rare smile. "I journeyed to Bando to have discussions with the head man and I learned of matters which would have been closed to me had we not met face to face." He gave me a knowing look but did not elucidate on the meaning of his words.

"I am gratified, Mr President, that you have found my little arrangement satisfactory."

"There are many things in this life which I don't understand and one of the many is why you should choose to do this for me. What is it you really want in return?" His smile this time has an edge to it.

"It is as I said, that I would like to build conference centres in Benejado and Golas Cities and I would like the permissions to be granted without delay."

"Of course you can have those permissions but I think it a small reward for the big favour you have done me. Be that as it may we will not continue this discussion and I will savour it later." He gives me another knowing smile which I find disturbing because I find it impossible to decipher.

Jacob Wellbeing:

I am sure that the permissions that L'Etranger seeks are a blind; there is something else he is looking for and for the moment I do not know what it is. An interesting side issue for me is that the he has asked me to keep knowledge of the origins of the aircraft to myself and not to let Dagobah know. I'm sure that he is astute enough to realise that this gives me a hold over him but still he has done it.

My first foray in the presidential aircraft has given me useful insight into the intentions of Dagobah – and Dagobah does not know that I know. It seems that Dagobah's heavies, after extorting high payment from the Bando businesses, threatened them with dire retribution if they breathe a word of it to any other person. The business men told the Mayor, feeling safe in the knowledge that the Mayor would not jeopardise them by confronting Dagobah, but the Mayor had no such qualms about telling me in the safety of a private conversation on the presidential aircraft. It is not my intention at this time to confront Dagobah, I will bide my time.

Abu Haider:

The cousin of Dagobah – Jabido – is acting suspiciously. Had I not known that he was Dagobah's cousin I would not have noticed his unusual activities but I do know – and I do notice. My associates have been watching Scar Face, following his return from Golas City, and he and Jabido are acting together. They are noticeable because they are such polar opposites; Jabil is cunning and secretive and Scar Face is brutish and a dullard. They have been noticed meeting covertly and they stop talking whenever anybody else is near.

Dagobah's personal guard also returned from Golas City and are a menacing presence which makes all around them nervous. Being here means they have a task to perform for their master and it is probably nothing to do with what Jabido and Scar Face are both doing. I feel I should talk to Simon but there is nothing concrete to tell him, I have suspicions but no more than that. Reports from my people fuel those feelings but to be assured that they are up to no good I must deal with this matter myself.

Jabido and I parted on bad terms after his visit to the café so a direct approach to him will be difficult and I don't think that talking to Scar Face will yield any worthwhile results. I need to get Jabido to come to me and to have him do that, means I must have something he wants – but what will that something be?

Dangajabido:

I'm required to work with the oaf Scar Face, but he is more of a hindrance than a help. I have to explain everything to him several times and I'm still not sure he gets what I want him to do. Whatever I tell him to do I need to take care that I don't expose myself to difficulties when he leaks the information to my cousin. My instructions to him need to be clear, simple, and non-toxic toward me when he eventually lets the cat out of the bag. I think it best to send him on fool's errands which will safeguard me, they will need to be carefully constructed because Cousin Dagobah is astute enough to spot a task that is meaningless.

I set him off on his first fool's errand to test my hypothesis by instructing him to follow the presidential guard to make sure they are doing a good job. I doubt that he would be able to make a judgement about the quality of their work but it will be an interesting test. He undertakes the task happily because it means he is following an order rather than creating one of his own; this should keep him out of my hair for long enough for me to dig the dirt on L'Etranger. I don't like him, neither do I like Abu Haider, they are Arabs and like Dagobah I detest foreigners, especially Arabs who suck the money out of my fellow pure-blood countrymen. When the New

Light revolution comes, Arabs will be stripped of their wealth and if they are lucky they will be deported, those who are not deported will face terminal consequences.

To melt into the background, I exchange my tribal robes for the uniform adopted by so many of the poor, a mixture of western-style clothes which are a washed out and ragged mish-mash, most of which originated in the USA even though the Americans are amongst our most deadly enemies. The Arab L'Etranger does not know me, so disguised or not I would mean nothing to him and when he meets with Abu Haider and I am close by them Abu does not recognise me because of my changed appearance. I am now set to watch them both and discover what it is they are conspiring to do. My confidence in the disguise I have adopted is shaken when, later, I receive a message from Abu Haider telling me that he has some information that he thinks will be of interest to me. He asks to see me which is not something to which I would normally acquiesce but in this instance, I need to know whether he has seen through my disguise so I agree to a meeting.

Abu Haider:

Jabido looks uneasy when he comes to see me. I can think of no reason why he should be and as we had parted on bad terms from his point of view I wonder why he has agreed to the meeting so readily. I had expected a refusal and not having received one is puzzling.

"You wish to speak to me." There is no warmth in

his tone.

"I do, and thank you for being so gracious in your acceptance. I fear that I upset you during our last discussion and I would like to put our relationship onto a sounder footing." I invite him into my private quarters where freshly brewed lemon tea awaits us, and offer him the chair that I would normally occupy myself. "Please forgive my lack of hospitality during your last visit. I was having some personal difficulties which made me act the way I did. You are, of course, welcome at any time in the House of Smoke and Tranquillity at any time, as are any of your friends and family."

"What do you know of my family?" He is immediately suspicious of my intentions.

I continue hastily. "I know nothing of your family, my offer of hospitality to you and your family members is my way of atoning for my transgressions."

It is not possible to detect any duplicity from his tone or facial expression. I feel less alarmed but I am far from totally convinced.

He continues. "I have noticed you around the town just recently. You have been in the company of the one known as Scar Face and I know something of this man – he is not one that you can trust. He is, if you will forgive my impertinence, a low-life who will do your reputation as an elder great harm. Unlike you, he would certainly not be welcome in my house."

Dangajabido:

I have a feeling of great relief on hearing Abu

Haider's words. I thought he had seen through my disguise but I have not been in the company of Scar Face while wearing it so he is referring to seeing me earlier with him while I was wearing my tribal costume. He is not apparently aware of my later deception. Safe in the knowledge that my trickery remains unrecognised, I sip and relish the lemon tea which only an Arab can brew satisfactorily.

There is the matter of why he should take the trouble to invite me into his house assuming, as he assures me, that he is not aware of my family connections. There will be opportunities later to dwell on what could lie behind his invitation; I believe from what he says that he is unaware of my keeping him and L'Etranger under constant surveillance. After I leave the café I return to Dagobah's villa and contact him by phone to tell him that I have put myself in a position where I can observe what the two Arabs are doing at will. He doesn't tell me that he is pleased at my initiative but I am sure that he cannot help but be impressed with my ingenuity.

Jubilee:

There is little comfort for me in Golas; this is a backward country when compared with Nematasulu. The accommodation I am given is basic and does not have the air conditioning to which I am accustomed. After the first night, I abandon my accommodation and set up living quarters in the helicopter where there is air conditioning and satellite television. I offer the same facilities to Nataly, my co-crew, but she inexplicably turns me down, saying that she prefers to stay in the poor accommodation that has been provided for her. She does not, she tells me, want to insult our hosts by ignoring their hospitality. I do not share he sensitivities but I do tell her that she can change her mind at any time.

Taking the president around his impoverished country serves to illustrate to me what Nematasulu was probably like before we threw in our lot with the Colony; that all happened before I was borne. Golacian infrastructure is virtually non-existent. I can see, as we overfly vast tracts of barren wasteland which exist between the cities, that there are strip roads joining the cities and ramshackle villages which are built using local materials producing buildings that have not changed for hundreds, probably thousands of years.

Flying low, I see no evidence of motor vehicles and only the occasional ox- or donkey-drawn cart which is usually overladen with an assortment of straw, leaves, stunted branches and other consumable materials. Calf paths wander across the undulations showing that there are wells but they are not productive enough to provide a regular supply of water which would justify building a village around the water source. When one water hole runs dry the children, who are the water carriers, choose an alternative location which they will use until it too runs out, after which they will move on yet again.

The president, who has taken to air travel like a duck to water, shows no awareness of the desperate conditions in which his people outside the main cities live. We have overcome the problem which probably existed in Nematasulu before the joint venture with the Colony by using the Colony's incredible technology to drill a series of interconnecting tunnels which join the underground water courses to give a central point of permanent supply.

Such facilities do not exist here and it is very likely that they never will under the present regime. My job is to fly the Hovering Jetstream which ferries the president around; I am not here to try to make changes to the way this country is run although it is very tempting.

We have flown further afield for this present tour; he is not visiting outlying villages but is limiting his attendance to larger towns and cities. The people are amazed by the technology their president has at his disposal and he is greeted like a deity. He basks in the glory of these accolades and promises his people that they are next in line for improvements at the government's expense. This is not a convincing argument for me because he says it at every location and unless he has divine assistance or is Santa Claus he can't do these things at the same time.

Everywhere he goes he hears tales of the cruel behaviour of New Light but it seems that he is not at all affected by what he hears; he seems not to have any sympathy for his people which in my view makes him a bad president and a person who would certainly not be tolerated in my homeland. On our return to Golas City the president is deep in thought and for a brief time his face betrays a concern for something. What that something is, is not obvious, but he is wrestling with a problem which troubles him.

Benningo Dagobah:

The sudden popular success being demonstrated by Jacob Wellbeing is bothering me. My plans to discredit him which are now well advanced have suddenly hit a brick wall; he is beginning to garner support through his programme of touring the country. He now enjoys more support from the ordinary people but that does not bother me so much as the increased support he is building in government circles. Some of the people to whom I have made significant payments are now wavering. How he managed to acquire what he calls his Presidential Air Transport System, PATS, is not something about which he is forthcoming and the waverers in my in-house support believe that he has outside financial support which is even greater than mine.

Wellbeing has offered me limited use of PATS to fulfil my governmental duties but accepting that weakens my position, it shows that I am beholden to him. I will need to do something which eclipses his current ascendancy and put me back towards the top of the heap. When I finally bring him down I will make sure that I have no rivals in government circles to take his place. To counteract this possibility there are two people who are not within my influence who will need to be removed from office; this is a further task I could do without but to which I must attend in person.

I begin immediate plans to counter the threat from my potential rivals and although I will be directing their removal from the fight I will not actually be carrying out the deed. Who it is I should get to accomplish the physical tasks comes to me in the form of a telephone conversation. Despite the president limiting satellite communications and even cell phone towers to himself alone, Dangajabido is able ultimately to contact me using the old and very unreliable landline systems. Wellbeing's reason for banning more flexible communication systems is that he fears that his opponents will use it to consolidate opposition to his position as president; he has an army of people monitoring landline calls as a form of insurance. Dangajabido is aware that his call may be listened to by the security services so he uses guarded words to convey some information to me.

"Cousin, greetings," he opens the call to me. "I have been taking care of the matters we discussed recently and can report that given a little time I can find out who caused the distressing outcome in your villa and by doing so I believe we will be able to test the truthfulness of those you have requested me to catalogue."

At first I think that not only is he confusing those who may be listening in, he is also confusing me and it takes me some time to unravel what he is saying. Taking out the obliqueness of his rhetoric, what he is saying is that he can find out who shot Oginga and if the perpetrator is in the pay of or connected to either of the two Arabs.

"Thank you, my cousin," I say to him. "It would be better if you were to join me here so that we can discuss your findings and plan for other activities."

He agrees to my suggestion and promises, again obliquely, to leave as soon as he has finished his assignment in observing the two Arabs whom he refers to as our two opponents. I am sure that if our conversation was overheard that the listener would have no clue to its meaning.

Nataly Obollah:

Noah's instructions to me were clear and to the point *'do what you have to do to maintain your cover story but find out what Simon Hunter is up to'*, so that's exactly what I am doing which is why I find myself, in a very disjointed way, trying to track him when we are not on flying duty. I have no other duties outside my job as cabin attendant but keeping tabs on somebody who doesn't stay in one place for long has its challenges.

Following him is not difficult; I can merge into the background whereas he does not merge so easily. He wears local tribal clothing including the headdress but his European features make him stand out. If Noah hadn't told me differently I would have believed Simon to be an Arab; his beard hides his face quite well, as does the sunburned dark skin of his face. The slender shape of his nose gives away his European heritage, but then many Arabs have European heritage.

As I watch him walking into the city's main square I begin to wonder what the rest of him looks like, presumably the rest of his body which is protected from the sun beneath his robes is the pale shade of northern Europeans. I stop that thought process because although he is much older than me he is still physically attractive, even though I know he is far older than he looks, and I must remain objective if I am to carry out my intelligence-gathering task. Fantasies must not cloud my judgement.

He enters an Arab-owned smoking café and exchanges greetings with the owner, and they spend some time exchanging pleasantries. After an hour or so of tea drinking but without smoking the hookah he departs the café and disappears into the narrow streets of the souk and in the melee, I lose him. I cast around in all directions at random but in this confusing labyrinth not only do I lose him but I lose myself. Call me paranoid but I get the distinct impression that he realised I was following him and he entered the souk to lose me. If that is the case, he succeeded with an ease which reveals me as an amateur.

Simon Hunter:

To confirm the tail, I dodge into the coffee shop owned by a friend of Abu Haider and talk to the owner to whom I had been introduced. While exchanging pleasantries, I glance occasionally into a mirror on the back wall of the bar and see the cabin attendant from the Hovering Jetstream looking nonchalantly into a trinket shop across the narrow street. She is still there an hour later when I leave and as I walk past her she peels herself away from the shop front and merges into the crowd behind me.

I walk at a leisurely pace up to one of the cross streets and turn into it. As soon as I am out of her sight I sprint along the narrow street and duck into a shop on my left which I know leads through to a parallel street. Reaching the parallel street, I turn left and head back the way I came. Turning left again, I complete the square in time to see her looking frantically right and left, but not behind, searching for me. I leave her to her own devices.

I doubt that she is following me for personal

reasons, indicating that she is motivated by a third party. The only people who could want her to do that are Jubil or Noah Gilliland. I rule out Jubil immediately, we have only recently met and he can have no axe to grind – that leaves Noah, but why would he want to have somebody spying on me? This is a distraction I could do without.

Dangajabido:

If Cousin Benningo is pleased to see me he hides it well. He has the air of one who is under pressure so extreme that he cannot deal with it. To further my cause, I offer to relieve him of some of his burdens by giving my unreserved help at any time – day or night. I can see from the changed look on his face that he is relieved to have an offer of help but at the same time he has a look of suspicion; he is a difficult man to read.

I indicate to my cousin that I will be able to identify the one who shot Oginga but I have so far been unable to keep that promise. With all my Benejaden contacts I thought it would be simple but uncharacteristically my contacts have been unable to find anybody boasting about the deed.

"Finding the identity of the assassin is going well and I expect results before too much longer. As soon as I have the answer I will pass it on to you without delay." I pre-empt the difficult question from him by anticipating it.

"You have not yet been successful?" He looks and sounds surprised.

I congratulate myself on having anticipated his

question and by doing so have taken the sting out of the outcome. Disapproval from him, I can handle, but being subjected to his wrath would be an entirely different matter.

Simon Hunter:

Time to take stock of what is becoming a very unpredictable operation; up to now I've shared the details of the operation with nobody, not Noah Gilliland nor anybody from the Colony, and I intend to keep it that way at least until the situation is clearer. The basis of my original plan was to use the weed-killer approach, that is to overfeed Dagobah which I knew would cause an over-rich feeding frenzy which would in turn lead to a growth spurt that he would be unable to sustain. Like an overfed weed he would outgrow his strength and collapse in a useless heap. That's the intention.

The overfeeding element was to provide him with some access to transportation which would be the envy of his people and lead him on to think that he is invincible, in addition to having already supplied him with arms which gives him a sense of power which, unbeknown to him, I can control. The ultimate intention is to have him rely totally on these two things to achieve his goals and then to withdraw them from him, to have his world collapse around him. Something upon which the people on whom he relies for support would take as a sign of his irreversible failure and would ultimately lead to his being disgraced deposed and abandoned.

Having achieved that goal discrediting New Light

will be a simple matter of its structural assassination. The basic approach would be successful but for the unpredictable way in which he works. I had not expected him to assume a position in the government of his country and then to rise to a senior position which would allow him to bribe ministers and become so influential. I am sure now that those members of government, ministers or otherwise, who refused to support him will be removed from their posts by dismissal or assassination.

A further nail in the coffin of my master plan is that providing an executive aircraft to the president to bolster him in the eyes of his cabinet, and his people to make him strong in their eyes, has backfired. It has only led to him to travelling around his country for long periods in a frenzy of self-promotion, unfortunately leaving the rest of the government in limbo and at the mercy of a power-hungry Dagobah. I need to rethink my tactics and bring this to a conclusion as soon as possible before it gets completely out of hand and does irreparable damage.

I talk in guarded terms to Abu Haider using the patchy local telephone system. The conversation is cryptic because of the possibility of it being overheard by security service personnel. I am counting on the likelihood of the listeners being relatively unsophisticated and therefore unable to untangle the hidden meanings in our words. I ask Abu to stir up and destabilise the citizens of Benejado City and restrict the amount of food available through the Arab stores and markets to the point where it makes the citizens angry but does not jeopardise their health. I also undertake to reimburse the traders for their loss in trade for doing this.

Having nurtured the seeds of unrest among the Benejadens, I leave the propagation of them to Abu Haider, in whom I have complete trust. I can now continue with my plans to get the administration of Jacob Wellbeing to work in my interest. I seek closer interaction with the president by pandering further to the ambitions which have been awoken in him by providing him with quality air travel.

Getting a private meeting with the president has become easier since I provided him with the air transport; his presumption in allowing an immediate meeting is undoubtedly that he expects me to offer more incentives. I take it as a good sign that the meeting takes place, not in Government House but at his private estate. This is a privilege he affords to very few; even Dagobah has not been given such an opportunity.

"What do you wish to offer me?" The president's expectations are made clear with his words of greeting.

"What I have to offer you is far more valuable than that which I have already given. My offering will safeguard you against deadly harm." My words were not what he is expecting to hear but they certainly get his immediate and focussed interest.

Jacob Wellbeing:

This Arab newcomer is skilled at getting my attention. How can I possibly ignore somebody who firstly provides me with luxurious travel at no cost, then he gives me access to other countries which have until now ignored me. Now he offers to protect me against a danger that I do not yet know of.

"What harm do you intend to protect me from that I cannot take care of myself?"

"Mr President, please forgive me if I hesitate but what I am about to tell you could put me in the very situation of danger from which I am offering to protect you."

"You may speak freely and in confidence, I wish you no harm – you have proved yourself to be a friend." I can see immediately that my words of encouragement have put his mind at rest. Events will determine whether I will eventually make good on my words.

"You know of my relationship with His Excellency Dagobah; I have been instrumental in promoting his interests. You are also aware that I have commercial interest in developing a business in Golas. If I continue supporting His Excellency and New Light it will be to the detriment of my business aims. If I support him in his political and societal aims, there will be no place in his society for people like me – foreigners."

I don't follow his logic. "Why must these things be exclusive? Surely you can support him and pursue your business objectives. These are matters which have no impact each on the other."

"This is where I must give you information which will harm me greatly if it should ever reach Dagobah's ears."

"We are speaking in the utmost confidence." Once

more, I attempt to put him at his ease. I am curious to discover where this is leading and I am becoming irritated by his hesitancy.

"Very well," he continues, "it is Dagobah's aim to convert this country to his chosen religion, New Light. To do this he needs to have complete control of the domestic situation and to get that control he has to deal with you because his religion is not of your choosing."

I interrupt him. "Dagobah is weak; he commands a minor city with a small inefficient police force and army and a small bodyguard. He is no match for my substantial army and police force and of course I have my government machinery behind me. He is in no position to mount a coup."

"He has complete control of Benejado City and he has a controlling interest in all of the states, towns, and villages adjacent to his city, in fact the whole of your northern territories. If he needs to he can call on a considerable number of able-bodied men to defend his interests and they are driven by a religious fervour which you will find difficult to match or contain."

His words are beginning to alarm me. "I have heard of unrest, during my recent travels, and the demands being made by New Light have led to a growing fear of what Dagobah represents but I am not aware that it is of any real substance. You are being alarmist."

"I wish that were so, Mr President, but the support from your government, on which you rely, is not as solid as you appear to suppose. It is my belief that Dagobah is rallying around him many of your former supporters and is bribing them to join him in his opposition to you. It is likely that he has sixty percent of your government on his payroll and the few who resist his wishes have either disappeared or soon will."

What he says to me begins to explain some strange disappearances recently and all the disappeared are long-standing supporters of my leadership. Since Dagobah's move to Golas City twelve of my most loyal followers no longer appear at government meetings and they do not offer any explanations as to why they are not attending. Now that this matter has been pointed out to me I am aware that other of my supporters have developed a tendency to abstain from voting on a whole raft of issues which I have put before government. I am putting two and two together and the four being produced is not to my liking.

"Monsieur L'Etranger, what you are implying is disturbing. Are you really saying that you think I am losing control of my government and that I am in danger of being displaced by Dagobah?"

"That is one word you can use, Mr President, although there are other far more permanent words that could be applied which would prevent you from ever returning to the presidency if you should lose it." He says this quietly so that I strain to hear him.

What was a quiet life is suddenly turning out to be less tranquil than is my wish. If what this man says is correct, and in truth I find his words credible, I am in serious – even terminal - danger. "You have issued me with a warning of danger. May I suppose that you have a solution to what might be my problem?"

Simon Hunter:

Jacob Wellbeing reacts to my warning initially with casual indifference but as I turn the screw on him I can see the concern he is beginning to feel. He has been president of Golas for over forty years and his position has softened from the harsh stance he took all those years ago, to one of benign superiority. My words of warning, once they have found their target begin gnawing at his complacency and his rheumy eyes begin to glitter with a mixture of surprise and resolve. His question to me about a possible solution to the danger he faces is telling.

"Far be it for me to advise a wise man such as yourself who has many years of success to call on, but I have some thoughts that that might help. Dagobah has collected enough local taxes to buy support from those in government who are weak in their support or who are grasping. It would perhaps be useful if you were to mount a counter offensive and buy back the support that is wavering."

"I can identify some of the waverers by looking at the voting registers to see who has recently abstained from voting or to voting against issues which support secular national issues. They are the people I should target for reintegration into my administration." This statement is made as if it were a thought process spoken out loud. He sits up straight and looks as though he has suddenly shed tens of years; he is a younger fighting man again.

I wait for him to settle before continuing. "There are other matters which should be addressed. Dagobah's support in the hinterland needs to be shaken loose and specifically in his stronghold in

Benejado. I can take care of Benejado City – that is if you want my help, but it will fall to you and your security forces to take care of the hinterland."

"If what you say is true I will welcome your help. I will need to assure myself that what you say his intentions are, is accurate. If I find it to be so I will act on your suggestion. However, if I find that what you say is untrue you will find yourself in a bad place."

With that threat ringing in my ears I am dismissed and told to keep myself in readiness for another meeting.

Jacob Wellbeing:

When the Arab is gone, I smoke my special brand of herb and reflect on our discussion. What had started out as a meeting of which I was in control descended into a one-sided affair. Once he had convinced me of the potential value of his words of warning and advice several things, which had been troubling me of late, begin to fall into place.

During my many recent visits to both near and remote parts of the country I was struck by the constant expressions of disquiet because Dagobah is fleecing local coffers. I had thought he was just lining his pockets, which is part of the local entrepreneurial culture which I foster, but now I see what he was doing in a different light. If the Arab is right what he is doing is building up a battle fund probably with the aim of overthrowing me. Forewarned is forearmed, I will put Dagobah to the test and give him enough rope to hang himself. At the same time, I will need to watch the Arab, if he turns on Dagobah there is nothing to stop him from doing the same to me. *Caveat emptor.*

Benningo Dagobah:

The president has lent me his executive Jetstream so that I can attend to some personal business on the eastern borders. He is being condescending by lending it to me but I don't let that influence me. Very soon this air transport will be mine to do with as I like. The Nematasulan pilot, Jubil, and the pretty cabin girl, Nataly, are very attentive and they look after me as though I am royalty which to them I suppose, I am. The cabin is very comfortable and stocked with imported food and drinks of all kinds. When all of this is mine, I will acquire a second larger craft to illustrate my superiority to Jacob Wellbeing who is well past his sell-by date.

My arrival at Nkando causes great excitement; the people there have never seen this or any other craft up close and there is a carnival atmosphere with music and dancing. I like the attention but the music and dancing are not approved by New Light and is a matter which I must attend to before my departure. Nkando is too small to have a mayor; in his place is a head man who receives no recompense for his position and who greets me with much bowing and subservience. I feel a great sense of superiority at the effusiveness of my reception and choose to hold off admonishing them for the singing and dancing until I have assumed the presidency.

My meeting with the head man goes well. He is frightened of me which is a good sign and when I tell him that my agents will be along within a week to collect the new taxes which are to be levied by the government he does not demur. The coffers of this town are in a healthy condition because the land within the village curtilage is rich in the minerals so much needed by the rest of the country. When I learn of the size of their cash reserves I double the tax. I will, when the time is right, sequester the mineral rights for New Light.

When I return to the aircraft after having been offered the best local food and strong drinks I see the head man in conversation with Jubil. He is looking with envy into the interior of the cabin which has the window shades down to keep out the harsh middle-day sun and is lit by soft cabin lights which makes it inviting. He is impressed by that and by the air conditioning which maintains the cabin temperature at a comfortable level. Seeing me arrive, he backs away from the aircraft and bows to me as he walks awkwardly backwards, nodding his head in recognition of my superiority. This is as it should be.

Jubilee:

On our return to Golas City I do as have been instructed and report back to the president in person. I give him chapter and verse about the conversation I had with the head man of Nkando following the meeting with Dagobah. The head man is a simple country person with no political bent; he shared the whole conversation including the taxation numbers without any understanding that he was being duped.

The president is happy with my report and he tells

me that it is not necessary for me to tell Dagobah of our conversation, it is a matter between the two of us and is confidential. As requested by the president I do not and have no intention of discussing these matters with Dagobah but he makes no mention of not discussing it with Simon Hunter. I repeated my conversation with the president to Simon, word for word.

Simon Hunter:

What Jubil divulges to me about Dagobah's visit to Nkando fits in very nicely with my developing plans. Now that Jacob Wellbeing knows about Dagobah's actions in Nkando I can leave it to him to make all the necessary arrangements to curtail Dagobah's Machiavellian activities. This leaves me free to join Abu Haider in Benejado City to drive further nails into the New Light coffin.

I don't want to face another bone-rattling trip to Benejado in the 4WD so I tell Jubil to advise the president and Dagobah that the Jetstream needs to undergo a scheduled service which must be carried out in Nematasulu, and as its sponsor I will need to accompany it. The president is relaxed about the event but Dagobah is less so. He does not want me to go and he does not want to lose use of the Jetstream even for the short time that is supposedly required for the service.

Jubil uses his imagination to overcome Dagobah's objections by telling him that if the period between services is exceeded the engines will refuse to start up and can only be reset by the Nematasulan engineers –

in Nematasulu City where the Jetstream laboratories are located. Reluctantly Dagobah agrees to the plan but demands that the three-day service be kept to the minimum so that a fully functioning craft will be returned to him with the least possible delay. I am impressed by Jubil's quick thinking and I tell him so; he merely shrugs and smiles, telling me that his flying training programme on the Colony included a section on quick thinking under duress. Once more I thank heavens for the thoroughness of Carlina Tanterelli's in-depth training programmes.

We take off from Golas 'International' Airport and head south and west as if we are going to the Nematasulu border. Once we are over the horizon we turn east and head out over the Atlantic, once offshore we turn again, heading north, and set a course for Benejado. The flight is arranged so that we arrive at night. Using a night vision array, we safely navigate in the darkness to a remote clearing in a palm grove where we are met by Abu Haider in a dilapidated vintage Jeep. The old Jeep has an eye-watering number of miles on the clock. The stealth afforded by the whispering engine ensures that our arrival goes unnoticed which is more than can be said for the Jeep.

Jubil stays behind to guard the Jetstream and undertakes to move on should the radar give any warning of discovery, and to return to the clearing at mid-day every day until my return. He has everything on board that he requires; food, drink, and Nataly Obollah. He tells me with a big-toothed grin not to hurry back. Nataly grins her approval of his words and reveals equally white teeth which contrast attractively with her dusky skin.

The ten-mile journey from the palm grove to Benejado is hair raising. Abu Haider's driver does not have the benefit of enhanced night vision technology and by the skill he demonstrates it seems he doesn't need it. We arrive with everything intact except for my shredded nerves. The House of Smoke and Tranquillity lives up to its name; the heavy scent from the hookahs hangs in the thick still air and only begins to disperse when Abu Haider switches on the ancient air conditioner and lazy fans. We have thick Arab coffee to dampen down the choking dust of the journey which coats us from head to foot and gives a red tinge to our exposed skin.

Before we start the business in hand I observe the Arab niceties of exchanging news of a general and polite nature since we last met. I tell him of what happened to me in Golas City with the exception of anything which will impinge on the serious subject we are about to discuss. He in turn fills me in with the day-to-day gossip of the city's Arab quarter. Having exchanged this news, we are set for the debriefing and Abu Haider is ready with the information I want to hear. This is a very one-sided affair, there is very little I can tell him but a lot that he can tell me.

"In accordance with your wishes, Simon, I have set my Arab brothers to work. Word has been spread among the native population in the bazaars and meeting places that Dagobah is more interested in teaming up with the government than the Benejadens. It is his intention to abandon them once he has extract extracted all the wealth from them that he can. We have been careful to avoid this message being leaked to Dagobah's supporters, but that is a situation which cannot be maintained indefinitely. We have identified those citizens who support him and advised the others to avoid discussion with them. Using this approach, we have also been able to compile a list of those who will support Dagobah no matter what and those who may ultimately be swayed."

He has done exactly what I had asked of him but I can see from his sad expression that there are matters which give him cause for concern.

"What troubles you, my friend?" I ask him gently.

"I fear for the safety of those whom I have involved in this mission. We are not trained as spies or insurgents, we are not armed and Dagobah's men are armed with the latest weapons."

I want to put his mind at rest without revealing to him details of how I can render them ineffective. "Let me put your mind at rest about the weapons I have provided for Dagobah's men. They are not standard weapon issue. I can influence their use but I cannot explain further. I need you to trust me and I need your assurance that you will not reveal this to anybody, not even your most trusted friends."

He looks at me long and hard, his eyes unfocussed in concentration. "I don't know why I trust you – but I do. Dagobah's men will be using the weapons you have supplied and your control of their use must be total." He continues to peer at me, waiting for my response.

"If it should come to it I will stand between your colleagues and the enemy guns which would be suicidal, and suicide is something I would never contemplate. There is one caveat; you must understand that I cannot control the firearms unless I am present."

He gives me a wolfish smile, revealing his berry-stained teeth. "Your word and warning is good enough to me. I will reassure my men as best I can without compromising your secret."

Abu Haider:

I trust Simon L'Etranger even though I hardly know him and I am putting my life and those of the people close to me in danger by supporting him against armed thugs; he inspires such trust. Simon is in Benejado on borrowed time and will be unable to stay long without facing the ire of Dagobah. My colleagues in the destabilisation project are as nervous as I am, about the repercussions that may accrue, but I will use my reputation to persuade them to continue.

Preparation of a schedule of citizens that we are compiling continues and identifies those who are against Dagobah, those for and those who are neutral. Those for and against Dagobah make up thirty percent of the population; of them sixty percent are against Dagobah and his aims, the remainder are devout unshakable followers. I accept that converting his avid followers is a lost cause. Converting any of those who don't follow him to support our cause is an uphill battle. Uphill or not, the task that has been set is vitally important to the lives of all Arabs in Benejado and ultimately other parts of the country.

Benningo Dagobah:

The absence of my air transport is annoying, as is the continued absence of L'Etranger. Without him I can't use the 4WD because it is tailored to his use alone and that confines me frustratingly to the precincts of Government House. In my enforced isolation, I think through my situation and the more I think of it the more I don't like the conclusions I reach about the activities of L'Etranger. He is closer to the president than I find comfortable; he has control of the 4WD and the Jetstream and while he is out of my sight and influence I do not trust his motivation. I am suspicious about the sudden need to have the Jetstream serviced.

Jacob Wellbeing is a doddering old fool and he will not be a problem now that I have so many of his cabinet working in my interests. My actual support on the ground right now is thin because we are in the heat of summer, which is the time for family vacations, and the corridors of power are nearly deserted. One thing that will change when I am in charge is that all cabinet members and general government officials will need to register their vacations so that not too many are away at one time, and when they are away there must be a means of contacting and recalling them. This will also enable me to make sure that any decisions I make which may meet with the disapproval of some cabinet members are only debated when such opponents have been granted leave of absence.

I want to return to Benejado City but without my usual land or air transport the thought of the journey is too daunting to contemplate. I make use of the spare time I now have, to consolidate my position and to continue undermining the president. As if he could read my mind Wellbeing sends a courier to me and summons me to a meeting in the presidential suite of Government House. Here is a further opportunity to continue to undermine I'Etranger and to get insight into the president's plans for the immediate future. Knowledge coupled with control is power.

Jacob Wellbeing:

Dagobah saunters into my chambers with an insolent swagger. He has exchanged his usual traditional ceremonial clothes for the more formal western business suit, the effect of which is spoiled by his wearing a gaudy T-shirt under the jacket. To complete the strange ensemble, he wears workers' sandals with brightly coloured socks.

"Good day to you, Jacob." His use of my familiar name is shocking; the only other people to use such familiarities are two of my leading wives.

The look I give him does not reveal my displeasure at his undue familiarity. "Good day to you too, Dagobah," I keep my voice neutral. "There are issues we should discuss without involving the cabinet." I can see immediately that he is thrilled to be singled out for confidential conversation.

"My thoughts are at your disposal." He puffs out his chest like a strutting pigeon and takes a seat without being invited to do so.

'Strike two,' he is down to his third and final transgression.

"I am considering making changes to the structure of my government." I lean forward conspiratorially. "Times are changing and the structure I initiated forty years ago is no longer relevant, it is time for a new broom."

"As the latest addition to your government I am in a unique position to advise you in these matters." His self-important words are matched by his look of pure arrogance.

"What I would like you to do is to consider how many and who should be in a new, more relevant cabinet, and what the portfolio for each cabinet member should be."

My suggestion is met by him with incredulity but the immobility of my features gives nothing away. The hook is baited. I await *strike three.*

Benningo Dagobah:

The old fool has gone completely gaga and this suits my purposes ideally. He has virtually asked me to form a government of my choice which gives me a great opportunity. I can shift him sideways into an ineffective role and assume the leadership for myself. After a little time, I can either put him out to pasture or have him thrown into jail as a traitor. I will never be so out of touch as to allow myself to fall into the same trap that he has.

Reports from Cousin Dangajabido about what is going on in Benejado lack the essential detail that I need. As soon as the Jetstream is back from having its service I will commandeer it to take me to Benejado to judge the situation there for myself. Until that happens I will continue working on getting the support of some of the waverers in the cabinet.

Jacob Wellbeing:

The upstart Dagobah thinks he is going to pull the wool over my eyes by initiating a cabinet structure which will support his own ambitions. He is too self-centred to realise that by structuring the new cabinet to suit his own ends he will be telling me who he believes will support him in his undoubted bid to wrest power from me. He fails to recognise that I have kept control of my country for some forty years by being one step ahead of any opposition. I will be keeping him close by, involving him in restructuring; a close enemy is controllable whereas a distant one is not.

He has already told me that he intends to use the Jetstream to attend to some pressing matters in Benejado City. I do not oppose his intentions to commandeer the presidential transport but I will need to have eyes and ears acting in my interest and the person I have in mind is L'Etranger. Dagobah does not have any knowledge that L'Etranger and I have reached an agreement about the level of support he is giving me.

Right on cue the Jetstream and L'Etranger return to Golas City and I watch it land in the compound in an angry swirl of fine red dust which eddies away on the gusting mid-day breeze. I summon L'Etranger to my chambers and tell him that he must accompany Dagobah to Benejado and act as my informant. He seems, curiously, to be relaxed about spying for me and promises to be vigilant and to keep me informed about Dagobah's activities.

Benningo Dagobah:

I'm back in full control of the situation now that the Jetstream is at my disposal and L'Etranger is back under my governance. I make haste to depart and take my guards with me. It is my intention to make an impact on my people when we arrive by landing outside the administrative compound so that my people can see me arrive in style with the flying machine and my personal guard. To make sure that my arrival is heralded I instruct the pilot to circle the landing area a few times to give time for an audience to assemble.

My arrival is the biggest thing to have happened for some time, maybe even forever, and I can see that my ardent supporters are in the crowd making sure that those assembled pay due homage to me. It would be proper for there to be serious music to mark my return and I will tell my people that this is to be observed whenever I do in future.

Not having the 4WD to transport me from the aircraft to Government House is very unsatisfactory and we are forced to suffer the indignity of having to walk to the compound gate. I make a further note to have a second 4WD to be left here for future use and to make sure that this one, unlike the one L'Etranger, can be driven by anybody of my choosing. I will make sure in the future that I have ownership of a larger aircraft more fitting to my purposes. A second 4WD will underline my position which will mean that the usefulness of L'Etranger will be at an end. Once he has been disposed of, my entourage will be pure-bred Golacian, which is as I want it to be.

My first port of call is to my cousin Dangajabido who has been keeping me up to date in his own unsatisfactory way with what is going on. I must seriously consider who will fill the soon to be vacant number two position; the only one who springs to mind is my head guard Kofi; if all else fails I will give him the opportunity. His ruthlessness which if anything, is greater than Oginga's was, could be of great value.

I call on my cousin's home unexpectedly only to find that he is not in residence and one of his junior wives tells me she does not know of his whereabouts. After asking around some of his other wives one suggests that he might be at the party warehouse. It surprises me that he might be partying at this early hour but I despatch one of my guards to collect him and send him to my living quarters.

Abu Haider:

I am taken aback when the Jetstream suddenly reappears on the same day as its departure. I join the crowds which have been attracted by the circling craft. The New Lighters ignore me and my Arab colleagues and concentrate on making sure that the Benejadens demonstrate their respect for their leader. Those who are reluctant to show sufficient fervour are persuaded to do so by the usual use of physical abuse. Their obedience is tangible when they are being watched but it collapses into undisguised resentment as soon as they are no longer observed.

My people are watching the reaction of the crowd carefully and noting those who resent the coercion from Dagobah's supporters and those who are showing respect bordering on adulation. I watch the passengers leave the aircraft; Dagobah leads the way followed by Simon and the bodyguards in quick succession and finally the air crew. Dagobah and Simon enter the compound followed by the guard detail; the air crew stay behind in the shadow of the fuselage. Simon nods to me as he passes by and points to his wrist watch, indicating that he will talk to me later.

Three hours later Simon appears at the café and he is looking disturbed, clearly something had happened which has made him very uncomfortable.

Simon Hunter:

I call on my friend Abu Haider to mull over my uneasy feelings about Dagobah and Dangajabido. I don't know which one of them makes me more uncomfortable. Dagobah is cold and inhuman and Dangajabido is just plain creepy. Between them they are a nightmare of fermenting hatred. Also at the meeting was Kofi, he is a well-matched bedfellow of the other two and he takes '*creepy*' to a whole new level. He said very little during the discussion and merely grunted in answer to questions. The lenses of his dark glasses glisten as he speaks, as does the gold eagle medallion at his forehead. I shake off the gloomy images of the meeting and turn my thoughts instead to the pressing business in hand with Abu Haider.

"We are getting close to the culmination of my work here," I say to him. "From being in the doldrums action is suddenly front and centre. Dagobah has been given the task of reforming a government which does not suit my purposes or yours. We are going to have to derail him quickly and permanently because if we don't it will lead to the total destabilisation of Golas and take its people back to medieval servitude."

"Much as I would like to help you with your fight I fail to see what I can do to assist you further." Abu looks unhappy.

"You have done as much as I could expect and more and you have my undying gratitude. You can retire from the fight and be proud that you have done your best to protect your society and that of the other citizens of Golas. From this point forward I must rely on my own efforts to do what needs to be done. This could get to be dirty and it is probably best if you and your colleagues were to melt into the background. Your work is complete."

It had not been my intention to do without the help of Abu Haider and his friends but even in my colder *binary one* state I am uncomfortably aware that I am abusing the trust shown by Abu by exploiting him in much the same way as Dagobah exploits his followers. It is rare than *binary zero* should influence my alter ego *binary one* decision processes but on reflection I think that this is a 'check and balance' feature that both personalities will welcome. Be that as it may, I have no time to analyse exactly what it means to me; these thoughts are for later once the objectives I have set have been achieved.

Benningo Dagobah:

Dangajabido is finally unearthed from the party warehouse and delivered to me by Kofi. He is dishevelled and slightly drunk and almost certainly under the influence of drugs but he still has the perceptiveness to greet me without displaying rancour at being disturbed at play. The more I think about it the more I realise that he will make an excellent number two; he is both totally immoral and subservient.

"Greetings, my cousin." I decide to calm him down. "What news do you have for me?"

"I did not expect you here now otherwise I would have placed myself immediately at your disposal." His words convey the subservience I value.

"It is not important; you should have time for enjoyment. New Light offers a man the right to enjoy himself without interference from his wives."

He relaxes visibly at my words and smiles. "The comfort I receive from my wives wears thin and they are not good at comfort, which is why I seek solace elsewhere."

I smile at him indulgently; I do not tell him that the fault is his rather than theirs. I know this because I have sampled all his wives and I found them to be satisfactory. "Tell me of any new information that you have."

"In accordance with your wishes I have been watching Abu Haider to see if he is likely to cause any problems. The night before last he took a car out into the brush-lands and returned a few hours later with a passenger. Although it was dark I could identify the visitor as he was taken back to the House of Smoke and Tranquillity. It was my intention to contact you this evening by telephone so your arrival here is fortuitous."

His obsequiousness is becoming tiresome and the look I give him stops him in his tracks. He continues, falling over his words in an effort to get them all out. "The visitor was the Arab." He spits out the last word.

"Which Arab?" I suspect the answer but I must be sure.

"The Arab L'Etranger. They were being clandestine but I outfoxed them." He puffs out his chest in self-congratulation.

"Are you sure it was him and this was the night before last?"

"I am, Excellency." Seeing my agitation, he reverts to his timorous self. "Did I do wrong?"

"No, you did the right thing by telling me but now you must leave me to think, unless you have more to tell me?"

"No, Excellency, there is no more to tell you." He scurries out of my apartment.

My dilemma is plain; L'Etranger told me he was going to have the Jetstream serviced in Nematasulu but instead he came here. Why did he lie to me and what was the purpose of his visit here? Whatever the answers are, L'Etranger is not being straight with me and as is my habit when such a thing happens, I must remove the offender from the equation.

Before I remove him, I must discover how his movements have affected me. His action of deceiving me means that I no longer have his whole-hearted support; a situation I will not tolerate. To start the ball rolling I instruct Kofi to take his guard detail to arrest Abu Haider and take him to the interrogation centre. Kofi accepts the order without displaying any emotion; he simply nods and grunts his understanding of what I want. If only L'Etranger was as loyal as Kofi, my life would be much simpler.

I am torn between two thoughts, do I have Cousin Dangajabido and his cunning as a second-in-command or do I opt for Kofi who is taciturn, implacable, and totally focussed in an evil way which even I find disquieting? This is an issue I will put on the back burner until the matter of L'Etranger is resolved.

Simon Hunter:

I am summoned into the Dagobah presence and the moment I see him my hackles are raised; I don't know why but there is a sixth sense telling me to beware of this man even more than usual. He sits in his chamber near to the table which had housed the hand gun which would have been the death of me but for the intervention of my unidentified saviour.

"We have work to do in Nkando and I require you to accompany me there. It is on a matter of some delicacy which I will explain to you once we have reached our destination."

I hope that none of my uncertainty is reflected in

my voice. "I am, of course, at your disposal, Excellency, as always."

He smiles without humour. "It is as well that you acquiesce because there is no alternative open to you." He looks at me unflinchingly mutely, prompting a reaction.

I make no response to his threat but I go with the flow and try to determine what is causing this hostility. "When is it your intention to go to Nkando, Excellency?"

"We will depart tomorrow an hour after sunrise. I will instruct the pilot to make the Jetstream ready." He dismisses me with a wave of his hand.

As soon as I leave his chambers I make my way to the House of Smoke and Tranquillity. When I enter the café Abu Haider is nowhere to be seen and his usual place behind the counter is occupied by one of his sons.

"Monsieur L'Etranger, I am concerned about my father, some of His Excellency's guards came here and took him away. They did not say where and I am worried about him." He makes a classic Arab gesture of distress by dry washing his face with his right hand only which also signifies tiredness or worry.

"How long ago was this?"

"An hour, maybe an hour and a half."

"Were they threatening him?"

"No, except they had weapons drawn but they were not pointing at him. Their leader took my father by his arm and guided him outside. They said nothing to me or to him about where they were going or how long they would be."

"How did your father react to this?"

"You know my father well enough to know that he does not show emotion."

"Yes, I do, and be assured that I will seek out your father and make sure he comes to no harm. In the meantime, tell his friends what has happened and tell them that I will secure his release."

I leave the café and walk to the quarters used by Dagobah's guards; they are empty. Next I go to the town's prison which is a festering broken-down building which, since its former colonial days, has descended into terminal decay. I am recognised by the people in the reception office as an officer in the Dagobah administration and they afford me what passes in their world for courtesy.

"Take me to His Excellency's guard, I will speak with them." This is issued as a direct order and the desk clerk scurries off into the rank interior of the forbidding building.

Within minutes he is back and he looks scared about the message he conveys. "Chief Kofi says that he is interrogating a prisoner and cannot be disturbed."

I purse my lips to show my displeasure and issue the clerk with a firm order. "Go back and tell Kofi that this is not a request but an order. I will speak with him and now."

Once more he scurries off and this time he is gone for some time. When he finally does return, he is accompanied by, not Kofi, but one of the other guards. He looks me up and down with an animal-like stare that is devoid of humanity.

"Chief Kofi will not be seeing you, he is too busy interrogating a prisoner. My instructions are that if you cause trouble I am to arrest you and throw you into a cell until he is ready to interrogate you." He delivers the words without a shred of emotion.

These words only serve to underline that I have done something to upset Dagobah, otherwise why would a mere chief of guards send me, Dagobah's lieutenant, such a disrespectful message of dismissal? It is obvious that my old friend Abu Haider is in deep trouble and the fault lies with me, as must the solution to his dilemma. A solution needs careful planning to be successful and I don't have the faintest idea where to start.

Benningo Dagobah:

The morning is, as ever, one of sunshine, and the smell of the red earth is delicious after a brief and unexpected rain storm; the storm is a sign from above and bodes well for me and my ambitions. As I had directed the Jetstream is prepared and ready for take-off and L'Etranger is in attendance. It is irksome to have to walk from my villa to the aircraft in the compound but this is mitigated by having an attendant with a huge umbrella to shade me from the burning sun. I am welcomed aboard by the cabin woman who is here to attend to my every wish, as befits the leader of his people.

Monsieur L'Etranger is unusually quiet, almost sullen, and I wonder what he is thinking; I do not like sullen people around me. He opts to sit far back in the cabin away from me and Kofi whom I have selected to take care of my personal security during my visit to Nkando. I would not normally have need of a bodyguard but I have become conscious that the people of Benejado are not as subservient as they were before I left for Golas City and I fear there may be those who are no longer frightened of my wrath. There is also a task that I wish Kofi to undertake when we arrive.

I will never tire of flying over my country and seeing what it is I am about to be master of. I even like the barren wastes which are dotted with dusty patches of vegetation which are home to brilliantly coloured vines which will ultimately strangle the vegetation. After this terminal cycle the whole event will start again; starved of vegetation, the vines will ultimately die and once they are dead the vegetation will re-establish itself on the nutrients of the dead vines and the sequence will repeat, as it has done since the creation of time.

Kofi sits, inscrutably staring into the middle distance behind his dark glasses. My gaze strays to the rear of the cabin where L'Etranger sits. Like Kofi he does not sleep through the noiseless flight, but unlike Kofi his eyes are visible and they betray his unease. It is my intention to play on his unease and make what remains of his life extremely miserable.

Simon Hunter:

I still don't comprehend why I am included in this visit to Nkando and I am uneasy about it. I am also uneasy about the presence of Kofi; why does Dagobah need a bodyguard to travel to a small town in the middle of nowhere – and does his presence have any bearing on my immediate future? I comfort myself by confirming that I still have my NLG Surekill strapped to my left hip under my robe and I also have the kill button on a chain around my neck. I feel reassured when I confirm that both items are in place. Whatever happens I know that at least I will not be shot to death using the weapons I have provided.

As soon as we arrive Dagobah talks to the head man but I am excluded from these proceedings. My exclusion does nothing to quiet my jangling nerves. Right now, I am still in my *binary one* persona which enables me to deal dispassionately with the vagaries of what is going on but does not prevent me from feeling caution concerning the possible outcome of the end game. I cannot hear what is being said in the meeting but I can hear the tone of the voices of the two men. Dagobah's voice is cold and withering, that of the head man conveys outrage and extreme alarm.

When the meeting between the two men is finally over they emerge from the palm frond roofed, mud walled hut, both blinking and screwing up their eyes against the harsh sunlight. Dagobah indicates to Nataly Obollah to bring forward the umbrella to give him shade. Once shaded he indicates to Kofi that he should join them and after a few words of instruction Kofi takes the elbow of the head man and marches him, at a speed which makes him stumble, towards a larger hut.

The head man and Kofi disappear into the dark interior of the hut and after a moment there is the sound of angry voices. The dissent continues for a short time and as quickly as it had started the hubbub stops. There is movement in the doorway and the head man, encouraged forwards by a side arm being held to his back, steps out into the sunlight. A dozen or so men, I presume to be elders, follow in their wake. The crocodile of people moves slowly forward and marches out of the village into a nearby palm grove. They halt at a refuse trench which is half full with the rotting detritus of village life.

Dagobah prods me forwards to the edge of the clearing which surrounds the trench where he tells me to stop. He takes the umbrella from Nataly and tells her to return to the Jetstream. When she has departed and there are just the two of us and the gaggle of people at the edge of the refuse pit, Dagobah signals to Kofi using what I presume to be a prearranged signal. Kofi, still holding the gun to the back of the head man, faces the assembled councillors; he addresses them and although I can't hear what he is saying I can deduce from their collective reaction that he is telling them something they don't believe and they look at him with horror.

At Kofi's instruction, they all line up along one edge of the trench, facing it with their backs to Kofi and to us. I can no longer see the fear on their faces but I can feel the terror in the air which surrounds them. Kofi says something to the head man which we are too far away to hear and pulls from under his tunic a second side arm, which he also points at the head man's back.

What he is about to do dawns on me and with a cold heart I reach inside my robe and grasp the kill button. I press it and hold it down. There is a flash and a sharp report and the head man pitches forward into the trench. Even as *binary one* I am beginning to feel unsettled, something is very wrong; the kill button has not worked. I release the button and press it again. There are several more flashes and reports and several more men pitch forward into the trench. I try frantically to reset the switch but to no avail and almost before it has begun it is over and the trench has become the final resting place of the town's councillors. I am horrified at the cold-blooded murder I have just witnessed. The explanation of the kill button not working is soon revealed when Kofi joins us at the edge of the clearing. As he puts his guns away I see clearly that they are not the ones which I had provided for them, they are a marque I have not seen before.

Benningo Dagobah:

Kofi has carried out the executions exactly as I ordered. It is amusing for me to see the affect this has had on L'Etranger; he is mesmerised by witnessing sudden and violent death, maybe for the first time. He denies any knowledge of the murder of Oginga. When we are joined by Kofi he is given a look of pure hatred by the Arab and that same look is transferred to me. His intensity is profound and I can read revenge in his mind. I have some things to use him for and then I will set Kofi on him to conclude our brief association.

"Why in God's name did you do that? It was barbaric, what have they done to you to warrant such a violent death?" The Arab is beside himself with fury which is far from his being stunned, which is what I had expected.

"They refused to sell me the mineral rights of the village and their ownership is vital to my finances." I explain this to him as if he were a child, for a sophisticated man he is very dumb.

"This is your way of negotiating? Comply or die!"

"Put it whichever way you like. Ownership of the minerals is not a request, it is a prerequisite. I have taken care of something which was necessary in much the same way as I will be doing with Abu Haider."

"Abu Haider?" This time he looks shocked. "How are you dealing with Abu Haider and why?"

"He has been working against me and is destabilising my organisation. He is in custody as we speak and he is to be interrogated to reveal the identities of his fellow conspirators before I find him guilty, in a fair court of course, of treason – the penalty for which will be death."

Seeing his reaction to my words, I signal to Kofi and he anticipates my wishes and once more deploys his formidable firearm, which is better than those provided by L'Etranger, to persuade him to go along with my wishes.

Simon Hunter:

Dagobah has noticeably cooled towards me. Including me in the barbaric acts of this day is, inexplicable. I would have thought that he would want to keep those who know what he has done to a minimum rather than allowing me to witness his barbarism.

Kofi is pointing his side arm at me and watching me like a hawk. Until today I had viewed him as a heartless thug and now I know he is a cold-blooded murderer who in the eyes of Dagobah is taking my place as number two in New Light.

When we board the Jetstream to return to Benejado and then on to Golas City, Jubil does a double take on seeing me being held at gunpoint. He confers with Nataly Obollah as he follows us into the cabin and they both ensure that we are seated and strapped in before Jubil takes the pilot's seat and Nataly the second pilot's seat. Jubil goes through the checking procedures prior to take-off and when they are completed takes his hands off the controls and hands over to Nataly. We lift off in a swirl of red dust and pirouette slowly until we are on the correct compass heading before she starts a smooth forward ascent.

Once at cruising altitude Jubil unbuckles his safety harness and walks back to the galley at the back of the passenger cabin. In doing so he passes me and by the inclination of his head he signals me to join him. I wait for a few minutes and then I stand up to move aft. Kofi has other ideas and blocks my path, side arm drawn, his blank visage turned to me. I shake my head at him slowly and insultingly rolling up my eyes in the universal signal of disdain. He grunts and pushes me back towards my seat; Dagobah indicates that I should return to my seat.

I look at them both with as much disdain as I can manage. "I need to use the head and I would be grateful, *Excellency*," I enunciate the word with venom, "if you would tell this mad dog to get out of my way before I disarm him and break his bones." I don't know how much of this Kofi understands because I am talking in French; he gives no indication that he does.

Dagobah sneers at me. "For one who is in so much trouble you do nothing to help yourself. Like all Arabs you are out of control and your arrogance will be the death of you."

"Let that mad dog loose and we will all be in trouble; this Jetstream is a flying incendiary, one bullet in the compressed sodium tanks and at best we will all be obliterated instantly and at worst the craft will be disabled and we will have a front seat at our own funerals which we will be able to watch in slow motion."

As I finish my untrue warning we are joined by Jubil who backs up my version of events. "Excellency, we are flying using an experimental fuel. It is entirely stable unless it is exposed to a sudden temperature increase such as would be caused by any of the fuel canisters being hit by a bullet. The discharging of a firearm could be catastrophic."

"Let him go," Dagobah snaps ill-temperedly at Kofi. "Put your gun away. And you," he turns to me. "Go to the bathroom and be quick about it and come straight back here. You are under arrest for treason."

Jacob Wellbeing:

I had expected to hear from the Arab L'Etranger by now. My instructions to him were clear and unambiguous; he was to keep me apprised of Dagobah's movements and actions, this has not happened. In Dagobah's absence, I have been doing some digging and as I expected he has been marshalling forces against me. Fortunately for me those he believes are supporting him and who are taking his bribe money are also, like him, not who they seem to be. A little persuasion from me by way of cash inducement and promises of advancement has caused them to see the error of *his* ways and return to my side – if they ever truly left it. Members of the cabinet are made uneasy by his sudden ascent to power; they do not understand that it is my intention to keep my enemies closer than I do my friends which is why I am president and they are not.

The only course left open to me is to contact the Jetstream by radio and find out where they are and what their intended programme of action is. My communications minister makes the necessary arrangements and I am patched through to the pilot who is currently airborne. To my surprise the pilot is a woman which goes against all regulations in our society. I tell her that I want to talk to the real pilot. I can hear her stifled laugh at my request and find it most inappropriate; women are for babies and cooking – not for doing a man's job. She tells me that she will locate him and ask him to contact me. I tell her this is not a request but an order and to mind her manners while talking to the president.

Simon Hunter:

After the kerfuffle and being arrested by Dagobah, I finally end up going to the bathroom. Jubil is in the galley, through which I pass to get to the head.

Jubil opens the door for me and speaks on low tones. "What is going on, Simon? What's with the gun being pointed at you?"

"Dagobah has discovered that he does not have my full support with what he's doing and he's getting ready to ditch me. He made me witness to a massacre back in Nkando and I don't yet know why. But more importantly, he knows that we didn't go to Nematasulu to have work done on the Jetstream so watch your back because you are implicated in the deception. Oh, and by the way thank you for backing me up with the story about the problems of discharging a gun inside the cabin, you saved my bacon."

"You're welcome and thanks for your warning, the little I know about Dagobah tells me he is cunning enough to say nothing while I'm the only one who can fly him back home but I have no doubt he will exact his revenge when I am no longer of use to him. The man is a psychopath." Jubil, far from being cowed by the potential trouble he could be in, appears to relish the battle.

I return to my seat and the watchful eyes – if only I could see them – of Kofi. Jubil returns to the flight deck to do whatever he can to neutralise what could be a very harmful situation. Dagobah ignores me and Kofi grunts and indicates by gesture that I should sit down, strap up, and keep quiet.

Jubilee:

This whole scene is bizarre. Dagobah and his thug of a bodyguard have assumed unilaterally the right to take command of the Jetstream. Without the cooperation of Nataly or me there is no way they can fly anywhere except straight into the ground. Simon's situation is a little more precarious; he is being held under open custody and it seems quite possible that they could put an end to him by the simple expedient of throwing him out of the cargo door. They have chosen not to which presumably means that he is still of use to them.

I return to the flight deck and drop into the still vacant pilot's seat. Nataly glances at me questioningly, wondering if I intend to take the controls. I shake my head.

"The president is trying to talk to you; you should contact him by radio." Nataly hands me a headset and a hand mic and switches on the transmitter.

I broadcast on a pre-set wave band. *"Jetstream captain Jubilee to President Wellbeing."* I wait ten seconds and repeat the greeting. After a further ten seconds or so the scratchy voice of the president responds and I immediately pass on an update to him making sure that I cannot be overheard in the passenger cabin. *"Simon L'Etranger is being held under arrest by Dagobah and Kofi. Something nasty happened during the visit to Nkando but I have no further details. If I can learn more I will update you. Do you have any further instructions for me?"*

"Yes, I have," his voice was suddenly authoritative. *"Tell Dagobah that I wish to speak to him straight away."*

I unbuckle and go through to the passenger cabin where Simon is being watched like a hawk by Kofi while Dagobah is availing himself of alcohol and snacks. "His Excellency, the president wants to talk to you straight away."

He looks up at me with disdain. "Tell him I am otherwise engaged and I will contact him when I am ready to do so." He waves me away with a dismissive gesture.

I return to the flight deck and don the headset without taking my seat. "*Mr President, his Excellency Dagobah does not wish to talk to you, he is too busy. He says he will contact you in his own time or maybe when we return to Golas City.*" I deliberately misrepresent what Dagobah said, to be antagonistic and to test Dagobah's assumed superiority.

"*Is that what His Excellency says?*" He pauses while he considers his next words carefully. "*Tell him that we must speak urgently on his return.*"

The mildness of his response surprises me; I had thought he would fly into a rage at Dagobah's rebuff.

I return to the passenger cabin and advise Dagobah of the president's response by juggling his words in my own way. "His Excellency, the president says that he will speak to you on your return if he can find the time."

Dagobah responds in frigid tones. "He has no choice, he will speak to me whether he can find the time of not. He is an old fool." The last part is said under his breath but I hear it quite clearly.

Simon has been listening to my exchanges with Dagobah without betraying any emotion except for the slightest twitch of a smile. He is leaning back in his reclined seat with his eyes closed, feigning sleep.

Jacob Wellbeing:

The Jetstream hovers just above the compound as I watch it through the window; it pirouettes gracefully and lands with its nose facing Government House. The engine is eerily quiet, all that can be heard is the diminishing soft *wop-wop* of the slowing rotor blades. The passenger door opens; the first off is Dagobah. He is dressed in an old-fashioned city gent's business suit and carries a fly swatch which he beats against his trouser leg in a tempo which has meaning only in his jangled mind. The cabin woman follows him out and unfurls an umbrella to shade him from the sun. Already since he has been resident in Golas City his skin has become several shades lighter, that and his change in garb style is a warning sign.

My PA hurries out to intercept him and his entourage. Dagobah shows his great displeasure at his return being heralded by a lowly servant of the government, which is my intention. There is a brief exchange between the two men and I can see that Dagobah is agitated by being told to come to my chambers before he does anything else.

Moments later he is shown into my chambers, his attitude is surly. "I have no time to discuss anything with you; my being here is delaying the real progress I am trying to make. You are just slowing me down." He gives vent to his irritation and glares at me.

It is time to put him in his place and that will mean opposing him at every turn, I will goad him into overreacting and leaving himself open to censure. "What progress have you made in the task I set you of recommending the restructuring of the cabinet to meet our developing needs?" I allow harshness to creep into my voice.

"I can't believe you have interrupted my progress to ask such an inconsequential question." His anger is rising.

With great difficulty, he curbs his tone when he realises from the intensity of my look that he has overstepped the mark and that his position is still at my whim. "It is not my wish to incur your displeasure but the tasks you have asked me to consider have far-reaching influences which need my absolute concentration. I cannot afford distractions." His voice has lost its angry edge.

"If you are to be a reckonable force in the modernisation of our government you must learn to handle these difficulties like a true leader." I notice with an inward smile that my implied criticism of his abilities has hit its mark. To drive home his discomfort, I continue with an order which underlines that I still consider him to be an inferior intellect. "I need you to continue with the task I have set you. I also wish to discuss issues with the Arab and my chief pilot which does not need your input. You may go!"

His former anger returns and I can see rebellion seething just under the surface. He is momentarily lost for words and for a fleeting moment I see the beginnings of unfamiliar doubt within him. As he leaves he turns to speak to me but changes his mind.

Benningo Dagobah:

My mind is made up; Wellbeing, like the two Arabs, must go. He is frustrating my every move. I was considering suggesting for him a comfortable position in the new government structure but the disrespect he has shown me has put a stop to those thoughts. He will be removed once and for all by the only means open to me; as far as I am concerned he has joined the forces of people who oppose my aspirations and I will treat him as I would any detractor, but for now I must let him think he has his way.

In due course I will tell Wellbeing that the Arab was entirely responsible for the massacre at Nkando and that his intention is to stage a coup to depose the present government and replace it with one populated by his own Arab cronies. When I return to my compound I find the Arab tied to a chair with Kofi standing threateningly over him, side arm drawn. The pilot and the cabin girl were sitting across the room from him, they were not restrained but both looked fearful.

"You can stand down, Kofi. The president has expressed the wish to talk to your prisoner and I need to explain the rules of engagement. Untie him while I explore some issues with him."

Kofi unties him and steps across the room to where the air crew are sitting; he positions himself leaning comfortably against the wall, from where he can see everybody at a single glance, with his weapon drawn.

"Listen to me very carefully, Arab scum. Whatever it is the president wants to talk to you about you will not recount to him what happened at Nkando today, and just in case you think about disobeying that order just remember that we have Abu Haider in our keeping and that his welfare is in your hands. If I even suspect that you are going to disobey me Abu Haider will suffer in a way that will have him begging to be put out of his misery. After that, it will be your turn and your punishment will take much longer and be excruciatingly painful. Kofi is a past master at tongue-loosening interrogation and will relish the opportunity to practice his skills. Is that not so, Kofi?" I turn to face Kofi who gives one of his Neanderthal grunts. L'Etranger obviously understands without me having to say more. "You," I point to the pilot, "will accompany this man to meet with the president and be careful that you do not say anything to him that will reflect badly on me. If you do, your little playmate here will suffer the same fate as this Arab and his Arab friend. Do I make myself clear?"

Jubil regards him unemotionally. "Your meaning is very clear."

"Good, so you will comply."

The pilot makes no comment but follows the Arab, who is prompted by Kofi's gun, on the journey to the president's chambers. I am happy that my threats have secured their cooperation.

Jacob Wellbeing:

"What news do you have for me?" I ask as soon as Dagobah's guard has left.

"I did the best I could sir to keep you informed of what was going on." The pilot answers quickly.

"I'm sure you did your best but my question was not directed at you but at Monsieur L'Etranger." I am amused by the look of surprise on the face of the pilot, he clearly has no knowledge of the understanding I have with L'Etranger.

"As you requested, Mr President, I went along with everything that Dagobah did without comment. What he had in mind was not what I expected and not what we expected." He describes to me the massacre that had taken place at the hand of Kofi and the direction of Dagobah.

I am sickened by the barbarism described and can see that the pilot is even more affected. "What was his motivation for doing such a thing?" I ask L'Etranger after the impact of his description has sunk in.

"He said it was because the head man refused to sign over the mineral rights to him and he included the whole town council in the massacre because they had agreed to oppose his ownership."

"That is high handed even for Dagobah."

"I believe there to be another reason why he did it. If he wants access to the minerals all he had to do was sequester the rights. The killing makes no sense."

"How do you propose we find out what his real motivation is?"

The Arab addresses both myself and the pilot "There is only one way to do that. We must let him think he has got away with it and wait to see what his next moves are. We must keep quiet about this, Jubil, otherwise Dagobah will carry out his threat to kill Abu Haider, me, and Nataly and you."

I cannot help showing my surprise at this news. "He has threatened three people with execution?"

"He's already massacred a dozen or so today, three more will mean nothing to him." L'Etranger looks grim.

"Dagobah will be informed by yourselves and a leak from my office that this meeting was to do with the supply of more aircraft to start the foundation of a Golacian Air Force. That should satisfy his curiosity."

Benningo Dagobah:

The meeting they had with the old fool of a president was brief and it is clear from their relaxed looks that it was unremarkable, but nevertheless I ask the question. "What was the purpose of this conversation with the president?"

"That is a matter between the president and us," L'Etranger says defiantly.

"For your own sakes and for the sake of your two friends I suggest you tell me of your conversation in detail."

"We talked about supply." The pilot responds quickly with timidity, beating L'Etranger to the response.

"Supply?" I am mystified. "What does that mean?"

"He means what he says," L'Etranger seems to want to provoke me but I do not rise to the bait. "The president intends to equip an Air Force for the protection of the country and he talked to me about the financing of such a project and to Jubil about aspects of the training.

"Is that all?"

"It's a bold move which will elevate your country up in the league of senior African countries. The president has vision and yes – that is all."

I consider what has been said and reach the opinion that I would have reached a similar but better conclusion than that of the president, but for the fact that I have other tasks to perform; even I have my limits. The old fool has nothing better to do than sit around and savour his out-of-touch pipe dreams.

The president is in the dark about today's events and seems to be oblivious to my undermining his position with his cabinet, which will soon be mine. I have dealt with him quite easily and now I must arrange for the punishment of L'Etranger and the pilot who disobeyed me and lied about having the Jetstream serviced. I telephone Kofi and tell him to make haste with the interrogation of Abu Haider and to prepare for his execution at a time of my choosing; the only adjunct to that task is that if his death is uncovered it must look like an accident.

Just as I think that everything is going my way I am told by Wellbeing that I am to lay off L'Etranger because he is doing many things in the interests of the country and detaining him would not be in the country's best interests. I return a message to him saying that there are very good reasons for my wanting to put him under arrest but they are waved aside. It is prudent for the time being for me to concede and allow him his freedom.

Simon L'Etranger, who does not know of my plans for him, advises me that the president has instructed him to go to Benejado City to set up deals to purchase strategic materials. During this conversation Kofi has been sitting nearby but he shows no interest in what we were discussing, probably because our conversation is in French.

I address him in a loud voice to wake him from his reverie. "Kofi, wake up and listen. You must accompany me to Benejado City; there are pressing issues I require you to take care of."

Kofi turns towards me and somehow manages to look disinterested even though I cannot see his expression.

L'Etranger goes to his quarters to prepare for tomorrow's journey and to alert the Jetstream crew that there is to be a flight to Benejado City. As soon as he has gone I give instructions to Kofi to keep a watch on L'Etranger and his followers to see what they get up to, and I instruct him to interrogate Abu Haider to build a plausible damning case against them.

Jubil:

The arrival of the Jetstream in Benejado no longer animates the crowds; they look up when they hear the muted sound of the engine and after a moment look away. We four walk from what has become accepted as the helipad into the city precincts. Dagobah is with us and his presence stops the dancing and the music instantly – all signs of frivolous enjoyment are extinguished.

Dagobah's New Light stance, that dancing and gender intermixing is forbidden, takes a firm hold and it is as if the sun has gone in and the temperature has suddenly plummeted. This makes me feel great empathy for the people of Benejado. They are governed by the whim of a self-appointed tyrant and the feelings I have about it make me wish I was back in Nematasulu where such social restrictions would never flourish. I have only a basic idea of what Simon is here to accomplish but I will do anything in my power to help him.

I spend the night sleeping in the crew cabin aft of the galley and Nataly occupies the slightly larger and more comfortable captain's cot in the forward cabin. At first light we have a breakfast fit for royalty from the guest galley, after which we prepare for the return flight to Golas City as ordered by the president. I have a feeling of deep foreboding about leaving Simon unsupported in this hostile place with only Dagobah and Kofi for company.

Simon Hunter:

I must locate where Abu Haider is being held and somehow free him. I don't want to involve anybody else in doing this because being found out will be catastrophic for those involved and I don't want any more deaths on the conscience of my *binary zero* personality which will, when I emerge from this, be devastated.

Dagobah is occupied by his own issues, leaving me free to follow my own. One way of finding Abu Haider is to follow Kofi, who will undoubtedly be instrumental in what is happening to Abu Haider. Following him is easy; he is sinister, dressed from head to ankle in black. He has the same effect on all who encounter him, they avoid him and he can sweep through dense crowds with ease as they scatter before him. I follow him at a distance because of the ripple of his wake through the dispersing crowds. It becomes a little more difficult when the crowds thin and I hang further back to escape his peripheral vision.

Even before we get to the destination I anticipate where we are going. It is a place devoid of people on the outside because those who go into the city jail very often do not re-emerge. Kofi walks in through the main entrance without being challenged by the guards. Like prisons in general this one is designed to keep the people inside from getting out rather than preventing those on the outside getting in. I circle the perimeter wall which has seen no maintenance since it was built over two hundred years ago; the plaster rendering is falling away from the clay block wall core which is weathering badly.

At intervals along the perimeter walls there are service doors which were once substantial, but like the walls the doors have fallen into disrepair and do not close properly, having dropped or sagged on the hinges. The whole structure is insecure and I can't help wondering why there are not mass breakouts. To test of the lack of security I join a group of labourers who are unloading a hand cart of straw mattresses and carry one into the interior of the building. I am not challenged and there appear to be no security personnel.

I hoist one of the mattresses over my head and drape it down my back and wander out of the mattress store to the interior of the prison. There is a powerful smell of unwashed bodies and worse lingering in the foetid air. Lighting is inadequate and the corridor has doors on either side with small steel grills set at eye level. I peer through one of the grills and in the gloom count eight occupants in a cramped furniture less cell. The next room is similar but with more people and this pattern is repeated along both sides of the corridor.

Having seen enough, I retrace my steps back to the store room and drop the mattress on top of one of the untidy piles left by the unloading team which has since departed. I now realise why the external doors are not secured; the prisoners are shackled to a centre ring in the cell floor. The shackle chains are long enough to enable the prisoners to reach a single slops bucket but not long enough to reach the door of the cell; with such a system of incarceration it would not be necessary to even lock the cell doors. Prisoners are shackled just as dangerous animals might be. Somewhere in the bowels of this prison Abu Haider is being held.

Benningo Dagobah:

Under the pretext of presenting my suggestions for the restructuring of the cabinet I telephone the president. My real reason is to further my plans for revenge against the Arab and now the air crew who have aided him in his duplicity. I begin to speak to him but he tells me to be quiet while he finishes breakfast. I bite my tongue.

"Jacob," I say when he indicates he has finished, "I have prepared a revised list of cabinet members of which I am sure you will approve. You will see that I have included some of the current members but not all. Some of them are past their peak and I will put them out to pasture."

"I have read the document you left for me; do you

presume that I am one of those who are past their peak?"

"No Jacob, you will see that I have placed you at the very top of the tree as Lifetime President in recognition of the great things you have done for our country."

"And where do you figure in all of this? You are not on the list."

"I will be your deputy and I will take responsibility for the day-to-day things which now stand in the way of you being free to take care of the decisions which are of strategic importance to our country and are currently hampered by the day-to-day trivia."

"I will consider your proposals at my leisure."

I am unable to detect whether his words are genuinely felt or if he is being sarcastic. "You are very gracious, Jacob, but on a cautionary note I must advise you of a situation which is most disturbing."

"This sounds serious, what is the situation?"

"The Arab L'Etranger and his aircrew have abused the position of trust which you granted them. When we were in Nkando they got into a dispute with the town councillors and a gun battle ensued in which the unarmed councillors were all slaughtered. I do not wish to make this matter generally known; it would be unsettling for our citizens to learn of this treachery and might make them think that your presidency is weak."

Now that I have sown the seeds in his mind it doesn't matter that they will attempt to defend themselves, I have pre-empted their defence postures.

Jacob Wellbeing:

If Dagobah only knew that I am aware of what he is trying to do, he would take a different tack. However, he doesn't know and the strategy he employs is self-serving. All he is doing is digging deeper the hole into which he will ultimately fall. Clearly he does think I am past my peak and that error will further compound his difficulties. I allow him latitude just to see how far he is prepared to go with his double dealings. Concluding the meeting, I allow him to presume that he has succeeded in his attempts to hoodwink me.

One further thing is clear from the indications emerging; Simon L'Etranger is perhaps not all he appears to be. I have learned to be wary of people who change sides in any kind of conflict if for no other reason that a person who changes his mind once will easily do so again. I do not find it at all plausible that he is doing as he is for me because he wants to start up a business complex in Golas, his motives will be much more complex than that. I will take what he has offered but I will not trust him with anything of importance.

Benningo Dagobah:

Getting anything out of Kofi is like getting blood from a stone. I ask him about progress being made with the interrogation of Abu Haider but I am unable to read anything from his tone of voice.

After several attempts, I lose patience with him. "Don't just stonewall me when I ask questions, do something – tell me what's going on."

His voice is, as usual, a chilling whisper when he finally replies. "He is still in the prison and I am doing what you asked me to do, I am extracting information. If I apply too much pressure I am likely to get lies. Doing it the way I am, slowly and steadily, the information he is leaking without realising it is good value." His look is one of insolent dismissal.

"So what information do you have to pass on to me?" I insist, ignoring his look.

He sighs impatiently. "When there is anything of value I will pass it to you but only when I have the whole story."

His attitude tells me that I will get nothing further from him and I take note for future reference that he does not appear to care that he is being disrespectful to me. The upside of that is that if he affects me that way I can imagine what effect he will have on others less assured than I. I congratulate myself once more for having the foresight to take him on as my chief guard and his actions confirm that he is the right choice to be my second-in-command to replace L'Etranger.

"Listen to me very carefully, Kofi." I lower my voice conspiratorially for effect. "After you have completed your interrogation of Abu Haider and there is nothing more you can get from him I want you to take him out of the prison and dispose of him. That will stop the other Arabs from following his example of opposing me. After that I will have L'Etranger taken care of also. You do not need to do this, I will get one of the others to dispose of him. You just concentrate on Abu Haider and leave the rest to me.

Kofi makes no further comment. It is as if I had

just asked him to carry out a minor chore. It seems that instructing him to interrogate and kill somebody and then telling him that a second person is to be killed are matters that will not cause him to lose any sleep.

Simon Hunter:

How I can set Abu Haider free does not spring immediately to mind. Approaching Dagobah is out of the question; it is by his order that Abu Haider has been detained. Equally I cannot appeal to Jacob Wellbeing; he would not wish to become embroiled in such a minor matter. Unfortunately, there is only me and I have no viable plan of action that would stand any chance of success, and even if I did and I managed to free Abu Haider, what could we then do? There is nowhere for him to go except back to the café and that is the first place that Dagobah and his cronies would look. The dusty streets are quiet as I walk back to my apartment in search of inspiration.

Hearing fast muted footsteps behind me, I turn to see who approaches but before I complete the turn there is a swishing sound and a grunt and a rag is held over my mouth. Darkness.

I am not awoken by smelling salts per se but by an alternative; the overpowering stench of human waste. I am in hot darkness and I put my hand up to my aching head to discover that I am shackled by wrist and ankles to a ring set in the centre of a cramped cell which is only too familiar to me from my earlier visit to the prison. Lying on the floor around me are half a dozen or so shapeless forms of sleeping prisoners, some snoring and some in the vocal grip of nightmares. I shake my head to clear away the mists of the anaesthetic but I have no means of clearing the foul taste in my mouth. My instinct is to shout out for the guards but I realise that there is nobody in the prison who can help me.

Not only do I not know who drugged me but I am equally clueless about why Dagobah is displeased with me, presuming it is he who orchestrated this situation. As I ponder my fate the first strands of dawn begin seeping through the high barred window and there is the dawn chorus of winged insects and birds. The stench in the cell attracts, among other things, flying insects whose incessant buzzing is just marginally better that the silence that ensues when they have found a fleshy target.

The inert forms around me begin to stir as the light increases; except for one they are all Benejaden as evidenced by their dress style. The exception is one who is dressed in hooded Arab garb, he is deep in slumber, apparently undisturbed by the increase in light and the stirring of humanity around him. One of the Benejaden prisoners calls out to the guards for food and water and endeavours to stand up; his attempt is unsuccessful and he falls to the filthy floor. A guard walks in through the unlocked cell door and deposits a bucket of water and a box of what looks like mouldy bread on the floor to one side of the door, and makes a quick exit before he can be caught up in the stampede which ensues. Some of the inmates take immediate action to procure both bread and water and in the melee the water is spilled onto the dusty floor where it is sucked in by the parched beaten earth.

The noise and confusion wakes up the Arab who sits with his back to me, not bothering to join in with the quest for food and water, like the others. His knees are drawn up as he sits and he rests his forehead on them in what looks like weary dejection.

"We should stick together," I say to his back in local Arabic. He suddenly sits up straight.

"Yes we should." He replies in the same language and I recognise the voice before he turns to face me.

It is Abu Haider, we are cellmates.

Benningo Dagobah:

Kofi is very slow to carry out my orders. He tells me that there is still no real progress with Abu Haider's interrogation and suggests forcefully that I should be patient and that the answers will be forthcoming. I do not have his patience and his surly attitude is grating to the point where I consider telling somebody else to take on the task, but I can think of nobody else who is cold blooded enough to do my bidding.

"Why are you here talking to me when you could be carrying out the interrogation and bringing this to a conclusion?" I use my most authoritative voice.

"He must first be made to sweat with the fear of anticipation. Once that has been done the interrogation will be more rewarding." He says this to me without any hint of subservience.

I find him frustrating but I cannot disagree with his tactics, my own experience tells me that fear will ultimately bring greater rewards than random precipitous actions. "Very well, but sooner rather than later, we do not have a great deal of time to spare. In the meantime, you must locate L'Etranger for me. He seems to have disappeared and he has missed a discussion we were supposed to have over breakfast this morning.

The sudden and unexplained disappearance of L'Etranger is vexing and does nothing to promote the smooth running of my plans. There is only one other person who could be the architect of his disappearance and that is the president, but there is no way I can ask him, or let him know that I am discomforted by the disappearance. My interests can only be served by Kofi who must add finding L'Etranger to his dealings with the other Arab, the café owner.

Simon Hunter:

To the disapproval of our cellmates, Abu and I scramble over them until we are side by side.

He whispers to me when we are close together. "Don't eat the food or drink the water, hygiene is not good and your body system has not yet had time to be conditioned to it."

I take heed of what he says, although I would have to be dying from hunger or dehydration to even consider ingesting any of what has been provided.

"How long have you been here?" I ask.

"Two days but it's not as bad for me as it is for these others." He shakes his manacles as he sweeps his arm around to encompass the poor wretches who lie hunched on the floor. “Some of my friends learned of my captivity and they bribe their way in with food and water for me twice a day. The others here rely solely on the slop that the prison provides. Few of them will leave here except in a winding sheet and they will end up in an unmarked mass grave outside of town. They will die of malnutrition or from torture but only one in twenty will leave under their own steam and that will be because they have somebody to pay what the warders refer to as an administrative release fee.”

“Do you know why you’re here? I have no idea why I am – my being here serves no purpose that I can think of.”

“I was brought here by Dagobah’s chief guard and he calls me out of the cell to an interrogation room, so far, twice a day. His interrogation technique is very strange; he issues me with many threats but does not ask any questions of substance apart from wanting to know about what I am doing for you.”

“I’m so sorry, my friend, that you are in trouble because you have been helping me. There was always a risk of what we are doing being discovered and reported to the authorities but I had hoped that my work would have been completed before we reached this stage.”

“It is true that I have been helping you but what you are trying to do is still a puzzle to me. I continue to help you because what you are doing will be for the good of my people.”

Our discussion is interrupted by two prison guards flinging the cell door open with a crash against the wall.

"Get up, prisoner Haider, you are to be interrogated." They advance on Abu and detach his ankle shackles from the long chain fixed to the centre ring by stretching the anchor chain taut and using two remote keys simultaneously, one at the centre anchor and one at his ankle shackle, and push him before them out into the corridor.

Abu Haider:

The surprise of seeing Simon in the cell must have shown on my face. I haven't been told why I am in captivity and I don't understand why he is. The guards sent to collect me interrupt our conversation before I can find out if Simon knows why either of us has been incarcerated. I don't have much time to consider why before I am thrust into a small room which has a wooden table and one chair which is occupied by Dagobah's chief guard, Kofi, the one who was responsible for bringing me to the prison.

"Stand still and be attentive." He says to me in his eerie whisper. "You have many questions to answer."

He is disturbingly comfortable with the situation we are in and although the way he is dressed and with his face is covered, he still manages to look and act menacing. He sits for long minutes just regarding me, without uttering a word. Somehow I can tell that his look is stern and unyielding and that he would have no compunction about inflicting pain should the situation demand.

"What were you doing for the traitor L'Etranger, why are you helping him?" His whisper is coldly emotionless.

"Simon L'Etranger is a customer at my café and what I do for him is serve tea." I am surprised that I can convey this lie in a convincing way; perhaps fear is lending me the ability. "I do not know him as a traitor. To me he is a customer with whom I share small talk and he is a confidante of His Excellency Dagobah."

He grunts noncommittally and it is impossible for me to judge whether he believes me. His questions continue for a further half an hour and I am surprised by the rambling nature of his enquiries. His approach appears to be unfocussed but I can't help thinking I am misreading his intentions. I find him frighteningly unreadable.

Simon Hunter:

About an hour after he left, I can't be more definite than that because my watch has been confiscated, Abu is returned to the cell by the same guards who push him into the room so forcibly that he stumbles over his ankle chains and falls heavily. One of the guards kicks him where he lies, forcing him to crawl to where his long restraint chain lies curled on the floor. He is re-secured.

Abu smiles ruefully at me when the guards have disappeared. "That was the most uncomfortable bit of the whole interview; the chief guard is still asking me inconsequential questions about you which appear to be leading nowhere. I'm confused."

"My treatment so far is puzzling also. I was anesthetised before being brought here, not bludgeoned as I would have expected under the circumstances. There must be fifty cells in here but I have been thrown into the same one as you; it can't be a coincidence because they are asking you questions about me. Where does that leave us?"

"In the dark, I'm afraid, and with very little hope, without assistance, of getting back into the light."

Jacob Wellbeing:

The intelligence report dossier which I receive once each week sits open on my desk and it is the transcript of a telephone conversation between Dagobah and the guard Kofi which interests me. Dagobah's intention to dispose of the Arab Abu Haider is of no consequence to me, but his intention to dispose of L'Etranger is not welcome. I instruct the chief of my intelligence service in Benejado City to find out where L'Etranger is and to advise me so that I can take whatever action is necessary.

This telephone conversation and others involving Dagobah would not have been intercepted under normal circumstances because the enormous task of doing so would require legions of listeners. This conversation has been recorded at my specific instruction because of my distrust of Dagobah and my suspicions about his motives. I had expected to be the subject of his aggression so it is a great surprise that his ire is directed to the two Arabs rather than me. I am on top of what he is trying to do with the cabinet and I can handle that, but for him to take out L'Etranger before I have fully exploited his potential is not acceptable. I must make a move on him soon to stop the rot.

Simon Hunter:

My first day of captivity ends. My expected interrogation has not happened. One of Abu Haider's Arab friend's visits bringing food and clean water. I recognise him from my many visits to the café as one of the regulars. His access to our cell is gained by daily bribes to the guards who are paid very poorly – sometimes not at all. They offer rewards for bribes to keep body, soul, and family together. The comings and goings of such emissaries is unrestricted and I am aware of several during my first day in captivity.

Our visitor carries a palm leaf basket containing bread, salted meat, root vegetables, fruit, and clean water. Those who do not have visitors are the ones who I observed scrabbling for the meagre rations which are delivered twice a day by the guards. Abu Haider's visitor has a generous quantity of rations which he commences to share with the needier prisoners. Abu shares the food with me and I am especially grateful for the water which soothes my chemically induced parched throat. The heavily salted meat opens my pores and perspiration clears them, and the evaporation in turn cools my skin to give momentary relief.

As the sun descends during my second night of captivity – the first night I missed because of the anaesthetic – we reflect on our situation. We agree that the reason for Abu's incarceration is because his opposition to Dagobah has been discovered and Dagobah would have no qualms about locking him up without trial or representation. As far as my situation is concerned the reason is less obvious. As far as I am aware Dagobah does not realise that my intention is to stop him in his tracks so it is unlikely that my incarceration would be of interest to him. Whoever is responsible for me being here has issues with me that differ from those of Dagobah. Who that may be and whether my reading of the situation is right is something I am yet to find out. Once my interrogation commences I may be able to fathom out the who and the why.

Benningo Dagobah:

Cousin Dangajabido visits me here in Golas City to give me his weekly report on what is going on in Benejado City. I do not allow him the luxury of a rest after his long and uncomfortable journey and put him straight to work. I ignore his protestations.

"The importance of your mission cannot be overstated," I tell him conspiratorially to get his full attention. "This is a very delicate matter which will need to be carefully planned and I am entrusting it to you as a valued and loyal family member. Do I make myself clear?"

"As ever you do, Cousin Benningo."

"Good, you are as smart as I thought. I must talk to you about a matter of assassination, in the national interest of course." As I tell him of my plans his face registers shock tinged with fear.

Jacob Wellbeing:

My security people in Benejado City inform me that Abu Haider is being held in the city prison, probably at the behest of Dagobah, and he is being interrogated by my informant Kofi. I am not concerned about Abu Haider's welfare, he is of no importance to me, but their other news is disturbing. The other prisoner being held is Simon L'Etranger and this does not suit my plans. I intend to hold Dagobah to account over this and get instructions to him to telephone me without delay.

When he makes contact he sounds annoyed and is once more discourteous. Rather than ask him outright about both prisoners I approach the subject in a more conversational fashion. "Do you have an update on the whereabouts of the Arab Abu Haider who has been causing you concern?"

"He is being held in the prison in Benejado City and is being interrogated by my head guard about the unrest that he and his people are causing among the city's population." He pauses for a moment. "Why do you ask?"

"I do not wish you to be distracted by trifling issues like this, you have the important task of reconfiguring the cabinet to complete. If there is anything I can do to help you with Abu Haider just let me know." He does not react to my contrived offer of help so I continue with the real point of my questions. "Simon L'Etranger has not been in touch with me for some days now. Tell him that he must contact me without delay, we have unfinished business."

"I too wish to speak with him, but his whereabouts is unknown to me and I find his absence very annoying. I am having Kofi look into it."

His reaction to my request appears genuine enough; maybe he doesn't know that L'Etranger is being held captive. This poses a question; if is not at the direction of Dagobah, then whose?"

"Mr President I have serious concerns about L'Etranger, as I have previously indicated. His loyalties are suspect. He slaughtered some of our countrymen because they refused to sign over to him the mineral rights of the region and now he has disappeared without trace."

The fact remains that L'Etranger is being held and if it is not Dagobah, who is responsible?

Simon Hunter:

Apart from the visits of Abu Haider's people I have no contact with the outside world and I still don't understand why I have not yet been questioned or been told of the reason for my imprisonment. One way of doing something about it would be to get free of my shackles and gain freedom. Simply looking at the locks yields no clues as to how I can do that or what tools I will need.

"That's not the way out." Abu has interpreted my thoughts. "I have had my people send a locksmith with my daily rations to see how I can be freed of these chains. His prognosis is that without a special coded key opening the lock will be impossible, and additionally the locks are fitted with a device which jams them if they are tampered with and the shackles can only be removed then using a blow torch.

"So, without the key we are stymied. What about bribing somebody to get the key?" I ask this question more in hope than expectation.

"I'm informed by my locksmith friend that it takes two keys to operate these special locks. The two keys are kept in different places and need to be operated by two different people."

"Where did that system come from?"

"I'm told that the prison was leaking inmates at an alarming rate and plugging all the loopholes in this old prison was more expensive than Dagobah was prepared to pay. He called in an American security expert who sold the shackle locking system at a fraction of the cost of updating the whole prison structure."

"How were the Americans paid for their work? The local currency has no international value."

"It all came down to bartering, in exchange for the work Dagobah arranged for the American company to be supplied with the only thing of value that is available in Golas, the rich minerals mined in the eastern province. I hear it cost a whole year's production and the president was most displeased, but it was too late for him to do anything about it. What I find surprising is that Dagobah is now part of central government. It doesn't make sense." He looks totally bemused.

"Strange goings on, but it doesn't help us get out of here, and we have to before things get worse. Getting out of here is a must and I'm hoping that your people are going to be able to do something about it, there are no other sources of help."

"My people can do nothing, nothing at all." He looks as dejected as I feel frustrated.

Dangajabido:

Cousin Dagobah is demanding that I do something which I find very unsettling and there is no way I can wriggle out of it; what Dagobah wants, he gets. I start the first part of my two-part task by taking some accommodation, which is in sight of thc presidential apartments in Government House. I have a week to keep a diary of the president's movements. My task is to determine any pattern in his daily activities which indicate a predictable course.

My work requires me to watch his quarters through powerful binoculars and record the movements of the president and his staff. After just an hour of doing this I realise that boredom will cause me to be inattentive. Cousin Benningo is ill informed when it comes to surveillance; he would have me rely on observation and handwritten notes. I am more progressive and I choose to use more up-to-date methods.

If I do well at this I will be given a senior position in my cousin's new administration. Maybe I can be minister of technology which will give me the opportunity to travel and become even more knowledgeable. But first I must update methods and make a good job of my initial task using video recording. I do not yet know what the second part of my work will be but anything my cousin wants but keeps secret from me, is not good.

Jacob Wellbeing:

I feel like a circus juggler. The balls I have in the air, apart from my presidential duties, are many and growing. The issues are: how I can stop Dagobah from taking over the government; how I can continue to open my international access to finance and goods for which I need the input of L'Etranger; and finding out who has incarcerated L'Etranger and the reason for the slaughtering of council members in Nkando.

I order the Jetstream and crew back to Golas City so that I may travel to Nkando in a way which will not allow enough time for those I am visiting to anticipate my arrival and hide things from me. There are no telephone communications between Golas City and Nkando so the only way for me to find out about the massacre is to go there.

When we arrive, my plans are immediately thrown into disarray. The situation is not at all as I expected and what I do find changes my plans immediately. At last I have the leverage over Dagobah that I have been seeking; it has dropped into my lap. On the return journey to Golas City I am a changed man, I now have the ammunition to protect myself from the predator Dagobah that is not just a surprise to me, but it will be for L'Etranger.

To bring matters to a head, I despatch the Jetstream to Benejado City with instructions that Dagobah, Kofi, and L'Etranger when he is found, are to be returned to me to answer some vital questions.

Simon Hunter:

Sleeping on my third night of imprisonment is close to impossible; I am chained up and expending no physical energy during the day, and secondly my mind is wrestling with thoughts of how we can get out of this dilemma in one piece. Lying on the hard floor is also not conducive to sleep and every time I turn to try and get into a more comfortable position my chains rattle and twist uncomfortably. Beside me Abu Haider sleeps like a baby; he is used to the mosquitos and the high temperature and humidity of the Golacian nights.

Sleep must have overtaken me because I come to and sense that there is another presence close by. For a moment, I am confused by what is happening. I sense the presence is moving but there is no rattling of chains and the odour the presence brings is alien to this situation, but at the same time familiar to me. The masked interloper is vaguely visible by the light of a few stars shining weakly through the high barred window. He, for his outline is masculine, does not speak, but puts his index finger to his lips in the universal sign for silence. Next he shakes Abu Haider awake and bids him in the same way to be silent. Now that my eyes have become adjusted to the light level I can see that the interloper is wearing a balaclava and that he is a local or at least is West African, I can see only the whites of his eyes and his hands.

He squats down on his hunkers – bare feet flat on the floor – and withdraws a long cylindrical item from his loose trousers pocket, which he gives to Abu Haider. Taking great care to be quiet, he gathers up Abu Haider's chains and indicates that they should both go to the central anchor point where he puts the cylindrical device into the keyhole, indicating wordlessly that Abu Haider should turn the key and keep it turned. Next he picks up my chains and making as little noise as possible, gathers them up and then pays them out as he ushers me away until the chain is taut. He then produces a second key and pushes it into the lock of my foot shackles. The lock clicks open as the key is turned; I am now free from the shackle chain and able to move around.

The performance is repeated for Abu Haider and apart from the chain handcuffs we both still have, we can move freely. Our liberator beckons us to follow him and we pick our way carefully between the supine figures that litter the floor, without disturbing them. He looks up and down the external corridor to make sure it is clear. We follow him past cell doors behind which prisoners sleep restlessly and occasionally cry out with night terrors.

Outside the side alley is lit only by the stars and a sickle moon which gives just enough illumination for us to negotiate the many obstacles which have been abandoned in the alley. We are startled by a figure emerging from a shadowed doorway and I immediately make a fighting pose. The figure steps forward and identifies himself as one of the Arabs who has been delivering our food and water.

"Follow me," he hisses urgently, clearly uncomfortable with what he is doing. "We must avoid all human contact, friend or foe."

We follow him closely as he runs barefoot along the alley and ducks into a side lane which discharges us into the maze of the local souk. The shop fronts are closed and boarded and the rickety free-standing stalls are covered. Apart from the isolated bark of a wild dog the night is silent. Freedom is a relief.

Our hooded guide leads us to one of the shops and we disappear inside, into the darkness. The dimmed light is turned up so that we can see each other clearly and our guide, who owns the shop, is the locksmith whom Abu had told me about. He opens a tool cupboard above one of the workbenches that line both sides of the room and extracts a leather pouch containing lock pick tools. After a brief glance at the locks, he unpicks our handcuffs with practiced ease. Abu and our guide begin nonstop chatter, releasing the tension that has been locked up in them, in a sudden burst of sound.

"Where is the man who released us?" I ask.

The guide shrugs. "He did not leave the prison with us; the last I saw of him was when he turned back inside and closed the door."

"Who was he?" I ask them both.

Abu shakes his head. "I have no idea who he is, isn't he one of yours? He was definitely local."

"He is not one of mine and if he's not one of yours, who is he one of?" I look to them both for an answer. "How did you contact with him?" I ask the guide.

"He contacted me and asked for my assistance to release both of you."

"What is his name and how do we contact him?"

"He gave me no name and I have no way of contacting him, it was not a two-way conversation. I did what he asked because there was no alternative way of getting your freedom. He must be very well connected though; he was able to get possession of both shackle keys and he knew the technique for unlocking the leg chains."

Something doesn't add up for me. "Have we been

released because we were inaccessible inside the prison or do we have a guardian angel? Until we know that we're not, the reason for our release is the kind of mystery that makes me uneasy."

Jacob Wellbeing:

My visit to Nkando proved to be both a surprise and a mystery and has done nothing to clear up the situation. Quite the reverse, in fact. I am now less clear about what's going on and what it means to me. One thing is for sure, Dagobah is lying to me.

Looking once more at Dagobah's recommendations for the cabinet reshuffle makes his agenda clear; he wants to take over the government and to take no prisoners. I have spoken to the people he names as candidates and they fall into two groups; one group is anti-me, although they will not admit this to me in so many words – the other group is neutral; they neither support me nor oppose me. His amateurish attempt to placate me by moving me sideways into a dead-end position from which he will be able to dispense with me entirely, is transparent and is typical of his shallow thinking. In the past others have tried to remove me from office and they all now occupy unmarked resting places in the surrounding countryside. Those responsible for the burials have since disappeared without trace.

I have yet more reports of strange goings on from my intelligence people in Benejado City; two prisoners have escaped from the prison and their whereabouts is unknown. This is not only puzzling but it poses the problem of who it is that has spirited away two prisoners from a cell which is protected by a most elaborate system and for which a fortune was paid by Dagobah – against my wishes. One of my local guards has been given the task of shadowing Dagobah and he advises me that Dagobah has received a visit from one who is believed to be his low-life cousin. They are plotting something I have yet to determine; I will allow them just enough rope to hang themselves.

Simon Hunter:

Without the freedom to roam, continuing with my task becomes infinitely more difficult. I must find somewhere to live from which I can continue my fight. Abu Haider also needs a safe house until Dagobah ceases to have any influence. Before anything else happens, I need to rest, which for the last three nights has been impossible. Ahmed, the locksmith who helped to rescue us, allows us to stay in the accommodation behind his workshop until we can make other arrangements. As I drift off to sleep I register the thought that Ahmed has placed himself in danger by harbouring us, and my first task after resting and eating some proper food will be to find alternative safe accommodation. From that location, wherever it might be, I intend to launch a final and definitive attack on Dagobah.

Twelve hours of sleep works wonders and I feel refreshed and a little euphoric at being free and able to continue with the one thing that is driving me. Abu Haider is already awake and eating a meal of dates, bananas, and Arab bread which he is washing down with sweet lemon tea. The aroma of his repast makes me realise how hungry I am myself; the locksmith gives me a platter bearing a similar meal.

"What is our next move, my friend?" Abu asks when I have finished eating.

"We should find somewhere else to stay; your friend is in danger while we are on his property. The first thing the authorities will do when our disappearance has been discovered is to find out the addresses of all your friends and contacts and raid them."

"I will get a message to my son Haider to find us a safe house to which we can travel under the cover of darkness."

"He should do that for you but I will need to make other arrangements. We must separate; if we are caught together you will be in danger. If you are captured by them while on your own, you can say that you were forced to escape with me against your will and that you were about to give yourself up having given me the slip. Until I can answer the question of why we were released and by whom, I must stay in hiding. You must go your own way, my friend. Knowing me has put you in danger. While I am no longer part of your life you will be safer." I give him a smile of encouragement to relieve the tension that is oozing from him.

Jubil:

Something happened during the president's visit to Nkando which caused him to cut the visit short and return early to Golas City. He descended from the Jetstream and scurried off at a speed that is quite remarkable for one of his age and apparent frailty. Nataly and I are left to our own devices. The president has a new distraction and it is to do with Dagobah being involved with Jabido. I have heard nothing from Simon since our earlier visit to Nkando and I am concerned for his welfare.

Using the Jetstream's radio, I contact Noah back in Nematasulu and fill him in with progress and tell him of the loss of contact with Simon. Like me, he expresses concern and tells me to investigate and find out what I can. Wellbeing and Dagobah are still heavily involved in pursuing their disparate agendas and Nataly and I are at a loose end. Acting on the suggestion of Noah that I should locate Simon, I decide to return to Benejado City.

In no time, we are back in Dagobah's remote and dysfunctional city which during Dagobah's absence appears to have taken on a lighter note. The people look more relaxed and are enjoying their newfound freedom. There are rickety tables set up under brightly coloured awnings offering shade from the cruel heat of the sun. There is music on the streets and in the squares which draws an appreciative audience who willingly join in by dancing, some solo and some partnered by pretty girls in traditional dress. When the people of the city realise that Dagobah is not with us they resume their enjoyment.

Simon Hunter:

We are waiting for darkness so that we can move

out of the locksmith's workshop annex and Abu Haider can be taken to a safe location outside of Benejado. The stress of the situation shows plainly on the faces of the locksmith and Abu Haider and the air inside the small hot shop crackles with pent-up tension. There is the sudden sound of running feet and the door to the workshop annex is flung open. Haider Al Haider bursts into the room.

"Abu, you are in danger." He is breathless. "Soldiers and police are scouring the souk in search of you and effendi L'Etranger, they are searching from building to building and they are in the next street. They have orders to shoot you and any supporters on sight."

"Be still, my son." Abu tries to placate him. "We must flee before they get here."

"That is not possible, my father, they have ringed the souk and are closing in from all directions. You must both hide where you cannot be found; they will be here in minutes. I pray that you are able to escape the clutches of these evil men; here," he thrusts a portmanteau he brought with him towards Abu Haider, "there is money in here that will help once you have escaped."

He flees from the workshop closely followed by the locksmith. I look around the small room; there is no hiding place for us. The front room of the two-roomed shop is the mirror of the one we are in; there is nowhere for us to hide.

"What do we do now?" Abu is distressed.

"Let us assess our options." I have an uneasy feeling that they are zero.

We move from the rear into the front room. The louvres on the street side openings throw zebra stripes across the dusty counter and the crude wooden floor; they give an oblique view up and down the street. I look in both directions and see to my left the uniforms of the police and to my right those of the army. At the head of the army contingent is the striking figure of Kofi. He has an assault rifle in one hand and a machete in the other. My heart sinks, it might have been possible to bribe the uniforms but with Kofi bribery is not an option.

The two converging groups are going into each building. If the doors are locked they are simply broken down and each property is ransacked and the occupants thrown out onto the street. Those carrying out the searches are enjoying the freedom of being thugs and throw themselves zealously into their destructive task.

I watch the two groups converging on us and we look to be the location at which they will both meet. They come ever closer and behind them the alley is strewn with the goods from the shops which have been ransacked. They are close enough now for me to be able to detect alcohol-induced speech slurring and they are all looking wild-eyed. Marginally, the police contingent is ahead of the army contingent and should reach us first; this gives me some hope. If Kofi gets to us first the cause is lost.

The police are in the shop next to us and Kofi and the army are still two shops away, at least there is a glimmer of hope. We can offer whichever policeman it is that discovers us the large bribe of the portmanteau of Abu Haider's money. Considering how little and infrequently the police are paid, there is a chance of success.

As the police to my left draw closer I breathe a sigh of relief. There is a flurry of sudden movement to my right and I see Kofi striding purposefully towards the entrance to our shop ahead of the police contingent as he waves them back imperiously. I hustle Abu Haider into the back workshop. I have a sinking feeling that something really bad is going to happen and there is no avenue of escape. I am acutely aware that Kofi knows that I was a witness to the slaughter he carried out in Nkando and I am a permanent threat to him. In his eyes, I am entirely dispensable and this exercise is a perfect cover for my assassination. Even worse, Abu Haider will be an innocent victim of my obsession.

We retreat into the back room and are both painfully aware of the total lack of cover it affords. The door crashes open and the muzzle of Kofi's assault rifle pokes into the room. I have my thumb on the kill button suspended around my neck but my heart sinks when I see that the muzzle is not from one of the guns that I provided, the kill button is useless. We have no defence against him. We are like fish in a barrel.

Abu Haider:

As the rifle pokes around the door we are totally exposed with no defence against what will inevitably happen. There is a muffled shout from out in the street and I hear Kofi's tortured whispered response. "I'll be right with you." His attempt to shout a reply comes out in a louder whisper. Suddenly he is gone and the silence inside the workshop is broken only by the diminishing sounds of the departing search parties.

I close my eyes and breathe raggedly in pure terror. "My heart cannot take such shocks." I hear myself say in a quivering voice. "My hands are shaking and my ears are ringing. Has he really gone?"

"He has gone, and when darkness falls so will we be." His voice reveals the relief that I feel.

When darkness eventually falls we leave the sanctuary of the workshop and venture out into the hostility of the city at night. Our journey to the café is cautious and before entering we ensure that there are no unwanted visitors in the café. My son greets us with affection.

"We have a friend here who will help us get you away to a safe place." Haider beckons to somebody in the next room whom I cannot see.

Jubil enters. "Noah asked me to be of assistance in any way I can." His unexpected presence has turned our options from zero to many.

We sit in the back room going over the possibilities that air transportation offers us. It is unsafe for me to hide in Benejado City but I don't want to be too far away from home. As for Simon, he wishes to pursue his obsession and that means staying in the city. I am reluctant to go but entreaties from Simon for me to take the safe option and be taken to a village to the north where members of my Arab brotherhood are domiciled, makes a lot of sense.

Dangajabido:

I am doing what my cousin demands of me. Over a three-day period, I have made a log of the president's movements and I have established that he has a predictable daily pattern around breakfast time. I have recorded this with a very old but reliable video camera. I will demonstrate to Dagobah that I am up with the latest techniques, as would befit a future technology minister in his government. I am concerned about what it is that he wants me to do after I have finished this first task. I am reluctant to ask him because I don't want to hear the answer.

It is worse than I thought, Cousin Dagobah has told me what he wants me to do. I am to use a sharpshooter rifle which the Arab has supplied and from my apartment I am to shoot and kill the president while he is at his breakfast on the terrace outside his apartments. I am no marksman but Dagobah has assured me that this is a special rifle which has laser guided bullets and all I must do is make sure, looking through the powerful telescopic sight, that I keep the red dot on the president's head before and after I pull the trigger.

My problem with that plan is that if I don't succeed and I am caught I will be executed as a failed assassin. If I succeed my life will be in danger because I will be the only person other than Dagobah who will know about the assassination and he will not want any witnesses. I have a little time to protect myself against the two possible fates because I am not required to carry out the assassination until my cousin has returned to Golas City; he wants to be in place to step into the vacant presidency without delay. If I fail I will need an escape plan and go to a country beyond the reach of Cousin Dagobah.

Benningo Dagobah:

I am now so close to being president I can almost taste it. Cousin Dangajabido has done what I demanded and the way to assassinating the president is fool proof. The one remaining thing for me to do is to find L'Etranger, take him to Golas City and present him to the cabinet as a trophy to show how much I have the interests of my country at heart. This will smooth the path of my unopposed acceptance of the presidency. As an extra I will have the aircrew of the Jetstream executed for complicity in the massacre of our brothers in Nkando. This will give me outright ownership of the Jetstream and the 4WD.

I make the offer of a king's ransom to any citizen who can lead me to the whereabouts of L'Etranger so that I may bring him to justice; the opportunity spreads around the city like wildfire through dry brush. Once I have flushed him out I will have him flown to Golas City where I can deal with him as I wish.

Cousin Dangajabido will carry out the assassination and plant evidence pointing to L'Etranger which when added to the evidence of massacre will ensure that he is executed and that I am seen to be the saviour of my country. A show trial with all the evidence I will invent will ensure that my actions in all of this are seen to be exemplary. My plan, as ever, will be a resounding success and L'Etranger will be no more.

Simon Hunter:

My situation is precarious. Abu is taken care of which leaves me unencumbered and able to focus on my own objectives, but without outside help I cannot meet the objectives I have set myself. Paradoxically the only possible source of assistance available is the president and I'm not sure that openly asking for his help is a viable proposition. He is a focussed man and he would sacrifice me in pursuit of his own interests in much the same way as Dagobah would. Catch 22.

I try to imagine what a formally trained intelligence officer would do in similar circumstances. An agent out on a limb as I am would evade capture and make his way by some means to Golas City, where he would get an audience with the president and blow the whistle on Dagobah in the hope of achieving some rapport with the president which can be used to some advantage. That's what an agent would do, so my approach must be the opposite to that to achieve success; he would avoid capture, make his way under his own steam to Golas City and rely on being able to persuade the president to help. My task therefore is to take the opposite course of action.

Benningo Dagobah:

My people are scouring the city to locate L'Etranger; the generosity of the reward I am offering has engendered a great deal of interest from ordinary people as well as those who would sell their own grandmothers for a pittance. It is the latter people whom I think will be of most benefit to my cause – they will shop L'Etranger without a second thought.

My ploy bears fruit on the first day of its execution and the source of the information leading to the discovery that he is in an empty shop in the souk. It is, surprisingly, Haider Al Haider, son of Abu, who is the giver of the location. He offers the information in the hope, not only of the generous reward but, of having his father forgiven for his opposition to me. The reward is in Golacian shillings which are worthless outside Golas and of limited value to me, and I part with them without demur. I promise to review his father's case and make a judgement; I do not let him know at this stage that I will still find Abu guilty as charged. That will come later after we locate him.

Picking up L'Etranger is a simple matter and my troops escort him to my quarters. He looks angry and when I tell him who it is that gave him away he becomes even angrier.

"Is this the way you treat people who have helped and supported you? You are treating me like a common criminal and I have done nothing to you except help." He is more agitated than I have ever seen him.

"Like all your kind you have tried to deceive me, you have made the mistake of thinking that you can outwit me but you are gravely mistaken, I can read you like an open book. You will be given a fair hearing which will be overseen by me but your fate is sealed and no amount of money or other forms of bribery will do you any good at all."

Simon Hunter:

When the troops come to get me in my temporary

hideaway I am ready for them. They take me to Dagobah and are none too gentle about it. I remonstrate with him about my treatment which of course he ignores. He believes he has me at a disadvantage, but it is I who hold the advantage.

The first tactic of my strategy is complete; he believes he is outwitting me using cunning but he is wrong. Now I must get him to take me to Golas City and the president, and this must appear to be his idea and not the fulfilment of my intention.

I start the ball rolling. “I have failed to do what the president has asked me to do and failure is not something he will tolerate. He has given me an ultimatum; get the materials he requires or face the consequences. You must allow me to continue with this work, I have no alternatives.” I give a look of contrition.

“What is this thing you are required to do that is so important?” he asks me through pursed lips.

“I am to acquire strategic materials for him which will give the new government he is forming a stronger international influence. He is doing this so that the new leader of the government, whoever he is, will have the necessary strength to see Golas through to the next stage of development. He has charged me with this and it is something I must follow it to its conclusion. Not to do so will lead to serious consequences for me and anybody who prevents me from doing the president’s bidding.”

“Who is the person of whom you speak, the one who will lead the next government?” He looks eager to know my thoughts.

"I don't know who it is but I do know that anybody who helps me to fulfil his wishes will be looked on with great favour by the president and could even replace the person who is his current choice." I say this with as much conviction as I can muster.

"What do you need to do to satisfy him?" He has taken the bait.

"I need to use the satellite radio in the Jetstream to arrange for the delivery of the strategic materials direct to Golas City, it will take me only half an hour to complete the transactions and if you will allow me to do this thing the president will be indebted to you. I will personally convey to him that you have greatly assisted me to fulfil his wishes." I give him another of my most theatrically earnest looks.

"I will grant you the freedom to make the arrangements required by the president but you will be under close guard and you will then accompany me back to Golas City. You will report to the president that without my assistance you would have been unable to accomplish your mission and that I aided you in the face of great personal danger by freeing you from prison." He is most impressed at the way he has manipulated me into commending him to the president.

Jubil:

As Simon forecasted he is escorted to the Jetstream by an armed guard. As earlier instructed I followed his other wishes even though I have no idea of what he is trying to achieve. One guard accompanies Simon onto the flight deck, the rest remain outside surrounding the Jetstream with their armaments on display.

"I would like to use the radio." Simon looks at me stern faced for the benefit of the guard. "Set the frequency for me to talk to the Swiss supply company and tell them I want to talk to the quartermaster. Do it now!"

I do so and hand Simon the mic.

"Monsieur l'Directeur?" Before he can continue the guard snatches the mic from him and places his hand over it. "I speak not French, you must English use." His accent is thick and difficult to follow.

He uncovers the mic and speaks into it. "Who you are and why speaking French, not English?"

The reply which crackles over the radio speaker is distant and equally heavily accented in French but the meaning is clear. "I am the Directeur d' Travail of the company Swissystems."

The guard grunts and handed the mic back to Simon. "All time speaking English only."

Simon Hunter:

Time stands still when the guard grabs the mic and demands to speak to the person I am calling; this was not part of my plan and the response he gets could scupper my ploy before it even starts. As it turns out I have no need to worry, Jubil has done a good job of briefing our imaginary contact. Adlibbing by the person on the other end was enough to put the guard at ease. I am so happy to be working with quick thinkers who can change tack seamlessly when the situation demands.

The conversation with them is without any meaning but to the uninitiated would seem to be very technical and is concluded with agreement on both sides. I terminate the call and gave the mic back to Jubil. The guard grunts and prods me with his gun to leave the Jetstream. The guards outside reforms and we march off to the three broken-down vehicles which had transported us from Dagobah's residence.

Noah Gilliland:

There was a sticky moment when it was not Simon who came on the radio link but an interloper speaking very bad English and asking who I was. I realise from the opening words that Simon's plan is beginning to run aground. His addressing me in French which was not part of the brief I had been given by Jubil.

Jubil advised me to expect a radio message from Simon and he would ask me questions that would mean nothing to me but that I was to answer in a way which would give the impression that it all made perfect sense. There would be somebody listening in who is not welcome. I was to answer as though I was a director of a fictitious company by the name of Swissystems and talk convincingly about mythical strategic supplies. Jubil also said to me that after the event, if the witness was present, he would talk to me and tell me what is going on. I await his radio call with bated breath.

Jacob Wellbeing:

My secret service protection detail has advised me that the cousin of Dagobah has taken up residence in a building across the compound from my residence. There is no evidence that he is up to mischief and he seldom leaves the residence in daylight – it seems that he is a night owl. I will ignore his presence but when Dagobah returns to the city I will quiz him on the matter.

I watch them land in the middle of the compound in a swirling mist of red dust. This simple act is, once more, made surreal by the absence of sound except for the muted swishing of the rotors while they slow and stop. I am once more struck by the other strange things about the Jetstream; it has no tail rotor which is used by many other helicopters as a means of orientation. The pilot had informed me during one of our many flights that the two main rotors which share a dual drive spindle spin in opposite directions, and that spinning the craft around its vertical axis is achieved by reducing the speed of the upper rotor to spin to the right and alternatively of the lower rotor to spin left.

The Jetstream's doors remain unopened until the dust settles once it is cleared away by the light breeze. The first out are a gaggle of guards surrounding L'Etranger, after them Dagobah's chief guard descends followed by Dagobah who is accompanied by the flying woman who is carrying a large sunshade over Dagobah.

They approach my compound where I am sitting in the shade of palm thatching enjoying my pre-lunch chilled lemon drink. The military personnel halt before entering the compound and Dagobah sweeps through their ranks through my security gate. He turns to the assembled guards and indicates by hand signal that L'Etranger should follow him. I sense that this is the moment when Dagobah's true intentions will begin to surface, the game is now well and truly on.

Benningo Dagobah:

Quick thinking is my forte and my thoughts on the matter of L'Etranger have changed my intentions. I have decided to allow him to live just as long as he is of value to me, and he is for the moment. The work he is doing for the president is not complete until the strategic materials ordered are delivered. Using L'Etranger to sing my praises to the president will open the path to my intended cabinet reshuffle which is a vital part of my strategy.

I revise my immediate plans by redirecting Dangajabido. "There is a change of plan," I tell him before he has a chance to update me on his investigations. "I have decided to delay your next task until a more appropriate time. Meanwhile you will continue observing the president's movements so that I can safely choose the time and place of his assassination."

My decision to let my cousin in on my plan is prompted by my understanding of the way he thinks. His thoughts will be that if I am to have the president assassinated I will also certainly not hesitate to assassinate him should he consider resisting me. It is this fear which will make him carry out my orders.

His response when I have finished and he has had

time to digest my meaning does not relate to what I have told him and his eyes give him away. "My cousin," fear has made him short of breath, "I have done what you asked and have observed the president's habits to establish what is predictable. It is his practise to breakfast on the covered terrace outside his residence for a full half hour before starting his day's work; there are no guards nearby and he is entirely alone and easily visible from my residence."

This news is very pleasing, it means that I can make arrangements to ensure that he is taken care of at a time when I have a cast-iron alibi. The disposal of L'Etranger will be next on the menu and I fancy that I might be able to carry this out myself and prove myself to be a guardian of the country and its population against foreign interlopers who are trying to line their own pockets at the expense of us Golacians.

Simon Hunter:

Having pointed out that he has been instrumental in making sure that I am fulfilling the president's instruction, Dagobah is taken aback by the president ordering him to leave the room so that he can talk to me about private matters. He leaves with bad grace after whispering something in the president's ear and glaring at me.

"Who was responsible for having you thrown into jail? Was it Dagobah?" the president asks as soon as the door closes.

"That is a mystery to me. My first thought was that it must be Dagobah but his subsequent actions convince me that he knew nothing of my being abducted and the method of abduction was too civilised for it to have been him."

"You must realise, of course, that he wants you dead and that is something he is easing towards." He delivers this information without emphasis.

"How do you know this?" I ask him.

"He is trying to convince me that you are the 'terrorist within' in the hope that I will take action against you or instruct him to take action against you."

"I still don't know what he has against me."

"He insists that you are responsible for the growing uprising in Benejado, and more importantly that you are responsible for the massacre of the councillors in Nkando."

"I have already told you that I have no responsibility for what happened in Nkando. The executions were carried out by Kofi at the instigation of Dagobah." I reaffirm my version of events.

"I listened to what you had to say about this matter and I listened to Dagobah's version. They are diametrically opposed and the only way I could reconcile the situation was to visit Nkando. I took the Jetstream to Nkando and carried out my own investigation and I am assured that your version is without foundation."

I began to protest but the president holds up his hand to discourage me.

"Just hear me out." He waited until I had calmed down. "Your version, as I have said, is not so, but neither was that of Dagobah. I know that you did not take any part in the massacre." He sat back in his chair and let his words sink in.

"If I didn't do it then he or rather Kofi, must be guilty. Which is it?"

"The answer is neither." His response is enigmatic and he chooses not to enlarge upon it.

I have no idea what he is talking about, he speaks in riddles.

Benningo Dagobah:

The old fool dismissed me in front of the Arab and that is an insult which I am not prepared to forgive or forget. Once more my plans must change; I decide to bring forward the assassination of both the president and the Arab before the week is out. I call on Kofi, the one true ally I have left and can trust, and take him into my confidence which I sweeten with the promise of a high position in the military; I have in mind his being the chief of staff and my right-hand man.

Once more he surprises me by showing no emotion when I offer him these positions in my new government; he simply grunts to show that he has heard me. His 'man of mystery' act is wearing thin and I find it difficult to resist snatching away his anonymous dark glasses to see what his expression might reveal. I resist mainly because he is one of the few that I can trust and I need his support, and such an action on my part would change the nature of our relationship.

"Kofi, I want you to listen to me very carefully.

There is going to be a very special event which will take place in the next few days. It involves the participation of my cousin Dangajabido but I have doubts about him being strong enough in character to do what needs to be done. He has been given the task of shooting the president which will clear the way for me to take over from him. I want you to make sure that when the time comes he carries out the act with resolve. I have provided him with a fool proof laser-guided sniper rifle which can be used with accuracy even by the uninitiated providing he follows the simple act of keeping the laser marker on the target through the sighting scope. The bullet will hit the target painted by the laser with one hundred percent accuracy.

Simon Hunter:

Jacob Wellbeing has a secret which he is not disposed to reveal. Benningo Dagobah has gone from openly wanting to dispose of me to being benign. Kofi, despite his reputation as a heartless thug, either didn't realise I was in jail in Benejado and at his disposal or he has another motive. I feel as though I am not in control of anything that's going on.

My attempts at discrediting Dagobah in the eyes of the president appear to have failed. He is still in government and he is still in line for taking over as president with the support of Jacob Wellbeing. I am no closer to dealing with New Light or Dagobah than I was before all of this started. All I seem to have achieved so far is to provide armaments to Dagobah and to provide the Golacian government with air transport which was intended to set the president and Dagobah at each other's throats but has failed completely. I have jeopardised the life and livelihood of my friend Abu Haider and probably destroyed his business and caused his family and friends potential harm. On top of this I have had an attempt made on my life and I have been thrown into jail. All in all, this has not been a success story; it is as well that my *binary one* character is not unduly influenced by such a desperate situation.

My philosophy is predicated on the belief that the tide will turn and something will come along to counteract the negative things that have happened. And it does, I receive a message from Haider al Haider in the form of an addendum to a report on Abu Haider's circumstances. Fortune has smiled on us at last and his report of a conversation which he overheard in the House of Smoke and Tranquillity opens the opportunity of a whole new scenario.

There is rumour of a plot afoot among supporters of Dangajabido, overheard during one of the drunken warehouse parties, to assassinate the president and soon; the details are hazy but it seems that he is to be shot while at breakfast. The shooter will be situated in a building in direct sight of the terrace where he takes breakfast and the gun being used is a Nuovostani sniper's special which, I know fires laser-guided bullets which do not miss. I now have for the first time since starting out a clear plan of action which will enable me to take out Dagobah as well as New Light. With this valuable piece of intelligence being made available by the Al Haider family my programme has been compressed.

In the back of my mind there is a niggle. I

subscribe to the notion that if something seems too good to be true it usually is. Having this conversation overheard by Haider enabling him to pass it on to me, falls into the category of being too good to be true. On the other hand, if the information is incorrect and the attempt does not take place I will not be put in any danger by taking precautions against it. That would be disappointing but not catastrophic.

Jacob Wellbeing:

I am looking forward to my life resuming its former tranquillity, of late it has become more fraught than I find desirable. As if to underline the unacceptable nature of the present situation my breakfast, which is the only solitary time in the day for reflection, is shattered by the unexpected arrival of L'Etranger.

"Jacob, please accept my apologies for disturbing you at such an hour but there is a matter of an extreme nature that I must discuss with you." He looks at me with such intensity that I do not admonish him immediately.

"What is so important that you disturb me at this, my only quiet time?"

"Your life is in danger and rather than just apprehend the person charged with taking your life I think we should take steps to apprehend those behind it." His words are chilling.

I can both see and hear the conviction in his assertions and I am horrified by what he says. He must believe what he is saying is true because if it is not his life would be in the jeopardy that he states mine to be, and there is no benefit to him in that.

"How sure of this are you – and what is the source of your information?"

"I am totally sure and my source is impeccable."

"And what or rather who is your source?"

"My source is confidential but it is based on an overheard conversation in Benejado City between two of Dagobah's men."

"You base your advice on a conversation heard at the other end of the country?"

"I do, and I believe this attempt will be made and very soon. I also have a way of preventing you from coming to any harm but it will need your complete co-operation and to protect you I must meet you every morning for breakfast."

Simon Hunter:

I had thought to protect the president using the kill switch in the event of an attempt being made but that plan turns out to be a non-starter. The range of the kill switch transmitter is not sufficient to prevent the rifle from firing its deadly laser-guided projectile. My premise assumes that any attempt made on the life of the president will be when he is predictably exposed to public view and with no guards in place.

I do not bother the president with these details simply because it will scare him off. I counter this by not telling him about the limited range of the kill switch but to give him some confidence I demonstrated the capability of the switch by firing a pistol shot into the compound wall. Without operating the kill switch, it blasts a large, deep crater which does not happen when I take a second shot with the switch depressed. This demonstration eases the fears of the president.

The kill button not being effective over such a long distance means I must come up with an alternative plan. I have a plan but it is fraught with snags and relies on my lightning reactions. If my ploy succeeds I will have the undying support from the president; if it fails the way for Dagobah to take over the country will be clear and I will have lost the opportunity to rid the world of a tyrant, I will have made him stronger. I am once more in the lonely position of being sole arbiter.

The exact programme for the president's execution is not known, although it's clear that his lone breakfast is the likely time. Even if I am with the president for the duration of his long breakfast the whole exercise will fail if I blink at the wrong time. To give myself a fighting chance there are several things I must do. First, I must change the time the president takes breakfast, this will delay the event while the perpetrators rethink their programme. Doing this gives me a chance to find out the location of the proposed firing point which will give me extra time to protect the president when the shot is fired. Lastly, I must reduce the time the president is exposed to danger by at least halving the time he takes to consume breakfast. I have insufficient concentration abilities to be vigilant over a long period.

A similar outcome to that which I propose could be achieved by simply having the president stop taking breakfast out in the open, but that will not serve the purpose of dealing with Dagobah. The president gives the impression of being an absent-minded old dodderer but the more I deal with him the more I realise that under his benign exterior there beats a heart of flint. He is, for example, only interested in my safety as long as I can continue to be of use to him by both influence and finance. Take away both of those attributes and he has no interest in me or my safety.

The hidden steely nature of the president is what I intend to use in not just defeating but crushing Dagobah and his evil organisation. My aim of setting them on a collision course, as a result of which only one of them will survive, is now under way and we are teetering on the final round of this competition. The culmination of the activities in the next few days will lead to a finale which is irreversible and it will be the end of Dagobah, the president, or me – or maybe even all of us.

Dangajabido:

I thought everything was set and on this, the last intended day of my surveillance, I was observing the president before getting the all-clear from Cousin Dagobah and then disaster. The president has L'Etranger as a guest and the time taken has reduced considerably. I don't know whether this is a one off or it is to become a pattern. Whatever it is, I will need to carry out more observations to see if he is adopting another programme. Cousin Dagobah is not happy when I tell him of the changes to Wellbeing's morning habits.

New instructions from him require me to establish

any permanent changes to the breakfast pattern. My work so far indicates that morning is the only time that the president is in the vulnerable position offering the opportunity we require.

Benningo Dagobah:

Dangajabido's news is not what I want to hear. The change in Wellbeing's habit is extremely annoying but there is a silver lining to this cloud. If L'Etranger is to become a breakfast companion, there is the possibility of killing two birds with one stone. I have given my cousin three more days to establish a new pattern so that we can be assured of success and of my having a suitable alibi for the time of execution.

Simon Hunter:

To set the president's mind at rest I have given him the kill switch so that he can operate it all the time he is in the exposed position. It took a few more demonstrations and a few more holes in the compound wall for him to be convinced that he will be safe from harm; he feels safer than he actually is. The task for me now is to be able to anticipate when the shot will be made and take the avoiding action required to save the president's life and to have him indebted to me.

There is only one building in line of sight over the wall into the area where the president's breakfast is set up and it is half a mile distant and the sniper could be on any of the four upper storeys. The time taken for the subsonic bullet from the sniper rifle to travel the half mile from the building to the compound will be, give or take, 2.5 seconds. Light travels at 186,000 miles per second so from the time of observing the muzzle flash I will have a smidgeon short of 2.5 seconds to move the president out of harm's way and earn his eternal gratitude. To be able to accomplish this there are things that I must do including putting the shooter's building under surveillance and consulting an ophthalmic surgeon in Nematasulu's excellent general hospital.

What I am about to do has no room for error. I must plan meticulously and take account of all possible variations which might compromise the planned outcome. I do these things with the full realisation that not all possibilities can be considered and despite my planning there can still be things that go astray which can lead to devastating consequences, and this does not account for the potential of bolts of lightning out of the blue.

Benningo Dagobah:

Kofi brings Dangajabido to me after two further days of his observing the movements of the president. Kofi prods my cousin into my chambers and then collapses in a chair awaiting further orders, all of this he does without speaking. Dangajabido is clearly in awe of Kofi, perhaps even more so than of me.

"Report to me," I say to my cowering family member even before greeting him.

"I have done everything you asked of me. The president only leaves himself vulnerable for a reduced time; he shares breakfasts every morning with L'Etranger after which he attends to his duties in

Government House in full view of his select guard and government officials."

"You have done well and you will be rewarded when my government is established. You will go over your plan of action with Kofi and he will tell you if there is any weakness in your approach. There is an additional task for you to carry out; after you have dealt with the president you will despatch L'Etranger in the same way, with a second shot which you must take quickly to keep the element of surprise." My cousin is weak and I can see the doubt in his eyes.

"One is difficult enough but two shots; I am not sure that I can do what you want me to do." He is quivering with uncertainty.

"Don't be alarmed, cousin. I will take care of you. You will have one of the best teachers in the world to look after you and make sure you are up to the task. Kofi will tutor you in the use of the sniper rifle and he will make sure that you are able to take both shots quickly and efficiently." I turn to Kofi. "Is that not so?"

Kofi turns his face in my direction and then swivels to face Dangajabido. After a reflective pause he grunts his assent and then relaxes back into his chair as if he has not a care in the world. I have now done all that needs to be done to assure my accession. I will no longer need to convert the waverers in the cabinet to my way of thinking; after this course of events I am about to be free and unencumbered.

Dangajabido:

The time has come; I am about to change the course and history of my country. The air is clear and the sun is low behind me. Through the scope of the sniper rifle I can see the president's breakfast table. Two places are set which has become the norm, one for the president and one for L'Etranger. They walk out from the apartment into the dappled shade of the terrace with its palm thatched roof. The dusty floor of the terrace has been doused in water to stop the dust from eddying in the light morning breeze and being a nuisance; this works in my favour. My view will be unhindered.

The two men emerge from the interior and take their places at the table side by side facing in my direction. If I could lip read I would be able to follow their conversation, so clear is the magnification of the electronically enhanced scope. Kofi has prepared the rifle to do its deadly deed; he has fashioned a tripod to prevent my shaking hands from interfering with my aiming sensitivity. He has modified the breech of the rifle so that it holds two bullets side by side, when the first bullet is fired and the used cartridge is expelled the second spring-loaded bullet is fed into the breach, making it possible to fire the second bullet within a few seconds of the first, allowing me to realign the sights for the second shot on L'Etranger.

Suddenly it is time and Kofi gets me to lie prone on a trestle table which elevates me to sill level where I can fire into the compound. He does this so quickly that I don't have time to allow any doubts to dull the edge of my training. Over the last two days Kofi has drummed into me the sequence of events using half-mile distant targets set side by side.

Aim, breathe out, fire one, hold the red dot on the president's forehead, count two seconds, shift the red dot to

L'Etranger, fire, hold the dot steady, breathe in. The whole episode is over in a flash. I feel nothing, neither elation or depression, I have accomplished the task that will assure my future under the stewardship of my cousin Benningo Dagobah, soon to be unopposed President of Golas.

Benningo Dagobah:

My forethought of having Kofi train my cousin was obviously the right thing, the whole episode will work like a well-oiled machine. From my vantage point in a ground-floor briefing room which I share with a dozen members of the cabinet we await the later arrival of the president. He will never actually come. Looking obliquely out of the window I can see the president and L'Etranger having breakfast and I can just see the distant room from which Dangajabido will fire his shots.

Simon Hunter:

For the third consecutive morning, we share our alfresco breakfast. There is no way of knowing if today is to be the day of reckoning. The president appears relaxed; the only sign of tension is that the knuckles of the hand that grasping the kill button are taut and white and his hand shakes imperceptibly. We are deep in conversation when I am jolted into adrenalin-fuelled action. My eyes open wide so that I can see on the president's deeply etched forehead an intense red dot caused by the sniper's laser sight. The time has come and my senses are fixated to the exclusion of everything except the tiny focussed red dot which follows his forehead as he moves slightly in the process of eating. He stops moving, my eyes remain wide open; my concentration is absolute. The eye drop recommendation I received from the Nematasulan oculist which has inhibited the blink response has paid dividends.

The red dot is steady for a full second and then it wavers almost imperceptibly. That is the sign my heightened senses have been waiting for, that and the distant muzzle flash observed from the corner of my eye coupled with the slight movement of the dot tells me that the sniper has squeezed the trigger and that the bullet has been launched on its deadly trajectory. I have less than two seconds to move the president out of the way of the path of the projectile. I do this by flinging out my left arm and tipping him and his chair over; his fall is broken by a sun bed mattress placed on the ground behind his chair, the only thing damaged is his dignity.

In the fraction of a second that follows I congratulate myself at having saved the president and immediately realise that I am the one who is now in danger. In the centre of my chest the now familiar red dot shows and I am aware that my two seconds is up and that I cannot react in time to save myself. My last recollection is crashing backwards and then sudden overwhelming, all-enveloping pain and blackness.

Benningo Dagobah:

I see them both fall and shout out to the other people in the room that we are under attack and that they should take shelter. They all see as me putting my own life at risk as I run out into the compound and call for the president's guards and instruct them to find the terrorists who are threatening the lawful government of our country. The guards appear from the building in complete disarray, they don't know what has happened or what they should do. I take command of the situation and tell them to secure the area against further attack and to report back to me when they have done so. I have assumed a command of the situation which is the precursor to assuming command of the country. I have established my alibi and I have moved so much closer to being president, so much closer to owning the country and promoting New Light. The end of my quest is so close I can almost taste it!

To keep up appearances I run to the aid of the president and be as surprised as my accompanying audience that he has been shot to death. I tell the captain of the guard to accompany me as I run around the outside of the building to the breakfast terrace. When we reach the terrace, I am surprised, I do not see what I expect to see. The Arab is there, as I expected, and he lies dead on the floor, still sitting in the chair but horizontally. The president is nowhere to be seen; his chair lies on its back on a sun seat cover.

The captain of the guard looks around, puzzled. "Where is the president?"

I look around but other than the dead Arab and the president's overturned chair there is nothing to indicate where his body is, I can only assume that one of his servants has dragged his body inside the chambers. I only have evidence of half of my plan working, there is more to find out.

Dangajabido:

My first instinct after the shootings is to cut and run but Kofi calms me down and tells me not to panic. After recovering from my prone position on the trestle table and dismounting the rifle from its tripod, I watch in fascination through the rifle's scope as guards swarm like disorientated worker ants outside the president's chambers. There is no purpose to what they are doing and leadership is absent until Cousin Benningo appears on the scene and gives orders to the panicking guards.

I am aware of a curious calm now that the deed is done and I feel a great surge of omnipotent power. I could do this for a living; the laser-guided bullets assured faultless accuracy and my remoteness from the scene of the crime is protection against discovery. The only two people who are aware of what I have done, my cousin and Kofi, are themselves implicated. It is also in their interests to keep my involvement confidential.

Cousin Benningo will become the new president – he always gets what he wants – and I will become a senior member in his cabinet but now, instead of being minister of technology I think I will be better suited by being head of internal security in which position I can execute those who annoy my cousin the president. My dreaming is interrupted by Kofi who has packed the dismantled rifle and tripod into a duffle bag which he slings over his shoulder. We leave the building together; I turn to go to Benningo's apartment so that he can thank me in person. Kofi walks away with the duffle bag back towards Government House. When I am head of internal security I will appoint Kofi as my assistant, I will need a man with no moral compass.

Benningo Dagobah:

The president's chambers are quiet as a mausoleum but unlike a mausoleum they are completely empty, not a body in sight. I am beginning to get an uneasy feeling; something is wrong. I hear a noise outside, the sound of scuffling and dragging and muffled voices; going back outside I see three guards picking up furniture and tidying up the mess left by the shootings. The body of the Arab is nowhere to be seen, it too has been taken away.

"What are you men doing? You are ruining a crime scene, destroying evidence." The admonished guards look at me in fear and say nothing. "Which of you gave orders to disturb the scene?" I shout at them not because I have any reason to do so but my unease grows with the realisation that I am not in control of the situation of which I am the architect.

They look at me dumbfounded, shuffling from foot to foot.

The voice that responds sends a chill through my bones. "I gave the orders, and what brings you here?" The voice is that of Jacob Wellbeing; he is far from dead.

"Mr President." I curse myself for stammering and sounding unsure of myself. "I am here to come to your rescue; I feared you had been shot. I have sent guards to rout out the shooter and bring him to justice." I realise that I am babbling and stop myself from digging a hole from which I cannot escape.

"Interesting," is all he says.

My senses are screaming out to ask what happened to the Arab but I resist and leave him to tell me what he wants to, when he is ready.

"How did you learn of this incident?" His question is mild but I detect something more behind it than the simple words.

"I saw what happened when I was with the rest of the cabinet in the side room across the compound; I saw you and the Arab were shot and I rushed to your aid." I realise immediately that I have made an error by not asking him how he survived, it is what he would expect of me and I hastily add, "It is good to see you have survived this attempt on your life. You may rest assured that I will leave no stone unturned until we find the assassin and bring him to justice." I think I have made good my error because he does not pursue the matter further.

"Your protégé saved me by pushing me out of the way but he paid a price for doing so and I am indebted to his memory." The old fool looks sad. His words are confirmation that my plan is half complete. Fifty percent success is better than none at all. One down and one to go and this time there will be no interfering Arab to come to his rescue.

Jacob Wellbeing:

Dagobah falters momentarily when he hears my voice; in that moment he confirms without question that it is he who orchestrated the attempt on my life. From his vantage point in the government chambers he had seen me crashing to the ground and had assumed me to be dead. It falls to me now to establish beyond all doubt that it is he who has been plotting against me. No doubt he thinks he is safe from discovery because he has a watertight alibi for the time of the attempted assassination but that is just cosmetic. He will have got somebody else to pull the trigger.

I give him an opportunity to establish his innocence which he fails to take. The sniper shots were too distant to be heard and he could not have known that we were being shot at, but his initial assumption that he feared I had been shot tells me that he had foreknowledge of what was supposed to happen. His assertion that he came to preserve the crime scene, when there was no opportunity for him to know that such a crime had been committed, is a further nail in his coffin.

"Tell me, Dagobah, what did you see? What were the events that you observed leading up to the attempt on my life and the shooting of Simon L'Etranger?"

"I saw very little, I just happened to glance out of the window and I saw sudden movement on the terrace. I didn't realise you had been fired on until much later." He changes his story slightly to distance himself from any perceived involvement, and in doing so unwittingly digs the hole deeper.

"Interesting," I give him an inscrutable look. "You were inside Government House; how did you know that shots had been fired? It puzzles me."

"That is simple, I heard the shots and I looked towards you in time to see you fall." He appears puzzled by my question.

"You were inside the building with doors and windows closed yet you heard gunshots which I could not hear even though I was in direct line with the shots and I was in the open. How can that be so?"

The reason for my line of questioning suddenly dawns on him and he sees that his story is losing credibility. His explanation is unconvincing.

"I know this because I heard the guards talking about it when I rushed to be by your side."

"Another interesting response; to my certain knowledge the guards did not know what had taken place until I told them after the event. You communicated with the guards after the event but before I told them what had happened, so it cannot be they from whom you learned that a sniper was involved." I leave my observation in the air with the thought that he could further undermine his own position.

"It was all happening so fast and it is difficult for me to remember exactly the sequence of events. Perhaps I learned of this from hearing it from another source, I was so worried for your safety that I am confused as to what exactly happened."

Once more I use a silence to invite him to say things off the cuff that will help incriminate him.

"At least one good thing came out of this." His worried expression softens as he attempts to change the unsafe direction in which our discussion is leading him. "Simon L'Etranger did not survive the attempt and I have no doubt that his actions in saving you were purely reflexive, prompted more by the heat of the moment than his concern for your welfare. He was no friend of yours; one of the things I must report to you following my recent visit to Benejado is that he was building up a rebel organisation that would have you murdered. In fact, it was they who undoubtedly are responsible for this failed attempt on your life."

"You are saying to me that his people are responsible for the attempt on my life and that they shot their own leader after he saved me. Does that make any kind of sense to you?"

Once more his facial expression shows indecision and doubt and he stumbles over an explanation which he is no doubt formulating on the move. "These people are crude and inefficient." He pauses while he articulates the next thing to say. "They have no hard and fast plans of action; unlike us they do not think ahead, they are incapable of logical planning." He pulls up short on the explanation as he realises he is now doing what he accuses them of. His words and his expressions fizzle out and he looks at me in mute appeal.

I refuse to let him off the hook. "I am not happy with your reasoning and I am wondering if it is a good idea to give you a higher position in government or even to allow you to continue in your present capacity."

"Mr President, your mind has been poisoned by L'Etranger. He is your enemy and I am your friend and supporter, not the other way around. I must remind you that he was responsible for the wholesale slaughter of the council in Nkando. It was he who was building up Arab resistance against you and he who has vowed to see you executed. One good thing that came out of today is the execution of L'Etranger; he is no longer a problem to you. You can rest assured that I am the right man to follow in your honoured footsteps."

Benningo Dagobah:

My triumph is turning to ashes. Not only has the president survived the attempt on his life but his quizzing of me is taking a turn which I do not like. He is talking about L'Etranger as if he were blameless in all of this. I take the opportunity to underline that he is accused of doing dreadful things which, as he is dead, he cannot refute.

The president continues to look at me with suspicion and distrust and what I expected to be a great step forward has turned into many steps backwards. I must come up with something to redress that situation. That or I must complete the job and have him executed; maybe I will do it – personally.

I try one more time. "Your welfare is my priority, Mr President. The person who was the greatest threat to you has been eliminated. What remains now is to find those who have tried to kill you and have them executed. Once we have done that you will be safe." It came to me in a flash; if I throw suspicion on the Arabs and he goes for it I can kill two birds with one stone, it will remove any threat towards me and it will allow me to rid my city and then the country of the despicable foreigners who are sucking the life out of our economy. A double kill, two birds with one stone.

He does not show that he appreciates the expression of my desire to ensure that his welfare is secured. If anything, he looks more sceptical and I am beginning to sense that this old fool is not such an old fool after all. Tripping me up because my story had not been thought through comes as a shock to me; his grasp of the complex situation is rapid and accurate. Time for him to go, he is now a serious threat.

Jacob Wellbeing:

Simon L'Etranger was right in thinking that Dagobah is out for my blood. I am now completely sure that the time has come for me to take care of Dagobah and his evil religion once and for all time. Luring him back into my den is not at all difficult but there are several things I need to set up first. I have two big surprises for him, not including that I have discovered his plot against me. It gives me great pleasure to be able to expose a plot against my presidency and to deal with it as I have had to do several times in the past when individuals decided to challenge me. They, like Dagobah, had assumed that my 'old timer' laid-back approach to the administration of the country was something they could take advantage of. Those before Dagobah paid the full price for their treachery and the countryside is littered with unmarked resting places which give testimony to my dedication to the cause.

The few things I had to do are accomplished simply in a matter of two days. The scene is set and all the players are assembled by the time Dagobah makes his appearance. As far as he is concerned he and I are the only two involved in this discussion. The other players in my deception are out of sight and have been fully primed about their part in this charade.

Dagobah enters my chambers looking unsure of the reason for our meeting but he obviously anticipates trouble. I derive great satisfaction in playing on the fear he is displaying simply by looking questionably at him and saying nothing.

"You asked to see me, Mr President." His voice quivers uncertainly.

I continue looking at him coldly and I see that my unsmiling face deepens his trepidation. "Yes, I asked to see you to discuss some troubling issues which have come to light." My face is purposely fixed and wooden.

"If there is anything I can do to assist you, all you need to do is ask." His eyes are opened wide and his pupils are dilated; his look and his words do not match.

I offer him no comfort. "It is my belief that you have been deceiving me and that you are not the friend you claim to be."

"That is not so, Mr President; I am your faithful servant and always will be."

"How can that be when you were the architect of an attempt on my life?"

His eyes widen even more. "That is not true." He suddenly becomes more assertive. "Your mind has been poisoned by the Arab L'Etranger and now it is not possible to interrogate him there is no defence I can mount to disprove his lies."

"Tell me again of the evil things he has done."

He looks slightly relieved at being given another

chance to defend himself against somebody who is not here to defend himself. "In addition to those things I have already revealed to you, I can tell you that he has been bribing members of your government to support your overthrow and I can name names. The things I have already indicated to you include bribing his way into government circles, slaughtering the innocent council members in Nkando, and of course plotting your assassination by shooting. It is only by the will of the God of New Light – which I lead for the salvation of our people – that you were spared and he was not." He warms to the situation by embellishing his previous accusations.

He deludes himself.

I continue to press my case. "It may interest you to know that during your absence in Benejado I took the Jetstream to Nkando and I made a very interesting discovery. The events you described as taking place were at odds with what I was told during my visit."

"Whatever you were told is not true, there were no witnesses to the massacre except L'Etranger the perpetrator, myself, and Kofi my chief guard. Both he and I were the only witnesses so I am at a loss to know who has told you differently and where their information comes from."

"I have a few little surprises for you that might help to explain. Are you ready?"

Benningo Dagobah:

When the president asks me 'are you ready?' I have an uncomfortable feeling in my bowels.

"Please come forward and inform Mr Dagobah of a few interesting facts." He shouts towards the door to a darkened anteroom into which I cannot see.

"Of course, Mr President. I will be happy to do so."

I am unable to see the owner of that voice but it is chillingly familiar; it is the voice of Simon L'Etranger but it cannot be, he is dead. My uncomfortable feeling is turning to one of dread. He walks into the room and stands legs akimbo looking at me.

"Good day, Excellency. I will be interested to hear what you have to say about the massacre at Nkando, especially the part you attribute to me."

I feel numb; I cannot believe that my carefully laid plans have gone so wrong. The president and L'Etranger have survived the attempts on their lives unscathed. Fortunately, there is no proof that I was in any way involved in what has happened in respect of either the massacre or the shooting. Providing I keep strong there is nothing that they can prove. I decide that attack is the best form of defence.

"Once more, Mr President, your perspective on all of this is being manipulated by this… this, foreigner. He has committed mass murder in Nkando and he has staged being shot simply to back up his story. He believes that he can discredit my truthful account of events by these means to give his lies credibility. Do not be intimidated by this charlatan."

"His version of the massacre is very different from yours."

"Of course it is, but you must ask yourself whose version you trust most; that of one of your trusted government ministers or that of a devious self-serving foreign criminal."

"Put like that, there is only one answer." He smiles a distant smile at me.

I feel a glimmer of hope; he is rethinking his opinion of L'Etranger, perhaps. I must strike while the iron is hot and not give him a chance to change his mind again. "I think it will be appropriate for me to take care of this Arab, he has been nothing but trouble since he arrived. At first I thought he was a friend but over a short time it has become obvious that it is his wish to destabilise our country by, for instance, massacring tribesmen and attempting to put the blame on me and even you so that our people will revolt against us."

"Perhaps so." He pauses thoughtfully. "But there are other issues which need to be addressed before we make that move."

He has agreed with my proposals and it is my intention to take the Arab back to Benejado where I can put him in prison together with Abu Haider and deal with him as I see fit. The tables have turned in my favour.

"The issues to be addressed that I just referred to, include a report from this man." He beckons to a second person that I cannot see who is in the adjacent room.

For a moment I do not recognise the person who enters but then it dawns on me; it is not possible but the man standing before me is the head man from Nkando – the man I had had executed. Here he stands glaring at me and he is very much alive. Now I am beginning to feel panic; this is the third person I thought to be dead but whom, together with the other two stands before me. My imagination goes into overdrive and I think frantically of a way out of this mess. An adrenalin-fuelled idea comes to me that can still save me.

"Thank goodness you are safe, I thought this man," I point to L'Etranger, "had you executed. How did you escape from the fate he had in store for you?" I take a hasty look at the president but I am unable to tell from his expression whether he has fallen for my ruse.

"Not only did I survive but all of my council men also survived."

"I saw you all shot and I saw you all fall into the trash pit. How can you all have survived?" I am now seriously worried. I saw them shot, I saw them fall, I observed them inert amongst the refuse. They were dead, I was sure they were dead, but it is obviously not so. How could they escape their fate?

"That can be explained by a third person." Once more the president beckons towards the anteroom and from the shadow within steps Kofi. I discover to my discomfort that the blank malevolent physiognomy he presented to my enemies to scare them had – when the tables were reversed – the same frightening effect on me.

"Mr Kofi," the president beckons him closer, "would you care to tell us what happened in Nkando?"

I need to go into full defence mode, if Kofi spills the beans I am done for. I make a pre-emptive strike. "Now that I recollect the situation more clearly I remember that the act of massacre was perpetrated by Kofi at the instigation of the Arab, they are in this together. No doubt they intended to share the spoils of their crime by commandeering the mineral rights in Nkando. They are obviously in this together." Despite the danger I am proud of my ability to conjure up a plausible story at the drop of a hat.

"Interesting." The president's voice is dripping with sarcasm. "If it is as you now say, they are working together, why are the members of Nkando council still alive? Why would they pretend to kill them?"

"I have no way of knowing what they hatch in their twisted and devious minds, perhaps they are trying to set you against me with their lies." This is another theme I think I can exploit given half an opportunity. "Yes, that's it; they intend to promote discord between us so that they can take over our country without opposition from its two greatest sons. Obviously, the head man is part of the conspiracy to mislead you and target me." I am definitely on a roll now; this is a story I can build on to my own advantage. Everything is not lost.

"There is the issue of the attempt on my life and that of Monsieur L'Etranger." Wellbeing's voice is icy and calm.

"I have already explained that, I saw what happened. I saw L'Etranger push you out of the way so that you would be grateful to him and not realise his evil intent, and I saw him fall so that the shot which was supposed to have been meant for him went harmlessly over his head. You were set up, Mr President, in much the same way as I was." I feel a surge of relief; I have now explained all the events and the finger of suspicion is pointing not at me but at L'Etranger and Kofi.

"And yet." The president gives me another lazy humourless smile. "There is a last person who has an interesting tale to tell. For the last time, he beckons somebody from the darkened anteroom.

One more thing for me to overcome and I am free and clear.

Of all the people who might have made an appearance I did not expect it to be him. Blinking in the brighter light in the chambers, Dangajabido stumbles into the room. He looks terrified and dishevelled.

He shades his eyes against the harsh light and looks at me with dread. "I am sorry, Cousin." He looks as if he is about to cry. "They made me give information, I feared for my life." He bows his head.

The president continues in a deadpan voice. "Your cousin Dangajabido Metula seems to be unable to tell his story so I will fill in for him. He was told to take up residence in a building some distance from my compound but in its sight. He was furnished with a sniper rifle and tutored in its use and he was instructed to execute me and Simon L'Etranger, and the person who gave those instructions is *you*." He emphasises the last word and his eyes which had been dull are suddenly shining.

I have fallen into the trap set by the wily old fox. He has trumped all my explanations. There is the faintest of a glimmer of salvation available to me but it is the last throw of the dice. "Once more, Mr President, you are being duped by these interlopers. It is not I who am a threat to you but they who wish you harm." My argument sounds weak even to me.

The president's voice is calm. "Let me summarise the case as I see it. We have heard testimony from the head man of Nkando, Simon L'Etranger, Kofi, and your cousin Dangajabido. Their version of events is at odds with yours. Your proposition is that they were the perpetrators of all the foul deeds and you are the victim of an orchestrated conspiracy by them. You have no corroborating witnesses to the events you describe being carried out by them. Their versions have an air of credibility about them; they corroborate as they overlap. It has become a matter of their collective word against your unsubstantiated singular account. My view is quite straightforward; on balance, I believe the four people who have undoubtedly been manipulated by you. It is not my intention to have you tried for your crimes, you are a member of my government and it is not my intention to allow you to voice your views in an open court. I am therefore your judge and jury and I find you guilty of all the things you have denied."

Simon Hunter:

I watch the emotions flitting across Dagobah's face. They have gone from the beginnings of a reprieve to knowing that his time is up and he has lost everything he has been striving for. With movements faster than I would have thought possible for one of his build, he pulls a handgun from his hidden belt clip and points it at me. The muzzle wavers but at this range he cannot possibly miss. His sudden movement takes us all by surprise and none of us can react to his threat without exacerbating the situation and its consequences. I recognise the pistol as a NLG

Surekill and I reach into my robe to make use of the kill button which will render the it inoperative but it is not around my neck, I had not considered the possibility of having to use it. If I were in *binary zero* mode I would have been beating myself to death for nor carrying the kill button and for not carrying a weapon, but as my *binary one* alter ego I am able to put aside recriminations and consider the situation coldly.

The tableau is frozen, including Dagobah. He is in a position of authority being the only one with a weapon drawn which is tempered by a position of weakness – he is acting alone and it is now him against everybody else. We are all at relatively close quarters and he is obviously aware the he might be able to shoot one of us and maybe even two, but he could not cope with the third fourth or fifth of us and if he were to take that option he would be torn limb from limb by at least two of the remaining antagonists. The indecision is etched deeply into his features.

Benningo Dagobah:

This is a terrible situation but at least I have my weapon drawn and the only other person who is armed is Kofi, whom up until now I had trusted as a confidante but it is now obvious that he is aligned with the president and therefore an enemy. He is armed but not with a pistol; he has an assault rifle which is leaning up against a wooden table in the centre of the room. The rifle is far from ideal at close quarters and it is out of immediate reach. If he goes for it I will shoot him – he is the most dangerous of my adversaries.

I weigh up my options quickly and my first move is to tell them all to back away from the centre of the room and turn their backs to me. This serves two purposes, it moves Kofi away from his firearm and with their backs to me the very act of turning to face me will give me enough time to take out two, maybe even three but still not enough. If I do have to end up shooting them I will take Kofi first followed by L'Etranger because he is the next most active. The president and the head man are both old and slow so they will not be a threat and cousin Dangajabido is a wimp who will crumble if I even look at him.

Within seconds I am in command of the situation once more and I marvel at my ability to overcome all odds even though I am outnumbered five to one; I am confident that I am invincible and can overcome whatever odds are pitted against me. I must make my escape in such a way that I cannot be followed and I will return to Benejado City where my police and army will protect me. Getting away will not be too difficult, I will simply commandeer the Jetstream and its crew and have them fly me back to the city. It will take days for any form of military unit to travel to the city and I will by then be ready to repel boarders. I am tempted to shoot the old fool of a president but if I do the panic that it might instil in the others may give them the courage to rush me and that would be catastrophic; I will bide my time.

My cunning has defeated them and will continue to do so. The chamber has only one door. The door is very old and the wood from which it is constructed is as hard as iron; the door lock has fixed into it a great iron key which I know works because the president often locks it for privacy. I usher my captives against the back wall of the chamber and collect Kofi's rifle. Once they are facing away from me I retreat to the door and tear the telephone off the wall mounting and dash it against the floor before exiting and locking the door behind me. I take the key as a delaying ploy; I am free and they are imprisoned.

Jubil:

Nataly and I are at a loose end. There is nothing for us to do and all the people who can give us instructions are at a pow-wow in the president's chambers. We are both beginning to feel homesick; this country is godforsaken and I can't imagine why anybody would want to live in such an awful place. We decide to stay inside the Jetstream and enjoy the benefits of air conditioning. There are no local television channels so we resort to satellite broadcasts from Nematasulu; they are entertaining but do nothing to alleviate the home sickness we feel, if anything it makes us feel worse.

Our tranquillity is shattered by the rocking of the fuselage as somebody climbs aboard. I jump up, ready to repel boarders, only to discover that the boarder is Dagobah and he looks dishevelled, red-faced and out of breath.

"We need to take off immediately and go to Benejado City as fast as you can. There is a crisis I must attend to without delay." He says this between taking in gulps of air.

"Yes sir; I will get clearance from the president and we will be on our way without further delay."

"I said I'm in a hurry. I authorise this flight, now get on with it immediately." He looks wild and his eyes are rolling.

"But what if the president needs to fly somewhere? I will get his permission very quickly." My suspicions deepen as he continues to look panicked.

"Did I not make myself clear? We need to take off immediately and fly to Benejado now! The president and all others in authority are indisposed in the president's chambers and must not be disturbed. Take off now or face imprisonment for you and the girl." He points to Nataly.

I still make no move to start the engines and with a look of pure hatred he takes a side arm from its belt clip and points it at Nataly. "Do it now or the girl dies slowly; do I make myself clear now?"

He has made himself very clear and I have no choice but to follow his orders. I take the pilot's seat and run through the pre-flight checks with Nataly. He shows impatience as I go slowly through the checks but this is a part of the protocol which I will not rush. He looks out of the flight deck window as though expecting other passengers but seeing none, he turns back to me.

"Take off now or the girl dies, the choice is simple. Fly or I will kill her and then you." He is cold and emotionless and I am convinced that he is mad enough to do as he threatens, "I want radio silence; switch it off and leave it off."

I follow his order and reluctantly initiate the fuel injectors to start up the engines. There is no engine noise from the compressed sodium drive, just the swishing as the contra-rotating blades build speed. The airframe lifts on its suspension and the inert variometer shows that buoyancy is equal to the weight of the Jetstream. We are but are balanced, the weight being balanced by the up-thrust of the rotors. I increase the revolutions and we lift easily into the air, steady as a rock. We pirouette until we face north and I ease the rotors to tilt drive and we ascend and begin to move forward at the same time. No matter how many times I take off in the Jetstream I am always impressed by the steady vibration-free ride as we move gracefully and quietly forward.

I enjoy the flying experience but I feel trepidation about what we are flying into. Something about Dagobah is even more creepy. I am flying us into the unknown, at gunpoint.

Simon Hunter:

Cursing at myself for not having the kill button with me serves no purpose, I must work with what I've got to get us out of the chambers. The old hardwood door is several inches thick and even if we had a firearm it would not have power enough to blow it open. The room has no windows and by virtue of the thickness of the walls and the door it is soundproof. Shouting will do nothing for us.

I make a quick inventory of the room and find nothing that will help us to escape. We must work with what we've got. We could wait until the president is missed and rely on his guard to use initiative and call a locksmith but time is of the essence and I must be inventive. Looking around once more, I conclude that there is only one possibility that may be faster than waiting for the guard.

Crossing the room to where the telephone had been smashed, I pick up the pieces to see if jury rigging it is possible. Discarding the plastic carcass, I am left with a broken handset and a host of separated wires. The others watch me eagerly as I begin to reassemble the wires and components. The wires are of different colours so re-joining them, colour to colour, requires no great skill; the skill is in stripping the snapped wires of their insulation, re-joining them and insulating them so that they don't short out. The wires are thin and my first attempts at stripping off the outer insulation with my teeth is unsuccessful; either the insulation just stretches but does not break or I bite through the insulation and the wires completely.

The president goes to a small writing desk and produces a cheap old-fashioned letter opener which I am about to reject as being too blunt when I notice that the flat rectangular handle has a penknife blade inset. I bare the ends of all the wires and insulate them with clear adhesive tape which the president ferrets out from his writing desk. After forty-five minutes of assembly and trial and error I get a dialling tone. After that, it is quite simple and the president telephones his guard post and a flustered locksmith is summoned to release us.

By the time we are free of the chambers almost an hour has passed and the guards tell us that the Jetstream has taken off and has gone they know not where. Dagobah has departed and we must divine where he has gone and what he intends to do. I do not lose sight of the fact that he is my primary concern; the discomfort of the president and any others is of no importance – my focus is on bringing down Dagobah.

Benningo Dagobah:

The flight to Benejado City is without setbacks. I feel euphoria at the success of my quick thinking. Time is now on my side; it will take the president days, if not weeks to assemble a force big enough to launch an attack on my city, which seems to be his logical next step. As far as they are concerned I could have taken the Jetstream to any of the neighbouring countries and beyond which is what they in their short-sightedness would do, but I have no such inhibited thought. My little deception to bring down the president has suffered a setback but the advantage to me now is that I no longer have to be subtle and secretive. I can come out into the open and fight in my own inimitable way – something about which I feel infinitely comfortable.

I arrive back at Benejado and set my military personnel to work digging trenches and building redoubts around the city so that when the time comes we can defend our position and with our superior weaponry, thanks to Simon L'Etranger, we will be able to defeat the puny army of the president. They will be far from home and their supply lines will be stretched to breaking point. During my term with the government in Golas City I took the opportunity to talk to the senior officers in the military and learned, by telling them that it is my intention to help them be more efficient, all about their training and tactics. They will be no match for me, my military people are kept on their toes by my constantly challenging them. I keep them in line and they do as they are told. If not, they suffer the consequences. The president is weak and his officers who follow his lead are therefore weak.

Simon Hunter:

Dagobah could have gone anywhere but my bet is he has returned to Benejado. His one driving force is the rigid control of New Light and that is more difficult to achieve if he is outside the city. Only when he has fully re-established the absolute control of his organisation in Benejado might he promote it from outside the Golacian borders. Finding out if he is in Benejado is not difficult, the president has his own people who can furnish that information. To be sure of what he is doing I need to observe his preparations first-hand.

A discussion with the president tells me that his attempt to speak to his people on the ground in Benejado is not possible because telephone communications in the city have been disabled. I tell the president that I intend to take the 4WD on the long and comparatively slow journey across the plains to Du Djado province, stopping shy of the city to approach it on foot. Under cover of darkness I will reconnoitre any defences that may have been put in place and will advise the president of their disposition so that he can consider a plan of attack.

I persuade the president to marshal his forces and commandeer whatever vehicles he can to make the long, slow journey and to equip the army with enough food, water, and ammunition to sustain them during what could be a sustained battle. At first he resists and wants to mount an immediate attack on Benejado City but I explain to him that it is more productive for him to wait for the arrival of the new military equipment I will order, which gives him weapon superiority. It takes me a week to set this up and when it is done I make the journey in the 4WD and time it so that I arrive in the dead of night.

I hike the last two miles on foot having parked the 4WD in a stand of palms and covered it with windfall palm fronds. The stand is in the middle of sandy open scrub land in a position which does not attract visitors because it is virtually waterless and remote. After half an hour of yomping I am in amongst the scattered crumbling buildings of the outskirts of Benejado City. Apart from the cicadas and the occasional sound of a night foraging animal, all is silent. The landscape is bathed in the eerie light of a half moon and a remarkable number of bright stars. I make use of the dark shadows cast by the moon glow and flit from building to building, peering out from the covering pools of darkness to see my way to the next obscuring deep shadow.

There is nothing to be seen of any defences between the sparsely populated scattering of buildings, most of which are defunct commercial enterprises and all of which are in poor repair. The closer I move towards the centre of the city, the closer together the buildings become and on the outskirts of the citadel there are groups of buildings joined together in terraces with gated gaps in between the blocks to allow roads through. It is in this ring of properties that I begin to see evidence of fortification work; there are part-constructed trenches some five feet deep with shallow earth redoubts facing away from the centre of the city. These are works in progress, there are trenching tools and timber shoring scattered in confusion in the spaces between the buildings; no guards or other people are present which indicates they do not expect an imminent attack. The trenches are bridged using bulk timbers which will allow vehicles to cross.

This level of work confirms that the city is preparing to defend against attack which underlines my thoughts that Dagobah is in residence. He is prepared to stand and fight in the city which leaves him open to siege. If he had any sense he would have set up camp in one of the neighbouring countries and marshalled his forces to perform lightning raids in random places. He is not a strategist; he does not have the patience to formulate a longer-term plan.

Setting up a ring defence as they are doing may protect those inside the encirclement but it also means they cannot easily break out. All of Dagobah's forces will be grouped together in focal points where they can do the least damage to the enemy and suffer the greatest damage from them. If they decide to try to break out from their ring defence system they will be funnelled through the narrow ways formed by the gaps in the outer ring of buildings where they can be picked off like fish in a barrel. A problem in dealing with incompetence of this kind is that his reactions under any scenario are unpredictable.

My only companions during my survey of the outer city limits are mosquitos and wild dogs. The dogs are free to roam because they have the freedom of the night; they are uneasy about my presence but their unease is secondary to their need to scavenge for food scraps left behind by the humans. The time I spend looking at the defences and weighing up opportunities open to government forces is surreal, it is like working in a ghost town. After three hours or so circling the outside of the citadel I have seen as much as I need. The preparations are inexpert and it will only take a small lightly armed force to contain the entirety of Dagobah's bottled-up fighting forces. The lack of guards tells me that they are not expecting an attack anytime soon.

The president must be told of the lack of preparedness his troops will face but communicating with him is no easy matter; the only means of secure communications is via the Jetstream radio network but I don't know where the Jetstream is. The area I need to search to find it is vast and I can only move around with any freedom at night. My assessment is that, as I had anticipated, time is not of the essence and strategic and tactical planning needs to be undertaken before jumping into a messy military battle. A day of quality planning can reduce the length of a battle by weeks and lead to fewer casualties for both sides. It is far better to capture the opposition soldiers than to kill them; dead bodies provide nothing of value.

Forty-five minutes later I am back at the stand of

palms at which I left the 4WD. I leave the palm fronds covering the vehicle in place and crawl into the vehicle through the back hatch, threading my way between the drums of fuel which will get me back to Golas City. I spend the rest of the night in discomfort, scrunched on the front bench seat; sleep does not come easily and I spend what is left of the night going over strategies that will give me what I want and limit collateral damage. I drift in and out of semi-consciousness until the sun appears above the horizon and begins to dry out the cloying humidity of the African night. Before the light is full I start the long drive which gives me plenty of time to consider my alternatives.

Jacob Wellbeing:

When L'Etranger returns from his reconnoitring task he looks like death warmed up. His face is drawn taut against his cheekbones, his shoulders are slumped, and he seems to have lost several centimetres in height. The only thing which remains alert are his liquid brown eyes. It is almost as if they are the eyes of another, more alert person. He gives me an overview of the preparations being made at the city's inner perimeter.

"Jacob," he uses my familiar name unexpectedly, "we should continue to make careful preparation before we rush into a conflict with Dagobah in Benejado City."

"So, he is there?"

"I did not see him but the activity there tells me at least that he has been there and it is reasonable to assume that if he is not he will be returning in time for what he expects to be a conflict."

"His presence there is supposition on your part?" I raise my eyebrows questioningly.

"No, not supposition. As I have just said, it is beyond doubt that he is or will soon be there because of the work which is going on. The people of Benejado, by a big majority, hate Dagobah and all he stands for; they will only work in his interests if he is there to drive them on. His leadership is based on fear of retribution if they fail to follow his diktats."

"Very well, accepting that your impressions are right, I propose we assemble the whole of my army and occupy the city by sheer force of numbers." Our course of action is simple and clear.

"May I suggest a slightly different approach; one which Dagobah will not be expecting?"

I am not used to my proposals being questioned but I decide it is prudent to listen to his intentions. "You are free to impress me with your knowledge of battle tactics." If he is aware of my intended sarcasm it doesn't show.

"There is nothing impressive about what I propose; it is simply doing logically what the enemy does not expect. Dagobah will expect us to do as you have proposed but what I propose is that we identify their defensive perimeter positions and police each one of them with a small force which can contain their narrow road openings. From what I observed the majority of the defence positions are wide enough to allow up to ten fighting men abreast to exit the town on foot at any one time. A small force of say, fifteen or twenty men at each pinch point, will enable us to prevent them from exiting the city. Twenty men on our side against ten men at a time from theirs will allow us to mow them down with ease." He pauses to give me time to digest his proposal.

"We can stop them getting out but what good is that to us? I want our troops to go in and take the city." My distrust of his tactics must be obvious from my tone of voice.

"The moment our men are inside the perimeter Dagobah's troops will have the upper hand. We will be on the narrow streets and they will be in the buildings where we cannot see them and we will be sitting ducks." His logic is impressive enough but I see a flaw.

"Thanks to you, Dagobah has firearms equal to those of my people. It is my intention to saturate the city with my troops and win by sheer force of numbers."

He sits down and unfolds a plan to me that is not anything I would have considered, and I am stunned by its simplicity.

Simon Hunter:

We are a rag-tag comical army travelling slowly along the single road between Golas City and Benejado. With the president on board the 4WD we lead a convoy of mismatched vehicles including agricultural tractors pulling trailers of soldiers and the trappings of the siege we are about to mount. Our speed is that of the slowest vehicle and we are progressing at little more than a fast walk; at this pace, it will take us many days to complete the journey. The president is along for the ride because he wants to be present when Dagobah is captured. I tried to discourage him because the siege I have in mind will take a month or more to be effective. The strategy is to starve them into submission and have them surrender willingly and with a minimum of bloodshed. I can hurry the process along by cutting off water and power supplies but even that will take more time than the president can take off and still maintain control of the country. But he is his own man and he sets his own agenda.

Benningo Dagobah:

My plans are progressing well and the pressure I applied at the beginning of preparing the defence works seems no longer to be necessary. I had anticipated that the president would follow with a minimum of delay after my escape from his inferior clutches but he is even weaker than I thought. I pulled the communications plug after contacting my informants in Golas City and learned that the president appears to be doing nothing; he is obviously in a blue funk.

I have posted guards from my most loyal divisions at a point twenty kilometres along the road from Benejado to Golas City. When the president's forces reach that point, if they ever do, I will know and will mount my defences accordingly. The fortifications are now complete and with the weapons provided by L'Etranger will be put to good use to prevent his troops from invading the city. It is my hope that the president himself leads the fight against us which will allow me, after victory, to be his judge, jury, and executioner. All I have to do now is wait and victory will be mine.

It has taken over two weeks for there to be any sighting of the president and his forces; they are in a slow-moving convoy about eighteen kilometres from the city and at their current speed they will probably not be with us for the next four hours which means they will arrive shortly after sunset. This gives me time to ready the defences; the redoubts we have built across all the roads and lanes feeding into and out of the city have been carefully concealed so that they are not immediately visible to the advancing column.

I call together my officers and the platoon leaders and instruct them in the art of war. I have their absolute attention and I tell them to take up position and make sure that they stay low so that they will remain invisible until the last moment when with our superior weapons we will massacre them before they can set foot inside the city. My final instruction to them is to post a lookout a kilometre from our defensive position so that they can make ready for the short, decisive, and victorious battle that will ensue. I see no reason why we should not be totally victorious by mid-morning tomorrow.

Simon Hunter:

As the sun touches the horizon we are in sight of the outskirts of the city. I become aware of movements on the road ahead as we approach the outer buildings of the city; no doubt they have sent out scouts who are scurrying back to warn of our approach. We are not difficult to spot; we have generated a huge plume of dust even travelling at this slow pace and it is a similar if smaller plume which is giving their position away. In my mind's eye, I can see the frantic making ready of their defensive positions; they will be making sure that their trenches have guns, ammunition and fighting men, making themselves ready for a frontal attack under cover of darkness.

I stop the convoy just kilometres away from where I know the defences to be. The convoy stretches behind me into the deepening darkness and silence descends as all the engines are switched off. There is no sign of either defences or men ahead but that does not mean they are not there. We are located on the only main route between Golas City and Benejado, this is the direction of attack they expect and it is my intention to use that as a first warning of our intentions. The convoy behind me remains silent; they have been instructed to stay in their vehicles until they are ordered otherwise.

Reconnoitring the situation, I take point and move forward, alone, to check for signs of activity. Donning night vision goggles which, among other vital things, were delivered to me through Nematasulu, I survey the terrain ahead. I can see the defences across the road between the flanking buildings; the road level is slightly raised and there are wooden poles three metres high on both flanks, the reason for which is not readily obvious. My preliminary foray towards the enemy positions is under cover of darkness and unless they also have night vision, which I have not provided for them, my approach will go unnoticed.

That they do not have such equipment is immediately apparent when my progress forward is unchallenged. The beer bottle I am carrying contains, not beer, but surgical spirit and the top is stopped with cotton wool both of which come from the 4WD first aid kit. I carry the bottle to within ten metres of the now pitch-dark moonless defence line and place it in the middle of the road.

Heading back towards the head of the convoy, I take a sniper's rifle and adjust the telescopic sight for night vision, and look at the lone bottle through it. The infrared reader tells me that the bottle is 386.58 metres away and through the sight I can read the name on the bottle illuminated by the red laser dot. Leaning against the 4WD to steady my aim, I exhale and hold steady before gently squeezing the trigger. I close my aiming eye as soon as I have fired to prevent retinal burn as the bottle of surgical spirit ignites. The echoes of the rifle shot are drowned out by the percussion of the shattered bottle which has been ignited by the incendiary bullet.

The redoubt is suddenly lost to view when the defending troops switch on dazzling spotlights set on the poles at either side of the redoubt. The lights are angled downwards and fifty metres of the foreground is bathed in bright incandescence. My reasons for taking this approach was to see what kind of response it would illicit. I had not expected the lights but at least we now know one of their defensive tactics. The lights were intended to catch the advancing troops and blind them, rendering us vulnerable to slaughter. Dagobah has more savvy than I had anticipated; a salutary thought.

Benningo Dagobah:

We have prevented the success of their first sortie and I was in the front-line trench to observe the success of my tactics. I point out to my soldiers in the redoubt that without my forethought there would have been many casualties; I have frightened them off and protected my troops. Tomorrow in daylight they will make another attempt and the cunning way in which I have set up the defences means that the incoming troops will be forced to use the narrow road which will consolidate them and make them an easy target even for those who are not marksmen. We, in the meantime, will be safe and out of sight in our trenches. I am pleased with the way our military superiority is unfolding.

The stillness of night is broken by the sound of engines starting and shortly after, the sound of those same engines retreating. The war is not yet won but the first battle is chalked up to me without a shot being fired by us and just one by them, ineffectually. I would just love to see the defeat on their faces. I feel somewhat let down; my adrenalin level is high because I expected something more challenging than for them to turn tail and run. I do not confess this to my men; I simply tell them that I had anticipated such an attack and my planned actions have proved to be superior to theirs.

Simon Hunter:

We withdraw from the forward position and move the transport back out of harm's way to an encampment in a circular depression which hides it from the road. While it is still dark I move groups of ten men, on foot, so that they are deployed around the citadel, one to each of the city's defensive redoubt locations. This part of the exercise takes more than three hours and by the time the men are in place the eastern sky is suffused with the rosy light of the approaching dawn. As the sun rises and visibility is clear the groups of armed men are prone in shallow trenches, fanned out around the city's defensive positions three hundred metres distant from them. Our troops are not readily visible; their shallow trenches are hidden under camouflaged ground sheets which provide shade and invisibility for the occupants.

From the perspective of the city defenders we have withdrawn our vehicles out of sight, together with our fighting forces, and we no longer pose a threat. I have instilled into our people the need for stealth; they must not make noise and movement must be kept to a minimum. This is a difficult concept for the invading soldiers whose instincts are telling them to make a full-on attack so that they can use their new weapons. A hasty somewhat rudimentary form of weapons training was given by Karin Pelochev, daughter of the Nuovostani President, and her small team, to ensure that the overeager troops are a danger to the enemy rather than each other.

With our people in place we wait to see the Benejadens' take on the situation. Three hours after sunrise the troops defending the main road between Benejado and Golas leave the safety of their redoubts and make nervous sorties beyond the blank walls of the citadel. They make no attempt to take evasive action and when they see no external activity they talk over each other; as there is no threat visible they bravely shout excited encouragement to each other.

I am in one of the trenches under the stifling shade of a ground sheet which has been covered with loose brush. Using binoculars, I watch the city troops milling about just outside the defence wall. They are clearly relieved that they are not met with the threat of attack from us. Seeing nothing of interest, they slowly return to their redoubts with the swagger of new-found courage; not all their number wear army uniforms, many them are untrained civilians.

Benningo Dagobah:

The new morning is an anti-climax. It seems that the president's army has been frightened off by the searchlights which lit up the no man's land, causing them to lick their wounds and retreat like the rabbits they are. It is unlikely that they will mount an attack in the light of day. It would lead to their immediate defeat.

I visit the main redoubt on the Golas Road and observe at first hand that the government forces have indeed been forced to retreat over the horizon. I congratulate the officers present on following my brilliant strategy to the letter and notice that even the civilians who had been forced into service are showing pride in the part they had played in forming and manning the defences of our glorious city. At the appropriate time I will declare Benejado City to be the true capital of the Golacian Republic and demote Golas City. With the support of not just the military but also the whole Benejaden population, I am further assured of complete success and I am once more making strides towards the presidency.

Once the invaders are thoroughly demoralised I will launch an attack on them and put them to route to consolidate my victory. To do this I must establish the location to which they have withdrawn so that I can direct my troops to underline my authority as a great tactician. I allow four of my senior officers to use one of my official motor vehicles to scour the countryside and locate the position to which they have withdrawn, and advise me of their numbers and equipment capabilities. The vehicle is the best I have available – the front half is a Ford pick-up truck and the rear is Chevrolet cargo platform. Both halves have been blended together with great skill by my own skilled mechanics. This is not as good as the 4WD but that is of no importance to me, as soon as this battle is won the 4WD will be mine to do with as I want. I set them off with implicit instructions and tell them not to fail in their task; I can tell by their demeanour that they recognise that failure is not an option.

Simon Hunter:

There is a flurry of activity at the Golas Road defence point; the central barrier of the redoubt is cleared sideways to allow an odd-looking pick-up truck through. I can see through my binoculars that there are four army officers on board. The single vehicle is no threat to us so I let it through without hindrance; it passes within ten metres of me and disappears along the Golas Road in a cloud of red dust from which the tortured sound of mechanical distress is loud and clear.

The rest of the day passes without incident until a little before sunset the noisy vehicle returns from its mission and causes a stir as it passes through the redoubt which is hastily adjusted to allow it through. As soon as it has passed through, the redoubt is made good and activity ceases. As usual in this part of the world sunset is rapid and within moments of the sun breaching the horizon it is completely swallowed up and rapid darkness comes accompanied by the rising crescendo of cicadas making their buzz of procreation.

As I had arranged with the president, one of the quieter vehicles of our rag-tag fleet arrives to collect me and take me back to camp. I hand the trench over to my replacement for his six-hour overnight half shift. The journey to our encampment is short and the breeze created by our travelling is a welcome relief from the stifling day I had spent under camouflage. The president is waiting for my arrival and he hastens me into his tent which is annexed to the back of the 4WD to take advantage of the air conditioning.

"We had visitors today." Jacob Wellbeing is accusative. "Why did you allow them to escape from the city? Is this not a siege?"

"One vehicle and four men, is that right?"

"Yes but how did they escape?"

"They didn't escape, I allowed them to go."

"What's the difference?" He is very annoyed.

"The difference is they sent out a probe to discover where we are and what we can do and that probe will report back that we have run away and formed a camp and Dagobah will assume that we are on the run and don't know what to do."

"Why is appearing to be weak a good thing?" He is both annoyed and puzzled.

"Because if he thinks we are weak he will relax his guard and that will give us the opportunity to destabilise his position." I can see that he does not understand the plan I have in mind which is good, because if he doesn't understand it neither will Dagobah.

Benningo Dagobah:

My returning officers have not failed me. After a long search, they found the president's encampment a kilometre or so to the east of Golas Road in a depression, which is not visible from the highway. There are hundreds of decrepit old vehicles in the depression in which they hide. There are broken down vehicles in various stages of decomposition around a tented encampment which can probably hold two to three thousand men.

This tells me so much about my enemy. They are ill-equipped and untrained and they have taken up a distant position which prevents them from making a lightening attack without giving me ample notice of their intent. I am feeling more and more comfortable about how I am handling this and my next step is clear. I can deploy my troops around the depression the government forces occupy and pick them off with encircling fire-power. Next I will have done a more detailed reconnoitre of their camp and move my forces into position overnight so that they can dig in and take the enemy with secure ease at sunrise when they will be at their most vulnerable.

This is my final plan and at its completion I shall rid myself of those who have dared to oppose me starting with the president, then L'Etranger, and then cousin Dangajabido followed by Kofi, who has betrayed me, and Abu Haider. The rest of my detractors will be taken care of at leisure when I am installed as president. Those who are not killed will be used as slave labour for the many projects I have in mind after my victory.

Simon Hunter:

Under cover of darkness I approach the defensive positions on foot to establish first-hand how ready they are to defend themselves against us. There are no guards posted at any of the places I visit although each position is manned. Lights are visible and the sound of the troops as they feast and enjoy the company of the local good-time girls is evident and unrestrained. They have no idea that I am within ten metres of their positions and our defensive cabals are just three hundred metres away.

Between the fortified positions, the blank walls of the ring of buildings face outwards and it is one such blank wall that catches my eye. The guard positions at each end of the wall have fallen silent probably because their occupants are in the arms of the girls or Bacchus, courtesy of the local beer. Coiled diagonally over my shoulder I have a thirty-metre length of light climbing rope with a three-pronged grappling hook at one end. I swing the weighted hook in fast circles before launching it to the top of the building wall. My first two attempts fall short; the third attempt is successful and I tug the hook to make sure it is firmly attached. Satisfied, I take a few tentative paces up the wall grasping the rope firmly. Confident that it is safe to do so, I commence the climb.

Thanks to my having swopped my Arab robes for combat pants, walking boots, and a long-sleeved shirt which covers my white arms, my movements as I climb are less restricted. The only part of my Arab uniform I retain is the head cloth which I use to keep the sweat out of my eyes. Once at the top of the wall I sit astride it to regain my breath, laying forward so that I am not silhouetted against the stars in the otherwise dark sky, and when my breathing calms, I survey my situation. I pull up the slack rope and drop it down the inside of the wall. After lowering myself down to the inside I send a running snakelike ripple up the rope to dislodge the hook. I descend to the ground and detach the hook. Most if not all the citizens are asleep, the only signs of humanity I encounter on my way across the city are noises of revelry from a moonshine club in the outskirts of the centre. I reach the House of Smoke and Tranquillity without encountering any people and move silently down the narrow side alley to the door of the al Haider living accommodation.

The door is locked as I expect so I move around to the back of the property into an enclosed courtyard which cannot be seen from the street. In the starlight, I can see the second-storey window of the main bedroom usually occupied by Abu Haider, and although I know Abu Haider is not in residence I am hopeful that the room will be occupied by his son.

My hope turns into reality when after several attempts the small stones I throw at the window elicit a response from within and I see Haider's head poke out of the window. "It is Simon." I hiss to him.

His head disappears from the window and moments later he opens the courtyard door to his home and lets me in. I can see as he lights candles that he is fearful; his eyes are large and dark and troubled. "Simon, why are you here? Your life is in danger. If you are discovered my life will be in danger also."

"I have no wish to put you in danger. I need your help but more importantly your people need your help. We must stop Dagobah from taking absolute control, if he does so the Arab population of Benejado and then the whole country will be in danger of the worst possible kind."

He leads me through to an inner room, the windows of which are high up so that we cannot be seen by anybody from the outside of the property. "I will do what I can to help you providing it does not put my family at any more risk. Already Dagobah's people have been here to search for my father and I have told them that I don't know of his whereabouts. I do not wish to antagonise them any more than I must."

"I respect your honesty, you are truly your father's son and without jeopardising your position I would ask you to give me the name of one of your father's most trusted friends to assist me stop Dagobah."

He chews his bottom lip in thoughtful agitation. "I cannot give you a name but I can ask one of his friends if he is prepared to help you."

"Please do that without delay. What has to be done needs to be accomplished quickly."

Once more he hesitates before answering. "I will contact him tomorrow and see if he is prepared to assist you. He is a man without a family to protect and he is a fierce supporter of my father's ideals."

"Tomorrow might be too late if anything is to be done, it needs to be now, I must see him quickly. Dawn is only two hours away and I need to be gone from this city before daylight. Please do what you can now."

"I will go to his home and see if I can rouse him. Wait here with the lights off and I will do my best to bring him to you."

Haider Al Haider:

It makes me feel like a coward to refuse direct help to Simon but the shame of my cowardice is eclipsed by my need to protect my family. I risk everything by going to see one of my father's close friends whom I know will have the courage to be of assistance. Half-awake, he lets me in and lights candles so that we may see as we speak and he is very soon wide awake when I tell him of my reason for waking him at this unearthly hour. He dresses hastily and we hurry back to my home where Simon awaits us.

"Please do not give me names." Simon holds up his hands to emphasise the point. "It is better that I don't know who you are. How much has Haider told you?"

"That you wish to help our people, that you are a friend of Abu Haider – which I already know. Haider thinks it better that the information comes from you."

"Haider is becoming as wise as his father." He pauses and turns to me. "If you wish to leave us please do so now."

I choose to stay and listen to what he proposes and at the culmination, both I and the un-named one are intrigued by what he proposes. Simon obviously thinks outside the box and the simple thing he proposes is brilliant in its concept.

Simon Hunter:

The reverse journey I take to get back to the citadel walls is accomplished with half an hour to spare before the sun makes its first appearance over the horizon. During my journey back to the wall there are the first signs of early risers as they open windows and light candles. The air is suffused with the aromas of stewing fruit and maize meal. I drop down onto the ground outside the citadel walls and make my way to the outlying scrub land to where I have hidden the battered bicycle which carries me along the Golas Road out to the depression where our invading army is bivouacked.

When I arrive I find Jacob Wellbeing outside his tent enjoying breakfast. The sun has now cleared the horizon and the red and mauve haze which distorts the shape of the sun, heralds yet another hot and cloudless day.

"Your night of work was fruitful?" Jacob looks at me enquiringly.

"I have put in place the tactics we discussed and I

believe we will have success with it."

"You still think we can achieve what we want without starting a full and bloody war?" He gives me a disbelieving look.

"Our argument is not with the people of Benejado, it is with Dagobah. The people of Benejado are your subjects and as their president I believe you will support the tactics which protect them from harm." I say this without believing that it will be his true intention, in the hope that he might rise to the occasion. Looking after his people is an alien concept to him.

Jacob Wellbeing:

This Arab is very strange. He shows compassion to my people that I do not comprehend. The people of my country are there to minister to the needs of their president and his chosen government; their welfare is only important if it enables them to fulfil their obligations to their country, president, and government. If they cannot fulfil these tasks, they are of no value. Our country does not have time for passengers who use up its resources without offering back more than their existence costs.

I have never spent time considering the differences between the Arab population and those born and bred of African stock, but the way L'Etranger acts I believe there are fundamental differences which make the two groups incompatible. I allow the Arabs to be part of our society because of their ability to employ locals and generate income which leads to taxes. After our successful battle against Dagobah I will make sure that local Africans become managers in these Arab companies. The ultimate aim will be to have locals replace the Arabs completely.

Benningo Dagobah:

The stalemate is now four days old and I tire of the situation. The time has come for me to take the next definitive step to bring about an end this one-sided standoff. The president's men seem to be content just to sit over the horizon and do nothing. Life in the citadel goes on and apart from the lack of the usual through traffic everything is the same. The citizens can move about freely within the walls and are doing so totally ignoring what had been perceived be a threat from a government attack.

My planning of the next military action is interrupted by one of my aids coming into my chambers looking distressed. The way he looks warns me that he has bad news and none of my people like giving me bad news.

"Excellency," he says, looking distraught, "there has been a catastrophe. You must come and see for yourself." He urges me out by wind-milling his arms.

"What is the nature of this emergency?" I demand. This is the kind of distraction which makes me angry.

"I don't know the details, I have just been told there is a big problem." His immediate aim is to get me outside of my chambers in the belief that with an audience his treatment by me will be less harsh. I am heartened that one of my senior people should be so afraid of me that he needs the support of others. The slight lift in my mood is of short duration, there is obviously something very wrong.

I am driven to the outer more industrial part of the town centre which is only just inside the citadel walls. We turn into the high walled compound which is the power and water centre which gives life to the city. Gasoline for the transport and electricity generation and to drive the pumps which provide water to my property and other strategic parts of the city are located here. As soon as we drive into the complex I can see the nature of the problem; the open reservoir which holds the city's drinking water is not muddy brown as it normally is before being pumped through the filtration units, but it has a silky blue black hue of turgid liquid.

"What is this? What has happened?" I demand of the driver.

"I don't know, Excellency; I was just asked to bring you here as quickly as possible." His voice quivers. He is the bringer of bad tidings and expects retribution.

"Take me immediately to somebody who does know what's going on." I am driven to the crumbling building which serves as the administration block. When we arrive he rapidly puts the car between himself and me as a form of shield. Storming into the administration block, I demand to see the site manager.

The manager scuttles out to meet me. "Excellency," he quivers. "There has been a catastrophe overnight. We have been sabotaged; somebody has broken in to the compound and opened the gasoline taps of the gasoline storage tanks and has allowed it to run into the fresh water lagoon.

All of the gasoline is lost and the water is completely contaminated, we have no clean drinking water and no gasoline." He cringes before me.

"How could you let this happen?" I scream at him.

"Excellency, there was nothing I could do, it happened overnight when nobody was here. It is an act of terrorism."

"Why were there not guards posted overnight?"

"We had no instructions to do so, Excellency."

"Do you not realise that we are in battle with the dogs of government troops? You don't need to be told to guard these facilities at such a time, you should be intelligent enough to do so without being told."

He hangs his head in terror and shame. I cannot permit this thing to happen without showing that I have zero tolerance of such stupidity. I must demonstrate my resolve in this matter. I take out my side arm and aim it between his eyes, and his look changes from terror to abject horror.

Simon Hunter:

At sunset, we have the shift change from the twelve-hour day shift to the two six-hour night shifts. Returning to camp from his day shift, the Golas Road observer reports that there was in the early morning an incident which caused sounds of panic from within the citadel. My presumption is that they have discovered what we have done to their fuel and water supplies. There is a report of a shot being heard and an unusual amount of activity at the Golas Road defence point which involves a queue of vehicles stretching back into the city. I check with the other observers, the defence points they are watching show no signs of unusual activity.

Knowing that Dagobah is an inexperienced military tactician and knowing that this makes him unpredictable, I try to understand what it is that he intends to do, both logically and illogically. I come up cold. The only way I can think of trying to understand his motivation is to talk to one of his fellow countrymen who might think in the same unstructured way; the candidate I have in mind is Jacob Wellbeing.

"That is quite simple." He looks at me as if I were an errant child. "Something has happened to force him into being an aggressor rather than adopting his intended defensive posture. He has been stung into moving forward and bringing the war to us and clearly he intends to make a frontal attack on us using the Golas Road to get his troops to us. He will throw all his resources into one definitive thrust. It is what I would do myself."

"But that is a suicidal plan. It's a tactic he cannot possibly win; his few against our many in an open field of battle." I find the illogicality of it incomprehensible, but Wellbeing obviously doesn't.

"You think like a foreigner." He talks to me again as if I am a child. "It will be his belief that he can creep up on us under cover of darkness, surround us and decimate our forces with the first sustained salvo of shots which will rain down on sleeping troops. It is what I would do."

"That is complete madness; it is not possible for

him to be successful."

"He will think it entirely possible because he does not know that we anticipate his plan."

I smile inwardly; the president knows his people and the way they think, so well. He uses a thought process that I would never consider. He thinks on a far less sophisticated level than I would adopt.

He continues with his theme. "We have him at our mercy. As soon as his convoy leaves the citadel defence our people will shoot them down like dogs and the victory he seeks will be ours." He is certain in his own mind that the battle will be over before it starts.

"We have a force of only ten men at the Golas Road position."

"This is a good battle plan and it is what we are doing. Our soldiers will pick off theirs one by one because we have defensive positions outside the gate and their fighters have no defence once they leave the redoubts."

"Our plan of action was satisfactory for preventing troop movements by using siege tactics but they will be using motor vehicles which can convey troops out at a faster rate than we can kill them and ultimately they will be able to outflank us. Remember we are a siege force not an attacking force."

The president looks crestfallen. "What you are saying is that we have a bad battle plan. Your bad battle plan."

Jacob Wellbeing:

Recently I have taken to looking at Simon L'Etranger as a useful ally; now I am not so sure. His plan to oust Dagobah and leave me free to run my country unhindered is falling apart around us. His initial idea sounded good, it was to lay siege to Dagobah and his troops and keep them locked up in their city using what is a relatively small force at each of their strong-points where the entrances through the citadel walls are narrow, allowing the defenders to attack through it just ten abreast which can be taken care of by our small teams armed with rapid-fire weapons.

The second thing he proposed was to sabotage the water and oil reserves in the city to shorten the duration of the battle. This also sounded good but is failing because rather than trying to defend their positions against our attack they have decided, because of the sabotage, to move from defence to attack mode. They are concentrating their attack using the Golas Road redoubt but not by deploying men whom we can defeat easily, but to use vehicles and troops which cannot be stopped by our small force. I am seriously revising my view of the capability of this Arab.

A further thing which bothers me is that he believes that Dagobah will be making an error if he tries to surround our camp and to attack us from the rim of the depression in which our encampment sits. My reading of that situation is that if Dagobah's troops have the high ground all around us he will be in command of the battle that will take place. My concern grows!

Simon Hunter:

Using darkness, I increase the number of troops at the Golas Road redoubt up to fifty in five fanned ranks of ten in camouflaged scrape holes. I give orders that if the enemy tries to break out of the city to concentrate fire on the vehicles, specifically the tyres and engine compartments rather than the troops. Some of the soldiers express the wish to take out the troops and so disable their foe. I instruct them to follow my orders to the letter.

I fully realised that the acts of terrorism that Abu Haider had persuaded his men to carry out might promote an abreaction rather than cause panic among Dagobah's people. This is the way it seems to be going; the massing of vehicles at the redoubt is clear evidence of their intent to go on the offensive. I am aware that both Dagobah and the president think along the same lines as far as the tactics of war are concerned. Being able to consult with the president about what he would do gives me a clear idea of how Dagobah thinks.

Using my night vision kit, I can see that the convoy at the redoubt is being prepared to launch an attack. The vehicles are full of troops their firearms are stowed rather than being at the ready. It is clearly their intention to bring their arms to bear once they are in position when they reach the camp site. They are still unaware that our men are in position within sight of the redoubt. I have instructed our fighting men to commence firing only when I fire the opening shot and each of the five ranks have been given a specific target to take care of. There is the sound of engines being fired up and vehicles begin to edge forward with lights switched off. As soon as the first five vehicles are clear of the redoubt I fire an opening shot at the lead vehicle and score a hit on the radiator which brings forward an eruption of steam.

The still of the night is shattered by all our troops opening up with their weapons. Our troops have been positioned so that firing on the first five vehicles emerging does not produce crossfire. After the initial salvo, the first five emerging vehicles are halted and the troops on board pile out onto the road; their firearms are stowed in the vehicles and in their desperation to get away from the withering fire they do not try to retrieve them, instead they run back to the redoubt in complete disarray.

The five abandoned vehicles with their cargo of guns have been disabled and they sit on the road either burning or on the rims of the wheels, the tyres shredded by gunfire. The salvos last less than ten seconds, after which there is silence broken only by the noises of the retreating enemy and the noisy engines of the vehicles waiting to leave the citadel. The road out of the citadel is now completely blocked by the abandoned vehicles, preventing the rest of the convoy from leaving. The remaining engines are switched off and silence descends.

Benningo Dagobah:

Disaster, and all because my military leaders failed to detect the presence of government forces immediately outside the Golas Road redoubt. They have made such basic errors in carrying out my faultless strategy that I cannot allow them to remain in command. When the six officers concerned with this dereliction of duty are assembled before me they rightly show fear. I demand an explanation of why they had not made sure that the road out was secure and that the launching of the convoy could be carried out safely and successfully. They greet my question with complete silence with much shuffling of feet and downcast eyes. I repeat the question.

The most senior of the officers is nudged forward by his companions and he stammers an excuse. "Excellency, we were not given orders to make sure the road out was clear. We were told to assemble the convoy to be ready to leave under cover of darkness, which we did to the letter."

"Did I tell you when you woke up this morning to be sure to wear your uniform?" I answer my own question. "No, I did not… and why did I not? Because, I expect you to wear it as a matter of course, without being told to do so! In the same way, I expect you to make sure that the road ahead is safe and clear without being told to do so. What do you all say to that?" I look at each one of them without compassion and invite them to answer my question.

"Excellency, you have always told us to follow your orders and not to question them. We were not ordered to clear the road and so we did not." This is said by the youngest of the officers who looked more indignant that afraid.

"So," I say to him frostily, "you are saying that your lack of basic judgement is my fault. Do I understand you correctly?" He should heed the warnings of my frosty words but does not.

"No, Excellency, that is not what I mean." His dark skin pales to an ashen colour when he realises the hole he has dug for himself.

I continue. "What you say can have no other meaning and you must suffer the consequences of your folly." I take my side arm from its holster and line it up between the eyes just as I had done to the manager of the fuel and water compound. I feel no compassion for this fool and look hard and long at his fellow officers. There is no way I can condone this insubordination and he and the remaining officers must suffer the same fate.

Simon Hunter:

We have just fought what must be the shortest battle in the history of warfare; the action lasted less than thirty seconds and the enemy were completely routed, and to add to its curiosity factor there are no fatalities. Further convoy activity using the Golas Road is now out of the question, the road is completely blocked by the five disabled vehicles. The troops remain in their foxholes waiting for further orders.

My night vision glasses show that there is some personnel activity at the redoubt but no evidence of a further attack being launched. Giving the situation ten minutes to see if there are any further developments, I wait. Nothing happens until minutes later when the stillness is shattered by a single gunshot from inside the citadel. At first I think they are about to launch an attack but nothing else happens. I observe and wait and fifteen minutes later there are more pistol shots followed by more silence. This silence is long-lived and I take the opportunity to replace the overnight troops with the first day shift before it gets light. The lack of response from Dagobah is an anti-climax and there are mutterings from the troops coming off shift that they had expected and looked forward to action which had not been forthcoming. Dagobah continues to demonstrate his fallibility as a military strategist.

We wait to see what Dagobah will do now that they realise they are securely barricaded in their citadel and cannot be attacked but neither are they able to mount an attack – they are held prisoner in their own fortress. This has now become a war of attrition; their drinking water is contaminated and their food supplies are limited to the dry goods they have stored in warehouses. The lack of fuel means they don't have any electricity and there is no cold storage for the same reason. They can feast on what they have in the freezers for perhaps three or four days after which the perishables will be ruined. My estimate of the siege taking months is downgraded to weeks or even days.

Jacob Wellbeing wants to storm the citadel and impress the country's population with a flourish of death and glory. It takes all my powers to dissuade him from this course of action. I convince him by telling him that he will be seen, after victory, as the saviour of his people against evil, and he has done so without shedding the blood of his fellow countryman. Being a hero appeals to his nature; he realises that it will bring him the stature to dissuade others from trying in the future to adopt the same course as Dagobah.

Benningo Dagobah:

Now that I have taken care of the traitors in my camp I must rebuild my powerbase and reassert my superiority over the president. I can see that the weak government forces have become parasitic and have used the tactics of my invention against me which has produced a stalemate which I will break. There is no sense in engaging in hand-to-hand fighting, the government forces outnumber us by at least two to one; I must use my formidable planning ability to achieve my goals.

First I will test the possibility of leaving the citadel through the other redoubts now that the Golas Road defence is blocked. A dozen men and a platoon leader are dispatched to each of the other defence positions with instructions to break out through the citadel walls to test the resolve of those guarding each of the exits. Within an hour and a half, they are all back reporting that it is not possible for any significant number of our soldiers to leave the confines of the walls because of the intensity of the pinning fire that they encounter.

Leaving during daylight hours is not a practical option so I will do so under cover of darkness. Once I have troops on the outside they can form a cordon around the outside of the government firing positions and we will have them covered front and rear. We can cut them down like the cowards they are with angled crossfire; this will leave us free to move towards their encampment and surround them. Surrounding them and having the advantage of the high ground will mean that there will be no defence they can use to defeat us. They will pay dearly for their folly. There will of course be losses on our side, but such is the lot of fighting men.

Jacob Wellbeing:

Simon L'Etranger has been lucky so far and has been able to avert disasters of his own making but I'm not confident that his luck will continue. I cannot afford to lose this battle and I need to make sure that Dagobah is not only defeated but he must also be vanquished. There is an alternative possibility that is more likely to lead to the success I must have and that is to replace Simon with Kofi. Kofi is a warrior; he doesn't possess any finesse and he is no Einstein but he will have no compunction about dealing decisively with Dagobah and New Light which must also be wiped out.

For an Arab Simon is like no other I know, there is a softness about him which he keeps well-hidden and I think it likely that under pressure he might crumble and lose his resolve. The most recent thing he has done to make me think this is that he has fought a battle with the intention of not inflicting undue injury on our enemy. This is not a move that Kofi will pursue and I intend to prepare him to take over the reins of command before disaster strikes. My thoughts are interrupted by L'Etranger walking into my tent.

"We have done well, Jacob; Dagobah's troops have been defeated without them firing a shot in anger. We have his total armed contingent trapped inside the citadel and they have little clean water and only the fuel that is contained in the tanks of the vehicles. Their access to food is limited and will very soon run out. Once that happens those inside the citadel will revolt against Dagobah and will be ready to negotiate surrender." He looks pleased with what he believes to be the road to victory.

I give away nothing of my thoughts. "Do not underestimate Dagobah. He is a wily fox and he can probably outthink you."

"He has not been successful so far."

"I disagree; you didn't expect him to try to attack us, you thought he would just want to defend his city. You have been lucky so far because his officers are not up to the standard required for such an engagement." I look into his eyes with a complete lack of emotion, challenging him to challenge me.

"Interesting that you should think that!" He gives me a wry smile. "What, in your estimation will be his next move?"

"I don't expect you, a non-military man, to understand the intricacies of Golacian tactics, but it is very clear to me what he will do. He will use his wiles to break out some of his men under cover of darkness and attack our troops where they lie in their fox holes."

"And how do you think he will achieve that? We will be under a full moon tonight and any moves he might make to break out and attack us will not have the cover of darkness to prevent his men from being shot." He gives me a look inviting comment.

"I cannot be sure of the details of his plan but I know him well enough to understand that he will sacrifice his men and overcome any of our moves by sheer weight of numbers. The battlefield will be small in area and our superiority in backup numbers will have no impact through sheer lack of space." I am sure that my words strike fear in his heart; there is no way he can outthink the Golacian mind.

I firmly believe that we should take the initiative and storm all the redoubts with heavy gunfire and overpower them by sheer numbers. Casualties will be heavy but in a war of this kind we have the superiority of numbers. I will locate Kofi and give him the authority to carry out the invasion my way.

Simon Hunter:

My strength in all of this is as was expressed by Sir Michael Westinghouse; he said that the reason I would succeed in the field of operational intelligence is that I have no formal training but that I can use my natural capabilities to do things which are not expected and defeat those who are well trained. I am applying that logic to this current situation; I cannot think in the same way as a Golacian but if one foxy Golacian tells me what he thinks another foxy Golacian will do under given circumstances, I have a fair chance of being able to think my way out of the problem.

After leaving Jacob I ponder on what he says. I would certainly not try the tactic of sacrificing my men to win a battle of this kind which would not necessarily lead to winning the war, and I would not have considered the action that Jacob thinks Dagobah will. Accepting what he says is the starting point for counter moves, I call a meeting of the senior military and outline a plan that I believe will prevent Dagobah from achieving the objectives that Jacob thinks he will attempt. I explain to them what I want done and they all give me looks that tell me they think my proposals are crazy. Nevertheless, I give them direct orders to do as commanded.

Once more the sun hurries below the horizon and following the afterglow the full moon makes its presence felt, and as the sun's afterglow disappears the stars join the moon in bathing the landscape in a soft silvery light with contrasting deep shadows in the folds of the undulating land. It is these dark pools which form the backbone of my tactics for this battle. My strategy is based on Jacob's understanding of Dagobah's probable course of action.

From my position outside of our trenches at the Golas Road position I have a clear view of any movements around the redoubt. I am certain, thinking like Dagobah, that the breakout will come from this location and this is where I have based the majority of our troops. The crippled and abandoned vehicles still litter the area outside the redoubt, looking ghostly in the silvery light. At 3am I detect the first signs of movement in the citadel; there is an accumulation of fighting men waiting inside the walls. They are armed with an assortment of hand guns, rifles, scimitars, and long knives.

They wait in silence. I cannot believe they are simply going to run out through the gates to be cut down by an inevitable fusillade; even Dagobah cannot be that naïve. They continue to wait and it becomes clear that something is about to happen when the men suddenly become still and look out into the silvery half-light expectantly. The next sequence takes me completely by surprise. The stillness is shattered by the start-up of engines but they are not vehicle engines, the tone is wrong; it takes me a minute to recognise the sound of generator engines and with an electrical squeal a large bank of powerful search lights pointed out towards us floods the entire area with viciously bright light which destroys the night vision of our troops and all but blinds me through my night vision equipment.

This is bad; I can see nothing but spangled multi-coloured blotches and that means the same thing is happening to our troops. We are blinded and at the mercy of Dagobah's ruthless troops.

Benningo Dagobah:

When I give the order with a sweep of my arm the search lights are switched on, flooding the land from the redoubt to five hundred metres out. It throws the undulating land into patches of bright light with valleys of darkness in stark contrast. That my plan is working is evident; there is no immediate gunfire from outside which means they are temporarily blinded and will take too long to recover to be able to inflict any damage on us.

Another signal from me and the lights are doused, enabling my men to go around behind their fox hole positions to fire on them from in front and behind without being silhouetted by the lights. They have been completely outfoxed; the sudden bright lights have blinded them so they are unable to see my men to fire on them and now with the lights off my forces have the upper hand and there is nothing they can do to prevent us from clearing the Golas Road entrance.

Simon Hunter:

I am aware that the searchlights have been switched off not because I can see yet, the retinal burn still prevents that, but my eyes are still sensitive enough to tell that the light level has been reduced considerably. The spangling of my vision has stopped but my retinal damage is such that I can see very little. From within the enveloping darkness I hear rapid gunshots and a lot of shouting; with a sinking feeling I realise that our blinded forces are being massacred and there is nothing that I or they can do to prevent it.

Benningo Dagobah:

Just as I think I have won, the things that are happening do not support the thought. After twenty or so of my men leave the redoubt there is sustained gunfire coming from our attackers' positions which is enough to stop the rest of my men from joining their comrades, but my plan is still holding together. I can see in the dim light that my twenty men have circled around behind the dugout positions occupied by the government troops and we now have them caught in a pincer movement. They are at our mercy; there is no escape for them.

Their firing on the redoubt to contain my men enables us, by virtue of muzzle flashes, to pin point their ground locations. The flashes show that there are dugouts in a semicircle around the redoubt which are much further away than I expected. I tell the men who are being pinned down by the incoming firepower to aim at the muzzle flashes and prepare to fire when the detail outside is in position to fire on them from behind. I raise my hand to signal for both those in front of and those behind to open fire simultaneously.

Then something totally unexpected happens.

Simon Hunter:

My instruction before the start of this engagement was for the firing trenches which we occupy to be widened slightly so that a second man could lie alongside the first man but facing away from the citadel. The idea of this was to cover the scenario of encirclement that Jacob Wellbeing had outlined. His supposition was that the first wave of Dagobah's men would be sacrificed as cannon fodder to enable a second wave to get behind our positions and ambush us from the rear. My plan was to have soldiers in the dugouts facing away from the citadel so that they could cover the troops behind the lines while the forward-facing contingent would keep the adversary pinned back at the redoubt.

The lights could have become a game changer except for the plan B which I had left for Jacob to handle. The plan was to position a ring of men two hundred metres beyond our ring of foxholes in case a mass breakout was made and Dagobah's men tried to encircle us, as they did.

When my vision returns to normal I can see that the contingent of Dagobah's men who had managed to encircle our position in the confusion caused by the searchlights. Their intent was to slaughter our troops using crossfire from the citadel wall and their outer ring. They are positioned some thirty metres behind our lines with their hands up, their firearms abandoned on the ground. From where I stand, using my night vision equipment, I can see a lone figure sporting a sniper's rifle which is held across his chest. He is in a dip which hides him from the view of those who are at the redoubt but he is clearly visible to those who have surrendered. He is shouting instructions to the men in Golacian, I can't hear the individual words but I can judge the clear intent of what is being intoned. Dagobah's men look completely dejected and they wait, heads bowed, to hear their fate. To my slight surprise Jacob has done his job well and the lone figure I see is Kofi, who is clearly in his element.

Benningo Dagobah:

When these failures of fighting men get back here, if they ever do, they will face a firing squad. I watch in total frustration as what I had thought to be my finest fighting men surrender to opposition which I cannot even see. They abandon their weapons and hold their hands up in complete surrender. Whatever the force is that has captured them must be more powerful than I would have thought to be available from within the forces of Jacob Wellbeing. I urge my men at the redoubt to break out and engage with the enemy but the moment they try to follow my orders they are met by a barrage of gunfire from two positions, one three hundred metres out and another in the far distance which I had not anticipated.

Another failed mission by my military leaders; they

must be made to pay for their cowardice and that payment must be public as a warning to the other troops and to the civilian population that I will not tolerate failure. I leave my failing troops to do what they can and return to my compound from where I will devise a master plan which will annihilate the government troops and the government itself.

As I leave I am conscious of an air of unrest amongst not only the officers but of the men as well. This is something I will also have to deal with as part of my master plan. When I tell my people to do something I expect them to carry out my orders to the letter or to die trying. Those who follow me without question will become brothers of the New Light; those who question me will suffer the ultimate consequence. As I make my way back I am formulating a plan which is brutal but cannot fail; it will mean great sacrifices being made by my people but it will lead to the salvation of the survivors. My plan is invincible and I will lead it.

Jacob Wellbeing:

I knew instinctively that instructing Kofi to back up the plans of Simon L'Etranger would lead to a good result. I had explained to him that L'Etranger required a fall-back plan should Dagobah's men break out from the citadel and that I had come up with a plan to back him up and that Kofi was qualified to carry out that task.

In his usual way, he had shrugged noncommittally and he had spoken a few words in his creepy hoarse voice. "You must be clear about what you want me to do."

"You must observe what he is doing and make sure that his planning is meticulous and if necessary you must use reinforcements to ensure his success." I have no interest in the detail of the plan. That, I leave to Kofi.

Just before the nightshift guard change and now in the early light of a new day, Kofi is back with me to report on the outcome of the night's exercise.

"I have brought captives – twenty of Dagobah's men."

"Don't tell me about captives, I want you to tell me that last night was successful." I peer at him to be intimidating.

"Last night was successful." His whispered reply is terse.

"And?"

"And nothing; last night was successful. There is nothing more to say." He looks bored with our conversation. "What do you want me to do with the captives?"

"Shoot them!"

"It's a waste of bullets, why don't you question them and see what you can find out about Dagobah's plans? That's what I would do – but you are president, what you do is up to you." He turns away without permission from me and leaves my tent to go out into the energy-sapping heat.

I poke my head outside the tent awning which is still attached to the 4WD and look at the captives. They are huddled together in the back of an old flatbed truck and they look completely defeated. They are not under guard and not shackled; I wonder why they have not tried to escape. Slowly it dawns on me – there is nowhere for them to run; they cannot disappear into the surrounding countryside, there is not another village for eighty kilometres and they would dehydrate before they could reach that sanctuary. Going back to Benejado City is clearly out of the question, were they to do so it is guaranteed that they would face a firing squad; Dagobah is unforgiving.

Maybe Kofi is right; I can interrogate them and find out more about Dagobah's plans but looking at the motley crew in the back of the truck does not give me great hope; there is no obvious officer material on board.

Simon Hunter:

When I get back to the encampment just before noon everything is quiet. In the shade of the few stunted thorn trees in the depression, government soldiers are sleeping or at least relaxing. The day is oppressive; it is one of the typical 100/100 days where the temperature is 100 degrees Fahrenheit and the humidity is 100 percent.

The flaps to the presidential tent are closed and the way it billows shows that the 4WD air conditioning unit is at full blast. As I approach the tent the 4WD's engine bursts into automatic life to top up the batteries which are running the air conditioning. Inside the tent the president is relaxing on a fold-up army cot; his eyes are closed and his breathing is even.

"What can I do for you, Monsieur L'Etranger?" He asks this question seemingly in his sleep; his eyes remain closed.

"Forgive me for interrupting your rest time but I have just returned from the city and I am ready to give you my report." I continue talking to a man who appears to be asleep.

"I am fully cognisant of the events of last night; there is nothing you can tell me that I don't already know."

"What is the source of your information?" I am puzzled that he has a report; as far as I know I am the only person who knows what went on last night and even I have gaps in my knowledge. "What is your understanding of what went on last night?"

Still with his eyes closed he recounts the events smoothly and with absolute assurance. He even fills in some of the blanks for me and makes sense of the hazy events that I had been unable to unravel. He had put an extra fifty men behind the dugouts occupied by our forward troops. It was they who had opened up with the pinning fire that had kept Dagobah's troops at the redoubt and it was the leader of that contingent that I had observed giving orders of surrender to them. Maybe I have underestimated him, what he did saved the operation.

My aim is to disable Dagobah and New Light. I suspect that the president's sole aim is simply to get rid of Dagobah period.

Benningo Dagobah:

I have held a court martial and found eight of my officers guilty of dereliction of duty. In other armies, their crime would be punished by a prison sentence but I need to set an example and my ultimate finding is that they must face a firing squad. The men who are sentenced are devastated and those soldiers in the court who are merely observers look uncomfortable, which is exactly my intention. After this the members of my army will carry out my orders without question. I convene the court martial on the morning after the failure of the overnight attack. The sentencing is immediate and is carried out without delay. This has concentrated the minds of the remaining officers and the new appointees are in no doubt about the price of failure.

How I address the next stage of my strategy is now foremost in my mind and I will use all means at my disposal to achieve my objectives. I need to break out of the citadel, overrun the president's forward troops, travel to the depression and surround the encampment. I have an ingenious plan which they will never suspect but I do not tell my officers of my plan because I don't know how trustworthy they are. What I have in mind is very unconventional in modern warfare terms. The enemy will have no defence against my tactics and assured victory will be mine. This plan, unlike my others is simple and fool proof and needs no special training to accomplish.

Simon Hunter:

My major concern at this juncture is that Dagobah

will react quickly and illogically, without regard for human life. He will sacrifice his own people to aggrandise himself. His only real course of action, it seems to me, is to make a mass breakout irrespective of the casualty level and attack the encampment with as many of his forces that survive the suicidal breakout. In my *binary one* alter ego state this does not greatly distress me but it seems to be the wasteful expenditure of life and I will do whatever it takes to contain the inevitable level of carnage.

Discovering his intentions is paramount if I am to structure a countermeasure and there is only one person I will trust to do that. Me. To achieve this I will need to get into the citadel again and gather as much intelligence as I can in a brief visit. I need to do this alone because as a single entity I will not pose a threat in the same way as a group would. Having entered once by climbing over the citadel wall I see no reason why I should not be able to do the same again with the same success.

Using the route of my previous incursion I scale the wall and find myself in the quiet of the night city, it seems that the laws of the New Light religion do not encourage colourful night-time activities which prevail in other Golacian cities. The town is deserted. Like the rest of the city's citizens, Haider is at home and I arouse him as before.

"Being here is very dangerous for you and for me. If Dagobah's men catch you here we will both end up dead," he hisses to me as he lets me into his home.

"I have no wish to endanger you but I would like

news of your father. Is he well?"

"My father is in a safe place and was well when I spoke with him yesterday. He is safer where he is than we are here."

I can see in the dim light that he is fearful of what my presence might mean for him. "I am glad Abu is well and I will only be with you for a short time because I understand the dangerous situation I put you in by being here. Are you aware of the activities of last night?"

"We have been told that the government troops mounted an attack on the Golas Road access to the city and that our troops fought them off showing extreme bravery," he says without conviction.

"I was there and that is not my interpretation of the situation." I laugh briefly and without humour.

"What you say is no surprise to me but do not tell me what really happened. If I don't know then I cannot be seen to know and I am safe from criticism. I will stick to the official line." There is no humour in his words.

"I understand." I pause and take a deep breath before continuing. "I would like to know if there have been any strange activities since the skirmish last night?"

"I know little, it is in my interest as the son of a proclaimed dissident to keep a low profile but I am told by the few customers who come into the café that Dagobah has ordered his troops and all other citizens to collect together empty wooden barrels and to empty any full barrels of their contents and take them to the water and fuel compound as part of the glorious war effort."

"Do you know what the empty barrels are to be used for?"

"I have no idea and neither do my customers or friends."

The role that empty barrels might play in the war effort is not obvious. I bid Haider farewell and leave him, much to his relief. Making my way to the fuel and water compound I circle the walls to see if there is some way to find out what is going on. At the back of the compound I find a double gate which is padlocked. The gates, much like the doors of the prison, are ill fitting and there are gaps at the hinge and joining positions. The stench coming from the compound is evil but familiar to me it is the smell of raw fuel, a cloying throat-catching smell. In the dim light, I can see a small army of men scooping up the fuel floating on the lagoon and putting it into barrels; they are overseen by armed uniformed troops whose presence is intimidating. The men work in silence which is occasionally broken by threatening words from the guards. There are scores of barrels which have been filled with fuel and hundreds of empty barrels waiting to be filled. Having seen enough I make my way back to where I have stowed my wall-climbing gear, through what is a poorly guarded ghost town.

I am stealthy when approaching the government encampment to see if I can get past our guards without arousing their suspicions. If there are any guards, they are incredibly well hidden so my assumption is that there are none or that they are asleep on duty. Obviously, night fighting is not a normal part of Golacian culture. I decide to turn in rather than waking the president two hours before dawn. The likelihood of being attacked at this hour is remote in the extreme as would be the likelihood of a daylight attack. I will talk with the president in the morning and see if he can unravel the tactic which uses barrels of fuel.

Jacob Wellbeing:

All was quiet last night; there was no activity by Dagobah's troops or ours. I will give Simon L'Etranger a last opportunity to mount an attack before I take over the direction of my troops personally. I discuss the issue with Kofi but he is a man of action rather than a planner. I believe he shares my view about going into action rather than sitting back and waiting to see what happens, although he refuses to discuss it.

L'Etranger reports back to me about his antics last night. He has found out that Dagobah is planning something but he doesn't know what. It involves barrels of fuel, hundreds of them, and he asks me what I think Dagobah has in mind.

"Leave it with me," I tell him. "When I've given it my consideration I'll let you know what I think."

He leaves me and I immediately summon Kofi to see if he can shed any light on Dagobah's intentions. The inevitable response he gives is a non-committal grunt and it is impossible for me to tell whether he has anything to offer.

I try to get comment from him. "Give me your best guess, what do you think his intentions are?"

"He intends to use the fuel for some purpose of war," he replies without emotion.

"That much is obvious." The heavy sarcasm in my voice is lost on him.

"You must fight fire with fire." With that cryptic remark, he walks out of my tent without asking my permission. He is one of the most disrespectful men I have ever met but right now I need him.

As soon as Kofi has gone I summon Simon to my tent and ask him if he has had any further thoughts about Dagobah's intended course of action; he confesses that he has not. I test his capacity for understanding Kofi's cryptic utterance by passing it on as my own. "We must fight fire with fire."

He gives me a very strange, speculative look.

Simon Hunter:

For as long as I have known Jacob Wellbeing, his intentions have been expressed very simply but these words are cryptic. His comment about fighting fire with fire is unusually obtuse. I look at him long and hard to see if he intends to elaborate but he chooses not to.

"How do you propose we respond to what Dagobah proposes to do?" I hope to get some insight into his meaning.

"That is a matter for you to find out and react to." He turns away dismissively.

I take my leave of the tent and go to the one that I am using which, unlike his is not air conditioned. In the hot and humid interior, but at least out of the burning sun, I ponder on what he has said. My thinking goes around in circles as I try to understand the meaning of what he has just said; ultimately I try a different approach. Whether what he has said comes from within him or from another source does not matter. Ultimately I analyse that what he says makes surprisingly good sense. Leaving my stifling tent, I go to the weapons trucks which hold the spare guns and ordnance supplied to me through Nematasulu by Nuovostan. The supplies are contained in five new seven and a half tonne box trucks which are air conditioned to stabilise the explosive items. There are side arms, assault rifles and sniper rifles, all of which are controllable by use of my kill switch. In addition to these there are machine guns and enhanced rocket-propelled grenade launchers (ERPG) which are standard, so not fitted with firing kill mechanisms.

If this situation develops into a fire fight we will certainly have the upper hand although I am reluctant to allow the unmodified weapons out of my sight. The deal I have with the Nuovostanis is that when these unmodified weapons are used in the theatre of war I will report back about their effectiveness and any shortcomings. I am hoping that I will not have to use them in anger because doing so will inevitably mean significant loss of life.

Taking inventory of the weapons clears my mind of its former confusion and leaves room for uncluttered rational thought. This leads me to the only conclusion that makes sense and I berate myself for not understanding the unsophisticated simplicity of Dagobah's thinking. I have been seeking a sophisticated solution to a simple problem and I have overlooked the old maxim that simple thinking leads to a complicated answer and, conversely, complicated thinking leads to a simple answer. I now believe I know what the simple answer is and I set about preparing for a stand-off with minimal casualties. I implement the first part of my defence strategy. The president is beside himself with fury at what I do without consulting him.

Benningo Dagobah:

Night comes and the Golas Road exit is littered with abandoned vehicles from the first skirmish so I line up the vehicles at two adjacent redoubts. Preceding the vehicles at these exit points will be one hundred men, fifty at each location. My plan is for these men to break out of the citadel and inundate the government defensive positions. Our casualty rate will be very heavy; I estimate 90 if not 100 percent of the first waves. I have told these men that they are going to fight a battle where they outnumber the government forces by at least ten to one which means that their victory is assured; I neglect to tell them that they will be totally exposed and the government men will be well dug in and near to being invulnerable. If the forward troops are too stupid to work this out for themselves; they deserve their grisly fate.

The start-up of the vehicles, as soon as it is dark, is coordinated between the two chosen exit redoubts. The noise of the start-up of these mostly ancient vehicles is deafening and will certainly get the attention of the government forces but there is nothing that can be done about that. At my command both columns of men emerge from the redoubts screaming blue murder and firing wildly into the direction of the dugouts. I wait for the crackle of return fire but it never comes.

Simon Hunter:

As far away as we are from the citadel I hear the frantic covering gunfire as Dagobah's people exit to make their way to us. I smile wryly to myself as I picture the confusion on the face of Dagobah when he realises that there is no opposition to his breakout. Halfway through their brief journey to our encampment the laboured sounds of the convoy reaches us on the still night air causing a stir in our camp.

"What is that noise?" The president, looking wild from having just woken, comes bustling out of the comfort of his tent.

"That will be Dagobah's convoy on its way to do battle," I inform him.

"I told you that withdrawing our troops was a bad move and if your plan, whatever it is, heralds our defeat, you will pay dearly for it." His voice is full of panic.

"Let's talk about it after we've defeated them and we can all go home to our families." I do my best to calm him.

"If I had a gun I would shoot you now, you are a traitor you have left us defenceless." He looks around with wide eyes. "Guards, guards, come here and arrest this man." His voice has reached a pitch which would challenge the hearing range of a bat.

"Your guards and all of your troops are deployed

to the perimeter of the encampment and they have full combat orders and they know exactly what to do."

The president looks at me and realisation dawns. "You have a plan." It is a statement rather than a question.

"I have a plan," I assure him with a placating smile.

Benningo Dagobah:

The first surprise of the night is a good one. The government troops have surrendered their positions without any attempt at resistance. Clearly they know that my strategy is superior to theirs and they have deserted rather than face the might of my forces. I urge my driver forward so that I can take point and lead my convoy of brave men to the unopposed victory my planning deserves. Jacob Wellbeing has thrown his lot in with losers and he will pay the penalty on this night.

I can hear the fluttering of the New Light flags which adorn the front of my vehicle, one on each side. The blue background with a white bolt of lightning of the flags will soon replace the meaningless Golas flag and it will fly over Government House soon after dawn when I instruct my people in Golas City to tear down the old one and destroy it. The moment of my triumph approaches and I will savour it with joy.

After our short journey the vehicles, as I had instructed, form a circle, equally spaced around the top of the depression in which the encampment sits. The troops on board pile out of the vehicles and begin unloading the barrels of fuel which they stack along the top of the incline leading down to the bottom of the basin and its tented city. My plan is now clear; even my lowliest troops can see the wisdom of my intentions. They prepare to ignite the rag fuses stuffed into the barrel bung holes in readiness to ignite them and roll them down into the encampment where they will wreak havoc and bring us victory. I hear my men murmuring in appreciation of my fool-proof plan.

Simon Hunter:

My night vision equipment shows quite clearly Dagobah's intention. I can see him standing up on the cargo deck of his ancient Peugeot hybrid pick-up. He has one arm raised, in his hand an assault rifle which at this distance is useless but it gives him an impressive and dramatic silhouette against the star-studded sky.

His arm drops and there is the immediate twinkling of a hundred lights as preparation is made to light the fuses. His final act is to fire a single shot into the sky. The sound of the shot echoes around the depression, turning one shot into many; the cacophony is added to by the jubilant whoops of his men as they scent victory. The lit fuses of the barrels begin a strange hypnotic dance as the barrels spin down all sides of the depression. It is a dance which increases in pace as the barrels gather speed.

President Wellbeing looks nervous. The sound of the first wave of barrels booming down the inclines is punctuated by three crisp shots from my side arm.

This is the signal that our men who are spread around the perimeter of the camp at regular intervals have been waiting for. They are prone and have newly delivered weapons, some on tripods, some nestled into their shoulders. At the sound of my shots they fire at the oncoming barrels. Rifle fire concentrated on the first barrels break them up, which scatters burning fuel, but they fight a losing battle by sheer numbers; the volume of shots required to break up the barrels is too great and barrels begin to get through the defences. Jacob Wellbeing looks at me in horror and I know that if he had a gun he would have used it on me.

Benningo Dagobah:

I have a nasty feeling when they open fire on the barrels and some are destroyed. For a moment, I don't think my tactic is going to work but then, as they are unable to have enough concentrated firing to deal with the influx from all around them, I relax again as more barrels get through the defences. I discover in the blink of an eye that war is fickle; just as I believe I am winning the game changes. I incite my men to speed up the barrel-lighting process to inundate the encampment.

A few barrels get through to the encampment but before they become numerous enough to create a destructive fire storm, the perimeter of the encampment lights up with a circle of flashes which are much different from normal weapons. I realise with dread that they are firing rocket-propelled missiles, not at the descending barrels but at the stockpiled barrels around the top of the rim of the depression. The projectiles are big enough to be seen in flight and produce a powerful explosion which ignites the stockpiled barrels, which in turn explode, throwing burning fuel over the adjacent piles of barrels. Within moments the whole of the rim of the depression forms a halo of fire. After the first explosion, my troops turn tail and run from the flames.

From my command position, I observe the fleeing men, their faces distorted in fear. I shout to those who run past me to stand their ground and act like real men but their fear of the fire and explosions is greater than their fear of me. I have two fully loaded pistols which I fire in the general direction of the fleeing masses. Their forward impetus is slowed as their comrades fall around them. I fire off more shots and command them to hold their ground; they stop and turn to face me. One of the officers brandishes his gun and shouts orders to the men which I cannot hear because of the raging battle behind me. At least one of my officers is loyal and appears to be reinforcing my exhortations and is admonishing his men for their cowardice. There is a lull in the sounds of battle and I hear the words of the rabble as they approach me. They are not listening to my orders; they slaughter the officer trying to defend me. An angry shout from the attacking men chills me and I feel an unaccustomed frisson of fear. They have for the first time in their miserable lives overcome their terror of me.

Simon Hunter:

Jacob is once more a happy man. His whole attitude changes when the troops I deployed around the perimeter of the encampment open up with their enhanced rocket-propelled grenades, ERPGs. We can see the launched grenades travelling as if in slow motion up to the stored barrels of fuel. The troops firing them do not need to be deadly accurate with their aim, the ERPG needs only to land in the proximity to ignite the barrels of gasoline. Once they are ignited they explode and set off a chain reaction with adjacent stockpiles and before long all the barrels are either destroyed or ablaze. The whole of the rim of the depression is on fire.

There is a ringing cheer from our soldiers when they see the carnage they have created and their jubilation is shared by the president who, despite his advanced years, dances an uncoordinated jig outside his tent. The brightness of the ring of fire precludes the use of night vision equipment and I look at the enemy through ordinary binoculars. Dagobah's troops are fleeing from the raging fires which are destroying their vehicles. Defeated, they leave the battle theatre by heading back to the city on foot. I can see a group of men who appear to be fighting among themselves and I am happy that the rout is complete; they are fighting themselves rather than us.

I turn to Jacob Wellbeing, who has stopped dancing. "The solution to this problem was your idea. When you said we should fight fire with fire it took me a while to realise that you had concluded, before me, what their tactics were and you planted the idea in my mind. I congratulate you on your perceptiveness. You are truly a military force to be reckoned with."

Jacob Wellbeing:

Like all good politicians I am happy to accept accolades even when they are not due. Simon Hunter congratulates me on my forward thinking that has led to our overwhelming victory. Why he thinks this is so is beyond me, but accolades are accolades. I simply repeated to him what Kofi had said to me: 'fight fire with fire'. I didn't know then what it meant then but now I do and I am more than happy for L'Etranger to think the idea is mine, but at the same time I wonder how Kofi knew what to do – he is an enigma.

By the time the sun rises above the horizon the surrounding fires are almost out. There are no flames but smoke rises from the glowing embers of the barrels and the destroyed vehicles. Dagobah's troops are gone; all that remains of them is a collection of those unfortunates who had not been quick enough to escape the burning onslaught. I use the binoculars of Simon Hunter to survey the scene of devastation; there is a tall, leaning, lone palm tree silhouetted against the deepening blue of the morning sky and hanging from it is what appears to be a naked inverted body which turns slowly in the wind of passing dust devils created by the increasing heat of the sun. Dagobah has lived up to his reputation and committed the great folly of hanging one of his men as a warning to others, and by so doing has lost the support of his troops, probably forever.

Otherwise the scene is quiet, the smoke of the dying embers is diminishing and the only evidence of what has happened overnight is the shimmering mirages caused by the hot embers as they cool and the lone body gyrating in the eddies as it hangs forlornly from the leaning palm.

Simon Hunter:

I cram twenty armed men into one of the seven and a half tonners which had been used to deliver the armaments that enabled us to win the battle. Approaching the outer walls of the citadel with caution, I send foot scouts ahead to see if there is any threat from the routed army. They return quickly and report that the redoubts are now empty of fighting men and the city, as far as they can tell, is blacked out and deathly quiet. No soldiers and no civilians.

It is still necessary to proceed with caution and I station one armed man on either side of our vehicle standing on the front bumper, six men on top of the box body, one facing forward, one backwards, and two on each long side. Driving slowly, I bounce the vehicle over the redoubts using the bridging planks. We meet no resistance and I continue forwards at walking pace while at the same time being ready to gun the engine should the situation demand. No such situations are presented; we are not challenged by anybody and the streets remain deserted.

Dagobah's compound is empty, as are the adjacent army barracks which are strewn with discarded uniforms and abandoned weapons. I stop and listen; the only sound is that of the breeze sighing over palm thatching. I gather together my troops and pair them up to search the city for any inhabitants. They are instructed to assemble anybody found in the town square where they will be addressed by the president later in the day. Alone, I go to the House of Smoke and Tranquillity in search of Haider. The café itself is deserted. I go around the building to the living quarters; the doors are locked and the shutters are closed. Like everywhere else in the city the building appears to be deserted. I turn to leave and become aware of a small movement behind one of the shutters.

I wait, saying nothing, for the inhabitant to make himself known. I remove my side arm and place it gently on the floor and hold my arms out to the side to indicate that I am here in peace. After a brief time the first small presence is joined by a bigger presence who obviously studies me to see that I do not pose a threat. Both disappear and after a brief pause the courtyard door opens slowly.

"Come in quickly, Simon." Haider's voice is barely more than a whisper.

I walk from the bright sunlight into the dark interior and wait for my vision to settle. When it does, I see Haider and a small boy of probably eight or nine.

"This is my son, Salman." He ruffles the hair of the small boy and keeps him close, protectively. "What is going on? Why are we prisoners in our own home?"

"The city is empty, you are not prisoners. Why do you think you are?"

"We were told by Dagobah's troops to remain in our houses until the battle is over and we will then be dealt with when the victorious troops return. That means we will be imprisoned at best and I do not wish to speculate about the worst that will happen. You being here will put us in great danger. I fear that Dagobah has lost all reason and he has murderous intent. Rumour has it that he has been executing his own troops." He clutches his son once more to protect him from unseen harm.

"Haider, my good friend, do not be afraid. Dagobah has been defeated and all his troops have fled. You are no longer in danger."

"His troops said that they could not be defeated and that Dagobah had a plan which would assure victory. He pressganged us into collecting barrels and filling them with gasoline which they said would give them a formidable weapon." He looks at me with doubt. "Are you sure that you have not been outmanoeuvred and that you have walked into a trap by entering the city?"

"Dagobah has been defeated and his army has been routed. Please believe me when I say that he is no longer a threat to you."

"Do you have him in custody?"

"No we don't, but he can't hide forever."

"If you do not have him in custody I cannot leave my house, he told me and everybody else who was not fighting alongside him to stay at home or to be executed."

Jacob Wellbeing:

Simon L'Etranger has cleared the city of all threats and has attempted to have the people assemble in the main city square. He has suggested that I talk to them and assure them that the situation is under government control. I agree with him that I will do so providing he can assure me that it is totally safe for me to enter the city; it is my intention to tell them, not that the government has the situation under control but, that I have the situation personally under my total control. They will love me for being their saviour.

The city square is full of civilians who look uneasy. There are no army uniforms on display, the soldiers have either changed into mufti or have left the city. There is one thing that bothers me and that is Dagobah has not been apprehended, and his still being at large is an uncomfortable situation. The crowd in the square is surrounded by my armed troops who face alternately inwards and outwards to protect me from harm from either direction. The great gathering is totally quiet in a disturbing and unnatural way.

I stand on a raised dais, facing the crowd; when I address them, the silence becomes absolute. I have no speech prepared and I speak to them off the cuff. There will be no record of what I say, I am a pragmatic politician.

"Friends, you have gone through difficult times and I feel it necessary to protect you from the evils of Benningo Dagobah and the despicable New Light. Dagobah is an outcast and New Light is, from this moment, a banned organisation, and I expect all citizens to sign a paper denouncing the man and his renegade organisation."

Having assured them of my support, I carry on with a speech that is worthy of an election for the post of president, which is unnecessary but it is good for me to practice rallying speeches.

Simon Hunter:

Jacob Wellbeing drones on about how much he has the interests of the citizens of Benejado at heart. As he continues to speak the crowd begins to look as though it believes what he is saying and slowly the belief that they are being freed from the influence of the Dagobah regime takes hold. The atmosphere changes to that of carnival as they continue to relax and the president warms to his boastful claims that he alone is responsible for freeing them from the oppressive yoke that has been their burden for so long.

I feel gentle pressure on my shoulder as I listen to the president and observe the crowd, and I turn to see the smiling face of Abu Haider. He kisses me on both cheeks. "I came as soon as I learned of the news; it is good to be back in my home town. I have missed my family and friends. Tell me what happened, I am excited about the news of freedom."

I give him a précis of the events of the last twenty-four hours without going into too much detail, and as I speak I see him scanning the crowd.

"You are looking for Haider?" I ask him.

"Yes, and my grandson. I believe they are safe but I would like to see with my own eyes."

I nod my head to where Haider stands with his son clutching onto his leg. Haider is wrapped up in the words of the president and has not noticed the arrival of his father. Abu Haider makes his way through the crowd and is seen first by his grandson, who releases his father's leg and runs towards him. Haider looks up and shouts joyfully to his father. The two men stand with little Salman between them, they are lost in the words of hope being spoken by their president.

After a further brief time, I lose interest in the president's words and my mind turns to what is to be done about Dagobah. Jacob Wellbeing has said that Dagobah and his New Light organisation are no more but that does not satisfy me. I need to see irrefutably that there is no way that Dagobah can ever return to power. I want to see him imprisoned or banished from this country to a place where he can do no more harm. While he is a free man he is a threat to civilisation.

The president is driven from the encampment to the city in my 4WD. I have undone the personalisation of the vehicle control system and set it for general use. The president's driver ferries me back to the encampment so that I can gather together all the weapons we used, especially those which do not have the shot kill control system. The soldiers using the ERPGs were so enthusiastic that they used all the grenades so there will be no temptation for them to commandeer the launchers, having no ammunition to fire. I send a detail to collect the launchers and to bring them back to me; I am pleasantly surprised to find that they are all accounted for; they are locked away in one of the box trailers. Completing this task I am aware of a whispering apparition in the sky and I watch as the Jetstream hovers overhead and slowly sinks to the ground in an explosion of red dust.

Jubil and Nataly step down onto the dusty ground. Jubil is unshaven, Nataly is just as she has always been – svelte and with the healthy glow of youth.

"Hear you did a good job, boss." Jubil says as he approaches with his hand outstretched; I shake it firmly.

"We had a little luck along the way." I give him with a lazy smile.

Nataly joins us and she kisses my cheek. The feel of her kiss brings back memories I had suppressed over the past months; she has a softness which I have forgotten about. Standing back, she looks at me uncomfortably, as though she has done something wrong.

"Sorry," I say to her when I realise why my reaction makes her uncomfortable. "It is so long since I have felt the soft skin of a woman that it came as a complete and very pleasant surprise."

She smiles coquettishly at my words and leans forward to give me a kiss on the other cheek and this one lingers a little longer and her skin feels a little softer.

Jubil smiles broadly. "Do you want to fill us in about what happened? I need to write up my pilot's log to keep the record straight. I've done our bit, we got thrown in jail by Dagobah's people and we only just got released."

As I had done for Haider, I gave them a précis.

Having secured the weapons and now having access to the Jetstream, I set about tracking down Dagobah; he is the last remaining fly in the ointment. Knowing where to look is the most difficult part and I don't know where to start. He has had most of the day to put distance between himself and us and he has a pick-up truck which in the fourteen-hour period of his disappearance will give him a range of 400 miles at best. What takes him fourteen hours to travel can be covered by the high-speed Jetstream in fifteen minutes with ease.

The Jetstream rises steadily into the air and heads south in the direction of Golas City. At 400 miles out we turn in a counter-clockwise circle and adjust to six thousand feet elevation which gives us vision of a broad swathe of terrain to our left and right as well as forward. Jubil scans ahead and Nataly and I take the left and right flanks. We see an occasional vehicle on the dusty tracks which pass for roads; descending for closer inspection enables us to see who occupies the vehicles. There are no desirable results.

We complete the circle as the sun sets and disappointingly we have failed to locate the whereabouts of Dagobah. The Jetstream settles on a flat area just outside the perimeter of the encampment and we alight as the last rays of daylight evaporate. Jacob Wellbeing has decided that the air-conditioned tent in the encampment is preferable to the accommodations available in Benejado City. He strolls towards us as we approach the encampment. "For somebody who has just won a great victory you do not look as pleased with yourself as I would expect. You have a problem that I don't know about?"

"You know about the problem I have." I look at him, grim-faced. "Dagobah has escaped and as long as he is at large my mission is incomplete."

"Dagobah is no longer a problem for me." He finds my discomfiture amusing and gives a distant smile.

"You don't understand, I need to know that Dagobah can do no further harm to his people, your country, and the rest of the world. Until that time I will not be able to rest."

"When I say that he will no longer be a problem, I mean just that. He will be buried tomorrow." He leaves the sentence hanging in the air.

"Do you mean you have found him and you're going to execute him?" I feel an overwhelming sense of relief at the thought of him being found but a deep sense of discomfort that he is about to be executed.

"We've found him but we will not be executing him."

"But you have said before that he is guilty of treason and that the penalty for that is execution."

"What you say is true." He gives a rare happy smile. "I must stop leading you on. We have located him; his mutilated corpse is hanging from a palm tree. He received retribution at the hands of his people who rebelled when he started shooting his own soldiers. He suffered the consequences of his own actions; justice has been done. His death was not pretty, as befits the way he led his life. He was given an ancient form of retribution; he was stripped naked, hung upside down and suffered the torture of a hundred cuts. He was then smeared with honey and covered with fire ants. It is difficult to know what actually killed him, whether it was the cuts, his drowning in his own blood, or the painful poison of the fire ants. Whichever it was, he will have endured extreme pain."

I am overcome by a feeling of relief that Dagobah will no longer be a threat. In the end his demise has been engineered by his own people; it is a fate that has applied to many despots in the past. He has reaped his just desserts. My work here is done.

Afterwards

At last I'm on my way back to my Berkshire home, *Riverside Roost,* or more accurately the boathouse apartment which is in the grounds of the *Roost.* I am persona non grata with my family and vacated the comforts of the main family home some time ago.

After all the danger encountered during this project, the last straw which opened the floodgates to hysterical laughter was my appearance. After living so long as an Arab, I and the photograph in my passport bear little resemblance to each other and I fell afoul of the Golacian emigration agency, almost not making my flight from Golas to Tangiers. They thought, because of my wild appearance and uncontrolled hysterical laughter, I was unhinged as well as using somebody else's passport. As ever, in this part of the world a donation to a carefully selected official enabled me to overcome what became an unimportant issue.

Using the bathroom during the flight from Tangiers to London, I understand the confusion I caused in the departure hall of Golas International Airport, a grand name for a private airfield which boasts one short grass runway and a ramshackle corrugated iron shack which doubles up as arrivals, departures, and many other functions. My hair which previously was straight is a cascade of unwashed ringlets reaching down below my shoulders. My skin is now Bedouin brown which makes my teeth florescent white by contrast because I have stopped eating the local berries which discoloured them. To add to the exotic blend, I have now removed my brown contact lenses, revealing my natural bright blues for all to see. I have lost a considerable amount of weight which has turned me from being slender to being skeletal, and my eyes are sunken into dark sockets. My cheek skin is tight across the now prominent bone structure.

What I see shocks even me.

I have to use a similar 'donations' ploy to get by the migration officials in Tangiers. Before departing for London, I telephone what was my London office before I was obliged to relinquish control of my company by the UK government – but that's another story. I arranged for the necessary wheels to be oiled to allow the changed me through UK customs. I may not own the company anymore but I am still a major shareholder and, unofficially, I have their ear. Off the record, I still advise the company on matters of commercial strategy, which is my true forte.

To my surprise, when I arrive at Heathrow I am greeted by Tefawa Belawa, my MI6 colleague, who enables me to bypass all the usual formalities. He meets me airside and escorts me through diplomatic channels, bypassing passport and customs. My scant luggage and I are reunited courtesy of a courier who has already collected them and has them stowed in the boot of a vehicle with diplomatic plates. It was my intention to go straight to the *Roost* from the airport but I am to be denied that intention by being whisked to MI6 headquarters, some thirty-five miles further down the river from *Riverside Roost*, by the courier/chauffeur who had collected my luggage.

Tefawa Belawa sits in the back with me.

"It's a good thing I know you well, Simon. You look unbelievably different. I doubt whether even your family will recognise you. Your old company contacted Sir Michael and asked for some assistance in getting you through customs and he thought it best that I smooth the way for you. By the looks of you it's a good thing he did, there is no way you would have got through customs screening looking the way you do. They would probably have clapped you in irons."

"I'm grateful to you for helping with this but I'm not so happy about being rushed to MI6. Above everything else I need sleep and proper food."

"Sir Michael just wants a quick debrief, he's been worried. There was a time when he thought you had gone over to the dark side. What you've done is fantastic and he wants to talk to you while it's still fresh in your mind."

"What does he know about what I've done? Most of it was under cover and it has been kept under wraps. It's a private thing between Jacob Wellbeing and me and I suspect he wants to know all about it, so he's sent you to soften me up and spill the beans?"

"Not so. You won't have to tell him anything from a cold start; he will make statements to you and you can confirm or deny his statements as you wish." He gives me his big friendly smile.

"Are you going to be in on the debriefing?"

"In the beginning probably but I'm sure there are things that he will want to discuss with you in private."

Traffic is light and our journey to the MI6 headquarters, *River House*, is brief. Driving through unmarked, bulletproof, outer roller shutter doors, we wait in the airlock for them to close before the inner doors open; we are now in the car park known affectionately by the fraternity as the lower bowels. A lift whisks us up from the car park to the executive floor and I find myself in the familiar surroundings leading to Sir Michael's office. We are shown in by his personal assistant who occupies the anteroom to his suite. She announces us on an intercom before showing us into the inner sanctum.

"The wanderer returns." Sir Michael smiles a greeting but behind the bonhomie I can detect the shock he experiences when he sees my appearance. To him I must look like the wild man of Borneo. "Please, both of you be seated." He recovers his composure with seamless diplomatic ease.

"As good as it is to see you, Michael, I would like to keep this brief. I need to get back home and relax." My *binary zero* more gentle personality is in the ascendancy once more and I endeavour to extend to him the politeness he offers me – but it is something of a strain.

"I will be brief and I apologise for dragging you here straight from the airport but there are a number of things I would like from you while they are still fresh in your mind."

"I presume the things you want to know are to do with New Light and Dagobah, in which case I must remind you that this has been a private venture for me and as such I owe you nothing to do with them or him." I say this firmly but without the edge of discourtesy.

"You are my guest here and I do not wish to disagree with you, but you will recall that I provided vital up-front intelligence to you before your departure, so in my opinion you at least owe me a little in return." He waits expectantly for my response.

Sir Michael Westinghouse:

Simon looks like a complete wreck. He is thin to the point of being emaciated and his eyes are dull. His usually well styled hair is a tangled mess and beneath the sun-damaged skin I detect the yellowing of jaundice which indicates dietary problems. When I tell him that I think he owes me something for the early assistance I gave him he pauses before answering but ultimately relents.

"I suppose I owe you something in return but I don't see why any of this would be important to you. I did what I set out to do and destroyed the vicious dreams of a despot. End of story."

"Not the end of the story but maybe the end of a chapter." I say this gently so as not to appear to criticise his success by completing what he set out to do. "You have taken Dagobah and New Light out of the equation but there is another dragon that has been awoken in the process. He is not a matter for you to pursue – that is for us – but just as we helped you at the beginning of your task I would ask you to return the favour by helping us at the beginning of ours." I can see that he is struggling to understand my intentions.

"Very well." He gives up the struggle. "How can I

help, if I can at all?"

"More so than you think; let me tell you what I know about your part in the downfall of Dagobah and New Light. You threw your hat in the ring with a café owner by the name of Abu Haider whom you used as a fifth columnist. You inveigled your way into the New Light organisation by subterfuge. To get their attention you provided them with arms which at first caused me a great deal of grief. It was only much later that it became clear that you were being even more underhand with Dagobah than he was with you."

Some forty-five minutes later I conclude my detailed monologue. I can see from the look of surprise that Simon was not aware that I know so much about the detail of his activities, and as he thought more on it his look of surprise turned to one of discomfort.

Before continuing with the debrief I indicated to Tefawa, N11, that he should leave Simon and I to our discussion. He rises from his chair and approaches my desk, making sure that his body is blocking Simon's view of me. He leans forwards with one knuckle on my desk and removes a small package from his breast pocket. He gives me the packet and whispers to me so softly that Simon cannot hear what he is saying.

He turns away from me and addresses Simon directly. "It was good to see you again, my friend; maybe our paths will cross again but should they not, I wish you luck in the dangerous and difficult path you have chosen to follow. I must return to duty and my next assignment." He leaves the room before Simon can respond.

Simon looks at the closed door and turns enquiringly to me. "What just happened?" N11's parting words had obviously made no sense to him.

"Later perhaps; first I must complete my understanding of what happened after your task in Golas." I did so and as I continue Simon becomes more and more unsettled. When I finish, he looks at me with deep suspicion and I can see that his willingness to co-operate is beginning to slip away.

"Michael, I don't know what the hell you think you're doing but as I said at the beginning of this conversation, this has been a private venture and it has nothing to do with the UK government and nothing to do with you. If you know so much about what went on over there why do you need to debrief me?"

"I know a lot about what you did with Dagobah and New Light for reasons which may soon become clear to you, but I do not have the same insight into the thoughts of Jacob Wellbeing, and he is potentially a greater threat now than Dagobah ever could have been and that is partly down to you."

"Oh, really!" His voice is heavy with sarcasm. "Your difficulty with Wellbeing is my fault? I gave you credit for more intelligence than that." Despite being desperately tired the set of his jaw is truculent.

"Not quite what I said." I keep my voice calm and level. "To expand on my meaning, you have inadvertently given Jacob Wellbeing access to what was previously dormant. By giving him a taste for air travel and international finance you have awoken the beast in him; he has acquired a taste for territorial gain. He has access to foreign money and he intends to arm his troops with modern weapons. Not the modified weapons that you provided for Dagobah, but the real McCoy supplied by the Eastern Federation. Deadly destructive weapons, in many cases more advanced than those readily available to us."

Simon Hunter:

My tired overloaded mind is reeling from the succession of revelations. Not only has he given me chapter and verse about the two attempts on my life and my incarceration, but he has laid bare all the details about what I have done to achieve the completion of my tasks. These were things which I thought only I knew. It is stunning that he knows so much and his knowledge is so accurate, I cannot fault what he says. This underlines why he is head of MI6.

"I need rest," I tell him dully. "There is too much for me to take in in my present state. We should continue this discussion later, after I have rested."

"You are quite right, Simon, and I apologise for taking so long at a time which is inappropriate." He offers me a small brown envelope which I had glimpsed when Tefawa Belawa gave to him just before leaving. "Open this in the car which I have arranged to take you to *Riverside Roost*; I think it might answer some of your unasked questions."

The comfortable limousine speeds me effortlessly along the M4 out of London, past Heathrow and over the Berkshire border. I struggle to stay awake in the warmth and comfort of my executive cocoon. I remember, as we turn off the M4 onto the A404M, the small envelope that Tefawa Belawa had given with some subterfuge to Michael which was passed on to me. I can feel two hard and rounded objects through the manila of the envelope; one is flat and about the size of an overcoat button, the second is larger and slightly elongated. I stick my finger under the gummed flap and tear it open, spilling the two objects onto the palm of my hand. In the soft interior light, I see the glint of what looks at first glance to be a gold coin; one side is flat and smooth and the other when I turn it over has a design which is so familiar to me; it is a forehead talisman bearing a soaring eagle impression. The second item is a kill switch, the mate to which is ever present on a chain around my neck. I have an epiphany; everything becomes clear. I now know how Sir Michael has so much knowledge about what went on between Dagobah and me and I also know the identity of my guardian angel, the one who saved my life by killing Oginga just as Oginga tried to kill me. He later released us from prison and engineered our escape from the army and police who were searching for us in the souk. It is suddenly all so clear and oh so simple. I should have known but until now it has been a mystery – but no longer. The many unexplained things which happened in Golas are easily made clear by the intervention of one person to whom I am, and always will be, grateful – Tefawa Belawa.

The limousine deposits me and my meagre luggage at *Riverside Roost*, or to be more accurate at the boathouse apartment. The driver takes pity on my obvious fatigue and carries my luggage to the boathouse entrance before disappearing off into the dark of night. The main house is in darkness, meaning that either everybody is asleep or they are not home. I hadn't told Isabella that I was returning home because it is not my way of doing things. So often, as has happened this time, my intended return home has been delayed unexpectedly – much to her disappointment; this time by my meeting with Sir Michel. The time of my homecoming is unpredictable and therefore unheralded – and for all I know, unwelcome.

The boathouse is stale and neglected, not having been entered by anybody since my departure what seems like a lifetime ago but is just six months. Nevertheless, it's good to be here again. Tomorrow I will contact Isabella and the children if they're home from university, but tonight is for deep, deep sleep. Before turning in I have a long, hot shower which takes some of the kinks out of my shoulders, neck and back. Comparatively relaxed, I slide into bed and fall immediately asleep; the sleep is deep and dreamless and I awaken as the sun rises feeling refreshed and trouble free, a state I haven't felt for a long time.

Later in the morning, after another shower I look out of the back window of the boathouse which gives me a complete view of the back of *Riverside Roost.* There is no sign of life and the windows look dead and empty. I cook brunch in my small but very efficient kitchen which is ideal for a single person, maybe even two. Having no bread or fresh vegetables brunch consists of scrambled powdered egg with canned butterbeans, canned tomatoes, and canned asparagus, an unholy mixture which tastes divine after the unfamiliar things I have been eating over the past months.

I hear a sound of footsteps from the path which leads from the house to the boathouse, and my hopes that it would be one of my family are dashed when I see Sir Michael approaching along the connecting path. My feelings of peace are shattered by his unheralded appearance and much as I like and respect him for who he is and what he does, he is not welcome here in his official capacity and only marginally so as a friend. I anticipate his arrival by going down the narrow stairway to the entrance to the apartment.

"Good morning Simon." His voice is hesitant; he does not know how I am going to react to his uninvited appearance.

"Good morning Sir Michael." I am formal and give him no indication of my feelings.

Sir Michael Westinghouse:

I am greeted by a stony look from Simon, which does not surprise me. I have intruded into his private domain. He barely acknowledges my greeting but stands back, allowing me in.

"I need to talk to you away from any possible surveillance," I say to him as I lead the way up the steep stairs.

"I don't like the sound of that, Sir Michael," he says to my back as I lead the way upstairs to the apartment. "As far as I am aware I owe MI6 nothing further and we have no formal or informal agreements which require me to say anything to you which requires secrecy."

We enter his small reception room and sit in armchairs which face each other across a small table.

"You at least owe me a hearing considering what we have done to assist you during your Golas adventure – don't you think?"

He considers my words carefully before responding. "I have already said that I am grateful for the intelligence I was given before I travelled to Golas and I am of course more than grateful for Tefawa Belawa saving my life, but that does not change the fact that we have no formal connections."

"As for the intelligence we passed on to you before your departure to Golas, it is the least we could do for a private citizen who has been of valuable service to the department in the past. The information imparted was not classified so there is no foul there. Regarding the other matter of somebody saving your life, I am delighted that it occurred but that cannot be a member of my team. It would be entirely inappropriate for one of my staff to commit murder to save the life of a privateer who is not strictly speaking a UK citizen. For me to condone such an action would totally compromise my position as head of MI6. I trust that you will never indicate to anybody that you believe such a thing to be true. Were such a thought to reach the ears of the authorities I would lose my job."

He smiles at my hyperbole and says tongue in cheek. "Obviously, I was mistaken about the events which occurred but should you ever discover who that person was I ask you to convey my thanks to him – or her."

"Be assured that if I discover who he or she, might be, I will pass your message on, but I believe that whoever it is, and for whatever reason they had, your gratitude will be considered rhetorical." His immediate grasp of the intent of my statement is gratifying and it simply reinforces that we have a level of understanding vital to the relationship I have in mind.

Simon Hunter:

Sir Michael has alluded to the assistance I was given by my 'unknown helper' but there is another issue which concerns me greatly and that I find it difficult to put into words because it relates to the part played by 'Kofi' in the slaughter of the villagers in Nkando village.

"There is the matter of the apparent massacre of a group of villagers. I saw them executed by the owner of the medallion and I learned later that they had not actually been executed, and it gave me sleepless nights even as my *binary one* alter ego until I learned that they were not executed at all. Can you shed any light on that?"

"I don't know the answer to that question but I can hazard a guess at what would have happened had I been in the shoes of the executioner and I was trying to impress on somebody my willingness to be ruthless." He pauses for a moment as if to gather his thoughts. "What I would have done is make sure that my words couldn't be heard by anybody but them as I address the villagers and tell them that they will be safe and unharmed if they do exactly as I say. I would tell them that my gun is loaded with blanks or is at least disabled in some way and that I will appear to shoot them individually in the back on the count of three and that they must fall forward into the pit and lie absolutely still." He smiles at me benevolently. "You understand of course that this is a hypothetical situation of which I have no knowledge, I am just using my imagination. It is one of what could be many different scenarios."

I feel relief knowing that my friend Kofi/Tefawa Belawa has his integrity intact. I can also now understand one of the minor things which puzzled me when I was taken and put into prison. The puzzling matter of why I was anaesthetised instead of being bludgeoned is that it was Kofi who abducted me and wanted to do so causing me the least injury. I surmise that he did so to hide me away from Dagobah whom I now know at this point was after my blood. Another mystery solved. A further mystery is also explained; after Jacob Wellbeing and I were shot at I was surprised that there were no bullet holes in the wall behind where we were sitting. I am puzzled no more; it is reasonable to assume that Tefawa was with Dangajabido at the time of the shooting and that he had the kill switch which now sits, along with the gold medallion, on the table in front of me.

The more I work with Sir Michael the more I realise that he is a person of impeccable integrity doing a job which requires him, on occasion, to subvert his natural inclination to being open and truthful. He is always ultimately on my side although it is not always apparent; I am beginning to suspect that he, like me, is a binary man but unlike me he fights against it. Tefawa Belawa has his own form of integrity which allows him to annihilate another human being if he detects imminent mortal danger to the things he holds dear. Hence the shooting of Oginga.

"Michael." I call him by his familiar name in private, a move of which he appears to approve. "The work I am now doing is gratifying but the depth of satisfaction changes from project to project. In the case of the battle against Dagobah and New Light I have strayed into unethical behaviour which is alien to me."

"Don't beat yourself up about it; what you are achieving far outweighs the infringements you are forced to make. Dagobah deserved to be brought to heel; he was a malignant growth on the body of humanity."

"What I did led to his death." I am painfully aware that my voice is weighed down by the overwhelming recrimination my *binary zero* persona makes me feel.

"What you did saved the lives of hundreds, perhaps even thousands of people whom you will never meet and will never know what you have done for them."

"That doesn't help the essential me. I have been instrumental in causing his death, not by my own hand but by influencing the hands that finally killed him."

Sir Michael Westinghouse:

The more humane side of Simon is pained by what he has done in much the same way as his other diametrically opposed side is gratified by the result he has achieved. He is able to separate the two sides of his character but has not yet come to terms with the overlap from his warmer *binary zero* personality with that of colder *binary one* element. It is this separation which I would like see developed so that he can continue be an unofficial asset to MI6. He will, if all goes well, become my secret weapon.

"I have a proposal to make to you," I continue when I have his attention. "You choose to intervene in situations where the authorities fail to uphold the interests of the defenceless."

"In a nutshell, yes." He looks at me with suspicion.

"You were able to hit the ground running at the start of your Golas project because we gave you intelligence which enabled you to do so."

"What you say is true." His look of suspicion deepens. "And you are now about to try to get me to agree to something that you know I will resist?"

"Not at all; what I am about to propose to you will be of significant help to you in the execution of your personally selected future projects. I will, unofficially, furnish you with up-front first-hand intelligence so that, as you did this time, you can hit the ground running. In return you will agree to be debriefed by me – completely off the record."

Simon Hunter:

As ever with Michael, what appears simple has a complex background which only he comprehends; I get up-front intelligence for future projects but inevitably there will be a *quid pro quo.*

"And what do I give you in return for this intelligence?"

"It is as I have said. You will permit me to debrief you after the event."

"When do you need an answer from me?" I am inclined to accept the offer because the inside intelligence he offers will be invaluable.

"What's to think about? You are getting everything for nothing." He grins at me like the wily old fox he is.

"As you so often say, if it sounds too good to be true then it probably is." I am giving myself time to think by stating the blindingly obvious.

"You're too suspicious; the offer is made in good faith and I am putting at your disposal some of the best intelligence gatherers in the world. For you, it's win-win."

I can see that Simon is hooked and I have no doubt that he will ultimately acquiesce. I feel badly about duping him but only a little, it's still a very good deal for him. I hope he will never discover that he is being manipulated.

The other purpose of the visit is to confirm our discussion of yesterday concerning Jacob Wellbeing and his probable intentions. I pursue this objective for the next hour. As my interrogation nears an end I receive a telephone call from the security detail that Simon is not aware of, who has been looking after Isabella Hunter in Simon's absence. She is on her way back from London and has reached the local train station from where she will take a taxi to *Riverside Roost.*

"Isabella will be here shortly so I will leave you to it. If she sees you looking like this she won't recognise you and you may get a face full of pepper spray."

"Thanks for the advice; I've looked like this for so long now that it feels quite normal but I don't want to scare her – or get a face full of pepper spray."

I hurry from the boathouse and drive away before Isabella appears. I don't want to get caught up in the conversation that they are likely to be having. I'm only just in time, our cars pass on River Road just a few hundred metres from the *Roost*, I am thankful for the tinted glass which hides me from her view.

Isabella Hunter:

The three-day conference felt more like a month. It's all part of running my growing publishing business but that doesn't mean I like doing it. I'm so glad to be nearing the tranquillity of home. It's a nice day and a cup of tea on the upper terrace will help repair the rigours of the last three days. The taxi pulls to one side on a narrow section of River Road to allow a sleek black limousine to pass.

The house has been shut up for three hot days and the interior has a slightly flat, stale smell which will be remedied in minutes when I switch the air conditioning on. As I do so there is a familiar soft sigh as the cool air seeps gently out from the grills.

I make tea and carry it on a tray out to the upper terrace. While I wait for the tea to draw I press the button set into the stem of the parasol in the middle of the table which deploys its large rectangular canopy, throwing the table into welcome shade. I feel a great peace descend over me which I pander to by taking a soft, plump cushion from its storage bin and placing it onto a recliner chair. Sitting down, I recline the chair and relax into its soft comfort.

I feel about *Riverside Roost* in a way I feel about no other inanimate thing. If it is possible for a human being to love a building, then that's what my feeling is – love. The only sounds I can hear are those coming from the passing river craft and the *slap, slap* of the wake from their passing as it reaches the sloping river bank and the jetty piling. I look up at the clear blue sky and watch a jetliner leaving vapour trails which are caught up by jet stream winds, causing them to evaporate. I wonder as I squint at the bright sky what exotic place it is going to.

My moment of tranquillity is shattered by my mobile phone ringing; I admonish myself for not having left it on charge back in the kitchen.

Simon Hunter:

I watch Isabella trying to locate he telephone in one of the many pockets of her characteristically voluminous shoulder bag. She answers my call without noting it is from me.

"You look so peaceful and in harmony with your surroundings, it is a shame to disturb you." She gives a sharp intake of breath as she recognises my voice.

"Simon!" She looks around for me. "Where are you?"

"I'm in the boathouse and the reason I'm calling you first is to make sure that when you see me you won't dial 999."

"What does that mean?"

"I look kind of different from when you last saw me and I don't want to frighten you."

"You're already frightening me, what's this all about?"

"I've been away on a project and I haven't had a chance to sort myself out. If you're up for it, I would like to talk to you."

"Okay, I'll get another teacup and we can share tea."

"No need to get up, I'll bring a cup with me."

Isabella Hunter:

I watch the door to the boathouse apartment as it opens and Simon steps out. He is too far away for me to see him in detail but it looks as though he still has all his limbs, which brings to me instant relief. There is something strange about the way he walks as he approaches the terrace; he is less upright than usual and his limbs seem to be slightly out of sync with the rest of his body movements.

As he draws closer I can see why he felt it necessary for me to be warned about his appearance. His clothes are hanging from his emaciated body and his face is gaunt. His hair is a shock to me – it is usually straight well coiffured but now is in stringy ringlets which fall untidily below shoulder level, and looks as though it is infested. The greatest shock as he comes closer still is the sun damage to his skin; his usually bronzed smooth complexion has been ravaged by overexposure, and the distinguished crow's feet laughter lines around his eyes are now deep, burnt grooves. His eye sockets are sunken. He looks like the walking dead.

"I didn't want to scare you," he says with a shrug and a shy smile which gives a glimpse of the Simon that I knew so well, so long ago it seems. The man who stands before me now looks like a broken shadow of his former self.

I try to hide it but the shock of his appearance makes me flinch reflexively. The Simon I met, knew, and married is no longer there. When we met, we looked the same age and as I grew older he still retained his youth in a way which I found infuriating. I discovered only after we had divorced that the secret of his prolonged youth was the influence of the living regime on his Colony homeland, and a special diet which he follows still. Until I went to the Colony and sampled the life and technology there I had no knowledge of his upbringing and the influence it had on his personality and appearance.

As I see him now he has not only caught up to me in age appearance but he has surpassed me. This frail ageing man who stands before me hands a cup to me and sits on the opposite side of the table under the shade of the parasol. In a moment of macabre humour, it occurs to me that his using the parasol is like shutting the barn door after the horse has bolted.

Simon Hunter:

"I'm sorry if the way I look distresses you but I have been through a bit of a difficult time and I will need a little time to recover. That's why I'm here but I don't want to be a burden to you." I nod towards the empty cup and raise my eyebrows by way of making a request. She smiles like a Madonna and gently pours a cup of tea for me. Her smile is in recognition of a family tradition which says that a teapot should only be poured from by one person, not passed around like a bottle of port. The superstition is that shared pouring leads to a falling out between the pourers.

"Your appearance does distress me; you look terrible. In fact, you look as though you need a doctor and I mean right now." She is concerned for my welfare.

"That can wait," I tell her. "I need a few days just to get myself into a position to accept medical advice that I can act on."

"Are you going to tell me what you have been doing or is it another one of your secrets?" A familiar bitterness creeps into her voice.

"Let me have some tea and a little relaxation and then maybe I can share with you some of what I have been doing."

"What I really want to know is not what you have been doing but what you will be doing. At the moment I can't forgive you for the way you have destroyed our marriage and how you have disappointed our children. They put a brave face on, rather better than I do, but they are deeply hurt that you have abandoned them to follow your own selfish dreams. They don't lack financial support thanks to your generosity but they lack the moral support of a father who really cares for them." She is saddened by the cutting nature of her own words but she speaks her mind unwaveringly. "Starting over seems to me to be the remotest of possibilities, so for the moment I don't pursue it."

I still have a mountain to climb or bridges to repair, fences to mend or something akin to these things, but my exhaustion is too great, my thinking too disjointed. I finish off my tea and stand up, painfully aware that my joints like my appearance are suffering sudden accelerated ageing. Not only must I repair the disappointment of my family relationships but I must also repair the ravages to my body and, I reluctantly admit, maybe even my mind.

Irrespective of personal pain, I am driven to go on with what has become a crusade against mindless evil. It is a struggle that is beyond my control; I have led a life which was once privileged and comfortable. I feel in some obscure way that I must atone for the privileges I have enjoyed by protecting those who are unable to protect themselves and who do not benefit from the shelter of the establishment. I have suffered the privations of following this philosophy over the last few years and cannot help myself from sharing pain with the disenfranchised.

With a sudden starburst of clarity, I know what I must do to continue the work I have started and for which I had not, until now, envisioned to have a conclusion. Having reached resolution, I can feel the shadows lifting from my soul and the corners of my mind and I have a clear, uninterrupted view of what I must do. But before I start on my new direction I must sleep, and now that I have a clear mind I know that I will sleep deep and long. When I awaken, I will follow my newfound philosophy and enable myself to live the fulfilling life that I so much desire.

Later, before sleeping, a random news broadcast brings me back to reality with a jolt. Revealed to me, there is one more opportunity to intervene in a situation that I must endeavour to help. It is an injustice which is out of the reach of internationally acceptable protocols. I must formulate my new approach to deal with it. It is as well that I have separated myself from my family. Each time I undertake a project my life is threatened; this last project caused the death of a despot and one of his cohorts and scores if not hundreds of troops.

A telephone call from Sir Michael sets the next project in motion; he has clearly seen the same broadcast as me and recognises that there is nothing he can do about it officially and that I am the only one he can call on to address it.

My next project, hopefully the last to be carried out under the previous rules, could prove to be more dangerous than its predecessors; it gives me pause for thought. With danger escalating from project to project it is possible that I will not survive this fourth sortie into the dark world of those who seek to control others by force and threat. I need to make sure that in the event of my demise there is somebody who can carry on the work I have begun. There is only one person I believe I can fully trust to carry on the work I have started. I pick up a telephone and make a call; my proposal is accepted and a new chapter is set to start.

ALSO BY ROBERT SWANN

THE RETROGENESIS TRILOGY

Retrogenesis 1: The Anomaly

Retrogenesis 2: The Journey

Retrogenesis 3: The Legacy

*

THE SIMON HUNTER SERIES

Hunter's Way

Binary Impact

Smoke and Tranquillity

*

And next:

(Working Titles)

Jamaica Quay

Game On

Overspill

Printed in Poland
by Amazon Fulfillment
Poland Sp. z o.o., Wrocław